The Night We Met

The Night We Met

zoë folbigg

HEAD
of ZEUS

An Aria Book

This edition first published in the United Kingdom in 2021 by Aria,
an imprint of Head of Zeus Ltd

9 7 5 3 1 2 4 6 8

A CIP catalogue record for this book is available from the
British Library.

ISBN (PB): 9781838930691
ISBN (E): 9781789542141

Cover design © Leah Jacobs-Gordon

Typeset by Siliconchips Services Ltd UK

Printed and bound in Great Britain by CPI Group (UK) Ltd,
Croydon CR0 4YY

Aria
c/o Head of Zeus
5–8 Hardwick Street
London EC1R 4RG
WWW.ARIAFICTION.COM

For Doc

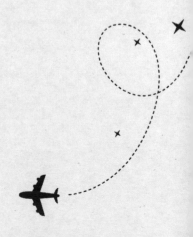

Part One

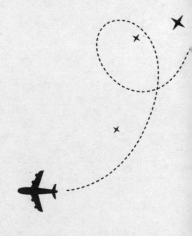

One

September 2018
Cambridgeshire, England

'Olivia Messina', said the red writing on a white board, above a pillow strewn in billowing hair. The script was fat, as if the magic marker had been lumbered upon with a heavy arm and a carefree hand as it pressed against the wall-mounted board. Fibres splayed. The jovial cursive script said more about the nurse who wrote it than the patient in the bed. The jolly writing didn't say that Olivia Messina was dying.

Cables and tubes went into veins and came out of cannulas. A machine beeped. A drip hung from a stand. A small rectangular bag poked out of the sheets from halfway down the side of the bed, its contents the same sepia shade as Olivia's freckles. Her husband Daniel tried not to look at the bag, he didn't like to think about how it was attached to his wife with a catheter. He didn't like to think about how dehydrated she was. The bag revealed too much. That time might be running out. Daniel didn't want to consider that, not when he was working so hard to find a solution.

A Glaswegian nurse called Fraser, a stout man with grey eyebrows and a dour charm, wearing a white tunic and a weathered smile, pushed his trolley full of pills and potions onto the ward. The squeak of four small wheels, under the weight of remedies and responsibility, announced his arrival. The cart creaked rhythmically as Fraser pushed it from its back end like an upright piano he didn't mind bumping. Bottles, scales, notebooks and clipboards hung from the trolley's ledges and edges, recording the inventory of his medicinal comings and goings. He gave Daniel and Olivia a nod as he passed her bed, noting the newspaper on Daniel's lap.

'Evening squire,' Fraser said. 'Don't read me that match report, will ya? I can't relive it.'

'Evening Fraser,' Daniel nodded back, while the crumpled sports section fell in a whisper to the floor. 'Shall I read you the Liverpool one instead? Mané and Firmino. Two beauties…'

'Get outta here!' Fraser said as he rolled his eyes.

Of all the consultants, nurses, radiographers and carers the family had met in the past – hideous – year, Daniel liked this apothecary the best. He wasn't quite sure why; they had come across some amazing medics along the journey from Ibiza to Addenbrooke's via Queen Square in London – but Fraser had a certain no-nonsense wit about him, an honesty to his compassion.

He didn't cock his head to one side when he asked Olivia how she was. He looked her straight in the eye, with the acerbic sparkle of his. He had pathos and patience, and talked to Olivia as a woman, not a cancer patient. His broad shoulders looked like they could weather anything for the Messina Bleeker family, that he would dig out his old boxing gloves and fight the fight for them, if only he could.

Fraser was a challenge to comprehend, but when Daniel could translate his thick Glaswegian tones and keep up with the fast and industrious pace at which he spoke, both men would come alive in conversation about politics, Brexit and sport. Fraser loved that Daniel knew as much about Scottish football as he; and he liked to jibe him for being one of those southern Liverpool fans.

'I was born in the shadows of Firhill Stadium you know,' Fraser told Daniel about his beloved Partick Thistle.

'I supported Liverpool through thick and thin,' Daniel would counter. 'Not just the Eighties.'

'Ach, gauen yersel!' Fraser would reply with a ruffian's smirk.

Fraser was solid, reliable, always dishing out pills at regular intervals, and the squeaking of his wheels brought respite and cheer from the turgid beeping of machines.

'I'll be back to see you in a bit, Botticelli,' Fraser said to Olivia with a wry smile. She closed her eyes. He had nicknames for all the patients. Portland Bill. Posh Spice. Agatha Christie. The Don. He called Olivia 'Botticelli' because her Renaissance-red hair reminded him of an Italian masterpiece. 'Just goin to see The Diva over there,' he said, as he clicked his pen and tucked it into his tunic pocket. Daniel picked the sports pages up from the floor and Fraser shook his head.

'Should never have been a goal,' he muttered under

his breath, as he unlocked the brake and continued to the woman at the end of the ward with brown skin, high cheekbones and a black and gold turban.

Daniel waved languidly as Fraser dished out his pilules and potions to the woman with one breast.

Olivia turned her head slowly, across the plump pillow it was slumped on, to look at Daniel. He gazed back like a tired and adoring child and mentally noted how Olivia looked both young and old. The mole at the end of her lip; her rich olive skin; the cascade of hair – they usually made her look youthful and vibrant. But her skin was paper-thin and pale, wrinkled beyond the laughter lines. Today she looked ten years older than she was.

She squeezed Daniel's hand.

'We've hit rock bottom huh?' she said thoughtfully, the once flame-freckled lids of her eyes closing and opening in slow blinks.

Daniel smiled, sat up and rearranged Olivia's hair so she didn't get hot. The open window enabled air to channel through the propped doors of the ward, but it was warm, the tail end of summer making both their brows bead with a slight sweat. He pushed her hair back off her face.

Rock bottom.

It had been a long time since Daniel first heard Olivia say that, but he sighed and smiled, awash with relief, to see a spark of humour.

She remembers.

Although English was Olivia's mother's mother tongue, Olivia grew up in Italy with English as a second language. Despite her fluency, she sometimes got things wrong – much to the amusement of Daniel and their daughters.

'Budgie up!' Olivia would say if she wanted to squeeze in on the sofa.

'It's a doggy dog world,' she would tell Flora, if she didn't get the part she wanted in the school play.

'Don't pop your clocks,' she would snap, when she wanted someone to calm down.

Rock bottom.

'This isn't rock bottom, my love,' Daniel said. His face handsome and earnest. 'Look around you, all this brilliant treatment! Not just Fraser and his wagon. The research Mimi is doing. The diet I've got everything ready for at home. I've been juicing like a bastard – even Flora liked the spinach and apple one I made yesterday. This is just the start.'

Olivia looked at Daniel with the same comforting smile she gave their youngest daughter Sofia, and stroked the hair on his forearm with her bony hand.

'"Crazy, sexy juicing" or whatever it's called isn't going to help me Daniel. You need to accept it.'

He swallowed.

'Don't be so negative. Elisabeth, at work – the health editor – she forwarded me something about a study in *Nature*. Some experimental drug that can inhibit cells from spread—'

A slight woman with lighter red hair, in a soft basin-like style, walked back into the ward to Olivia's bed by the open doors.

'Got them!' she interrupted, thrusting a notebook and pen into the air.

'It's called AMD 3100 apparently...' Daniel added in hushed tones, quickly trying to sneak it in, so Olivia knew about the breakthrough but his mother-in-law wouldn't get carried away before he'd had the chance to do more research.

Olivia looked at her mother and smiled gratefully, her prettiest of noses crinkling at the bridge. She looked more galvanised by the pen and notepad Nancy had just brought her, more eager to prop herself on her pillow and sit up, than she was by talk of miracle cures, curative juices and new drug cocktails Daniel had been trying to drop into conversation.

Nancy put the pen and notepad on the thin wooden table that lay across the bed and gestured to Olivia to sit forward.

'There you go, love,' she said as she plumped up the crisp pillows. Nancy was both matronly and warm, a small woman in mustard trousers and a burgundy shirt, a thin silk scarf tied around her pale, wrinkled neck, despite the warm evening.

'It's not for me!' Olivia laughed wanly. 'It's for him!' She gestured to Daniel. 'The pen and notepad.'

'Oh, I thought you wanted it,' Nancy said, puzzled. 'For lists and things.' Her Edinburgh accent was soft and rolling, and so different to Fraser's.

'No, it's for Daniel.'

'For me?' Daniel rubbed his eyes and tried to hide his sleepiness. He wasn't the one *in* hospital. 'I've got my laptop!'

Olivia nodded, her hair tumbling, and some colour seemed to capture across her cheeks again, excited by the prospect of her idea.

'For you! A separate journal. So you can write our story.

For the girls. I always wanted to tell them our story. You know, properly.'

'Our story?'

Daniel looked from Nancy to Olivia in bewilderment. '*You* can tell the girls our story.'

'No I can't. I don't have time.'

Two

Nancy stopped plumping up the pillows behind her daughter's head and froze.

'I'll go refill that water jug,' she said, fussing and distracting herself from the water welling up in her eyes.

Olivia and Daniel watched Nancy walk into the corridor with the half-empty Britax jug, her gaze firmly on the nurses' station ahead of her, the cooler next to it with its blue button offering the cold water Olivia preferred. Nancy liked to keep busy.

Daniel frowned, his dark brows lowering over soft, khaki-coloured eyes.

'You do! I'm going to get us more time.'

'With what, spinach and apple juice?!' Olivia had a mutinous look, but she tried to go easy on Daniel. 'Really Dan—'

'But I read a case study of one woman in Albuquerque or somewhere, she had it worse than you and they trialled this drug on her, plus changing her—'

'Daniel!' Olivia shot. Silencing him as she always could.

Nancy walked back in with the water jug as Fraser finished tending to Dionne, who was far from a diva in her silent curtained chamber. The caustic colour of his pale eyes brightened a little.

'Ah! Lady Spencer!' Fraser smiled.

'Good evening Fraser,' Nancy replied.

Fraser nodded to Olivia. 'I'll be back in a wee while with your Keppra meds, just heading to the men's ward, see what those ne'er do wells are up to...'

Nancy looked flustered.

'I'll leave you lovebirds to it then,' Nancy said, a flush in her cheeks. As she said it, she didn't recall the first time she uttered those words to Olivia and Daniel, at the threshold of a light and bright apartment in a bourgeois district of Milan. Daniel remembered though. He could never forget the feelings of awkwardness and hope – even if he hadn't just seen them in Fraser. 'I'd better get back to Maria and the girls, make sure they're ready for "Back To School",' she said, making her fingers into inverted commas, as if it were a new holiday she didn't approve of. 'Honestly, the fuss in town today and having to have "new this" and "new that",' Nancy wittered, still keeping busy. She re-tied her silk neckerchief and smoothed down her tailored trousers, before kissing Olivia's cheek and squeezing Daniel's shoulder.

'Say hi to Mamma for me,' Olivia said. Olivia Messina was a curious case of having had two mothers from the day she was born.

'Of course,' Nancy replied. 'She'll come see you in the morning.'

Olivia smiled.

'Love you,' Nancy said, towards the air between them both.

'See you back at home,' Daniel answered.

*

Daniel and Olivia looked at each other and almost blushed. Both were struck by the weird sensation of finally being alone and able to talk, as if they had both been taken back to the nerves of the apartment in Milan and this were the first night of the rest of their lives, even though Dionne The Diva was now asleep in her bed behind the curtain.

I'll leave you lovebirds to it then.

But the giddiness stopped there.

Daniel knew there was a quiet conversation to be resumed.

With a shaky hand, Olivia took a sip of cold water and leaned back on her pillows.

'Here, let me help.'

'No, it's fine.'

The iciness of the cold water relieved her parched mouth but she couldn't take in much liquid without feeling queasy, so she carefully placed the beaker back on the table. The queasiness had worsened over the past couple of days, making Olivia's shrinking throat feel even more vulnerable, to gagging, to vomiting, to choking. The basic human function of swallowing was starting to become traumatic. Daniel wanted to tell Olivia about his research – all the brilliant hope he had found – but he knew she wanted to get back to the issue of the pen and notepad on the table. That seemed to excite her more.

'Listen, I want you to write it up.'

'Write what up?'

'Our story.'

'Really?' Daniel sighed. He didn't like this defeatist talk.

As if Olivia wouldn't be able to tell the girls herself. He was working, investigating, researching, day and night, and he was getting closer and closer.

'Yes! You're a writer. It's best coming from you. Write down our love story, from the bottom of the world to the top of the Matterhorn.'

She remembers.

'It's a cool story. I want the girls to know it all.'

'All?' Daniel raised a playful eyebrow that was quickly pulled back down by red-raw fibres and capillaries coming from his heart. Levers and pulleys, as if his inside was on the outside. He worried Olivia would see through him, see that he really was scared.

'Why don't *you* write it, while you're stuck in here?'

Daniel realised how clumsy that sounded. Olivia would struggle to hold a pen in a grip, she hadn't been able to for weeks. 'I could bring in my old laptop. It works perfectly well. Or your one if you'd prefer.'

'I can't, I'm too tired.' Olivia struggled to swallow and picked up the beaker again. It was a beige sippy cup with the image of a raised bear on its barrel. The vessel had been used by kids with childhood cancers, men after throat surgery and centenarians who had outlived their partners by almost fifty years. Daniel hated the sippy cup. His 43-year-old wife should not be drinking from a sippy cup. 'And *you're* too tired. For now,' she added, gingerly reaching her arm out to stroke his stubble with the back of her hand. 'But you have time.'

The blood drained from Daniel's face and he imagined those bright red capillaries emptying. Time.

Don't pop your clocks.

He stood up and paced the ward, with a rising anger that made him want to throw the sippy cup and smash it against the equipment. To pull out the cannulas from her hands and rip out the catheter attached to her urinary tract. He was overcome by an urge to unplug every wire and tube and smuggle Olivia out of the room, over his shoulder. He wanted to smash in Fraser's cart the next time he saw his merry face wheeling it from the back. But he couldn't do any of these things, so he clasped his hands, fingers splayed, to his face, shook his head to mute his scream, and sat back down.

'Darling—' Olivia tried to put a placatory hand on his arm, the way she always did when her floaty charms were calming the demons of Daniel's more anxious mind. But Daniel shook it off in desperation.

'How the FUCK—'

'Shhhhhh, *tesoro*...' she persisted.

They both looked over to Dionne's bay and Daniel lowered his voice. 'How the *fuck* do I write anything so significant? I can't write anything more than a match report. How do I write something that comes anywhere near doing us – doing you – some kind of...'

'Justice?' Olivia levelled him with a look. 'None of this is just, but I want you to write a document. An account. So the girls have more than a sense of injustice. So they have a lovely story. So their memories are more than of their family being at the fruit.'

'Huh?'

'*Essere alla fruta*. Hitting rock bottom.'

Daniel rubbed his eyes with the knuckles of his right hand.

'I thought we'd been there. I thought we hit rock bottom when we lost Jude.'

Olivia gave a laboured swallow, but said nothing.

'And we climbed our way out of the bleakness. We can do it again. We're strong. You're strong!'

Olivia's silence spoke volumes; it unnerved Daniel, who carried on, in despair.

'I dunno, my love. It's too big. It's too important. I'm not sure I can.'

Daniel looked away and picked up the rest of the newspaper from where it had fallen and blown, now under the metal bed on wheels, and flattened it on top of the polyester blanket over Olivia's feet. He pressed it down again in an attempt to neaten it. To make it readable. 'I just think it's beyond me.'

Olivia laughed from out of nowhere. A punch of a laugh that took the wind out of her sails and made her rattle. She coughed and swallowed hard again.

'Are you OK?'

'Daniel, you're a writer.' Her tone was that of a woman telling a man he was being ridiculous. But she wanted to be kind. 'You're a father. My lover. My husband. I know you can.'

Daniel felt all the hot embarrassment and anger of a teenage boy, as his kind face turned to petulance, and suddenly, lost for anywhere to hide, he brimmed to the boil and slumped his face onto Olivia's blanketed thigh. To muffle the sobs more than anything.

'I can't, I just can't...' he sobbed, as he shook his head into the hospital blankets, building friction between face and synthetic fibre. Electric currents raged.

'I *can't* write about you as if you're not around. I *can't* bring up two girls without you. I *can't* do this. I don't know how.'

Olivia was startled to see Daniel sob and put her hand on the back of his head as he cried into her leg. The touch of his hair felt soothing, even when she was trying to calm him. The crown of his soft hair, a thousand shades of brown, was swishy and swirly like the fur of a brown bear rippling in the wind.

'Shhhh, it's OK *tesoro mio*, it's OK.'

Daniel raised his hopeless face. For months he had held it together, but he just couldn't now.

'How can I bring up two girls without you?'

Dionne stirred from behind her curtain and Daniel and Olivia heard her call button buzz from the nurses' station in the corridor. Before a nurse could walk past and disrupt them, Olivia leaned into Daniel who was now sitting up, still clutching her thigh, and pressed her forehead to his.

'You already know how.'

Three

'Sofia's asleep in your bed, Flora's still up.' Nancy stood in the open atrium of the Huf Haus hallway, smoothing her shirt down in the reflection of the long mirror on the wall, while the girls' Italian grandma Maria fussed in the large open living room, checking the contents of the two backpacks that were propped up on the sofa. 'I think she's worried about tomorrow,' Nancy added matter-of-factly, as if she were telling her reflection. 'Although she's not admitting it.'

'Flora's worried about everything,' Daniel said as he hung his keys on a hook by the large modern door. 'She just doesn't like to show it.'

To make it known that she could in fact hear hushed whisperings and chatter about her, Flora opened her bedroom door and padded along the glass balustrade of the long landing in her pyjama vest and shorts.

'Oh, hi Dad,' she said casually, before slipping into the bathroom.

'Hi gorgeous,' he gazed up. Before Daniel could ask Flora if she were OK, she shut the bathroom door behind her.

Maria, a middle-aged woman with lustrous black curls, a tiny waist and fleece-lined slippers despite the balmy September evening, shuffled towards the front door, putting on her beige mac as she checked off her mental tick-list.

'*Andiamo?*' she said to Nancy, who nodded, before both women fixed their concerned looks on Daniel, to check whether he was OK to be left. They paused, searching his face for a miracle.

'Oh, yes, go! I'll be fine!' Daniel assured them.

They unfroze – for Maria to fasten her mac, and for Nancy to put her reading glasses into her handbag.

'Their bags are all packed and on the sofa,' Maria said, as she fixed a silk scarf around her head and tied it under her neck. Daniel would think she were a Sicilian peasant if he didn't know her mac came from Aquascutum, and her scarf and slippers from Liberty, bought on one of their many trips to London in the past year. 'Sofia was very particular about a certain special pencil case she wanted to use tomorrow, but I just couldn't find it Daniel,' she gestured with exasperated hands, pronouncing Daniel as if it had three syllables; the way Olivia had when they first met.

Dan-i-el.

'I can get her a new one in Cambridge tomorrow if she's that set on it.' Maria liked any excuse to go shopping.

Daniel scratched his head.

'The unicorn one?'

Maria nodded.

'*Si siiiii*, of course, *unicorno*, I couldn't find it anywhere. I looked in the kitchen... her bedroom... under the sofa

– nowhere!' she said, raising her hands to a higher power – in the form of a modern chandelier made of Perspex.

'I think it's in my car. Don't worry, Maria.'

'We ought to be getting back,' Nancy said, disinterested in the mystery of the unicorn pencil case. 'You should have an evening.'

Some evening Daniel was going to have – it was almost ten o'clock, he noticed. Flora really should be asleep by now.

'*Si si*,' concurred Maria, slinging her designer handbag over the crook of her arm.

They looked around the spacious hallway, its glass walls either side of the door looking out to the sheltered driveway at the front, and picked up a collection of hessian shoppers, laundry bags, Tupperware, books, magazines and all the things they ferried between the Huf Haus in Guildington and their Airbnb apartment in Cambridge, which they'd become accustomed to as the trips from Milan became more frequent; as their need for washing machines and stoves and somewhere to *be practical* became more apparent and the spare room or the Travelodge didn't cut the mustard.

'We're off!' Nancy half whispered up the stairs. She didn't expect a response from Flora and she knew Sofia was fast asleep.

'Good luck tomorrow, *cara mia*!' Maria added with an expectant smile, but there was no answer.

Daniel kissed both women on each cheek as they stepped out into the pale night sky and loaded up the hire car. Nancy got into the driver seat for the fifteen-minute journey back to the city centre. Maria had never learned to drive.

So much stuff. Daniel thought, as he tucked all their

shoppers into the boot, feeling guilty that most of it was for his benefit. For the girls. For Olivia.

He was certainly grateful to his mothers-in-law, but Daniel couldn't wait to be on his own. To crack open a beer. To put the telly on. To think about what Olivia had asked of him. To do some more research into promising studies. To check up on the woman from Albuquerque. To click on all the links Mimi had forwarded him over the weekend, about veganism and crazy sexy juicing and living clean and CBD oil – which he didn't want to revisit after Flora's dalliance with it at the start of the summer. He wanted peace and solitude so he could watch TV, get back to his iPad and scroll scroll scroll for answers and a cure.

Maria stopped in her tracks on the gravel drive and raised a finger.

'*Si*. Oh Dan-i-el.' Three syllables. Daniel leaned against the door frame, his hands in his pockets. 'Mimi called the house phone. Said she'd try you on your mobile.' Daniel remembered the three texts from Mimi he had received at Olivia's bedside.

'*Grazie* Maria,' he said with a nod. He loved the women dearly, but couldn't wait to close the front door on them.

Daniel kicked off his trainers, leaving them on the floor by the shoe rack and walked up the floating staircase in his socks. He wanted to put on *Match of the Day 2*, but he felt the pull to check on his girls first. As he walked up the stairs his feet felt sweaty, leaving a misty imprint on each step as he rose, and he cursed himself for overdressing today in jeans and a top when shorts and a T-shirt would have done.

He opened his bedroom door to see Sofia lying face down, cheek pressed on the mattress just below the pillow, a picture of purity. Her mouth was open in a small circle and she was wearing little pants and no vest – standard night attire for their hot bod, who always worked up a sweat while sleeping. Daniel unravelled *Harry Potter and the Prisoner of Azkaban* from under Sofia's arm, placed it on the bedside table, turned off the lamp and kissed her cheek with dry lips and a broken heart.

Sofia stirred and Daniel froze by the door, not wanting to wake her. She'd slept so fretfully for the past few weeks and months, he'd stopped protesting about her padding into her parents' room and edging him across the big double bed.

It doesn't matter.

Daniel – eyes already wrung from having sobbed into Olivia's thigh in the hospital – wanted to cry again, but he put his hand to his dry mouth as he looked at his little girl: his bear cub with brown hair like his. He walked back to the bed and half covered her, for comfort more than warmth, and closed the door gently behind him. Past the spare bedroom, Sofia's bedroom and the family bathroom, at the other end of the landing, Daniel tapped Flora's bedroom door twice gently and opened it.

'Hey…'

'Hi.'

'You ought to get some sleep you know.'

Flora groaned.

'You'll want to feel your very best for the first day back.'

Daniel tried to not sound pressurising, then had a sudden flash of panic about uniforms, bags and packed-lunch boxes, before reminding himself that Maria would definitely have taken care of it all.

'Their bags are all packed and on the sofa.'

Flora lay on her side, one arm under her head, gazing into the lava lamp on her bedside table. Daniel perched on her bed by her knees. Up close he could see Flora's irises illuminated by the light, like the swishes and swirls in brown and orange marbles he played with as a child, as she watched red orbs of wax rise gently.

'Whatcha looking at?'

He rued himself for trying to sound cool.

Daniel followed Flora's gaze and examined the mutating globules of wax as they rose like balloons at a fiesta before reconsidering; they started to look like haemoglobin sharpening into focus under a microscope. The water in the lamp like the bags of fluid, drugs and saline that weaved in and out of Flora's mother. Daniel didn't find the lamp as soothing to look at as Flora seemed to.

'I don't want to go back.'

'But it's Year 10!' Daniel said, as if galvanising her into battle. 'GCSEs start here! My big girl needs to glide into that school like the goddess she is, refreshed from the summer. Ready to take on the—'

'Not school.'

'What?'

'I don't want to go back to that place. To Mum.'

Flora gave a guilty sideways glance in the direction of her dad then looked back quickly at the rising red blood cells.

Daniel ruffled the back of his hair, trying to hold back a groan. He desperately wanted to stroke Flora's hair, lighter as it usually was at the end of the summer, not the deep russet it turned in midwinter. Flora hadn't spent this summer in Camogli or Ibiza or Scotland. This summer had been spent at the local lido, her hair turning lighter as her freckled face turned pink with blushes caused by the boys doing their A levels, many of whom fancied Flora but didn't know what to say to her because of her mum.

Daniel hadn't stroked her hair in so long, he didn't want her to feel awkward. She had been increasingly standoffish since her mother's illness; even worse since her incident with four friends and a bottle of CBD oil.

'Aww, don't say that princess. Mamma loves seeing you. She loves you so much. Your visits are the best thing about her day.'

As he said it, Daniel realised he was piling too much pressure on his daughter, adding to the million reasons he already felt wretched. Wretched about being a bad dad. About palming the girls off on Nancy and Maria. About the fact there seemed to be nothing he could do to make Olivia better.

She is still a child.

'I know Papa. But I want her here. Where she should be.'

'I know, and she will...'

Flora rolled onto her back and flashed her father a look of mistrust and doubt.

'And that's great you're keen to go back to school. After the shit summer we've had, some normality will do you good – to see Amelie and Jessie and do all the brilliant things you love. Get back to basketball. Get back to guitar. I get it. You need routine and fresh air and to not be sitting in that place with your sister and your *nonnas*.'

Flora gave a conciliatory frown as if to say, 'I know.'

'Come on.' Daniel straightened the duvet over his daughter's long limbs, kissed her forehead and briefly stroked her mane of hair scattered on the pillow above her scalp, as her mother's was in the hospital.

Flora rolled back onto her side in a foetal ball and returned her focus to the lava lamp, giving Daniel his cue to go.

'I love you princess.'

'I know,' she said, as she shut her eyes and tried not to cry.

Daniel turned the main light off at the door and closed it, leaving only the red glow of the lamp softly lighting the room.

'I love you too,' came a flat and little voice from the other side of the door.

In the open downstairs living space, Daniel leaned into the abundant fridge and scoured it for beers. He couldn't see any Peroni, Moretti or Brew Dog for the food his mothers-in-law had filled it with: a large earthenware dish bursting with *melanzane alla parmigiana* and covered in cling film; leftover fig cake; tubs of yogurt and cartons of smoothies for the girls' packed lunches. Bags of gnocchi next to Tupperware packed with Maria's ragu. A tray of tiramisu. A bountiful cheese box and some tins of fizzy orange.

Beer.

Daniel felt the salve of coolness on his hot face and took a can from the back of the fridge before shutting the door. The kitchen was large and modern, as was all of the downstairs, with vast glass walls, some of them all the way up to the roof, all looking out onto decking, the garden, Olivia's studio and the fields beyond it. It was an open and exposed space, but Daniel liked to think that only deer, badgers and hedgehogs would be peering in as he slumped into the L-shaped sofa and put on the TV.

Crack.

The hiss of the cool can brought little comfort to shoulders weighed down by a task, a truth, he didn't want to face. Next to the girls' new backpacks was Daniel's own bag he'd slung on the sofa, which he opened, and slid his laptop out of its case.

Olivia used to joke that Daniel was surgically attached to his computer, but he hadn't needed it so much lately, not since his site editor had told him to go on leave just before the World Cup. The emails had started to slow down. He was taken off editorial groups about Russia, strategy, story planning and tickets going spare. Now he only tended to get messages from friends, although they'd been less frequent given how poor he was at replying. He was grateful for the enquiries, he just hated not having good news to impart. So he only spoke to the odd close colleague. His deputy sports editor at BBC Online, who was currently stepping up and covering for him. The chief football correspondent, who predicted big things for his beloved Cardiff City this season and spent the summer trying to distract Daniel with transfer news, Fantasy Football and Predict The Score commitments. The fashion editor at Daniel's former paper, who had championed Olivia's clothing line from the get-go. And Jim. Jim still called and messaged daily, even when Daniel didn't answer.

He put the beer down, a pool of condensation forming

on the glass coffee table, and turned on the TV, letting out a sigh that turned into a yawn. Mark Chapman in the *Match of the Day* 2 studio provided some welcome normality, some rhythm to a topsy-turvy time. Since he had been on leave, in a world without deadlines, interviews and breaking sports news, Daniel was surprised by how easy it was to forget which day of the week it was.

Sunday.

He leaned back, fired up his MacBook, minimised the internet and its tabs about living strong, juicing and wonder drugs, and opened Word. Command + N. A new document. It's how he usually began writing up a story about the Lions' tour or the Ashes, or an exclusive interview with Bradley Wiggins or Usain Bolt. The blank white rectangle still put fear into him, still gave him imposter syndrome after all those documents written, after all these years, but never had he felt the fear as sharply, and wondered how the hell he should begin, as he did now.

How the fuck?

He thought about the first time he saw her. No, not the first. It was the fourth, but it was the first time they had held each other's gaze. It was the first time Daniel realised that Olivia was more than just a crush, that there was something deeper behind those fiery eyes.

I'll write it as a love letter to her.

He stared at the white rectangle.

No, I'll write it to the girls.

Daniel's fingers hovered over the keys and he looked up at the screen. Cardiff City were losing to Arsenal.

Fuck.

Four

I looked out of the window and there she was. Beyond the dust swirling in the air, through the smears arching across the glass, I saw a bronzed leg, long and carefree, stretching out of the passenger window of a battered orange campervan. The colours of the road, the sand, her skin, were all genuinely as golden as the halcyon image of my memory. She crossed her other leg over it, her dusty brown boots looking like they might fly off in the wind, and from my vantage point and the height of my seat on the Greyhound bus, I had a view into their van. There were people in the back, bags and pillows scattered around. From their movements I could tell music was playing even though I couldn't hear it. Although her face was obscured by her hair, I knew it was your mother. There is no other hair colour in the world like it, apart from yours, Flora.

I sat bolt upright and pressed my hand against the window. It was cold, despite the heat of the dry highway outside. Air conditioning blasted against the glass, messing with my senses and the red and gold parched earth outside it. I couldn't open the windows, they were locked and useless and I felt trapped. But I had seen her again. That brought me some comfort.

I thought about her jewellery, nestled inside my bag, and felt frustrated I couldn't open a window and shout out. Not that I would have known what to say. Even at 20 – wayward, unpolished and slightly gawkish – she was the sort of woman who left men a bit speechless. But she looked so carefree! Men – boys, I was just a boy – didn't know what to say to a girl like her, and I was envious of anyone who did.

'Hey!' perhaps. I wished I could just shout 'Hey!', and my shout would burst open the glass, but I sat up, my mouth dry and my voice silenced. My Walkman headphones fell out of my ears. I don't know exactly what I was listening to – Uncle Matt had given me his *Pulp Fiction* soundtrack tape as a parting gift. But it was probably a mixtape. The Fugees. Pulp. Beck and Björk.

That's it.

It was Björk – 'Hyperballad'. I had that album too – *Post* – and her cries tumbled out of my earphones and onto my lap as I sat up and pressed my palm flat against the window.

Björk galvanised me through the solitude and heartache of travelling alone, as glimpses of your mother had. It was the soundtrack to my trip.

I placed the music back in my ears and drowned in the comfort of it, then your mother looked up, out of the campervan window. She was laughing about something, looking inland, perhaps she was checking to see if the sky really was cloudless all the way from the east coast to the west. She was attempting to roll a cigarette – she smoked back then, though not very often; she wouldn't want you to think she was a smoker – but she lost her grip on the cigarette paper and it flew out of the window. She looked up to follow the paper's fast and delicate trail as it spiralled up into the air and saw it land, slapping and rippling against the bus window, just below my face, level with my mouth, like a gag. I gasped and felt my throat tighten. I was mesmerised and knew we didn't have very long. But there she was. Trying to tame her Titian hair in the wind – you remember Titian, my loves? He was Italian too.

She stopped talking to her friends in the van, or singing along with them, and I was tempted to look at them more studiously, to see the company she kept – but I didn't want to take my eyes off her.

There she was, moving her hair out of her eyes and looking up at me as her campervan gained on my cumbersome Greyhound bus. We both laughed. Her mute laugh looked like it was still trailing from a conversation in the van. Mine came from out of nowhere and I worried other passengers on the bus might think I was mad.

Then her laughter dropped to a look of puzzlement, as if she might recognise me, and her smile faded. We just stared at each other for what felt like an eternity but must have been just seconds, until we both looked to the white rectangle under my nose, a thin white Rizla paper separating us, fragile and determined. A bemused smile crept back across her lips and then, as fast as the paper whipped up in the wind on the highway and took off, she gave a half wave, and the campervan flew off ahead too. She was gone.

Five

It's her.

Daniel watched the orange campervan zoom off up the dusty highway, beyond his silver rattling coach, past giant fruit made of concrete and fibreglass; past kangaroo roadkill squished into the verges. Off to a destination he hoped was the same as his. He rubbed his eyes, dry from the cold air conditioning firing down from the vents between the window and the bus roof, and he thought of Kelly. Whether she might be at the next stop too. He was glad, for the first time, that she wouldn't be. He only wanted to see the girl with the long bronze legs and deep red hair.

He had seen her three times already in recent weeks, and this was the first time she had seemed to really *notice* him.

Three times! He totted up.

Three times in obscure corners of the planet, far from the other side of the world, the continent they both called home. *OK*, he conceded, *maybe not such a coincidence if we're treading the same beaten track*. But even so, for his

30

uncomplicated English mind, a brain that didn't look for chance encounters of significance and serendipity, Daniel had a weird and unusual sensation that the universe might be conspiring for him to see her, and so hoped she would be in Cairns, where his bus was terminating.

It's just a coincidence. We're all treading the same path.

The first time Daniel had seen her was on his second day in Sydney. It was late afternoon and he was walking down the Blues Point Road, the smell of coffee, freshly cooked pastries and optimism propping him up as he explored the energetic and sociable city draped elegantly around its sparkling harbour. Trying to get his head around jetlag and the fact he had done it. He had gone to the other side of the world on his own. Trying to get his head around the fact that his girlfriend was there too.

Ex-girlfriend.

Two weeks before Daniel and Kelly were due to go travelling, Kelly summonsed Daniel to Brighton, to her student digs. It was a Sunday night during finals week and he thought Kelly was panicking and needed his support, his arms around her. So he took two trains from his beige university house share in Farnham to Brighton, so he could rub Kelly's back and tell her it was all going to be OK. That she would ace her speech and language therapy exams. She was a diligent and bright student.

Except it wasn't all going to be OK. Kelly was dumping Daniel for a guy called Ian, who she had met at a gig on Brighton beach, and she was really sorry about it all – but would Daniel mind if Ian went travelling with her instead?

'Erm, yes,' said Daniel, baffled, as he stroked his messy brown hair. 'It's *my* ticket. In *my* name.' Kelly's insolence and surprise delayed Daniel's heartbreak for the moment; he was so confused he was unable to take it all in.

'*You* wouldn't still go on your own, would you?' Kelly spat. 'Travelling was *my* idea.'

Daniel leaned back on Kelly's single bed, with tiny ditsy flowers on the duvet cover, and looked up at the Alanis Morissette poster on the wall as he tried to hold the tears in. They had made it, from A levels all the way through to the last week of university, without splitting up. Without cheating on each other, despite the temptations of lads' holidays, freshers' weeks and years of getting drunk in the student union. Despite all the advances that had been pressed upon him. Well, Daniel had made it anyway. He had been loyal.

'He'll pay you for the name change fee of course.'

'That's nice of him.'

'I asked the travel agent, it's £104. Plus the flights. Of course he'll give you the money for the flights. He's come into some money since his gran died, so it won't be a problem.'

'Oh great,' Daniel said sarcastically.

He could feel his hands shaking as he sat awkwardly on the bed, hunched under the slope of the attic room ceiling. 'But still. No.'

'What?'

Kelly's long mousy brown ponytail swung from side to side as she stood up to close her bedroom door. This was going to be more difficult than she expected and she didn't want her housemates to hear. They had all been on Team

Daniel and urged her not to do it.

'What did you say?' she repeated.

Kelly had a proactive, head girl way about her, which Daniel had always found endearing. But now her cold efficiency in wanting to sign Daniel's round-the-world ticket over to a guy called Ian was tearing into him, as was the thought of a faceless man having squeezed into the single bed he was sitting on.

'No, sorry Kelly. I'm not letting him have my ticket. I'm still going.'

Daniel didn't want to go travelling by himself. He was terrified. At 22, he'd never travelled on his own before, except the journeys from his family home in Elmworth to uni in Farnham, to see Kelly in Brighton, and back again. Staying at home for the summer and watching Euro 96 with his brother and schoolmates back in the pub seemed far more appealing, and would have been a good tonic, he knew that. But Daniel was more stubborn than he was terrified. He had worked every university holiday, either in the Co-op in Farnham or the Red Hart in Elmworth, so he could save up enough money to go travelling with Kelly at the end of his degree. They had planned it for four years, he didn't even remember that it was her idea, they had both looked forward to it too much. A few months in Australia, travelling up the coast as lots of their friends had done, going to foam parties and surfing shitfaced; then to New Zealand and the Cook Islands before coming back home via LA and settling down; getting proper jobs and maybe buying a place together. And when Daniel planned something, something that had taken time and research and consideration, he saw it through.

'No. I'm going. If Ian wants to go travelling with you, he can buy his own fucking ticket.'

Daniel stood firm, finished his post-grad course in journalism, packed up his room, returned to Elmworth where he bought insect repellent and had his jabs, and a week later his older brother Matt dropped him at Heathrow and shook his hand at the check-in desk.

'Good luck mate. Hope you get to watch the matches Down Under.' Matt wasn't one to get emotional – but he admired Daniel for doing something he never would. Matt was a homebody and liked to know his favourite tea bags (PG Tips) were always to hand, which they were (aisle five, opposite the biscuits), in his job as assistant store manager of the Elmworth branch of Safeway. Matt had started working there aged 15, stacking shelves in the evenings, then as a Saturday boy, before leaving school at 16 and working his way up, through dairy, then head of the fish counter (which Daniel and their parents weren't so keen on – the smell of fish was impossible to shake) to checkout manager and assistant store manager, all by the age of 24.

Matt was the kind of boy who took great pride in wearing his black blazer, red tie and name badge. In Being Official. He met his girlfriend Annabel there too, while she worked weekends on the cheese counter to fund her accountancy training. Their lives were simple, provincial, and they always knew where they could get a good cup of tea. That was how Matt liked it. He had no wanderlust whatsoever. Daniel wanted to see the world and live it – to do a bungee jump, to go night swimming, to drink from freshly cut coconut on an island – with some planning, of course – and their parents were extremely proud of both sons.

As he paced Sydney, Daniel tried to process all of what had happened in the past few weeks: the shock dumping, the jealousy, the rage, the indignance, the heartache and the loneliness. He walked and walked, taking in the sight of the Harbour Bridge and Opera House from every angle he could, the white pearl gleaming on the harbour, always reminding him of his coordinates. Walking and processing and sightseeing, so he could distract himself from the pain in his stomach. So he could get used to the idea of three terrifying months on his own.

On that tiring second day, he ducked into a bohemian-looking coffee shop next door to the youth hostel he was staying in, in search of a caffeine boost before a rest on his bunk.

'Killing Me Softly' was playing on the speakers, and a girl with hair like a bonfire, bronze skin and straight dark brows over burning eyes was sitting at a rectangular wooden table, her back to the wall, holding court over the whole cafe. Her face was sprinkled with a dusting of freckles which sparkled at the back of the place. She was speaking Spanish or Italian, Daniel didn't know the difference then. Of the group she sat with, this girl was laughing the loudest, gesticulating the most enthusiastically, chinking cups the most heartily. All eyes were on her and she seemed completely comfortable with that. A boy with curly hair and little round glasses stood as he responded to her anecdote with one of his own and the whole group fell about laughing. The group – an assortment of nationalities in an assortment of vests, hareem pants, crochet tops and board shorts – looked like they hadn't all known each other long, but they were all united by the ease at which they made friends. Most people were interjecting in English but they all seemed to know what each other was talking about. Daniel didn't have a clue.

He felt very *boring*, and quietly ordered an iced coffee from a woman with intricate henna patterns on her hands. As she made his drink, Daniel tried not to look at the group at the back, the Proper Travellers, lest he seem lonely. But he couldn't help it, the girl with the wild arms and hair was too compelling. She stood up, and Daniel looked away sharply as she made her way around the table, helping a girl with jet-black hair lift a backpack as they made their way to the front of the cafe. Daniel kept his eyes on the drink in progress, but did his best to eavesdrop as they spoke in English.

'Sorry to love ya and leave ya,' said the girl with the backpack; her voice was soft and high and her accent Australian. 'I'm worried about missing my bus.'

'No worries!' the redhead purred, sounding not at all Australian. 'Safe trip, heh?'

Daniel stared at the creamy coffee, captivated by its centrifugal force, straining to listen. The girls said something about meeting in Melbourne, which Daniel struggled to hear over the whizz of his drink being made.

'Don't run off with any of those cute guys huh?' Daniel couldn't see it, but he could tell the Australian was gesturing to the backpackers at the table. 'Mike is looking forward to seeing you!'

Who's Mike?

'Ha!' the girl laughed, the sound of it knocking Daniel for six.

'The olds can't wait to see you either. Dad is desperate to show you what a real pizza tastes like…'

The redhead mumbled something in another language as the girls laughed and hugged each other tight, one much taller than the other, and the shorter one left.

'Five dollars please,' said the barista with beautiful hands. Daniel paid with a plastic banknote he hadn't seen before, picked up his drink, and glanced sheepishly over his shoulder at the redhead as she returned to the big table. As he stepped into the late afternoon sunshine he heard the girl's laugh punch the air, echoed by the cries on the rollercoaster rolling on the wind from Luna Park across the harbour. That distant cheer, the rise and fall of excitement and intrigue, tumbling in the breeze with the smell of suburban Sydney's frangipani trees, all made Daniel feel like a terrible humbug. For being antisocial. For not having any friends. For wishing that *he* was the funny guy with the little round glasses and that the redhead was laughing at *his* jokes. For feeling a stab of jealousy that someone called Mike knew her. For hoping that Kelly and Ian were having a worse time than him. That *they* hadn't made any friends either.

They don't need to. They have each other.

Daniel walked and walked that day. To tire himself out of jetlag more than anything. To distract himself so he was too exhausted to think about Kelly and Ian – who had pressed on with their plans to travel despite the inconvenience of Daniel not giving up his ticket – and which attractions they had hit first. Taking in the city, visiting Mrs Macquarie's

Chair and Darling Harbour, slumping on his bunk with a copy of *The Beach* and wondering if the girl in the cafe next door to his hostel might be staying at his hostel too. She hadn't noticed him in the cafe, there were more exuberant people there.

The second time Daniel saw her was six days later, at a nightclub across the city in King's Cross, a steamy suburb where walking down the street was a colourful joyride for the senses – especially for a Home Counties boy. Daniel had transferred to a hostel in Woolloomooloo, which cost less and had more cockroaches, and he was on a night out, a short walk away from the hostel with a crowd of backpackers he'd got chatting to while heating some Super Noodles in the communal kitchen.

'Come out mate,' said a man with an Essex accent and hair like Dougal from *The Magic Roundabout*. 'I'm going to a club wiv some French geezers and a couple of birds from the birds' dorm. It's fancy-dress film night. Alcopops are two for one during happy hour.' Daniel looked unsure. 'Catch the football if you stay up late enough? Miss the football if you pull…' he added with a wink.

Daniel didn't really want to go and drink alcopops in a fancy-dress theme night at a club with a guy who called women birds, and he couldn't really face chitchat. He wasn't very good at small talk; he wasn't interested in hearing people's travelling routes, just as he didn't expect people to be interested in his. But he didn't want to stay in the hostel common room watching *The Simpsons* or *Friends* all evening with the other backpackers without any friends.

Plus, walking into a bar or club with people he didn't really know was easier than walking into one on his own. Daniel knew he had to dig deep, and he had to make an effort.

I'll try.

'Sure thing mate.'

He was a week into his trip and becoming accepting of his new single status, getting used to not having anyone to share sights, experiences and snacks with. Sometimes he even felt a little bit proud of himself, as he walked through leafy Hyde Park eating a prosciutto panini, taking in the sights. Although he wasn't as keen as Dougal to 'pull' – the thought of it terrified him as he'd only ever slept with Kelly.

Daniel politely declined the kind offer of being Dougal's wingman and he didn't want any of Dougal's pills he was offering, so he stood awkwardly around a tall round table with the rest of the Woolloomooloo backpackers – two English girls from Leeds and the French guys, who didn't seem to want to talk to anyone – sipping from a bottle of something called Sub Zero he'd not seen in the student union at the University of Creative Arts in Surrey. What he really wanted was a beer and to find a bar where he could watch England v Scotland or France v Spain in the Euros later. Surely Dougal and the French guys would fancy that. Or maybe he could do that on his own. Sport was that wonderfully unifying thing where Daniel found he could make friends of strangers in a bar and feel a little less self-conscious.

'Heyyyyy,' slurred Lou, one of the English girls from the hostel. She apologised for her little red swing dress, that swished flirtatiously at her cocktail-stick thighs, and said she just didn't have anything in her rucksack that could double as a film character, but mumbled something about her friend Sally being someone from *Hairspray*. Daniel hadn't seen *Hairspray* but he could tell from Lou's tone that she wasn't being kind.

'Don't worry, this isn't fancy dress either,' he shrugged. Daniel was never one for costume parties.

'You could pass for Keanu Reeves in *Point Break* if your T-shirt was tighter,' Lou said with an intent in her eye, as she pressed his chest as if to make it so. 'And if your hair was a bit darker. And if you shaved.'

Nonsense.

Daniel laughed politely, as he rubbed his traveller's stubble. His features were gentler. His hair was messier. The soft undulating brown of a grizzly bear's coat was nothing like a Hollywood film star.

'Well, I do have two eyes, a nose *and* a mouth,' Daniel replied. Lou narrowed her eyes to check if Daniel were joking – and he felt a bit mean about being rude. 'And I am booked into surf school in Byron Bay in a few weeks.' He softened the situation with a smile, which he then worried would be perceived as flirty.

Lou's hair was tied back in a ballerina bun and her narrow face and chest were sunburned, even though it was winter in Australia. 'I've always fancied Keanu Reeves,' she slurred, still pressing onto his T-shirt. 'Since *Bill & Ted's Bogus Journey*.' She fixed her dilated pupils on him. Daniel leaned back against a speaker, raising his bottle so it was a little barrier between his chest and her obtrusive body. Even when he remembered he wasn't in a relationship and could do what he wanted, he didn't want any of this. Plus he had a feeling Lou might do this every night – that she was just trying to get one up on Sally, sitting alone and self-conscious on a bar stool while her friend kept trying to prove she was more popular.

As Daniel pressed his spine against the high back of the speaker, a woman hopped up onto a little platform on the other side of it. It was her metallic leather sandals Daniel noticed first, and a gold chain caressing one ankle, sparkling under the blue and purple hue of the nightclub lights. Then her long bare legs as he looked up. She wasn't in fancy dress either, but she was jiving like Uma Thurman in *Pulp Fiction*, to the song Uma Thurman jives to in *Pulp Fiction*. She twisted her bottom in well-worn denim cutoffs. Her hair was big and unkempt.

It's her.

Suddenly Daniel felt single. And it was OK. He looked up at the woman from the cafe as she sang every word of the song, although he couldn't hear her under the sound of the nightclub speaker. Daniel looked at her lips. He could see from the way her mouth moved that her English was perfect too. This made her even more exotic and alien to him.

On her back was a tiny backpack and her loose paisley shirt was tied in a knot at her stomach. She looked down at Daniel, inconvenienced by the small plastic cup of something and Coke in her hand that kept sploshing drops on her fingers and toes, and thrust it into his as if to say 'Hold this for me,' without saying a word. They looked at each other for a second. Her eyes were speckled and mischievous, but perhaps that was the illumination of the UV lights.

'Buddy?' Lou asked. Trying to get Daniel's attention back. He couldn't take his eyes off the girl on the speaker. He looked up at her and gawped, his mouth open in a half smile. He watched her jive even more freely now she wasn't holding the drink, her bottom twisting artfully to the raucous chords of the boogie-woogie piano, and he forgot all of his words, not that she would have heard any.

For some reason Daniel wanted to take a sip of her drink but didn't. He just stood there feeling voiceless, mesmerised; bottle in one hand, plastic cup in the other.

'Buddy?!'

Lou looked from Daniel to the woman on the podium and raised her arms above her head to dance a sexier dance. She started writhing against Daniel to distract him, rubbing her groin up and down his thigh to get his attention. He frowned briefly in discomfort but still didn't draw his eyes away as Lou dry-humped his leg.

The Essex man, who turned out to be called Terry, not Dougal, jumped up on the speaker, pretending to be John Travolta, but his Madchester moves were unwelcome and the girl with the tiny backpack turned her back on him.

'Excuse me BITCH!' said a drag queen in a black bobbed wig, white fitted shirt and black cropped trousers, as he almost picked up Terry by the scruff of his neck, dropped him on the floor off the podium and started jiving with the redhead. They got closer, he being careful not to spike her toes between the gold straps of her gladiator sandals with the sharp end of a platform stiletto; she enjoying the fact that most of the club were watching.

As Chuck Berry played, Daniel knew she had forgotten all about him holding her drink.

The dancefloor was packed with reverent clubbers, all facing the unlikely coupling on the podium. As the song finished, the girl took the drag queen's hand and did a polite curtsey as he brought her to his neat cleavage then kissed her hand and then her forehead, careful not to smudge his makeup. They hugged and laughed before she jumped down, straightened her backpack and weaved back to the bar to get a new drink. The old one was long forgotten.

'You Got The Love' came on and the crowd cheered to the drag queen, who started lip-syncing theatrically on the podium. At his huge black stilettos, Daniel noticed the sparkle of the girl's ankle chain glimmering on the flat speaker surface, level with Daniel's eyeline.

'Hey!' Daniel shouted. Looking from the speaker to the girl as he watched her walk away. He grabbed the chain, which felt weightier than its delicate appearance would have him believe, and followed her; so he could give her the chain back, and her drink too – or buy her a new one if she fancied.

He apologised to Lou and excused himself without saying much, smoothed down his T-shirt, downed his alcopop for Dutch courage, winced, put down the bottle and walked at a fast pace so he could catch up with her, so he could get to the bar and talk to her before anyone else could start talking to her. Having seen her on the Blues Point Road, having seen her on the podium, he knew his odds weren't great.

'*Hey, you lost this!*' he was thinking he could say, imagining himself dangling the chain and raising one eyebrow in a heroic and sexy manner.

'*And your drink. Perhaps I can buy you a new one?*'

In his head he tried to channel James Bond, cool and composed. In reality, he weaved awkwardly, clutching the chain in one hand and her half-finished drink in the other, bumping into people as the bustle grew near the bar.

'Hey!' he called, losing on her.

Daniel watched her snake through the club, to some applause, pats on the back and admiring glances, as he followed with a sense that he was falling back.

A group of tall men in an assortment of German football tops past and present unwittingly blocked his way.

'Excuse me please,' Daniel said too quietly to one of their shoulder blades.

Shit.

'Excuse me please, mate…'

I can't see her.

As Daniel thought about tapping the guy on the back, he was interrupted by the forceful jabbing of a finger on his own shoulder blade.

Eh?

He turned around to an angry scrunched-up face.

'What are you doing here?' the face demanded to know.

'Kelly!' Daniel felt almost pleased to see her, then realised she wasn't pleased to see him. He closed his hand around the chain to protect it and downed the rest of the girl's warm Jack Daniel's and Coke, and a sickness rose in his stomach. 'What are the chances?!'

Daniel craned his neck to see if Ian were around. He'd seen him on the plane out; he was tall and gangly, with black hair sticking upright like a toilet brush and he had the kind of mouth that looked like he'd eat crisps in an annoyingly loud way. Which surely Kelly wouldn't tolerate for very long, she didn't have any time for loud eaters.

Kelly didn't answer his question. Her waspish face waited for an answer to hers.

Daniel shrugged. He didn't know what to say, but he wanted to ask Kelly if she were OK. Which sights she'd been to. How long it had taken *her* to get over the jetlag. He was surprised by how much he cared about her.

'Are you following me, Daniel?'

'No. Of course not.'

The conflict inside made him feel dizzy.

'Well, if you are it's embarrassing and I suggest you accept the situation.'

'I have accepted it – it's pure coincidence. I'm here with some mates from my hostel.'

Daniel looked around but couldn't see any of them now. He did however see the toilet brush lingering in the shadows by the dancefloor, craning his neck while pretending he wasn't.

Coward.

'You're only making it worse for yourself.'

What?

'I'm not sure why I'm the bad guy Kel – Kelly. Look—'

He held the chain tighter in his clenched fist, steeling himself through the power of rock and metal.

'I wasn't going to just give up my flights, to give up my plan because of your...'

He couldn't bring himself to say cheating, it almost felt a bit cruel on her. 'Look, this is what we both wanted. To go travelling. We both planned this trip for years. Am I not entitled to hang out in Sydney because it's a bit inconvenient for you?'

Daniel remembered he had other business at the bar and felt a sudden urgency to make this as short and as polite as possible.

Kelly shook her head and swung her ponytail, making sure her angry face looked *really* angry, so Ian The Bog Brush could tell she was Dealing With It from his corner of the club. Her face was angrier than Daniel had ever seen.

'It just seems a bit weird to me. Sydney is a big city, I'm sure we can *not* bump into each other. Who are you even here with?' Kelly asked, looking around, her hands gesturing vehemently.

'I'm out with friends,' Daniel said, nodding his head towards no one in particular, when he just wanted to get away in the direction of the bar.

Kelly pointed her finger at Daniel, her round pale eyes on stalks while she waited for an answer she liked better. Daniel conceded.

'Don't worry,' he said, looking around the dry ice and fluoro lights glowing in the dark. His back was to the bar, he couldn't see that someone else had got there first. 'I'm going up the coast soon anyway, think I'll keep moving.'

'I think that's for the best. Ian and I are going to try to get jobs here. Extend the trip. Stay a year if we can.'

'Oh OK, good luck,' Daniel said, nodding towards Ian. 'Hope it all works out for you.'

He waved and walked off. Kelly was irked by how keen Daniel was to get away, that he had turned his back on her and walked off to the bar before she had a chance to swish her pony and turn on her heel and walk back to Ian. By the time Daniel passed the tall Germans, the French guys, and

Terry whispering in the ear of a guy he was dealing pills to, by the time he finally made it to the bar, there was a gap where the redhead had been. And gone.

The third time Daniel saw her was during sunrise in Byron Bay, the cash-rich creative haven where hippies and healers shared tables at bohemian cafes with artists, artisans and actresses. He had set the alarm on his Casio watch and woken in the darkness of his bottom bunk, cumbersomely unzipping and zipping his backpack as he endeavoured not to wake his dormmates before sloping out. None of them were planning on seeing sunrise that morning, not after the *savage* night drinking mushroom shakes and smoking weed in a bar until 2 a.m.

Daniel had had an early night. He was exhausted after three days of surf school. It had been another leap for him, learning a new skill, learning to rely on himself and his body, remembering that he was OK on his own. But it had started badly. On the golden sand at Belongil Bay, Daniel had forgotten his ankle was attached by a Velcro-tight cord to his rented surfboard, and when his instructor told the group to run to the shore and back three times to warm up, his board had whipped into him, violently following his trail and knocking him over – before Daniel had even touched the water. By the end of day three he had ridden a turquoise wave over a rusty shipwreck, surprising himself not only that he physically could, but that he was thinking of the girl whose ankle chain was safely tucked inside his backpack in the surf shack. As he rode the wave, looking back at Byron Bay ahead of him, he beamed.

The next morning his body ached and his muscles felt worn, but he was determined to fight the fatigue. Determined to hike to the edge of the town, to a lighthouse, to the country's most easterly point – to channel the confidence surf school had given him to get up again and go out alone, at 4 a.m. So he threw on his Levi's, a T-shirt, a shirt and a fleece to beat the morning chill as quietly as he could and headed out, bypassing the empty communal kitchen. He walked out of town, past juice bars, surf shacks and art galleries, noting that the town smelled healthy – of mango smoothies, cress and hemp – even when the haute hippie eateries were closed, and headed on the quiet road towards the sea. He turned right at the beach he had learned to surf on, past the mast of the shipwrecked Wollongbar, jutting out like a rusty finger pointing him in the right direction, and he walked along a track towards Wategos Beach and the Lighthouse Road, three kilometres out of town.

As he walked past low buildings with orange roofs and white picket fences, the clean white lines of a lighthouse came into view, and below it a small gathering of tourists congregating on the knolls and in the car park. Some were holding cans of VB, Coopers and Tooheys; others were meditating. Someone was sizzling corn on a disposable barbecue and the smell of it mixed with the salty air felt invigorating, even at 6 a.m. A middle-aged couple were doing tai chi on the grass. A young couple huddled like penguins into the cold of the morning that would soon warm up. Everyone was gazing out towards the Pacific, waiting, as if they were waiting for the rest of their lives to start once the sun burst up. An older man wearing a fisherman's hat sat with a sketchbook, stroking his beard with one hand, drawing in charcoal with the other. Soft strokes forming a horizon. Daniel wondered how you drew a sunrise in black and white.

And there she was. Waiting for the sun to rise too.

She was speaking English in a slightly American accent as she talked to an American or Canadian man with long dreaded hair and no shoes.

In this cold?

Daniel stole a glance and kept walking.

The ankle chain!

He didn't know how he was going to tell her he had it without sounding weird, or how to even talk to her and interrupt her intimate huddle, so he stopped at the adjacent wall of the lighthouse's base, leaned back against it, and looked out to the Pacific.

Is he her boyfriend?

Daniel struggled to hear; the girl and the guy without shoes on were trying to speak in hushed tones – everyone was, as if speaking loudly might stop the sun from rising – but these two were struggling to keep their voices low.

'That was *so* funny!' drawled the man. He was slightly louder than she was. 'You totally, like, nailed, eight ball. You were awesome.'

Is he Mike?

She said something too quiet for Daniel to hear but the tone was husky and effervescent. The American or Canadian laughed overly loudly.

Wanker.

Daniel leaned back against the wall of the Cape Byron lighthouse and gazed up above his head. The cylindrical tower looked powerful and majestic, jutting out from a miniature castle with neat decorative battlements, all whitewashed bright, even in the twilight. He inhaled a deep breath as the prismatic lens emitted a beam out to sea.

How do I do it?

He turned his head towards the wall edge she was leaning against, desperately trying to eavesdrop. He heard cosy mumblings; the guy said something about 'tribes'. The girl mentioned the word 'Fiji' – and Daniel wondered if she had come from there – or perhaps that's where she was heading.

'Look!' gasped one of a group of seniors who had just arrived and formed a circle within the fence of their walking poles. 'It's coming!' said another, with a jolly chuckle. Daniel doubted whether the group of elderly walkers had slept in a hostel last night, listening to lumbering, stumbling, snoring and farting. He hoped they were staying somewhere more comfortable.

As the sun sizzled on the horizon, everyone came out of their shady corners, leaving their walls and their whispers, chants and private jokes, and turned to look at the same spot out to sea. As the light tinkled over the water, and the fisherman sketched furiously, Daniel faced out towards the sun, pretending to be mesmerised by the burst while he was in fact giving a sideways glance to her.

'Wow!' gasped the man who was doing tai chi. 'We don't see that often!'

'A whale?' said the redhead, stepping out of the shadows. Daniel followed her gaze and saw it too, out to sea, powering its mottled body out of the water in front of the rising sun.

Oh my god.

'A humpback,' said one of the seniors authoritatively, and everyone gasped as it blew a spray to the heavens.

Daniel looked back at the girl, noticing that her eyes were the same colour as the fire beyond the whale's water in the sky.

Now he had seen her, for a fourth time, overtaking his bus on the Bruce Highway – she had looked at him, *actually* acknowledged him and given him a playful wave.

So Daniel made a promise to himself, on his grandad's grave, that if he saw her again (and wasn't restricted by Kelly, groups of German football fans, or a glass window barrier), that he would go over and say hello. Because what could be wrong with that? He had to get her jewellery back to her anyway, it's not like he didn't have a reason.

She's so out of my league.

She might think I stole it.

As the dusty greyness of tarmac, roadkill and concrete fruit turned to lush jungle vegetation and low-rise buildings, Daniel arrived at the bus station in Cairns and stepped off his last Greyhound bus in Australia with a spring in his step.

She's here, I know it.

After navigating his way to his hostel and laying his heavy backpack down on the floor under his dorm bunk, Daniel grabbed the chain and went to look for the girl with the red hair in the hostel common room, kitchen and dorms.

He looked for her in local pubs, bars and even one of the clubs you had to pay to get into. He spent a whole evening popping his head around doorframes, pretending he was looking for his mates, when really he was just checking to see if she were there. If she had arrived yet. His handsome face meek yet friendly, his eyes hopeful. But she wasn't anywhere.

Six

'You know, I remember the first thing she ever said to me,' Mimi whispered from a wooden chair, as she looked up from her magazine. She was a small woman with black hair, pale blue eyes and a soft, high voice. Daniel hadn't seen her face back in the cafe in Sydney, but he'd never forgotten her voice.

'Huh?'

Daniel had been close to falling asleep on Olivia's still arm. The room was so warm – it was always overheated and had a stifling and soporific pull – and Mimi was reading so quietly, he'd almost forgotten she was there. Machines weren't beeping today. Dionne no longer pressed her button. Everything was quiet and the ward felt empty. Even Fraser hadn't passed through for a while with the rhythmic squeak of his trolley wheels.

Mimi, Olivia's best friend from school, was staring dreamily into the mid-distance, to the wall beyond Olivia's shoulder.

'What's that?' Daniel asked again, as he rubbed his eyes.

'The first thing she ever said to me. Livvi. On my first day at high school. I still remember it as if it were yesterday.' Mimi's Australian lilt made her statement seem like a question. She looked from the wall to Olivia's face as her friend slept, and gave a wan smile. 'It was my first full day in Europe. I was so tired – so scared! But Livvi had such an assurance about her. She bowled over, all sassy and stuff. Full of attitude. She was wearing one of those puffball skirts and long socks. She looked so cool! She kind of walked *at* me and said "I'm Olivia", as if I had been expecting her, waiting for her all my life. I suppose I had. All eleven years of it anyway. I'd never had a best friend before Livvi.'

Daniel smiled and sat up.

'She said in this quite deep and serious voice, as if she was a news announcer or something, "I'm going to be a fashion designer."'

Daniel laughed.

'I know, right! I laughed, of course. In Melbourne, kids like me didn't even know what a bloody fashion designer was! All I knew was my mum would buy me daggy dungas from Best & Less or Kmart – clothes were just something I played in so people wouldn't see my foof. I was just a little tomboy...'

'Oh really?' Daniel asked, as the lines around his eyes crinkled. He was amused to imagine what Mimi might have looked like as a boyish little girl in Eighties terry-towelling shorts and neon T-shirts.

'Yeah, I didn't know what the hell she was talking about. But I did know she was gonna do whatever it was she said she would. She had this magic about her. The conviction. The bluntness, I guess.'

Daniel frowned. He didn't like Mimi talking about Olivia in the past tense, even though she were talking about her in the past.

Olivia stirred in her sleep and Daniel spoke quietly so as not to disturb her.

'Yeah, she said she always knew; that it was in her blood.'

'Except it wasn't... was it?' Mimi said wistfully and shook her head a little in bafflement. 'Has Liv seen this?' she asked, changing the subject. Her face morphed from thoughtful to excited as she held up the double page spread from a Sunday supplement fashion special. She gestured to the model wearing a grandiose blush pink dress with biker boots in the middle of the Atacama Desert.

'Yeah, Nancy brought it in yesterday.'

'Did she clock it was one of hers?'

'Yeah, she was really lifted by it. It was cool. She asked me to text Vaani about it but even she hadn't known it was going in – they must have bypassed the PR and called it in for themselves, it's great.'

'So great,' Mimi sighed, clasping the magazine open and admiring it. 'Amazing coverage. And they've shot it beautifully.' She stroked the page once with a small hand before turning over to the next spread.

Daniel's lids started to droop as he looked back to Olivia and he felt bad that he envied her for being able to sleep whenever she wanted to. He felt wretched for having even thought it, for being so tired, for having so much yet so little to do at the same time. All he needed was to be here. But the girls needed him too. Flora had a county basketball match on Thursday; Sofia was booked into a street dance workshop on Saturday. Plus all the other clubs, homework and playdates they had in the diary. Daniel had so much to remember. He sat looking at Olivia, one part resentful, two parts in awe, as he stared at the sleeping face he adored. Olivia's mouth in a state of silence used to be a wondrous thing – so different to her punchy laugh and exaggerated gestures – but now her peace was disconcerting. It wasn't right.

He looked at her and felt guilty for worrying about all the things he should be doing right now rather than sitting here; guilty about the fact two women were running around after them, when really they should be putting their feet up. Guilty because he knew what Olivia would give to be doing these things, to be the one watching the girls play basketball, guitar, drums or dance. Mimi was lost in an article on the world's most impressive bedrooms, so Daniel gazed at Olivia and pondered the first words she had said to him.

He panicked for a second. *What if I can't remember them?* Panicked that he might have missed something significant. Panicked about what if Olivia never spoke again and he couldn't even remember her last words to him, let alone her first. He panicked about how easily Mimi recalled Olivia's first words to her, and that was a good ten years before Daniel had met her; ten years further back in the depths of the past.

Daniel mentally scrolled back through the timeline of their relationship, from sitting in the uncomfortable wooden chair he was on, to the highs and lows of hospital appointments as if they were scenes from a film he was watching. The euphoria of the all-clear. The fear in Ibiza. The times he couldn't take his eyes off Olivia as doctors spoke, as if he were a bystander.

He pictured Olivia in a karaoke bar in Tokyo; he saw her strolling towards him in a park in Milan. He saw her throwing up all over him in an apartment in Soho. He saw her storming out of a pub, leather biker jacket thrown in her face. He saw Olivia standing, wearing a cagoule, on the edge of a peninsula, looking out to sea, in a place as quiet and as silent as the room he and Mimi were sitting in now. Although that place, that precipice, was much more beautiful and much more calming.

Then the words came back to him.

Part Two

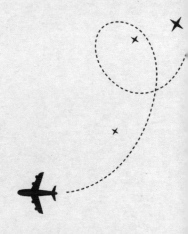

Seven

'Rock bottom, hey?'
Daniel turned to the woman emerging into his peripheral vision.

It's her!

He was awestruck, silenced to see her, even though he had been quietly absorbing the view anyway: the rolling hills, secluded sandy beaches, and occasional royal albatross floating over the headland as he looked out to sea from this barren and refreshing ledge. Daniel hadn't spoken to anyone for hours, and his surprise made it hard for him to find his voice. All he could manage was a Neanderthal grunt that sounded something like, 'Huh?'

'Rock bottom,' she repeated with a smile. 'We've hit rock bottom. We're at the end of the world, or at least it seems like it.' She let out her punch of a laugh, the one that he remembered from the cafe on the Blues Point Road in Sydney. It was so sudden and all-encompassing, it washed the smile off her face and hurt Daniel somewhere inside his ribcage.

It was the girl he had seen at four different spots on Australia's east coast, the girl who had punctuated his time there and given him the impetus, the strength and the confidence to move on when, sometimes, he didn't feel up to it. The girl whose ankle chain was zipped securely within the interior pocket of his daypack, hugging his shoulder blades as he looked out to sea.

Daniel hadn't expected to see her ever again, let alone in another country, but he felt an overwhelming sensation of awe and relief.

He gazed at her, in her cagoule and long trousers. A nose ring looped around the freckles of a neat nostril. He hadn't noticed that before. He hadn't been that close before.

Daniel knew he shouldn't look so intently, so he stared back out, to where her eye had drifted to, not noticing that her face had dropped a little – sadness fluttering across her eyes with the reflection of the thunderous clouds on the horizon.

'It certainly feels like the end of the world,' Daniel finally answered, as he marvelled at the view and just stopped short of putting his hand to his brow. He didn't want to look like a catalogue man.

'Like you could just drop off the end of it,' she said contemplatively.

For a few moments they looked out from the Otago Peninsula opening out into the Pacific Ocean beyond it. A grey fuzz on the horizon indicated a storm at sea. The girl made a box with her forefingers and thumbs and pretended to take a photo of the scene in front of her with a clicking sound of her tongue against her teeth.

'What's on the horizontal?' she asked.

Daniel found her use of words cute; it made her even more *different*. To him and to what he knew. To Kelly. To the girls in Elmworth or at Farnham. To anyone he had ever met.

'Antarctica,' said Daniel, keen to impress her. 'Around the corner a bit though. Beyond Invercargill and across the Southern Ocean. Zucchelli Station perhaps.'

'Zucchelli...' she lingered. 'Sounds Italian.'

'Or maybe McMurdo Station.'

'Sounds Scottish,' she said, arching one straight, dark eyebrow.

She turned to him and hit him on the arm like an old friend realising something. Daniel was taken aback and laughed at her forwardness as he put a hand to where she had struck, in mock pain and shock, but suddenly felt self-conscious and dishevelled when he realised she was actually looking at him now.

'Isn't it mad?' she said, studying his face enthusiastically. *Might she recognise me?*

Daniel straightened out his red checked shirt and ruffled his grizzly bear hair.

'How *weird* this place is. The city centre, the grey sky out there... It looks eerily like... home.' She was waving her arms around her head to accentuate the point. Her accent sounded both American and European, Daniel just couldn't place where *home* might be. 'Well, my *mom's* home. The city centre. Did you go into the city centre?' she asked, flitting from one idea to another, realising that of course he had, as all the trains, cars and buses would have had to. She brushed her wind-whipped hair out of her face and exhaled a sigh of wonder.

Daniel wondered where such a goddess, or her mother, could come from but didn't take the cue to ask; he was almost too scared to make eye contact, so he looked back out to the horizon.

'I thought the city centre looked strangely like Edinburgh,' he said in a small voice. 'Only smaller.'

'Exactly!' she said, again going to hit him on the arm, only this time she didn't quite make contact and Daniel silently cursed the invisible forcefield of reserve he had conjured, a barrier to protect him from another rejection. 'A miniature version of Edinburgh. Like Legoworld.'

Scottish?

She really didn't sound Scottish.

'Legoland,' Daniel corrected, kicking himself for sounding pedantic. Luckily she didn't seem to care.

'That's right. Legoland. It's even called Princes Street. I thought I was going crrrrazy.' She rolled her 'r' as she said crazy. 'Somewhere so like home, yet so far away. On the rock bottom of the world.'

Daniel eyed her with friendly suspicion and clutched his arm.

'Oh, sorry,' she laughed, giving it a rub.

'Don't worry about it, I was just kidding,' he smiled.

He wanted to know her name and where she was from. It couldn't be Scotland. Her accent definitely wasn't Scottish. He wanted to know whether she recognised him or whether *she* thought it strange that they had seen each other before. Four times in four different locations. Or maybe she didn't remember him at all. Perhaps she wouldn't find it funny, and if he pointed it out he might seem creepy and scare her. It definitely didn't seem like the right time to tell her about her jewellery.

He could see her rampant beauty up close now. Her thick dark eyebrows were the same colour as her lashes, and a mole teased at one corner of her lip.

She didn't look all that Scottish, red hair aside. But it was a deep red of a shade he'd never seen before; her skin was too swarthy to be considered Caledonian. He couldn't picture this woman in Edinburgh.

Daniel remembered Hogmanay in Edinburgh. He and Kelly had been, the New Year's Eve before their A levels. A group of sixth-form friends had taken the train from King's Cross and it had got very messy. They stayed in a hostel, ate KFC and drank Buckfast, and Kelly snogged a police officer on Princes Street and got annoyed that Daniel had minded.

He gazed back out to sea and studied the view, trying not to look across at her as she un-self-consciously held her hand to her brow. Her hair rippling to the sound of her cagoule rippling in the wind.

Edinburgh.

That's where the similarities ended. The Otago Peninsula, with its shags, sea lions and penguins; the sandy flats between rocky heads. A burst of red poked out from behind the storm, signalling the start of sunset. Daniel hadn't seen colours in the sky like this before anywhere.

'Are you *Scottish*?' he plucked up the courage to ask.

'No, my mamma is. One of my mammas anyway.'

Daniel didn't know which facial expression to show. He'd never met anyone with gay mums before. He tried to be cool, but looked down at his walking shoes.

'Oh cool.'

Olivia looked to Daniel and saw the familiar assumption.

'Oh, I have two moms. They're not lesbians. I was just brought up by two women.'

Daniel was surprised by her boldness – and embarrassed she had read his mind.

'Oh cool,' Daniel repeated. Lost for different words. Almost too nervous to look her in the eye. This… goddess… he had seen in all of these strange places. He wanted to ask her so many questions: where she *was* from, what her name was, who she was travelling with. Whether the guy with the dreads and no shoes was her boyfriend. Why would she have two mothers? Perhaps one was a stepmum.

They paused for a beat. She didn't make it easy. She was both friendly yet out of reach.

'Where *are* you from then?' Daniel finally asked.

The girl with two mums looked at the colourful Swatch watch on her left wrist and let out a sigh, as if she was trying to decide whether to bother answering. Daniel waited on tenterhooks, feeling strangely comforted, excited, by the fact that he had no idea what she was going to say next.

'Look I have, oooh…' She counted in another language under her breath. 'Five hours. Before my train leaves. Wanna get a drink?'

Daniel's legs were tired – he had hiked almost all day, a lonely but pleasant walk to Larnach Castle and the tip of the peninsula beyond it, and he felt in need of a shower and his bed.

But his heart soared.

Strangers from a faraway continent meandered along the cove back towards Dunedin, the sedate and slightly shabby

Gothic mirror of a European capital: Daniel, hands in his pockets looking at his walking boots, Olivia, tactile and wide-eyed as they passed stately weatherboard houses, coffee shops and student digs. The sight of the grand Victorian bluestone train station, with its Italianate clock tower, lured them into the city centre and its sports bars. It might have been summer holidays in the northern hemisphere, but at the bottom of the world, student life was in full swing.

'Where is your train heading tonight?' Daniel asked, trying not to sound disappointed.

'Christchurch.'

'Oh right.'

'We-llll,' she lingered on her lllls. 'Christchurch for a flight to *Milano*. Via Singapore and London. Then back to London for school in the fall.'

Daniel could barely keep up, but the twang of her accent, the way she said *Milano*, the way she spoke English as if she wasn't English, despite being confident and fluent, made him conclude she must be Italian.

'Oh cool.'

'Not so cool, my train leaves at half past midnight. I thought it was twelve-thirty lunchtime, so I got to the station half a day too early.' She rolled her eyes as if timekeeping errors were a common occurrence, but one she had become accustomed to.

'Oh no! Bummer.'

'Luckily I have enough time to get my flight; I was going to spend the night in Christchurch but now I don't need to. Saves on a hotel I guess,' she laughed and looked up at an aeroplane, heading north up the globe. There was nowhere else to go.

'Did you fancy a coffee?' Daniel gestured to one of the cafes closing up on the long road back to town, a sense of urgency and anxiety in him that it might be too late.

'Oh please! Something stronger, thank you. I have a six-hour train journey, a twenty-four-hour flight via Singapore, a changeover at Heathrow, and I won't be home until...'

'Yesterday?' Daniel offered, relaxing in his stride, noticing that lights were coming on and starting to twinkle in houses and the city ahead.

The girl laughed and started humming The Beatles. She started to sing 'Yesterday' blithely and out of tune, and laughed again, making Daniel laugh too, she was that infectious. Her enthusiasm and spirit filled Daniel with a delight he couldn't remember having ever felt.

'What's your name?' he interrupted her singing, overcome by the compulsion to know.

'Olivia. My name is Olivia. Yours?'

'Daniel. Nice to meet you.' Daniel raised a hand awkwardly as if he were accepting blame for something, and was relieved Olivia didn't notice as her excited gazed took in the day turning into night.

'Dan-i-el,' she said, lingering on it. Three syllables. 'I like the name Daniel,' she decided, having tried it out for size. Daniel felt like he'd won a prize.

'Thanks.'

'You're welcome.'

Olivia looked at her watch again.

'Come on, let's get a proper drink, Daniel.'

Windswept and weather-beaten, Daniel and Olivia walked

into a bar that looked like it had once been a bank or a church or another grandiose Baroque building, with high ceilings and bad burgundy carpet covering the intricate mosaic floors hidden beneath it. Sport was on TV, big green rectangles of something Daniel tried to ignore.

On the walk to town Daniel was surprised to learn Olivia was also travelling on her own, given he had mostly seen her surrounded by people. She had started in LA and gone to Fiji, before Australia – coinciding with her friend Mimi in Sydney for a few days, later joining Mimi's family in Melbourne before her flight to New Zealand. They had discussed their well-trodden routes and compared notes on the best fish and chips of their trips (Daniel's was at Mangonui on the North Island; Olivia's was at a beach on the Great Ocean Road in Australia), before stopping on the threshold of the grand yet slightly soulless bar. Not once had Olivia acknowledged seeing Daniel at any of the places they had both been, and he didn't know how to mention it.

'This is so weird!' Olivia marvelled. 'It's like a bar Mamma Una took me to, in Edinburgh, just a couple months ago, before I left for LA.'

'Oh right.'

'I was there seeing family...' Olivia's eyes glazed over for a second. The wild zest in them wore a veil of sadness that made Daniel decide to keep it chatty.

'But you live in Milan, right?' he asked cheerily.

'*Milano*, yes. I grew up there.'

Olivia didn't look like she wanted to explain her complex life story right now – traces of black mascara fibres smudged under her eyes and she fiddled with her nose ring as she stared at the ceiling.

Daniel felt boring. He didn't hop from Milan to Edinburgh and London. He wasn't well-travelled. Until now anyway. But his lack of adventure, the functionality of his shirt, jeans and walking boots didn't seem to bother Olivia; she seemed keen to get a drink with him.

Her gaze landed on Daniel while she waited for him to go to the bar. There was something comforting in his ruffled hair, gracious face and green-brown eyes that made her not mind retelling her story. But she wanted – she needed – a drink first.

'Shall we?' she said, as she nodded towards the bar.

'Oh yes, of course, what would you like?'

'Jack Daniel's and Coke please.'

'OK, I'll be right back…'

'I'll get us a chair,' she breezed gaily.

As Daniel walked to the bar he passed a large-headed man with a pink face who already had one eye on Olivia as he headed to the toilet, loosening the belt buckle on his thick waist. Daniel felt a momentary panic about losing sight of her again, about someone more bullish or more confident becoming her friend, but he knew this was different to Sydney. They had spoken. She had punched him on the arm.

Daniel ordered their drinks and looked back at Olivia, who was setting her cloth bag down on the high round table she had pulled a stool up at. It was the first time she had seemed alone, not surrounded by a group of admirers, and she looked different. She took off her cagoule and screwed it up on a stool opposite, leaving the one by her side free for Daniel, and untangled her hair from her funnel-neck jumper. She wore long, loose, tie-dye trousers that looked like she might have bought them on another world adventure, to somewhere even more exotic.

Daniel paid and walked cheerily back to the table, hoping his beer would revive him. Hoping it would give him the confidence to give her back her ankle chain without seeming weird.

'She asked if you wanted a double.'

'I do.'

'Oh, shit, I just got you a single.' Daniel felt inadequate again. He wasn't used to this. To buying girls drinks. To having to make friends. 'I can go back and get another m—'

'No, no, no,' she gesticulated for him to sit down. '*Tranquillo*, it's fine,' she said, taking a big slurp. 'Next time.'

Daniel set his daypack down on the floor at his feet and positioned himself on his stool next to Olivia and took a sip from his pint.

Next time.

'Cheers,' he said raising his glass.

'*Saluti*,' she winked.

'So, Daniel—'

Dan. Ee. El.

'Why are you following me?' Olivia asked with a wry smile.

She noticed.

'What?! I'm—'

'I'm just kidding. But I'm pretty sure I saw you in Australia, no?'

'Yeah, I sort of recognise you,' Daniel tried to say it airily, but it just sounded apologetic. Olivia sat up.

'*Siiiiiii!* At the beach in Byron Bay!'

Sunrise. She must have seen me.

'Yes, beautiful, wasn't it?'

'Beautiful?!' Olivia laughed. 'It looked pretty painful to me!'

'Painful?'

'Yes, I'm sure you were the guy running on the beach, still attached to your surfboard.'

Shit.

'Oh. You were there?'

'Yes, everyone on the terrace kinda… cringed. We were surprised you got back up.'

Daniel's shoulders dropped in defeat.

'Yes, I got back up.'

Daniel had rather hoped she would have picked a more romantic happenstance: Daniel the hero who held her drink. Daniel, pensive and self-sufficient watching the sun rise at Byron Bay. Daniel the stranger locking eyes with her on the highway. But of course, she saw his excruciating slapstick fail on the first morning of surf school. She didn't even know he had learned to ride a barrel.

'Yes, not my finest moment.'

Olivia stirred the ice in her drink and laughed.

'You looked cute.'

Daniel's tanned cheeks flushed pink.

He didn't know how to mention Sydney – twice – but tried to keep it casual.

'Yeah, I think that was you on the highway in Queensland, wasn't it?'

Olivia lit a cigarette and nodded.

'And I'm sure I saw you at Poste Restante in Auckland last week, but I was preoccupied,' she laughed to herself as if she had a secret she wanted to share, but Daniel didn't take the bait, he was too taken aback. Gutted to have missed her, even though he was with her now.

'Auckland? Oh I didn't see you.' He looked troubled.

'Yeah, you were ahead of me in the queue and I thought I recognised you... from the surfboard thing,' she said flirtatiously.

'From the highway,' Daniel corrected with a quiet twinkle.

'No, I *definitely* recognised you from the beach.'

Olivia could see Daniel was actually embarrassed by his beach calamity, so she playfully nudged into his arm with hers as they sat side by side on the stools looking out to the bar.

'And you're at the end of your trip. How does it feel to be going home?'

'Hmmm...' She twirled her nose ring. 'I have mixed emotions,' she replied bluntly. Daniel was too shy to ask why, he didn't want to pry, but kicked himself for not.

'I don't go home for another month,' he said. 'I have a job starting in September.'

Olivia didn't ask him what his new job was, she looked like she was still worried about going home, and he felt stuck. He wanted to tell her. Impress her with his new post, as a news reporter on the *Elmworth Echo*. She didn't look the type to be impressed by that though; Olivia looked like it took more to wow her than working for a provincial newspaper. So Daniel changed the subject back to Olivia.

'What do you do in Milan?'

'I finished school there. International school.'

'What's "international school"?'

'Oh, like a private one, with lots of kids from all round the world. It's why people *always* ask me if I'm fucking American.'

'I don't think you sound American.'

'Good.'

He didn't know what she sounded. Not Italian. Other than when she said the word *Milano*.

'So why didn't you go to an Italian school?'

'My parents are social climbers.'

'Oh cool. My parents have no ambition whatsoever.'

They laughed, and Daniel felt a bit guilty. Silvia and John Bleeker would do anything for their sons, as long as they followed a standard path, a binary choice. Co-ed or the boys' school? Mashed or boiled potatoes? Football or rugby? French or German? His mum was a primary school teacher and his dad was the manager of the Barclays Bank on the high street – Daniel had broken the family mould with this trip, but they were terribly proud of him for doing so.

'So have you just graduated?'

'We-lll, I finished a couple years ago, been fuckin' around really, working here and there. Drinking too much. Did my foundation. But I start college in London in the fall.'

'Whereabouts?' Daniel asked, trying not to sound hopeful that they might meet up back home.

'Central Saint Martins. I'm doing fashion design. Womenswear.'

'Oh wow.' Daniel pulled at the denim on his thighs to straighten his jeans.

'Yeah I kinda blew my baccalaureate and had to retake, do work experience and then my foundation. I messed up.'

'Doesn't sound like you messed up to me.'

Olivia shrugged. She sounded quite casual about messing up, like it was a rite of passage, one that all her friends did as if it were a gap year. Then the glaze appeared over her eyes again, the one Daniel had seen looking out to sea, and she downed her drink.

'So where is Central Saint Martins?' Daniel tried to sound breezy again. 'I've heard of it but not sure...'

'Soho – Mamma Una and I took a trip to look at it, after Edinburgh actually. See the university. I've got a little flat in the centre of the city. On Lexington Street, just a few blocks from college. Do you know Lexington? You are English, right?'

Olivia looked Daniel up and down and he felt so terribly English and so terribly inadequate. To him, London was the place he would go to see football matches, or take school exchange students to Camden Market, or go Christmas shopping on Oxford Street, or get the train to Farnham or Brighton from Waterloo or Victoria – although he wouldn't be doing that again. Olivia made London sound like New York.

'Yeah, I know Soho,' he replied, trying to sound worldly. 'Living there sounds ace.'

And expensive.

Daniel didn't realise people actually lived in Central London. Olivia nodded.

'Yeah it's near college and all the bars and stores and things.' She took another sip and finished her drink.

'And fashion sounds cool. How did you get into fashion?'

'Oh, you know,' she waved. 'It's just something I've always been surrounded by.' Olivia swirled the ice in her empty glass. 'Ever since I can remember.' She closed her eyes briefly. 'You know how your senses can take you back to a place in your past and it fills you with comfort?'

Daniel inhaled the smell of his dad's Old Spice aftershave and nodded.

'Well, for me it is the sound, the hum, of the sewing machine. It's the most comforting sound in the world.' Olivia closed her eyes again as she searched for it in the rolodex of her brain. Edwyn Collins came over the speaker, 'A Girl Like You', and Daniel's heart ached as he looked at her. Olivia's brow furrowed as she tried to remember; her face looked scared, something about her looked like she had suffered a car crash, but Daniel could tell she had wings hidden in all that hair.

Olivia Messina was something of a phoenix born out of the ashes of an accident. Her mother Nancy, herself flame-haired and feisty, travelled through Milan in the early Seventies – and decided to stay. She'd been broken-hearted after the boy next door in Edinburgh turned out to be a let-down and she'd decided to go interrailing, 'to show him'.

Nancy's mother, Jean, Olivia's Scottish grandmother, who was originally from the Hebrides and thought that the test of a woman was whether she could cut peat or not, pleaded with her 20-year-old daughter not to go.

'You're so naïve!' she said.

'Well, this will make a woman of me.'

'Staying here and learning a trade will make a woman of you! Anyway, if you're doing this to punish Hughie, you're wasting your time. Better to get revenge right under his nose.' Nancy's mother did always have a bitter streak.

But Nancy had a thirst for adventure that her mother didn't. She didn't need to go to the islands and learn to cut peat; she didn't need to learn another trade, she was already an excellent typist; and she didn't need to get revenge under Hughie's nose. Finding love in Antwerp, Valencia or Munich would be even more satisfying. And anyway, she wasn't going travelling to find love.

'I want to see Europe,' she protested. 'Look at the new opportunities there!'

So her mother and father, austere in manner but enchanted by their daughter, agreed that she could go, to get it out of her system, and they gave Nancy fifty pounds and waved her goodbye at Waverley Station, as she started her European odyssey clutching a small brown suitcase.

Nancy didn't expect to fall quite so spectacularly in love with Milan as she did. But the moment she arrived, under the cylindrical glass roof of Centrale station, and walked through the hulking portals into the city, she knew it would be a while before she would be leaving. It was so spectacular! The fascist flush that commissioned such a space had fallen, but the faded grandeur sat well with Nancy. It felt strangely more like home than the house on Montgomery Street ever had, and that's where her interrailing stopped. She rented lodgings in the bourgeois Wagner district of the city, with bustling boulevards and neighbourhood gelaterias, and enrolled in an Italian course until she got a nannying job with a wealthy family.

When Nancy's Italian was strong enough she left nannying – '*I bambini non sono per me*,' she apologised to the lady of the house – and took a job in the typing pool at the Pirelli Tower. The excitement of working there was immense; typing in another language kept her on her toes, and she was super useful when her boss, Alessandro

Messina, needed someone to help him compose a letter in English.

Alessandro was a charming and dapper man who wore Zegna suits and smoked Toscano cigars. A social climber from Sicily, Alessandro was a senior accountant at Pirelli, who soon fell for the Scottish typist, who he revered as if she were a magical creature. Nancy wasn't that unusual-looking in Scotland – her soft pageboy cut and neat neckerchiefs gave her delicate face a business-like gravitas – but in the Pirelli Tower she turned heads; many of the men walking the corridors in their wide lapels and flared suit trousers, hair slicked and a cigarette dangling from their lips, gawped at Nancy as if she were the first redhead they had ever seen. Alessandro picked Nancy out of the typing pool for her bilingual skills and her beauty, and she became his PA, typing his letters, popping out for his *piadina* and cigars, going for drinks after work with him, and soon La Scala. By 1974 Nancy was sleeping with Alessandro, while also arranging his holidays with his wife to the Dolomites, Camogli and Sicily.

She didn't think of Hughie once.

In the autumn of 1974, when Nancy realised they had slipped up and she was pregnant, she sat in Alessandro's office and they cried together.

'What are we to do?' he begged.

Nancy was lost for words.

Alessandro and his wife Maria had been longing for a baby for seven years without any success. 'This will break her.'

Nancy sat on the sofa clutching a handkerchief, for the first time in her life unsure. Of what to do. Of what it would mean for her future with Alessandro. Of what it would do to a job she loved. She had made so many friends in the Pirelli Tower, she didn't want to give it up.

'I can't do this to her,' Alessandro sobbed, conflicted by the treachery he was about to admit to but elated to have the child he'd assumed was impossible.

The showdown came on the yellow and blue tiled floor of the kitchen in the lofty apartment on Via Tiziano. Maria sat at her kitchen table, the Necchi sewing machine surrounded by lemons she had picked in the garden, and she looked her husband's lover in the eye.

'You have the baby, and I will nurture it,' she said, her eyes black and steely. Nancy wasn't sure if it was a suggestion or a command, and her hackles rose under the guilty sheen of her peachy skin. But the humiliation rendered her speechless. 'You want to be a working woman? Well, I want more than anything to be a mother, to hear laughter and noise in this lonely place.' Maria shot Alessandro a look to let him know her loneliness was his fault.

Nancy shook her head, unsure of what she had just heard, while Alessandro stood at the window, looking at the view of Milan beyond the balcony, oblivious to the tooting and the traffic below, his hands in his pockets and his dark brow furrowed. He couldn't believe Maria wasn't wailing.

'Maria, with respect,' Nancy trod carefully, 'I'm just not sure it would work.'

'Why not?'

And Nancy couldn't think of a single reason. It would certainly save her going back to her parents – she remembered their disapproval when abortion was legalised in her teens. She didn't want to go back to Edinburgh when she had made such a vibrant life for herself in Milan. And her inquisitive, intrepid mind was intrigued to know what a half-Scottish, half-Sicilian child would look like. Her biggest worry had been losing her job; perhaps this way, she wouldn't have to.

'I will not let you lose my husband's child,' Maria added.

She knew this was her one shot to be a mother.

And Nancy had been told.

Nancy, Alessandro and Maria agreed that Nancy would have the baby and they would live together in the spacious apartment on Tiziano while Nancy was convalescing. Then the baby would live with Maria and Alessandro during the week, and its birth mother at weekends. Maria, a seamstress, who could take as much or as little work as she wanted, would look after the baby during the days and long nights of Nancy's working week at the Pirelli Tower; growing into homework, ballet, swimming and horse-riding as their child got older. Nancy would have her baby at the weekends, some holiday time to visit her parents in Scotland. But there was a condition. The affair had to stop.

'I'm a proud woman,' Maria said, playing with an empty bobbin between her forefinger and thumb. 'A gift has come from this embarrassment. Don't make me go through it ever again.'

Nancy agreed. She was fond of Alessandro, but she didn't love him the way she would hope to love a man: wholeheartedly, without limits, terms and conditions.

Olivia was born in July 1975 and so the arrangement began. Maria was a tender and caring doula to Nancy while the battle cries of birth tore her apart. Alessandro sat in Bar Basso nursing a negroni and bought each woman a Bulgari diamond pendant for their travails. Maria might have looked rustic with her large bust and wild curly black hair, but her expensive clothes, cinched-in waist and subtle gems discreetly told the world she was an executive's wife.

Nancy recovered in the top-floor apartment while Maria got the nursery tip-top and Olivia gurgled in her crib. Alessandro had a Silver Cross pram with swirling, ostentatious wheels, shipped out from England, much to the amusement of his Pirelli colleagues, who said the tyres looked Stone Age, but there was nothing Olivia would want for. Two mammas. One doting father. A phoenix rising from the ashes of a marriage on the brink, bringing joy and normality to these otherwise unusual of circumstances.

Once Nancy was back at work, Olivia would kick and gurgle in her baby basket atop Maria's sewing table, the hum of the machine sending her off to sleep. At weekends Nancy would take her daughter to Parco Sempione, where old women would marvel at the little girl with olive skin and deep red hair, as if she were a firefly darting between the verbena bushes.

'*Che belleza!*'

'*Che magica!*'

'*Affascinante!*'

At school plays and musical recitals, Mamma Una and Mamma Due would clap proudly, and Alessandro would turn up if he could, beaming at his daughter; bestowing her with a Gucci watch or a Damiani ribbon-tied bag. It was a happy childhood for the adored girl, who felt extremely comfortable being the centre of three people's universes, until her teenage years brought rebellion and turmoil at the International School.

The man with the pink face returned from a second visit to the toilet and propped himself up at a fruit machine nearby, but Daniel didn't notice, he was too lost in Olivia's story.

'One of my mothers is an atelier.'

Daniel didn't know what that meant, but nodded because it sounded very impressive and he was too embarrassed to ask.

'She worked for the big houses before I was born: Versace, Dolce & Gabbana, Ferré... She was so good, so precise, so fast, they didn't want to let her go, so they let her work from home, with me in my basket on the sewing table. It was the early days for some of those houses.'

'What, she made all those expensive dresses from home?'

'Well, when she was at home and not in the studio she'd make the toiles. The prototypes.'

Prototypes. Models. Precision. They were words both Alessandro and Maria used in their very different sectors; motoring and fashion, two pillars of Milan's booming economy.

'She had a little sewing machine in the kitchen, and a bigger one, her favourite Necchi, was in the studio room.'

Olivia thought of the sewing machine under the window that looked out onto the fig trees of the manicured communal garden below. The room was light and bright with long windows and high ceilings; white fabric cut-outs of suits, skirts and dresses, some pinned with paper adornments where patterns, sequins and feathers might be added. All worn by faceless mannequins. Notes and dimensions, fabric codes and swatches, chalk and pencil markings, all pinned to great boards on the walls, designating which fashion house the item was for, which season, which collection. Secrets Maria kept for each designer, final incarnations of which she only saw in the *Corriere della Sera* or *Vogue Italia* after Milan Fashion Week had blazed through town. The seamstresses were never invited to the shows.

Olivia told Daniel how she would have tea parties with the mannequins: silent, impeccably dressed playmates and he smiled, picturing what a cute child Olivia might have looked like.

'I *loved* that studio room as a kid. I suppose it was meant to be another bedroom, but it was the best playroom ever. And there weren't any more children coming along – at least that's what we hoped…' Olivia rolled her eyes at Daniel.

Alessandro wasn't allowed to smoke in the toile room, lest the patterns turn yellow or pick up the scent of Kentucky tobacco, but he stopped in the 1980s anyway, after his first heart attack.

Daniel finished his pint and gestured to Olivia.

'Want another? I'll get you a double this time.'

She looked to the man at the fruit machine.

'Yes! But let's go somewhere else.'

'Cool. We should probably eat too,' Daniel said sagely.

In a similar, smaller sports bar, further down Princes Street, Daniel and Olivia sat opposite each other, each eating a burger. Double Jack Daniel's and Coke next to each plate.

Daniel was definitely getting a second wind.

'So what did you grow up thinking – about your... situation?' Daniel asked, while he put down his vast burger for a pause. Olivia stopped short of taking a bite, put her burger down, and tied her hair in a bun on top of her head, ready to go into battle. The mac'n'cheese burger they both ordered was no mean feat. A towering cheeseburger with bacon, lettuce, tomatoes and gherkins, then a square of macaroni cheese plonked on top of it, and sealed in by a burger bun.

'I thought it was normal. It was all I knew.'

'Wow.'

'I suppose when I got to *elementare*, maybe I wondered why my friends' families were more... *nucleare*. I suppose I started asking questions. Maybe I assumed all dads had these "blips". Or maybe because it happened before I was born made me not put any significance on it. As if nothing exists before you exist.'

Daniel looked at Olivia swiping mustard from the corner of her mouth and forgot that life existed before tonight.

'Maybe I assumed other dads had also... what's the word... squeered other children.'

'Squired?'

'Yes that's it. And that it was perfectly normal.'

Daniel picked up his burger again.

'It *was* perfectly normal, until I went to International School and realised it wasn't a very nice way to treat either of my mothers. But I made friends with people whose lives were a lot crazier than mine. And we all have our cross to wear...'

Daniel didn't correct her as he thought about his. He

didn't really have any. His mum and dad *were* pretty nuclear. He and his older brother Matt always fitted neatly into life, into bunk beds, into cars and family tickets to theme parks. They still lived in the neat semi Daniel and Matt grew up in. The only family heartache they had known was the death of Daniel's beloved grandad in the spring.

'Anyway,' she said casually as she looked at her watch again and tutted. 'Enough about this, I don't really want to talk about my dad.'

Daniel got the impression Olivia always wanted to move on; that she liked to talk and then suddenly didn't.

'What about you? Tell me your life story.'

Daniel lifted his burger but paused at his lips and looked a bit nervous. He was much happier talking about other people. Asking the questions.

'Me? Well I've just graduated. In journalism. Undergraduate and then post-grad. At Surrey.'

Olivia looked blank. 'Sorry?'

'Surrey. It's basically London.'

'Ah, OK.'

'I'm travelling for the summer before I start a job on my local newspaper. Again, basically London, just the other side of it. To the north. It's the paper in the town I grew up in.'

Daniel suddenly thought of Elmworth and Kelly and realised he didn't give a *fuck* where she was in the world. Whether she'd got a job in a bar or in telesales in Sydney. Whether she and Ian were going great guns or whether her foibles – the way she twisted her ponytail or pulled at the skin around her fingernails – bothered him more than they'd bothered Daniel, which wasn't much.

'Cool,' Olivia said, sounding more American now, as if it

was quaint. 'Where's that?'

'Near Cambridge. Have you heard of Cambridge?'

'For sure. Some of my friends went there.'

'Oh yes. Well, I live in a little town near there. Elmworth, it's called, you won't have heard of it.'

He didn't mention that he would be living back at home with his mum, dad and brother. That Matt would go off to work at the local Safeway supermarket while Daniel went to the newspaper office, his mum to school and his dad to the bank. His nuclear family. It didn't sound nearly as cool as a flat in Soho paid for by a Pirelli tycoon.

'What sort of thing will you write about?'

'Oh, I'm not sure.' Daniel dabbed ketchup off the corner of his mouth onto his red check shirt, a little more demurely than Olivia had with her mustard. 'I imagine cats stuck up trees, potholes, refuse collection. Although I guess I'll be making the tea to start with...' Daniel winced as he realised he was selling himself short and not making his best impression. 'But I hope to move into sports writing one day. I specialised in sports journalism. You have to work your way up.'

'Sounds cool.'

'Maybe one day I'll work for that pink paper you guys have. The sports one?'

'*La Gazzetta dello Sport?*'

'That's the one.'

'All the life is rosy.'

'Hmm, it really isn't,' shrugged Daniel, not getting the joke. Then a brief panic passed over him while he was chastising himself about underselling himself: what if he *hadn't* actually got the job; what if it *wasn't* secure?

He'd been offered the role of junior news reporter by Viv

Hart, the paper's editor, the day before he went travelling, and he hadn't heard from her since. No email follow-up. No contract had come in the post. There would be nothing rosy about getting home from travelling and returning to live with his parents and being jobless.

He made a mental note to call home tomorrow – when Olivia had gone – and ask his mum if a contract had come through. He hoped the job was still there, and that he could work his way up to being a sports reporter on a national paper during the time Olivia was doing her course in London. Then he could really impress her.

A karaoke DJ started setting up his equipment and Pulp's 'Disco 2000' came over the speakers.

'How old are you Olivia?' Daniel asked, changing the subject, embarrassed by how formal he sounded.

'Twenty. You?'

'Twenty-two.'

'Well, I'm only 20 for a few hours more.'

'Huh?'

'I'll be 21 tomorrow.'

Daniel cleared his throat.

'What? Actually, tomorrow?' He looked at his Casio. 'In less than four hours' time?'

'Yes!' Olivia said through a mouthful of burger.

'Happy birthday!'

'Thanks. It's not yet though. It's bad luck to say it beforehand.'

'Oh sorry.'

'That's OK.'

'So you're travelling all day on your twenty-first birthday? That sucks.'

'No, I'm pretty sure I get this birthday twice, International Date Line you see. That's why I'm going home. My mammas have organised a party.'

It was a party Daniel wished he could go to, but he wondered why her father hadn't had a hand in organising it: did he always leave the hard labour to the women?

'Then we should do something momentous! To celebrate tonight. What do you want to do?'

'It's bad luck to celebrate before your actual birthday!' Olivia protested.

'You look like a rule breaker to me,' Daniel said, surprising himself by how flirty he sounded.

'We-lll…' Olivia said, in a long and thoughtful way, as she leaned across the table, put her hand on Daniel's face, and wiped the final residue of ketchup from the corner of his mouth with her thumb.

He was taken aback.

'I want to do karaoke. For sure,' she said, nodding to the DJ. 'And then I might want to kiss you.'

'Right,' said the DJ with a mullet and a shiny suit, into a handheld microphone as he looked at his clipboard. 'We've got Livvi and Danielle – they're up next singing "Islands in the Stream". Livvi and Danielle? Come on girls, you're up!' The DJ looked around the bar, his mullet shaking in the breeze of his small and rickety wind machine.

'Ooh, that's us!' said Olivia, as she widened her eyes and unleashed her bun.

'What?'

Despite the steady flow of lager, whisky, and now sambuca,

Daniel still wasn't willing to sing karaoke. He'd never done it before.

'Nahhh, sorry, I'll sit this out – you go. I'll cheer the loudest I promise!'

Olivia took off her jumper and flung it on her cloth bag, not caring that her passport was inside it. The bar was warm and she looked like a Proper Backpacker again, in her vest and multicoloured trousers.

'*Andiamo*,' she ordered, hands on her narrow hips.

'No!' Daniel protested.

'Yes!' she barked. 'Look!' She gestured wildly to the watch on her wrist without taking her eyes off Daniel. 'In two hours it will be my twenty-first birthday – and *you*—' she pointed accusingly and almost stumbled '—*you*, are the last friend of my trip.'

Daniel felt a stab of jealousy, for all the other friends she had made. What if she had actually kissed them? He bet she kissed the man at the lighthouse without any shoes. 'You have no choice, you *have* to sing karaoke with me or you ruin my whole birthday.'

'I thought it was bad luck to celebrate before...?'

Olivia rose on the balls of her feet like a peahen, almost level with Daniel she was so tall. She gave him a disarming look he knew then he would never forget.

Daniel put up his palms in defeat.

'Really, I'm not a singer.'

Olivia studied Daniel's face through drunken eyes. She wasn't sure if his fear was genuine or not. She'd never met anyone like him before – the boys at school were never so modest. But they were the sons of Milan's finest. The bankers. The fashion elite. The motoring heirs. The sons of footballing legends. None of them would talk themselves down as Daniel did. The boys Olivia knew all had an air of entitlement about them that meant they would never consider themselves the tea boy, or be too embarrassed to sing to a half-empty sports bar.

'Livvi and Danielle? Come on girls! Make me happy!' said the DJ in clipped Kiwi vowels.

Olivia held out her hand.

'Please…?'

'Can't I just watch?'

She burned into his khaki eyes. Daniel stood up and took her hand.

'*Allora,*' Olivia said commandingly. 'You're Kenny, I'm Dolly, although in that check shirt it should be you who is Dolly.'

What?!

Daniel laughed at the ridiculousness of it.

'I can't sing!'

'Nor can I!' Olivia howled. 'That's the beautiful of karaoke.'

They approached the DJ and his PA system to a limp applause from the bar. The DJ looked at the pair of them.

'Danielle?' he asked Olivia.

'Daniel – she's Livvi, I'm Daniel.'

'OK Livvi and Daniel, Dolly and Kenny – whoever you are – take it away!'

Daniel's warm palms turned cold and clammy as a cheesy backing track struck up and Olivia started to sway confidently as the first chords started. Daniel ruffled his hair, missed his cue and started to panic, as Olivia watched words change from white to blue on a small monitor. As

Daniel's mouth went dry and a ball bounced over the words, Olivia came in and rescued him.

'OK I'm Kenny!' she ordered, as she took Daniel's hand, started singing and he joined in apprehensively.

For four clunky minutes they sang 'Islands in the Stream', badly, in unison, wide eyes looking at each other, scouring each other's souls for fragments of comfort they could sense within them.

Sitting on stone steps under a portal outside the imposing train station, Olivia checked her bag to make sure she hadn't lost anything. Disappointingly, the sports bar – seemingly all bars in Dunedin – closed at 11.30 p.m., so Olivia and Daniel had an hour to kill. An hour to amble to the nearby station and wait for Olivia's train; an hour for Daniel to eke out their evening to the very last moment.

'You sure you didn't leave anything in the bar?' Daniel asked, worried by how drunk and giddy he was feeling.

'Only my *dignità*,' Olivia joked.

'You got your plane tickets?'

Olivia rummaged in her cloth bag.

'*Passaporto*, train ticket, plane ticket, Walkman, headphones... money. Yes! All good. Don't worry, all my treasures are here.'

Then Daniel remembered.

'Shit!' he said.

'What?' Olivia gasped. Daniel's sharp realisation had made her jump. And then laugh.

Daniel had been so caught up in getting to know Olivia, fearful of the grains of sand ebbing away in a timer that was constantly on his shoulder, that he had forgotten about Olivia's ankle chain, safely stowed in the inside pocket of his bag.

'I have something of yours! I'm so sorry, I meant to…'

Olivia half smiled, half frowned, as she watched him open the bag on the stone step between his feet.

He felt the familiar shape of the chain. Its links and gems he had caressed and examined, imagining the life of its owner, and pulled it out of his bag.

Olivia saw it, her eyes widening in disbelief.

'My necklace!'

'Necklace?'

'How did you get this?'

'In Sydney. In the club. You gave me your drink to hold, so you could dance.'

'I don't remember.'

'A drag queen. *Pulp Fiction*. You were dancing together.'

'Her! I remember *her*! That's when I lost it?'

'You danced so hard your jewellery flew off!' Daniel chuckled to himself. 'I tried to catch up with you…'

Olivia's eyes welled up as she lifted the chain weaving through Daniel's fingers, threading it into hers. She stroked one of the stones with her forefinger and thumb.

'My necklace.'

She looked adoringly at it, then adoringly at Daniel.

'Thank you thank you thank you! I cannot believe it!'

'Well, I wanted to tell you – at sunrise in Byron Bay. After the whale had stopped leaping, but I turned back and you'd gone.'

'Oh.'

'And then on the highway, I wanted to tell you – I looked

for you in Cairns...'

Olivia silenced Daniel with an emphatic hug, her arms looping around his neck next to her. She squeezed him tight, in a wholehearted embrace.

'This is amazing, I thought I'd never see it again. I can't believe I'm reunited with it on the last night of my trip. Thank you, Daniel.'

Daniel was relieved she wasn't angry.

'I'm just sorry I didn't remember earlier tonight.'

A tear trickled down one of Olivia's cheeks.

'Are you OK?'

She nodded.

'Very OK. This is wonderful. You are wonderful. This necklace – my father gave it to me when I was a little girl. These are ruby, peridot and citrine – the birth stones of me and my mothers.'

Daniel looked at the chain under the pale glow of the streetlight. It was sparkling more now that it was in her hands. He was so obsessed with the girl it belonged to, he hadn't noticed the beauty in the gemstones. He hadn't realised it were so precious.

'I loved it so much, that as I got bigger and it became tight around my neck, I had it made smaller, a few links taken out so I could wear it on my wrist. But I wear it on my ankle. My father always anchoring me to the ground.'

Daniel smiled.

'I knew it was careless to bring it backpacking.' Olivia shook her head, as if she were chastising herself, looking like she was sobering up. She fastened the chain to her ankle, safely under her trousers, and shook her head again.

'Are you OK?' Daniel asked, nudging his arm into hers.

Wishing he had the confidence to hug her.

'Not really.'

'What's wrong?'

'My dad... He died in April.'

'Oh god Olivia, I'm so sorry.'

'A heart attack. He was 64. Older than my mothers – twenty years older than Mamma Una anyway...'

'Shit.'

'But too young for a heart attack. It was his second one!' she shrugged, as if it was funny, when clearly she didn't think it was.

Olivia looked up and her eyes met Daniel's. They were honest and heartfelt and she didn't feel drunk enough anymore.

'I'm so fucking sorry.' Daniel felt moved enough to pull her in, and she placed her face in the curve of his neck and let out a quiet cry. They sat in silence for a couple of minutes, Olivia's gentle sobs slowing. Daniel, conscious of the time and wishing he could stop it, stroked her arm under her cagoule, before Olivia pulled back, pushing her tears up to the wisps of baby hair on her forehead.

'That's why I came travelling really. To get some breathing space. To meet men and have distractions.'

She laughed bittersweetly.

Daniel didn't like the thought of Olivia meeting men and being distracted, even if he might be one of them.

'To drink hard and party hard. Ah!' Which reminded Olivia of the hipflask she hadn't mentioned when she did the inventory of her bag. She whipped it out to lighten the mood.

'One for the road?'

Daniel marvelled and nodded while Olivia took a swig

ot astringent vodka. She handed the hipflask to Daniel and he followed suit.

'Shit man,' he said, wincing. 'And I really am sorry, about your dad.'

'Thanks.'

'I would never have made such a fuss about being Kenny Rogers had I known.'

Olivia smiled gratefully.

'Have you got your passport?'

Olivia's heavy lids drooped as she felt for the rectangle inside her cloth bag.

'Uh-huh,' she nodded. 'And you asked me this already. You're fussier than my nonna.'

Daniel looked at the large train station clock. She had six minutes to haul the backpack she had clumsily pulled out of the locker in the left luggage area, onto her back and up to platform one, but she didn't seem bothered, Jack Daniel's, Dolly and a vodka reviver all coursing through her veins. The revelation about Olivia's father and the ticking clock was sobering Daniel up. The vodka hadn't worked for him.

'Your train terminates at Christchurch, yes? You won't fall asleep and miss your stop?'

'I will fall asleep – but I won't miss my stop. Christchurch is the last one, *si*.'

She pulled her Walkman and a cassette box out of her bag. 'I got my bedtime ballad to listen to.'

'Huh?'

'"Hyperballad".'

'What?'

She shook the rattling cassette box as she turned it around. It was 'Post' by Björk.

'It's my sleeping album.'

'No way! That's my "in transit" album. I listen to it on the longer journeys. I love her.'

Olivia was silenced, surprised by the English boy with a soft heart. They stood alone in the middle of the station, neither knowing how to end their brief encounter.

Four minutes.

The elaborate mosaic floor under their walking boots and the Royal Doulton tiles up to the circular balcony above the bookings hall made Olivia feel as if she were a diva on stage at La Scala, and remembered she would soon be back in Milan. But she already had her audience, Daniel's eyes were firmly on her face.

'You'd better go. You'll miss your train and your flight.'

Daniel heaved the backpack off the tiles and onto Olivia's back, the weight of it almost making her topple backwards.

'Whoa!' she laughed as Daniel caught her by her two outstretched hands and pulled her back up in his.

'Want me to carry your bag to the train? It's massive.'

'No, no, no, I'll be fine.'

Three minutes.

They paused, and Daniel looked around self-consciously, at the empty and ornate ticket hall, and then back to Olivia in their bubble in the middle of it. Both were surprised by how empty the train station was for the last departure to the island's largest city.

'*Allora,*' she said, thoughtfully. 'Thank you for my

necklace. I can't tell you what it means to me. How happy I am to be going home with it.'

Daniel smiled.

I don't want you to go.

'You'd really better go. Have a safe trip yeah?'

Olivia nodded.

'And a brilliant party. Save me some cake, right?'

'I'll see you in London,' Olivia replied, without much conviction.

As Daniel looked to see if Olivia was joking, she pressed her lips onto his, his gasp silenced by her mouth. Her lips were wet and plump and her tongue tasted of liquorice and honey. She pulled back again, the weight of her backpack and the ticking clock drawing her away. '*Ciao.*'

Two minutes.

'See you in London,' Daniel smiled and nodded, scratching the back of his head, as he watched Olivia zig-zag to her train on platform one, backpack dragging her down, travel documents and world possessions carelessly slung across her front in a flimsy cloth bag. He desperately hoped he would. 'Oh and happy birthday!' he shouted, up towards the platform beyond the barrier. 'It's your birthday now!' he yelled louder, his face full of hope that she would turn around and smile.

But Olivia didn't look back.

Eight

August 2017
Ibiza, Spain

'Girls! Are your cases packed?'
Olivia flitted around the villa, gathering bottles of suncream, trinkets, phone chargers and the few magazines she wanted to take home.

Flora was flopped on the sofa in a loveheart print playsuit, looking at her phone.

'Did you hear me?'

'Huh?'

'Your case. Is it ready for Dad to put in the car?'

'Erm...' Flora looked vague, as if she didn't have a clue where she was or why her mother was hassling her to get her suitcase together. From the distraction of Snapchat, Flora had forgotten she was even in Spain, and not on the L-shaped sofa at home. That she wasn't actually an animated puppy with enormous eyes and a long protruding tongue.

'Your case? Your stuff? Your new bomber jacket?' Olivia said, appealing to her daughter's sense of priority, even though it had been too hot to wear it all holiday.

'Erm, sure,' Flora shrugged unconvincingly.

'Well, go check. And where's your sister?' Olivia asked, although she didn't really need to. Sofia had spent most of the holiday doing cartwheels around the pool's edge. Daring to get closer to the blue and white tiled lip of the pool with each starburst of her limbs.

Flora rolled her eyes and stood up, to go and finish packing. True. She didn't want to forget her Love Moschino bomber jacket, the pride and joy her parents got her for her birthday in the spring.

Olivia, hair piled on her head, walked back into the bedroom where Daniel was stuffing charging cables and battery packs into a leather holdall.

'I don't know, I thought we'd made a leap yesterday. Now it's back to monosyllables and attitude.'

'She's 13. I'm sure you were the same at 13,' Daniel reassured.

'Yes, but yesterday was so... perfect. Like it was a glimpse into the future.' Olivia padded onto the stone floor of the rustic ensuite bathroom to gather the toiletries around the sink, wiping damp bottle bases onto a hand towel strewn next to it and putting them into a washbag. She stopped to examine her reflection in the mirror above it. To envisage what she might look like when her daughters were adults. She stared at herself, imagining lines creeping around her face like ivy climbing a withered wall, and she felt no fear in ageing. She saw Flora's face on hers, and imagined what a wonderful grandmother she might make.

Yesterday *had* been lovely. For the first time in the entire holiday, Olivia had got Flora to put down her phone and actually *engage* with her.

'Wanna go on an adventure?' she had asked poolside after breakfast, as Daniel patiently played bat and ball with Sofia. To Olivia's utter surprise Flora said yes. So they jumped in the hire car and drove from the clifftop villa to Santa Gertrudis, where they bought pottery and ate wild beets and goats' cheese in the village square, then to San Juan market to buy local honey, a necklace each and listen to live music, followed by the boutiques in Ibiza Town. Olivia stopped to look at dresses, fabrics and patterns, draping some of them around Flora and making mental illustrations of how she would shape them, how she would cut the fabric. How good they would look on her daughter. They stopped for a glass of rosé and a mocktail at a little finca on the way home, and Flora tipped her head back and beamed a smile Olivia wished she could bottle. Flora was even more beautiful than her mother, even though she didn't smile as much. Her skin was more olive, her hair more lustrous; the whites of her dark brown eyes sparkled against the terracotta tones of her face. Maria always said she was born a wise and cynical soul, and she adored her.

'I've had the most perfect day,' Olivia said, as an earthenware bowl of prawns in garlic sauce sizzled between them, hoping her enthusiasm wouldn't make her daughter recoil.

'Me too,' Flora replied, and Olivia felt like she had cracked a nut.

'Well, I'm sure the teenage angst doesn't end there!' Daniel called out from within a cloud of cable spaghetti on the bed. 'Plus we've got it in another five years with Sofia.'

'Hmmm, true,' Olivia said, still examining her reflection. The laughter lines around her eyes that she hadn't noticed before. Freckles that had married and morphed into bigger sun splatters after ten days in the Balearic sunshine. The sun-kissed streaks of her hair, as it went every summer, as it was when she first met Daniel. She tugged at her face and noted that her skin was almost as dark as her own paternal grandmother, Nonna Renata – a Sicilian peasant who was almost 100. Alessandro would take Olivia to visit his parents, Vincenzo and Renata, every winter when she was a little girl, and Renata would marvel at the redhead playing around the orange groves. Nonna Renata seemed old to Olivia thirty years ago, so she imagined how ancient she must seem now – as shrivelled and as soft as a sultana – to Flora and Sofia on their half-term trips to Sicily.

Alessandro had left the island to study in Milan, and took great pride in returning in his shirts, ties, dapper suits and paler skin, as if no one could tell he ought to be a farmer. The Pirelli building had a way of making men pale, but there was no mistaking Olivia's Sicilian heritage, smothering her Scottish roots at the end of a summer holiday, reflected back in the mirror today, making her feel both aged and revived.

The shopping trip with Flora had given her so many ideas, so much inspiration. Most of the dresses she created were flouncy but neutral, in muted tones, but for some embroidery or beading, usually in the same shade as the net, silk or tulle fabric. But yesterday's trip, the milestone with Flora, gave her new inspiration. The Balearic tiles and fabrics had reminded her of Sicilian majolica at Vincenzo and Renata's house: patterned earthenware covered in blues, yellows and golds, adorned with pictures of cherubs, saints and fruits. Stories that the Moors had painted and the potters of Sicily took as their own as the trade winds from north Africa blew ships through the Balearics en route to the Renaissance. Draping Flora in such prints inspired Olivia to create a whole line of clothes with more colour, more pattern: an ode to majolica, her nonna and her heritage.

Mi famiglia.

Olivia undid her topknot and let her hair tumble down. She considered brushing it, though she rarely brushed it because it looked better unkempt than bushy. She picked up the big paddle hairbrush next to the copper sink, and dropped it on the floor, taking a small bottle of face oil with it, and smashing it on the tiles.

'Shit.'

'Are you OK?'

'Avere le mani di pasta frolla...' Olivia muttered to herself.

Olivia rarely spoke Italian outside of Italy anymore – and it had been almost two decades since she'd lived there.

'Huh?'

'Pastry hands, I have pastry hands, it's OK,' Olivia said, as she bent down to pick the oil up, but she got stuck halfway. 'I... I dropped a hairbrush.'

Daniel walked into the bathroom.

'You OK?'

Olivia stared at the brush and the leaking oil on the floor at her feet but didn't say anything. She couldn't even turn the bottle to stem the small slick of oil. It was as if she had frozen, bent over, in the shape of a question mark. Daniel's question lingered in the air but he didn't think much about the severity of it, and tried to lighten the mood.

'I won't tell the girls it was pills and not hairbrushes you used to drop...'

It wasn't very funny, but Olivia could feel in her face that she wouldn't have been able to smile even if she had wanted to. She was frozen, and a burning sensation struck her like a lightning bolt in her right temple.

'Daniel... Daniel, I can't feel my...'

'Hey hey, come here.' Daniel carefully rubbed Olivia's back as he gently straightened her and turned her to face the sink's ledge so she could lean on it.

'Daniel!' she shouted, her voice echoing in the curved copper as she threw up into it. 'I can't—' She heaved again violently. 'I'm spinning.'

'Shhh, shhh it's OK, it's OK...' Daniel propped Olivia's elbows up on the smooth stone around the sink. 'Lean on this, don't move. I'll just grab the flannel.' Daniel reached out to the bath.

It wasn't pain Olivia felt, not after the lightning bolt, but a dizziness that sent her spinning, and a tingling numbness in her face and down one side.

'Just lean there, let it out. I'm going to pick up that glass on the floor or you'll cut yourself.'

Olivia stood on her tiptoes and clung to the sink.

'That's it, mind your toes...'

Sofia came running in, alarmed by the sound of her mother's echoed retching.

'Mummy! Mummy! What's wrong?!'

Sofia was bouncing at the door like an anxious puppy trying to catch a ball.

'Are you OK?!'

Olivia vomited her answer.

'Oh Mummy!' Sofia gasped.

'She's just a bit sick princess, she'll be fine – go and get the dustpan and brush from the cupboard under the sink for me, will you? There's a good girl.'

Sofia lingered at the doorframe.

'Oh Mummy, I don't like it!'

'Then go and get the dustpan and brush,' Daniel said more sternly, torn between picking up the glass at Olivia's feet and rubbing her back while she continued to vomit.

'It's OK my love, it's OK.'

'What... what about... packing?' she cried through tears and bile.

'Shhh, shhh, don't worry, just get this out. Deep breaths.'

'My head.'

'You're OK.'

Flora marched into the bedroom with a scowl.

'What's going on?' she said, as if she were about to reprimand her parents.

'It's OK, your mother's a bit poorly, she'll be right in a second.'

Over the basin, Olivia took deep breaths as the urge to vomit abated, the zoetrope in her head slowed down and her breathing started to regulate. As Daniel held her hair back and tucked it behind her ears, he thought of the flat in Lexington Street.

'Shall I call a doctor?' Daniel asked in a low whisper, into Olivia's ringing ear.

'No, no, no, it's passing. And we need to get going.'

'You can't travel like this,' Daniel urged.

'Is your case packed, *tesora*?' Olivia asked Flora in the

mirror, wiping her face with the flannel. 'We need to get to the airport.'

'Don't come in,' Daniel advised, 'there's glass on the floor.'

Flora clutched the door frame and stared at her mother's reflection.

'What's wrong with your face?' she asked.

'Right, drink the water or we lose it,' Olivia instructed to the brood following her, as they all wheeled little cases through to security.

Flora eyed her mother's face suspiciously, checking to see if it was going back to normal as she insisted it was in the car on the way to the airport.

'Are you sure you should be flying?' Daniel whispered as the queue snaked at a pace around metal posts. A never-ending stream of tanned people clutching straw trilbies, *artesania* souvenirs and metal cases packed with records, slinked towards the X-ray machines in the departures hall. It seemed the whole world was leaving Ibiza on the last Monday in August, and suddenly Olivia couldn't wait.

Home.

The Huf Haus. Its peace. Her studio. She had so much to be getting on with.

'Yes!' Olivia hissed, giving Daniel a look of *don't frighten the girls*. 'It passed. I'm *fine*.'

Daniel shrugged and looked at his feet anxiously. He knew there wasn't much point arguing with his wife when she was so certain of something. Flora begrudgingly took off her headphones and put them with her phone and bag in the tray, her little sister buzzing around her, seemingly having forgotten the little drama back at the villa. Sofia put her cuddly dog in another tray, kissed it and waved it goodbye, as Olivia slung her makeup in a clear bag next to it. Daniel pulled a tray out for his bag and laptop, and Flora threw a cherry lip balm from her pocket on top of it. As they walked through the metal archway Daniel winced. He so hoped that whatever it was that happened to Olivia back at the villa, whatever it was that made her temple sear, her head spin and her stomach pump itself, wouldn't be triggered by machinery, beeping, X-rays and scans. He didn't want the security guards to detect anything sinister in his wife, and was relieved when they all passed through with nothing more than a smile for Sofia.

'Come on,' Olivia beckoned through tense teeth. Daniel nodded back to keep the girls calm and appearances up. Flora willowy and gawkish. Sofia bouncing like a rubber ball. 'Duty Free?' Olivia said cheerily. 'Come on, I'll get you a treat.'

Flora's frown unravelled as they weaved through makeup and perfume.

'Oh Mamma, there's this really cool Urban Decay palette...' she enthused quietly. Sofia ran over to a shelf full of teddy bears with the Spanish flag on their tummies and deliberated between one of those and a keepsake tin of M&Ms.

'I'll go get us a seat, yeah?' Daniel looked at Olivia nervously. 'I need to get online. Check the site.'

'Sure.'

While Daniel paused at the electricals, Olivia studied the wall of glass bottles in front of her. She fancied a change to go with her feeling of newness, her new ideas. Her usual purple fig parfum from Liberty was feeling a little tired against her summer skin, so she perused the cornucopia of potions in front of her, hoping to find something that would help ignite her inspiration. Something curative.

She picked up a large square bottle, knowing she wasn't even going to buy it, mainly to make it look she was doing something normal, to ease the girls, as she thought of her dressing table in the light-flooded bedroom back home.

Get me home.

'Mamma, this is it!' Flora always called Olivia mamma when she wanted something. 'There are tons of colours I would wear. Look, browns, greens, even a cool orange one, the one I tried from Amelie's palette and you said it looked nice? Amelie got it for...'

The name Amelie echoed in Olivia's ears as the lightning struck her temple again and her head felt like it was on fire. She let out a pained yelp as a cold sweat bubbled over her skin like a clammy mask and she hit the floor at the same time as the perfume bottle smashed against it.

Nine

September 1996
Cambridgeshire, England

'Look, I can come back another time if it isn't good... if there's been some kind of mix-up.'

Daniel sat on the stiff little sofa for two, right in front of the welcome desk in the cramped loft office with a low ceiling. It was the top floor of a 1980s building that also housed a doctor's surgery and a stationery supplies company (handy for when the *Elmworth Echo* staff needed hole punchers and pens). Daniel knew he was so close to the young receptionist who had introduced himself as Lee, that Lee could probably see inside Daniel's ear canal if he wanted to. Not that he would – he was looking at the big screen of his computer, waiting for the dial-up to resume.

'No, you're all right, I'm still trying to get hold of her,' Lee said calmly, phone wedged under his chin. 'I'm sure she won't be long...'

Lee must have been around the same age as Daniel, but had a quiet sensibility and wore a neat sweater that made him look older than his years. Perhaps he'd just been working there for a long time and wasn't fresh from adventure as Daniel was.

'Blimming thing...' Lee muttered, rolling his eyes at Daniel as he clicked a mouse with his free hand. The black curly phone cable knocked over the pen pot on his desk (also from the stationery supplier downstairs) and Lee rolled his eyes again as he propped it back up. Daniel knew Lee was trying to make him feel at ease; that his boss keeping people waiting might be a common occurrence. But surely not a new member of staff on day one.

That's if the job was secure. Viv Hart hadn't sent that contract in the post but she did confirm in an email to Daniel that he was to come in on Monday the 9th of September and they could sort all that out then. Lee shook the mouse again, embarrassed more than anything.

'Well, she's not answering at home. Sometimes she does work from home. And maybe she's not getting her emails. The internet might be down. I'll reset the box.' Lee hung up the phone and untangled the cable. 'I suppose she might be at the gym...'

Gym?

Lee got up, straightened his slacks, and walked to the back of the office, to a towering stack of boxes and cables.

'I'm just restarting the internet!' he announced in a polite and monotonous voice to a groan from both the sales and the editorial sides of the *Elmworth Echo*.

'Urgh!' snapped a blond man at the back of the office as he stared at his screen and tried not to look at Daniel, twiddling his thumbs on the sofa.

Daniel felt self-conscious being left waiting. He had never been late for an interview or a meeting or a day's work in his life. When he did work experience in his dad's bank; when he sat at the checkout next to Matt at Safeway; when he'd worked in the Co-op at uni; when he pulled pints at the Red Hart; when he'd done his placement on *The News* in Portsmouth. He was always punctual, diligent and respectful. He always took the role seriously, whether he was swiping tins of beans or reporting on house fires in Southsea. He couldn't believe that now he was here, to start his first Proper Job with a post-grad degree in journalism, his new boss seemed to have forgotten about his existence.

They'd had a good meeting at the start of summer. Daniel had called the editor of the *Elmworth Echo* speculatively. First stop: local paper. It's what all his lecturers had said when doling out career advice. That and always be willing to make the tea. Daniel had remembered his tutor's advice and called Viv Hart to try his luck. He couldn't believe it when the quiet male receptionist put him straight through to the editor.

He thought their chat had gone well: she liked the fact he was local, he had grown up in the town. She even seemed to like the fact he was about to go travelling for the summer – more so when he said he was going on his own. And Viv arranged to meet Daniel at the new Café Rouge on the high street the day before his flight, where she flipped through his portfolio and quizzed him on his parents, his upbringing, and how well he knew the community. When Viv said she'd like to get Daniel in when he got back in September, he thought he was being offered a job. Except maybe he wasn't. Or maybe she had and changed her mind. She had definitely said come in on the 9th of September on an email he picked up in an internet cafe in the Cook Islands. And here he was, in the suit he wore to his grandad's funeral, portfolio propped between his legs, just in case Viv had wanted to see it again. Except she had clearly forgotten the whole thing.

The blond man's head kept bobbing to look over his screen like an inquisitive marmoset; he couldn't keep his nosiness in check, so he got up and walked with Lee, back to the reception desk.

'Hi,' he nodded.

'Hello,' Daniel said back.

The blond man had a large forehead and piercing, blue, far-apart eyes that made him look like a cross between Bing Crosby and a Disney baby. He was even wearing sailor-boy stripes.

'She not about?' he said in a loud, Welsh voice, mortified for the nervous-looking graduate sitting awkwardly on the sofa. Daniel looked up and smiled. Lee looked tense.

'No, I tried…'

'For fuck's sake,' the sailor boy said behind clenched teeth.

He looked to Daniel, who was rubbing his clammy palms together. Daniel couldn't take the embarrassment anymore.

'Shall I just go?' he asked in polite defeat. He'd been waiting for over an hour.

'I'm so sorry,' said the Welshman matter-of-factly. He was clearly as mortified as Daniel was. He extended a hand. 'I'm Jim. Jim Beck.'

'Hi Jim,' Daniel said, standing slightly as he shook his hand before sitting back down, not sure whether to get up and go. 'Daniel Bleeker.'

'Do you want a glass of water or something Daniel Bleeker? Perhaps a gin?' Jim Beck let out a booming laugh that made Daniel smile and lifted the tension. Jim couldn't have been that much older than Daniel either. Late twenties perhaps with that baby face. His hair was blond and slicked up like a matinee idol, the whites around his blue eyes dazzled despite the exasperation he showed, as if he was in a constant battle with a boss who might have done this before.

A woman with crisp blonde curls and a pencil skirt too tight for the bottom it restrained walked past the desk. Daniel had seen her passing several times already, going to and from the kitchen.

'Is she not about?' said the woman, with an air of disapproval and authority, as if she were the only person allowed to say it out loud. 'Honestly. Get the poor boy some water, will you Lee. And something to read.' She gestured to Daniel with a tanned hand and nails painted a shade of coral.

Jim gave an apologetic smile while Lee headed to the little kitchen by the lifts.

'Jim, I'm just off to meet JP from Autoglint about next year's rates. Tell Viv I'll be back for our midday classifieds update. If she—'

As the woman swiped a slick of fuchsia lip gloss from a fruity smelling tube across her lips, the boss walked in. She had short silver hair, big white teeth and she was eating a crunchy green apple.

'Hello, hiiiiiiii,' she said, sliding the pack down from her back, to the assembled group at the entrance.

Lee returned with a glass of water and the woman with

the tight curls nodded to everyone and left.

'Oh Viv, I'm not sure if you got my messages…'

Lee motioned to Daniel, sitting back on the sofa, feeling like a lemon.

'No I haven't yet.' Viv looked down at Daniel and gave a hearty, puzzled smile.

'Oh, this is Daniel Bleeker, he's here about the junior news reporter job.'

Daniel had the weird sensation that he was at an interview, not here for his first day, and he was confused by the vagueness of it all. He looked up at the editor, her smile was perplexed and icy. He wanted to say, 'June. Café Rouge. You offered me a job?' But didn't. He was hopeful that this was the part when Viv Hart might look aghast, that she might feel terrible about having forgotten an appointment almost ninety minutes ago. That she would feel so terrible, she would give him another £5,000 on top of the £16,000 she'd mentioned when they met.

We agreed a salary, I must be starting.

But she didn't send that contract.

Or maybe it was just a chat.

Viv looked down at Daniel, nervous and sweaty in a suit full of sad memories, and gave him a look as if she were trying to place him, as if he had arrived early and she needed *just a minute.*

Daniel was too needy to protest.

Viv took another bite of her apple and nodded with a full mouth.

'Yes, hiiiiiii…'

Daniel didn't know whether she remembered him or not. Whether to stand up or stay seated. Then a flash changed her expression as she remembered something.

'Oh Jim, there's an ambulance outside Woolworths, do you want to see if there's a story there? I'm thinking the cover could do with something more dramatic and gory than the darned Town Hall development...'

Jim raised an eyebrow, his face eager and hopeful.

'Did it look bloody?' he asked keenly.

Viv didn't answer while Jim grabbed his Harrington jacket from the back of his chair, slid his Dictaphone in his pocket and picked up his pen and notepad.

'Excuse me,' he said, giving Daniel a broad smile as he headed out, skipping like Dexter Haven in *High Society*. Daniel envisaged Jim sliding down the stair rail and swinging around a lamppost on his way out and smiled to himself for the first time that day.

'Do you want to come this way?' Viv asked, although it wasn't really a question. 'Lee, we'll take the meeting room.'

And as Daniel stood up and picked up his bag and portfolio, as he followed Viv while she took another noisy bite of her apple, Daniel wished he could rewind, to that precipice on the Otago Peninsula, and have that night all over again.

Ten

August 2017
Ibiza, Spain

'Daddy! Daddy! What's wrong with her?'

Sofia threw herself onto the floor next to her mother, not minding the wetness oozing out of the smashed perfume bottle, or the broken glass and plastic that dotted the puddle.

Daniel ran over as fast as he could, from electricals through watches to fragrances, to see a commotion he already had a sinking feeling, he already knew, was to do with his wife. Olivia was lying on her back, her body twisted, her face and arm twitching.

'Liv!' he cried, as he crouched down and carefully felt her head, to see if that too had smashed on impact, but he couldn't feel any wetness behind her hair, there wasn't a stream of blood snaking out. Just the sickly sweetness of a flinching body doused in top notes of bergamot and orange.

A member of security came rushing over, his lanyard hitting seven-year-old Sofia in the face.

'*Qué pasó?*' he said, in a gruff voice.

'Ambulance, my wife needs an ambulance!' Daniel shouted, knowing they wouldn't be flying anywhere today; his panic was further compounded by what had happened back at the villa.

'Get up, Mum,' Flora quietly said to herself, exasperation in her voice. Until she realised her mother wasn't doing this to be funny, or to get a reaction from her, or to embarrass her. She had collapsed on the floor involuntarily and was clearly in pain.

A woman in a Duty-Free uniform and neckerchief spoke into her walkie talkie. From Daniel's basic understanding of Italian he could work out some of her Spanish.

Ayuda.

Ambulancia.

Urgencia.

The woman, crouched and cramped, turned to Daniel.

'Wha fli jew on, sir?'

'Pardon?'

'Fli?'

'Oh, Stansted. The 1420. EasyJet.'

The woman spoke into her walkie talkie.

'OK sir, you cannot fli today, sir.'

'I know that. When's the ambulance coming?'

A small man with a bald head ran over and started tending to Olivia, checking her vitals.

'Soon, we need jour boarding pass and *pasaporte*, sir.'

'What?'

'So I can get your equipment taken off the plane. For all of your group.'

The woman spoke to the gruff security official, who was holding out his hand.

'Oh, right.' Daniel handed over the passports and boarding passes, except Olivia's, which was inside the little leather saddle bag slung across her body on the floor.

'And jer?'

'My wife, is she OK?' Daniel asked the bald man.

'Jer *pasaporte*, sir?'

'For fuck's sake, it's in her bag! I don't think we should move her!' Daniel looked up to the crowd and shouted. 'Has someone actually called an ambulance?!'

Sofia sobbed as tourists started to crowd around. A Swedish woman said she was a doctor and offered to help. The bald man nodded, to both Daniel and the Swedish doctor, as he listened to Olivia's pulse.

'Daddy! Is she dying?' begged Sofia. 'Please don't let her die!'

Flora started crying now and pulled Sofia into her waist. Daniel shook his head.

'No sweetheart, Mummy just fainted, she'll be fine. But I don't think we're flying home today.'

Eleven

'Thank you so much for having us Mrs Cruddup, your home is adorable,' Jim said, with earnest baby blues and a dashing smile, as he handed the woman with thick false eyelashes a Charles and Diana mug. His Fred Astaire charm was a veil for the scathing thoughts inside his head: that there was *no fuckin' way* (as Jim often said in his sweet Valleys diction), he would touch the tepid tea inside the commemorative royal wedding cup, not after he saw Mrs Cruddup pouring UHT milk into it. *On top* of the teabag. So he tipped it out onto the pansies in the front garden when only Daniel was looking. 'And thanks a million for showing us your gate,' he added with a beam.

'You're welcome love,' she said, touched to have been visited after all these months calling the paper.

Ever since Mrs Cruddup's new gate had been fitted in the spring, and she noticed something different about it, she had been calling Lee on reception at the *Elmworth Echo* and asking him to put her through to someone on the news desk. After months of being fobbed off and Jim putting it off, they finally paid her a visit.

Jim, Daniel and Alan the photographer couldn't deny that the gate to the neat front garden did indeed sound like Chewbacca from *Star Wars* mid-roar, as it opened and closed, and Jim was already thinking of the headline he could write to accompany the story.

'WOOKIE WHAT WE HAVE HEAR!'

'CHEWIE ON THAT, POSTMAN!'

'HEAR THIS GATE, YOU MUST!'

'THIS GATE NEEDS NO WOO-KEY!'

OK, they needed work, but it was a slow news week.

Daniel finished his glass of water and checked over his shorthand notes.

'Yes, I think that's everything. Thanks Mrs Cruddup, it's been... a revelation.'

The woman gazed adoringly at the handsome young men in her hallway, before her eyes settled on Alan the photographer, who slurped down the last dregs of anaemic tea to fill a silence. Jim shot Daniel a quick look of repulsion and pretended to puke.

'My pleasure! It's been a long time since I had three handsome men in my house!' Mrs Cruddup let out a saucy giggle, as Jim's high forehead crinkled all the way up to his quiff and his eyes widened in alarm. Alan pulled his trousers up from under his girth, and handed his mug with a barn owl on it back to the genial host. Alan had enjoyed getting an array of shots of Mrs Cruddup lingering over the gate, her heavy false lashes fluttering and her frosty pink lipstick shimmering in the sunshine. Especially after she had pointedly told Daniel in his interview that Mr Cruddup wasn't on the scene anymore.

'Gross,' Jim had whispered to Daniel, as they stood in the porch watching Alan at work, stifled by carpet and flocked wallpaper on a warm September afternoon.

'Thanks for having us Beverly,' Alan tried to smoulder.

'Unless something major happens, it'll run in Thursday's issue,' Jim said quickly, keen to leave.

'Oh wonderful!' The woman clasped her manicured hands together. 'I shall look out for it. Thanks so much for coming,' she said with an adoring smile. 'Bye boys.'

'Bye Mrs Cruddup,' they echoed.

'Bye Alan,' she mouthed seductively as her hand gave a regal wave. Alan took out his handkerchief from his pocket and mopped the sweat beading under his combover.

'I've just been sick in my mouth,' Jim whispered behind clenched teeth as he and Daniel walked down the garden path ahead of Alan, lumbering under the weight of his body and his camera. Daniel tried not to laugh.

Mrs Cruddup closed the front door and they stopped at Alan's low Citroen BX at the pavement.

'Want a lift back to the office fellas?' he asked as he unravelled his camera lead from his thick neck and leaned on the bonnet to catch his breath.

Daniel looked up and down the nondescript cul-de-sac, its 1960s houses with their identikit white uPVC doors.

'I'm all right thanks Alan,' he said gratefully.

'Yes, we'll walk back to town,' Jim concurred. 'It'll do us good.'

Town was just a fifteen-minute walk out of the cul-de-sacs, under a railway bridge and down a hill: Jim and Daniel would rather that than find space for themselves among the discarded McDonald's polystyrene, black 35mm film cases, crushed cans of Diet Coke (to offset the McDonald's), camera bags, newspapers and a battered London A-Z.

'As you will,' said Alan slightly huffily, as he mopped his combover again, waved farewell and wheezed into the low seat.

Jim threw his courier bag over his crisp white T-shirt while Daniel put his pen and notepad into his backpack and slung it over his shoulder. They watched Alan drive off at an angle, his driver's side skimming perilously close to the road.

'*Fuckin*' hell,' exclaimed Jim. 'I mean, no wonder he's morbidly obese.'

Daniel knew he shouldn't laugh.

'Seriously, it will take Alan more bloody time to go round two sets of traffic lights, park, get to the building and squeeze his sweaty arse into that lift and up to the top floor than it will take us to walk it.'

'He does have all his equipment,' Daniel said, playing devil's advocate.

'And did you *smell* him?' Jim's lightly freckled nose turned upwards, ignoring Daniel's point. 'The BO is just dire. You would have to pay me a *lot* of money to get in that car. "We'll walk thanks"' he added, doing an impression of himself and chuckling.

Daniel felt a bit bad for Alan. Life couldn't be easy shuffling around under his weight, carrying all his photography gear, getting from house to house, Scout parades, fun runs and the council offices, all in the name of being the *Echo*'s only staff photographer.

'Anyway, it's almost five. Fuck the office. Wanna get a drink?' Jim asked, looking like he'd planned this all along.

'Yeah, ace,' Daniel said, a bit confused by the fact his new boss already felt more like a mate.

In the courtyard garden of a town-centre pub, Jim and Daniel sat drinking cider.

'She's not always such a cunny, you know,' said Jim, as he savoured the taste of the end of summer.

Daniel nearly spat his out as he burst into laughter.

'Who?' he asked, knowing full well who Jim was talking about.

'You know!' he laughed. 'She can *occasionally* show flashes of generosity, but she does love a mind game, does our Viv. You know... make you jump through hoops.' Daniel rolled his eyes as if to say *that much I guessed*. In the three weeks he'd been working at the *Echo*, across the two issues he had contributed to, Viv Hart had sent every piece of copy Daniel filed back to him, riddled with red pen, asking him to rejig each story at least five times before another eleventh-hour change (and as a consequence, a late night putting the paper to bed). The most frustrating part? Each story had gone to print looking rather like the piece Daniel had originally submitted. It seemed an awful waste of time and energy.

Jim couldn't help but notice that Viv was 'pulling a Viv'

on poor Daniel, as they sat opposite each other on the news desk in the editorial half of the office.

'Even if you filed something the way it was printed – she would have changed it. She's a mindfuck. I wish I could bend space and time to test her on it – get a story she's happy with in the future, bring it back, file it, and see how she tears it apart.'

'Alan doesn't have a flux capacitor in that Citroen of his then?' Daniel asked, mopping the thin line of Magners from his upper lip. The feeling of bristles under his thumb reminded him to shave tomorrow.

'Not unless it's powered by McNuggets.'

Daniel smiled and flipped the bar mat next to his drink.

'Look,' said Jim conspiratorially, his Welsh voice oozing volume and clarity, even when he was trying to be quiet and candid. 'I don't want to dishearten you. You're doing a great job – and everyone likes you.'

Daniel made a keen face as if to say, *really*?

'Gail in sales *definitely* likes you.' Daniel raised an eyebrow even though he couldn't remember which one Gail was. 'Well, who can blame her? And don't do that raising one eyebrow thing Daniel Bleeker or I will fancy you too...'

Daniel blushed.

'I guess what I mean is, write what *you're* happy with. And leave it at that. She's an awkward bugger and she'll change it anyway. I spent too many hours busting a gut to write stories I was proud of, only to have this tussle. It's sooooo tedious.'

'How long have you been at the *Echo*?' Daniel asked.

'Five years.' Jim looked sheepish for once, and glanced around the pub garden to check no one was listening. 'To be honest Daniel, I'm trying to get onto a national. That's why I feel a bit better about it since you started. I don't feel so guilty. Don't get me wrong, I've enjoyed living in Elmworth. And walking to work is super handy – I know working on a national paper will be a bigger slog and a bigger commute – but don't let that trap you. Like Alan. He's been there thirty-six years! Not that *he* walks to work…'

'Thirty-six years? Fucking hell.'

'How old are you Daniel?'

'Twenty-two. You?'

'Twenty-six. Don't still be here when you're Alan's age.'

'Don't worry, it's only been a few weeks!'

'I know, I just see how Viv gets people in her clutches…'

'I'm just grateful to have the job. It's been a weird few months since I graduated,' Daniel confessed.

'You moved back in with your parents?'

Daniel was embarrassed, but Jim's face was nothing but open and kind.

'Yeah, my mum, dad and brother. On Albert Road.'

'Now that *is* a handy walk to work.'

'I know. Lucked out really. Although I'd love to work on a national too, I'm grateful for this for now.'

'Ahhh, you're too nice Daniel Bleeker. You don't have to pretend that the *Echo* is your dream job, even if you said as much to Viv. I don't want to be writing about gates that sound like fucking Chewbacca, or the man who didn't know what to do with his four-foot courgette. Or the kitten who looks like Hitler. I'm sure you won't want to soon either.'

'Yeah, I guess. It's a good start though.'

'Just be careful – everyone at the *Echo* has been there forever. Bill and Andy on Art – at least thirty years between them. The salesgirls have been there since they finished their O *levels*,' he said, to make a point about just how long ago that was. 'Viv makes it very easy to stay because it's so convenient, all the while why she chips away at your confidence, to make you think you can't ever leave.'

Daniel looked nervy.

'Just a caution, that's all.'

'Noted,' Daniel nodded, looking like he was settling in and ready for another pint.

A man with high cheekbones and floppy hair came to collect the empties and Jim gave the bum of his low-slung jeans a cursory glance.

'So, are you dating anyone? Gotta girlfriend?'

Jim could tell that Daniel was brooding over someone. A girl probably. He had that slightly forlorn look about him. And he hadn't seemed that keen in pursuing the Gail piece of intel; his mind was clearly elsewhere.

'I did have. But it's…'

'Complicated?' they both said in unison, and laughed.

Jim Beck's face looked sad and sympathetic at the same time.

'I was, sort of, dumped. Rather, I *was* dumped. At the start of summer.'

'Bitch. I don't like her.'

Jim's acerbic tongue jarred with his cute Disney baby face.

'We'd been together five years…'

'Shit! You were young.'

'I know,' Daniel lamented.

'The uni years! She robbed you of your uni years?!'

'Yeah, and the lads' holiday to Magaluf,' Daniel mourned. 'Although that's no bad thing, I guess.'

'No, I've been. It isn't.'

'We got together during our A levels, she went to the girls' school here; I went to the boys' school – then I went to do journalism and she studied speech and language in Brighton.'

Daniel told Jim about the travelling part, how Kelly had scuppered their big trip Down Under when they both finished their degrees; about her expecting him to give up his ticket for a dork called Ian.

'What a cow! How dare she?!'

'Well, it's fine – we weren't right,' Daniel said philosophically, not saying out loud that Kelly had already knocked the confidence out of him – Viv Hart really didn't have too much of a task on her hands. 'I was gutted, but it's OK.'

'Good for you.'

'And I kind of met someone while I was travelling.'

'Even better! What's she like? Aussie surfer babe with big knockers and mermaid hair…?'

Daniel pondered Olivia for a second. Describing her wasn't easy.

'…like a Botticelli, rising from the ocean on a shell?' Jim asked keenly.

Daniel ruffled his hair. She certainly looked like an Italian masterpiece. But one with swarthy skin and a Cindy C mole.

'She was a babe, that I can say.'

'Nice.'

'Not a surfer, I don't think so anyway. She's Italian actually.'

'Fit,' Jim said, annunciating his t.

'And coming to London to study this autumn. She might

already be here.' Daniel pre-empted the excitement on Jim's face. 'I don't have any contact details for her though.'

'Oh.'

Jim looked as disappointed as Daniel felt, but tried to think of a solution.

'Electoral register?'

'Could an Italian be on it?'

'For the local elections, I think so,' nodded Jim assuredly, finishing off his pint.

'Well, she wouldn't be on it yet. She has family in Scotland though. Edinburgh.'

'What's her name?'

Then Daniel realised. He didn't know it. He really didn't know much about her, other than the fact she was called Olivia. She went to an international school in Milan. Her birth mother was Scottish. She liked karaoke and Dolly Parton. And making clothes. She could jive. Her dad worked at Pirelli but died earlier this year. She was about to go to Central Saint Martins. Oh and her date of birth must be 29th July 1975.

'Olivia.'

Olivia. He said it out loud for the first time since their night at the bottom of the world and it made him sit up on his barstool a little taller.

'Anything else? Did you get an email?'

'No, no email. I just know she's going to be studying at Central Saint Martins from the "fall". I know nothing else.'

'Do you want to track her down?'

'Do you know how I can?'

Come on, Daniel thought. He was a reporter now. He had to think big. Surely it was within his grasp to find out a way of contacting an Olivia at Central Saint Martins. He looked at Jim hopefully.

'I don't really know, without a surname you're a bit screwed.'

Daniel frowned and flipped the bar mat again.

'It's fine, she wasn't that into me anyway. I was just the only person around that day to talk to.'

Jim looked aghast and gasped.

'None of that defeatist talk please. Of course she must have fancied you!'

Daniel laughed and shrugged it off. 'Well, I don't know...'

'Nonsense Daniel! Are you the Clark Kent to my Lois Lane or what? I don't know how to find a foreign national based only on her first name, but between us we will find a bloody way, I can assure you.'

Daniel raised an eyebrow again and Jim raised a finger as if to say *stop it*.

'Now if she lived in bloody Elmworth I'd be able to sniff her out in a second. Freaky natives—' Jim cut himself short, remembering he was talking to one – although Daniel had been to university and travelling, so he didn't count.

'Don't worry about it,' said Daniel cocking his empty pint glass. 'Another? It's my round.'

'Yeah I'll have a gin and tonic please. I need something stronger after that horny old biddy and her gate.' Jim shuddered melodramatically.

Daniel laughed and slouched inside to the bar, while Jim picked up a copy of *The Mirror* from the next table, unfolded the front page, and did a Chewbacca-style roar to himself.

Twelve

Mimi walked swiftly down a sunlit corridor, little feet making big strides against large shiny tiles that captured the sun's sparkle. In a room on the seventh floor she saw Flora, curled up in a chair looking at her phone. Daniel was sitting behind her, in a large ledge of a window that wouldn't open, a long pane of glass overlooking the beige exterior of a brewery and a concrete flyover on a parched August afternoon. He was sending emails from his window seat, updating his editor on The Situation in Spain and why he hadn't come back to work today as planned, as Sofia lay against Olivia on the bed, playing Harry Potter Top Trumps with her mother.

'Yesss! I've got Voldemort. Hand it over, Mamma...'

'Heyyy,' said a high and soft Australian voice as Mimi gently peered through the open door.

Daniel and Flora noticed her first from their perches.

A second later Olivia looked across and her face lit up in surprise.

'Mimi!'

Mimi tried not to cry as she looked at the peaceful idyll. Mother and daughter nose-to-nose playing cards.

'How are you doing?'

Daniel closed the lid on his laptop and Sofia sprang off the bed.

'Hey!'

'Aunty Mimi!' she squeaked, flinging her arms around a woman who was barely taller than her, in her white vest and black skintight jeans. Flora glanced up and smiled a casual, 'Hi,' before looking back down at her phone.

Sofia hugged Mimi's waist and rested her head on her shoulder. Mimi stroked her soft brown hair.

'Hey beautiful. How are my girrrrls? How's my favourite goddaughter?'

'Er, aren't I your only goddaughter?!' Sofia chuckled.

'Oh no! I have five in Australia. And another twenty in Switzerland. And a couple I forgot about along the way,' she said with a wink.

'Youuuuuuuu!' Sofia laughed, before remembering her news. 'I'm beating Mummy. She was winning but I had Voldemort and went "evil rating" when I knew she only had Ron...'

'*How* did you know I only had Ron?' Olivia asked with a raised eyebrow. Sofia looked between Olivia and Mimi with a guilty expression and giggled.

'I saw!' she confessed, as if it were a surprise to anybody.

Olivia and Mimi both gasped in mock shock, Mimi's mirth helping veil the water filling her eyes, which she soon hid in Daniel's T-shirt, as he walked over and pulled her in for a hug.

Mimi rubbed Daniel's back with her small hands, both comforting each other in the fright.

Daniel kissed Mimi's head and released her, so she could tentatively approach the bed.

'Look at you!' she said in an almost whisper. 'You look really... well?!'

Mimi wasn't lying. Olivia was tanned from her holiday, rested from having spent the past twenty-four hours in bed, and the blue hospital gown suited her glow. Olivia had always looked good in blue.

'I know, right?' said Olivia, dismissing the severity of the situation.

Mimi Sorrentino was Olivia's best friend at the International School in Milan, having been sent over from Australia when she was 11 'to get a European education'. Her grandparents were from the Amalfi coast but had moved to Australia from the Gulf of Naples with their young children as part of the 'populate or perish' programme of assisted migration after the Second World War. The family settled in St Kilda in Melbourne, where Mimi's father Nicola met her Australian mother Carol, and where he opened his first pizzeria, before taking on Lygon Street and Little Italy. Nicola Sorrentino was CEO of Australia's largest pizzeria chain (made to the highest Neapolitan standard of course) and had made a lot of dough from dough. When Mimi's older brother Mike hit his teens, started doing drugs and skipping school for cigarettes on the promenade at St Kilda, Nicola and Carol decided to send their children to Europe, for a private education in their *terra natale*, even though neither Mike nor Mimi had ever been.

Mimi and Olivia were thrown together on the first day of seventh grade when they were paired up in form room and Olivia walked over to Mimi, said hi, and declared she was going to be a fashion designer. Both girls were intrigued by and drawn to the other's differences.

Mimi was a boarder but loved that Olivia wasn't and that she had a home from home in Milan where Mimi, too, was welcome for hearty suppers and sleepovers. Olivia stayed with her parents in the top-floor apartment on Via Tiziano, but loved that she could spend nights in school if she wanted to, making out with Mimi's brother Mike, or any other overseas boy she fancied. Both girls could have the best of both worlds, staying on campus if they liked, eating homecooked dinners in Maria's kitchen when they preferred.

Their differences were the glue that bound them and made them a great double act. At 11, Olivia was already pretty tall – although her height came with an awkwardness, before she knew how covetable her long legs would become. Mimi was shorter than your average seventh-grader, still flat-chested and childlike. Olivia had rich eyes, olive skin and rusty hair. Mimi had black hair, pale blue eyes and porcelain skin like her mother – whose diktat was to always use sunscreen and wear a hat. Olivia was into boys, partying and happy house music. Mimi was into rock, and would studiously learn her bass guitar while listening to Queen, The Pretenders and Guns N' Roses. Olivia fancied Calvin Klein models and Marky Mark. Mimi's idols were Bruce Springsteen and Prince.

As teens, they both secreted bottles of cheap booze in their lockers and smoked weed with the gorgeous boys with curtains hair. But as Olivia's partying increased, Mimi put her work ethic and musical talent to good use, playing gigs in Milan, and Melbourne during Christmas holidays; moving to London after graduation to make a go of it and find a career in music; later touring the world with her band The Horizontals from her base in Brixton.

After twenty years of life on the road, Mimi was asked to write a musical with a Swiss songwriter called Udo Schär, they fell in love, and settled in the Alps – becoming the world's most successful songwriting duo, a Taupin and John for the movies. They even went to the Oscars last February. Today she took the Glacier Express, a Schweizerische Bundesbahnen train and two flights to be by Olivia's side in the hospital in Ibiza.

'How are you feeling?' Mimi asked quietly.

Olivia looked at Daniel, to give him a signal, and he scratched his brown-bear hair.

'Hey girls... Wanna get a shake from that gelateria on the corner?'

'Yay!' sprang Sofia.

'Actually, Dad, they're called *heladerias* here.' Flora almost tutted.

'Even better. Let me get my wallet.' Daniel rummaged in his daypack as he urged Flora up off the chair. 'Come on.'

'Ooh, can I have rum and raisin, Daddy?' Sofia asked.

'Cheeky. You already look drunk to me.'

'Hey!' she said, angling to jump on his back.

Daniel kissed Olivia on the lips. 'Back in a bit. Want anything?'

'No, thanks. I'm good for European royals and magdalenas,' she replied, wafting a pristine copy of *Hola!* above the white cotton bedsheets.

'I'm fine.' Mimi shook her head, looking far from it as Daniel, Flora and Sofia walked out in search of food and fresh air.

'Bye Mamma!'

'Bye. Love you.'

Mimi looked around the quiet room and pulled Flora's vacated chair up to the bed. The sun was beating through the long, closed window, but the air conditioning made the room feel temperate.

'Wow, you get your own digs on the Spanish NHS.'

'Yup.'

'And the sheets are cleaner than at King's...'

'Yep. We – well, *I* – even had hake for lunch. Nice sauce, fresh tomato and capers. It tasted good too. Flora didn't get that when they took her tonsils out in Addenbrooke's.'

Mimi squeezed Olivia's hand.

'But are you OK?'

'I think so. I *feel* OK.'

'You look bloody amazing, you bitch.'

'I know! I feel like such a fraud.'

'So what happened?'

'I don't know. They've run a load of tests – the doctors are really nice. I just sort of... fainted.'

Mimi frowned. People weren't usually admitted to rooms like this for fainting, but she didn't say anything. Olivia peppered her silence.

'I'm probably run down. I've had so much going on with the business, all the expansion, all the new appointments, moving into bridal... I've been super exhausted.'

Mimi still wasn't sure.

'I'm just worried for Daniel and the girls, for giving them a scare.' Olivia talked about it in the past tense, as if it was an inconvenience or a misunderstanding they had moved on from.

'What's happening with the business? Does Vaani know you're stuck here?'

'Yeah, I've been speaking to her, she's on the case.'

'What about Fashion Week?'

'Oh, I'll be back in time for that! I just need a couple of days – should have gone to a spa!' Olivia was wittering. Mimi knew Olivia wittered when she was worried. 'I've been rushing all over the place lately, running on empty. Daniel just panicked because I hit my head when I fell. That's what they were most worried about.'

'Daniel said you were fitting.'

Olivia looked puzzled.

'Did he?'

'Yeah, he said you had, like, fits. At the villa and at the airport.'

'I don't know about fits... You know me, I'm a drama queen. Anyway, you should see the hot doctors here.'

Mimi didn't take the bait. She was more troubled by this than Olivia. Her friend was usually honest and matter-of-fact about things. Now it seemed she was trying to brush it under the carpet.

'Do you want me to take the girls home? I can take them

back to the UK, or the mountains if they fancy an Alpine adventure for the rest of the holidays?'

Olivia squeezed Mimi's hand back.

'Thanks, but that's not necessary, I'll be out of here in a day or two I'm sure.'

Thirteen

December 1996
London

In the upstairs function room of a downbeat Soho pub, Olivia stood wearing a dress that looked like a binbag. Mainly because it had been fashioned out of binbags. She had been to the annual freshers' Christmas party – a Central Saint Martins tradition, where all first-year fashion students were given a roll of black binbags and charged with creating an outfit of any description. The lecturers, who once taught the fashion designers the students grew up admiring, critiqued the outfits, usually worn by the students themselves or model friends, in an old warehouse behind Poland Street, before the after-parties would commence at Soho's dingiest pubs.

'Nice dress,' said Vaani Bhalla, with scrutinising eyes. 'Not *my* style, of course…'

Olivia had turned her roll of binbags into a Marie Antoinette style creation (with the help of a bustle made from old wire coat hangers) shaping stinky black plastic into rococo ruffles, frills, ruching and a corset – to great plaudits from her hard-to-please tutors. But still she was having a shit night, alternating glasses of vermouth with tequila shots to get through it.

'Nice suit,' Olivia replied flatly, though she was genuinely impressed by how sharp Vaani's lines were. She had tailored her roll of black binbags into a tux Yves Saint Laurent might be proud of.

Vaani gave a nonchalant nod as if to say *I know*.

'Chin up, I reckon this Versaille... ensemble... will propel you to the top of the class next term.' Even when Vaani was saying something supportive, her face had a look of disdain.

Olivia rolled her eyes as if to say she didn't care.

'What's wrong?' Vaani asked rather impatiently.

'They're all arseholes Vaani. Privileged, superior arseholes.'

Olivia looked around the room, almost in panic, in a dress that didn't suit her insecurity when she should have been feeling royally triumphant. The tequila wasn't doing its usual trick either.

Vaani Bhalla was the daughter of a Mumbai steel magnate, and another Milan International School alumni who didn't quite fit in with the rock stars' daughters or the down-at-heel artists studying at Central Saint Martins.

Vaani had already spent a year in London doing her foundation, so although they weren't that close in Milan, Olivia had drifted to her for advice on living in the city; for someone to hang out with in the early months when she was becoming accustomed to the strange sensation of not having any friends. Vaani had a flat in Belsize Park paid for by her dad, and was comfortable with being an outcast. Her harsh but beautiful resting face and large dissecting eyes didn't make Vaani friends easily, but she was more comfortable in her own company than Olivia was in hers.

'*We're* privileged arseholes Olivia,' Vaani shrugged unapologetically. 'I mean, if you look at us from the outside. Take her...' Vaani nodded towards Edie, a girl from the northeast with blue skin and a space-age-looking outfit. 'That girl on my course... erm... Whatshername—'

'Edie.'

'That's it, Evie.'

'It's Edic.'

'Whatever,' Vaani said with a wave of her arm and a curl of her nose. She didn't care much for people with blue skin. 'Well, she must hate spoilt students like us. And you hate people like *them*...' Vaani nodded over to the rock stars' daughters, all coked up and chain-smoking Marlboro Lights around the fireplace in slip-like binbags which were surely about to melt.

'Edie would hate you even more if she knew you didn't know her name – she's on *your* course not mine!' Olivia had sat next to her in a few History of Fashion lectures they all shared.

'Well, just look around the pub. Or any of the other after-parties. Pockets of people in their tribes, and most of them see us as privileged arseholes. "The International Students",' Vaani added with a snarl in finger commas. 'It's all just a hierarchy of hate.' She couldn't help but laugh at her own joke.

'Well, I hate them,' nodded Olivia. 'In Technical Skills last week they were totally mocking me. Made me scrabble around for cutting scissors when they had three pairs on their worktop; laughed and cackled when I admitted I didn't know who Hussein Chalayan was...'

Olivia didn't admit to Vaani that she'd gone back to her flat that night and got through two bottles of wine on her own while watching *ER*.

'Olivia, *everyone* knows who Hussein Chalayan is around here,' she said, rolling her eyes fondly.

'Well, *now* I do!'

The pecking order was thick in the stagnant pub room as Olivia inhaled a cigarette nervously and Vaani batted the smoke out of her eyes with a frown. But unlike Olivia, Vaani didn't give a hoot about where she stood in it. She was just there to study fashion communication and business. She loved London and she loved the course.

Like Mimi, Vaani was petite and looked odd standing next to Olivia. But her boyish cropped haircut, slight silhouette and androgynous wardrobe gave her a gravitas in the leaky corridors of Charing Cross Road, even if people often called her 'young man' at art galleries, book launches and in lectures. Vaani was so comfortable in her skin, so accustomed to being mistaken for a boy, it didn't bother her, and she made the gentlewoman style all her own.

Vaani put her hands in her pockets and looked down at her Russell & Bromley brogues (bought from the boys' section, her feet were that delicate).

'Everyone will have settled down after Christmas,' she said authoritatively.

'You think?'

'Yeah, give them a chance...'

Olivia hadn't ever struggled to make friends before. She had a terrible feeling of discomfort in the pit of her stomach and quashed it by downing her Martini Rosso as if it were lemonade. She looked like she might cry.

Vaani didn't drink alcohol, so she nursed a tonic water in a plastic half-pint glass. It went quite well with the binbag fabric. 'Look, are you going home for Christmas?' Vaani wasn't very soft and she certainly wasn't going to hug Olivia, but she could tell she might need one.

Olivia nodded, lost for words.

'A few weeks in Milan will make you miss London, I'm sure.'

Olivia shook her head. She thought of her birth city, its Baroque piazzas, Art Nouveau mansions and Gothic churches – a city where everyone looked good and everything smelled good, from the ristretto vendors serving syrupy black coffee to the perfume of the women wafting through ornate shopping *gallerias*. She thought of her happy place in Parco Sempione, but she didn't feel joy – she was dreading going back. Her forehead kept crumpling as she tried to stifle a cry.

Vaani's enormous round eyes widened.

'It'll be good for you. Eat a shitload of *panettone*...' Vaani surveyed Olivia's meagre bones.

'I'm not sure I can face it. Christmas without my dad won't be Christmas.'

Vaani stopped short of putting her hand on Olivia's.

'The mean girls get me down... but at least they're a distraction.'

'It'll be good for you.'

Olivia didn't look sure.

'You can stock up on Baci – bring me some back. None of this Cadbury's shit.' Vaani's family still lived in Mumbai, she had no reason to go back to Milan in the holidays and stock up on her favourite confectionery. Olivia cracked a reluctant smile and Marie Antoinette started to loosen up. 'The chocolate's just not the same here, Italians do it better…' Vaani mused. 'Anyway, can you smell melting plastic?!' Vaani and Olivia looked over to the rock chicks and models draped around the armchairs by the fireplace, and started to giggle.

Fourteen

August 2017
Ibiza, Spain

'You sure about this?'

'Don't worry! Udo wasn't expecting me back in a hurry. The whole of Switzerland shuts down in August, and we write better apart anyway.' Mimi nodded reassuringly. 'I'll stay at yours as long as you need. Feed the cats. I can work from your gorgeous house – it feels like a chalet anyway!'

'We don't have cats,' Daniel said with a concerned frown.

'Goody. In which case I won't accidentally feed the cats Weetabix and the girls Whiskas. I did that with Mike's two…' Mimi gave Daniel a playful nudge. '*Really*, it's fine! They can show me around. Maybe I'll take them into London, see a show. I could do with checking in on my flat too. And it'd be nice to see Jim and Wesley and the boys.'

'Are you sure?'

'Really, take as long as you need.'

Daniel and Mimi stood in the lobby of the bland and unremarkable Holiday Inn Express on the highway between the airport, the hospital and Ibiza Town. Flora and Sofia's cases were repacked and propped up against the dark brown sofas the girls were slouching on.

'I just don't know how long these tests and results will take – when they'll let her go.'

'It doesn't matter how long they take. Really. Everything is in hand.'

Mimi squeezed Daniel on the arm then tiptoed to wrap her arms around him.

'You're gonna be OK, you know?' she said, bright eyes lucid in the cool air-conditioned lobby.

Daniel nodded.

'And the girls and I are gonna have a great time, aren't we girls?' Mimi called out while she adjusted her straw hat. Sofia looked up from her position – like a cat herself – on the top of the armchair over her sister, so they could both see the filters she was putting on her face.

'Huh?' Sofia asked, while Flora pouted, eyes firmly on her phone screen so she could angle an animated arch of flowers neatly on her head.

'Come on little minxes, we have a flight to catch. The shuttle is here!'

Sofia jumped up.

Mimi lifted a handbag that was almost as big as she was and wheeled her case to the automatic doors. A blast of hot air came from outside to hit them. 'Uff!' she sighed. Daniel walked over to get Flora and Sofia's suitcases and wheeled them out to the shuttle bus, where he lifted them into the open doors at the back. He walked back to the front, now trailed by his daughters like ducklings. Flora stopped, with her beach-battered backpack slung over her shoulder, knowing that her dad would want to say something to her even if she didn't want to hear it.

'Look after your sister, yeah?'

Flora nodded.

'And Mimi, she adores you girls, so be nice to her and just do what she asks of you. It won't be much.'

'O-K. I get it,' Flora said quietly, trying not to roll her eyes.

'Mamma will be OK you know,' Daniel reassured, putting his hands on her shoulders. Flora looked confused and defensive, as if there hadn't been any doubt about Mamma being OK, until now. Her father's words irritated and scared her more than anything.

'All right!' she snapped, before proffering a cheek for her father to kiss before she stepped up into the van. Sofia jumped up and wrapped her legs around Daniel's waist and smothered his face in kisses.

'Daddy I miss you already. Mwah mwah mwah mwah mwah!' she said, as she dotted her small mouth haphazardly around his cheeks, nose, forehead and stubble. One left a wet mark on his eyelid. 'Although we're going to have LOTS of fun with Aunty Mimi!' There was an excitement in his little girl that comforted Daniel – they would be all right.

'You no come, *señor?*' asked the doughy bus driver, as Sofia took the seat next to Mimi and waved to her dad through the window.

'No, I'm staying here.'

'OK, Papi staying in Ibisssssssa. *Felices vacaciónes!*' the driver said, as he pulled off. Flora looked out of the window at her father and the last thing Daniel saw as the bus disappeared towards the airport was the wash of fear that haunted his daughter's face.

Fifteen

'Can you talk?'

Daniel sat at his desk, staring at the empty chair opposite where Jim used to sit, confused that it was Jim's voice at the other end of the phone. Daniel was so very tired, he rubbed his eyes and looked around.

In January, Jim had left to become showbiz reporter at *The Sun*, and now if Jim wasn't partying with the 3AM Girls at the Shadow Lounge, he was trying to get one over them with exclusives. Stories about which soap star had been doing coke in the toilets; which comedian had thrown his pager at his PA and bloodied her nose; and which angel-faced boybander had gone down on Jim the night before – although, alas, he couldn't write that one up.

Jim's departure had made the stagnant home of local news feel even more stifling.

Daniel had been up for most of the night, first at the Elmworth count, witnessing the local Tory re-elected for the 400th time – the New Labour tide hadn't quite washed over this corner of the Home Counties, even if its spray caused a light mist – later watching the rest of the results roll in while Matt cracked open another beer and their parents slept upstairs.

'Not easily... You OK?'

Daniel looked around the office sheepishly. His editor Viv was leaning over Andy the art director's desk while she ate a nectarine; head of sales Jill walked through editorial on her way to the kitchen for her midmorning Cup-a-Soup, her pencil skirt straining under her stride; the advertising girls were taking advantage of this by resuming their discussion about Michael Hutchence and Paula Yates through the archway; and the TV on a bracket from the ceiling was showing Tony and Cherie Blair walking to rapturous applause along Downing Street – muted of course – just to accentuate the silence and highlight the volume of Jim's voice on the other end of the line. Daniel moved the receiver from one ear to the other to make a barrier, make it less likely that his boss might hear.

'Oooh, Jill, can I just talk to you about ratecards?' Viv asked, as she followed her to the kitchen, although it was more of a command than a question. 'Be right back,' she said to Andy with a shallow smile.

'Oh, hang on,' Daniel said, with some suppressed cheer as he watched Viv walk off. 'Yeah I've got about two minutes.'

'Can you believe the result?!'

'I know!'

'All my fucking life I can only remember a Tory government, it feels very, very weird.'

'I didn't realise men could be prime minister until 1990,' Daniel quietly laughed, remembering his Thatcher childhood.

'Obviously my editor is taking the credit for it, even though *The Sun* has been laying into Labour for decades.'

'You have to back a winner, eh? You bloody shape-shifters.' Daniel laughed and craned his neck. Through the archway that separated the editorial desks from the advertising side of the office, Viv and Jill were back at her desk, pondering the flatplan as if it were a strategic wartime map.

'Anyway!' Jim said eagerly. 'Speaking of shape-shifters... You know the hot sports editor here, the one I have a crush on? Ex-rugby player? Thighs of steel?'

'Yeah...'

'Well, I was chatting to him while we watched Dimbleby—'

'Sounds romantic.'

'No he's married, to a really dull woman, and they have two very plain kids.'

'Oh.'

Daniel could see that Viv was aware of him on the phone, probably on a personal call, as she glanced through the archway at him, and knew he didn't have long.

'*Anyway*, Hot Will needs some extra night shifters on the sports desk. Decent money, 10 p.m. to 6 a.m. sort of thing. Fancy it? We could even coincide!'

'Jim, between 10 p.m. and 6 a.m. you're out stalking celebs and scavenging for stories – we'd never coincide.'

'OK, maybe not, but this could be your in.'

Daniel looked around the office guiltily. Bill and Andy on the art desk were looking at layouts on their screens, and Kathy, Duncan and Denise on the bank of desks behind him were gathering death notices, transcribing interviews, writing football reports and paying invoices in total silence.

The advertising girls had stopped talking about Paula and Michael. The only noise was the quiet whirr of the photocopier warming up since Lee had reloaded the paper tray.

'I mean, *I'd* even pretend to give a shit about football if it meant spending long steamy nights with Will Simpson, but alas I have proper work to do.'

Daniel could hear the sarcasm in Jim's voice.

'I appreciate it mate, but I've not even been here a year.'

'You wouldn't be leaving! You could just tell Viv you're pulling some extra shifts; you really need the cash because she's such a tight arsehole you're sooooo skint.'

'I live at home with my mum and dad.'

'Say you're saving up for your first flat. Surely you don't want to live with your parents, Matt and his mizz girlfriend forever?'

Daniel thought of nights on the sofa with Matt and his girlfriend Annabel, who had taken to sitting in Daniel's favourite chair, reading Catherine Cookson novels and talking to no one. He was even glad to go to the General Election count last night so he didn't have to watch *EastEnders* with Matt and Annabel while his dad pottered in the shed and mum prepped a Great Fire Of London display at the dining-room table.

'When would I sleep?'

'Sleep is for the weak.'

'You say that as someone who probably only just got up. It's almost lunchtime.'

'It'd be a brilliant way in. On a national. In *sports* Daniel.'

Viv weaved back through to the editorial side of the office and sat down at Jim's old desk as she gnawed a leafy stick of celery. Daniel was grateful the crunch might drown out Jim's voice. Viv leaned in.

'Look – I'd better go,' Daniel said. He wasn't sure if he should pretend he was talking to a story lead or just admit it was Jim. He went with story lead.

'Thanks for the tip-off Mr, er, Johnson-son. I'll have a look into it and get back to you, just as soon as I can.'

Jim laughed on the other end.

'My cat looks like Hitler!' he shouted, before Daniel could put his hand over the mouthpiece.

'Buh-bye now.'

Daniel hung up and wrote some fake notes on his spiral-bound notepad, knowing that Viv was watching his every move. He really would rather write about his sporting heroes than cats who looked like Hitler, in an office where talking was discouraged, you were only allowed to eat at your desk if it were fruit or veg sticks, and visitors were left sitting on the awkward little sofa in front of Lee for an embarrassingly long time.

'How's Jim?' Viv asked with a knowing smile. Daniel rubbed his soft swirl of hair and gave a gentle laugh. Luckily Viv didn't dwell on things and moved the conversation along.

'Have you seen the *Mercury*?' The whites of her eyes were wide and loaded.

'No, I've been so busy going over my Nigel Dilley story, I haven't had the chance...' Daniel knew something was coming from the smiling assassin.

'Their man – Rob Hanlon – you must know Rob...'

Daniel thought of a weedy guy who always had a spot that needed lancing – his counterpart on their rival paper, the *Elmworth Sunday Mercury*.

'Yes, I've seen him at a few things,' Daniel said keenly through the gap between their monitors.

A man in a suit walked into the office and introduced himself to Lee.

'Well, Rob procured a *lot* more soundbites from Dilley at the count last night than you seem to have. Unless that's what you're writing up now... is there more to come?'

'Oh no, I filed everything I had. I could only get a couple of lines from him; he was out of there as soon as the returning officer had finished.'

'Well, the *Mercury* have their story up on their online website.'

'Online?' Daniel asked, flummoxed. The *Elmworth Echo* didn't have that facility. Jim had tried to convince Viv that online was the way forward – her antipathy towards it had been another catalyst in him leaving. As well as Jim Beck being too big a personality for the parochial office.

Now Viv had changed her tune, and was obviously scouring her rival paper's website regularly for stories and soundbites Daniel hadn't sourced.

'Yes, they have their election stories up already – and Rob Hanlon's has a lot more, shall we say, meat, to it, than you seem to have Daniel. Which is fine...' she added, passive aggressively.

Daniel wished Lee would interrupt them, to announce the visitor's arrival. 'But perhaps I should come with you to the next one?' she suggested. 'Help you get something better.'

Daniel hoped he wouldn't still be working at the *Echo* in another four years. The thought of Viv Hart holding his hand through a count in 2001 made him shiver.

I have to get out.

'Or perhaps we find you a course.'

'A course?' Daniel smiled and nodded to show willing. Viv stood up and Lee saw his chance.

'Oh Viv, your midday meeting is here. Geoff Tree from…?' Lee looked back to the bald man in the pale grey suit.

'The Rotary,' said the man, rising on shiny shoes as he said it.

Viv nodded to Lee, not acknowledging Geoff standing next to him.

'I'll be with you in a minute Lee,' she said. 'I'm just going to move to Jim's old desk. It's a nicer view overlooking the office and you can bounce ideas off me more easily here Daniel. If you're struggling.'

'Thanks.'

'Apparently we'll all be hot desking one day,' Viv said with a laugh, as she rolled up her sleeves and started moving a pile of papers without any urgency.

Geoff from the Rotary looked irked, and lifted the creases of his pressed trousers as he sat back down on the sofa.

This is shit.

Under the guise of work, Daniel composed an email to Jim, grateful that Viv had recently conceded to installing an external internet, cables that connected them to the outside world, a world beyond the office intranet. It was just one line:

Thanks Jim. I'll email you my updated CV tonight.

Sixteen

August 2017
Ibiza, Spain

'So you see Mr and Mrs Bleeker, from this area here, you can see you have a, how do you say… a *mass* on the outer part of the *cerebro*, sorry, cerebrum. Here…' A handsome Spanish consultant in a white coat and a grey beard held a flimsy X-ray up to the window, while Daniel and Olivia looked gobsmacked from the bed. The sunshine tore through a grey blob that looked like a small cauliflower on the outer part of Olivia's brain.

'This has to be a joke,' Daniel said. But all Olivia could think about was how the medic looked like Antonio Banderas; he was too handsome to be delivering such a blow, his eyes too warm.

No, this definitely wasn't happening to her.

She turned to Daniel, who looked more grave, which in turn puzzled her.

'Is call an astro-cy-toma…'

Even the way he said astrocytoma was sexy; Olivia couldn't take it seriously and almost laughed, as a horror washed over her at the realisation that a 'mass' meant a tumour.

'What?' Daniel almost spat.

'An astrocyte is a cell in the shape of a star. It has kind of far-reaching claws like an asteroid. If it mutates then it becomes a glioma, or an astrocytoma more *especifically*. This is what we suggest it is, but you need further tests to find out more about it, to grade it.'

'So is it cancer?' Daniel asked, looking so pale Olivia thought he might puke.

'It's a glioma, yes, a tumour. But it could be very low grade – whoop, taken out.' Dr Lorca put his fingers together and opened them out like a flower, as if it was so simple. 'It might not be too *serio*.'

Nothing about this conversation made Daniel think it wasn't *serio*.

'Does it *have* to be taken out?'

Olivia still couldn't speak.

'Well, even low-grade gliomas need to be looked at closely *Señor* Bleeker, because of the pressure and the impact they could have on the rest of the brain.'

Daniel shook his head.

'So yes, your lovely wife will need to have an operation.'

'Fuck,' Olivia whispered. Dr Lorca suddenly stopped being sexy. Someone was going to open up her brain.

'You will need to have some more tests, more details, more investigations at an *especialist* department. The good news is, we think this is a primary tumour, not a secondary one.'

'Wh-what do you mean?' Daniel stuttered.

'We couldn't find tumours anywhere else, in all those

tests your wife had. So it's more likely that it's just in the brain.'

'"Just" in the brain,' Daniel said, at the same time as Olivia thought it.

Fuck.

Neither could speak, so Dr Lorca continued.

'So what I would suggest is you return to the UK, I will give you permission to fly just as soon as the swelling abates a bit more from the seizure, the fall, but you will need to see your family doctor as soon as you arrive home, and they will get you the next steps, which will be scans and surgery.'

'But I feel fine!' Olivia protested, tearing at her hair.

'That is good, but you need this little asteroid out of your brain in case it grows, or in case it give you another seizure, or in case it *is* one of the bad guys.'

All the air in Daniel's lungs shot out.

'Oh Christ,' he said, slumping his head in his hands.

'But you are young! You're healthy! You are 42 and fit, not 82 and weak. You're in a good position.'

Nothing about this situation, from where Olivia was lying and Daniel was sitting, felt like being in a good position.

'Daniel, I feel fine!' Olivia repeated, as she turned to her husband, dismissing everything the good doctor had just said.

Seventeen

June 1998
London

'I've met someone!' burst Jim. He couldn't wait for Daniel to sit down with the balloon glasses of Pimm's and lemonade he was holding in each hand.

'Hang on hang on...' Daniel said, trying not to spill anything as he straddled a small pub stool and lowered himself onto it. Crowds were gathering for the football in the Fitzrovia tavern and it had been a mission to weave through without anyone knocking into him and spilling his drinks. 'Slow down...' He made his elbows big and placed the glasses on the crumb-strewn table. They had met there early, to get a seat and a vantage point, even though Jim didn't give a hoot about the United States versus Yugoslavia in the World Cup, although he did get excited about the Netherlands beating South Korea 5-0 last Saturday, for reasons he was about to explain.

'He's Dutch. Well, half-Dutch. He's called Wesley. Lived in London for almost twenty years.'

'Twenty years?!'

'He's older,' Jim confided.

'How old?'

'Thirty-eight. I'm 28. It's OK. Hardly dad issues.'

'I guess,' Daniel shrugged, as if he were giving Jim and Wesley his blessing. Jim was four years older than him too – maybe 38 didn't seem so old as you approached your thirties.

'He works for *Cosmo*. Writes about clits and G-spots all day.'

'Bit weird.'

'He was once even their male centrefold.'

'What a con!'

Jim battled with a sprig of mint as he took a sip of Pimm's and lemonade. 'Straight women can lust over gay men you know? Look at Ricky Martin.'

'True,' Daniel said, rolling his eyes. Leather trousers weren't his thing.

'Mr April. He's had it blown up, put on his flat wall. Had a bunch of tulips strategically placed in front of his cock.' Jim beamed with pride.

'Beautiful,' Daniel said, raising his glass and trying not to picture it.

Jim Beck had snogged many men in the two years Daniel had known him, but there had never been anyone significant enough to be actually named. It was always Boyband Bitch, PR With The Big Prick, Human Rights Guy or The Tory. Wesley being called Wesley was certainly a significant development.

'We met at a Steps showcase at Virgin Megastore. Went to G-A-Y after. Barely been apart since.'

'Wow, that's brilliant Jim. Is he coming here? Do I get to meet him before my shift?'

'He's at the Women of the Year Awards right now – might meet me at Chinawhite later. Shame you can't pull a sickie and join us.'

For a year now, Daniel had been working night shifts on the sports desk at *The Sun*, fixed by eternal matchmaker Jim. The sports editor Will Simpson had been nice – settling Daniel in with his tasks before handing over to the night editor Larry at 11 p.m., and Larry was nice enough too, despite smelling of stale cigarettes and rainwater. Daniel was usually tasked with the next day's World Cup round-up, Wimbledon match previews and Tour de France build-up, while tomorrow's paper was already rolling through the huge printing presses in the middle of the vast complex. Head down. Get on. There wasn't much time for chitchat but the money was good – at £200 a night he was earning three times his day rate on *The Echo*, then sleeping briefly on the train home before getting changed – at *The Sun* you could wear whatever the hell you wanted, it was only on a local newspaper that Daniel had to dress smartly. He'd have another hour's kip on his bed before turning up for work at 9 a.m. to face a gruelling onslaught from Viv Hart. At lunchtime he would go home, shower and power nap. After a year of stealing sleep where he could, Daniel was struggling, although the nights he met Jim for a pint before a shift were definitely better.

'Oh and he *loves* football!' Jim announced this as if it ensured Daniel would love Wesley too. 'So obviously I'm having to pretend – but that Holland game the other night… wow! Those guys can play soccer!'

Daniel laughed and threw a beer coaster at Jim.

'You fool!'

'A fool in love,' Jim smiled proudly.

Daniel looked down at his drink and stirred the limp strawberries and cucumber into a whirlpool as he remembered his own pitiful love life.

It had been almost two years since Olivia lifted his night and his life at the bottom of the world. It would soon be her birthday again, and he remembered her twenty-first the night after she had gone. He had spent the evening nursing a pint of Speights, back in the sports bar they had started in the night before, watching cricket on the large television screens above the bar and feeling lonely. It felt businesslike and empty. He imagined every room felt businesslike and empty after Olivia had left it.

Last year, on her twenty-second birthday, he wondered where she was in London, as he spent the night writing about transfer news at *The Sun* while 'I'll Be Missing You' by Puff Daddy played on Capital FM more times than Daniel thought funny. Now her twenty-third birthday was approaching, and Daniel lamented that he still didn't even know her surname.

Jim knew Daniel was thinking about her.

'Did you try AOL?'

They both knew what he was talking about. 'Honestly, I use it for stalking and searching up things all the time. You can even use a dictionary on it to look up spellings,' he confessed, a hack he didn't think any other hack had cottoned onto yet. Jim could access AOL at work to look up the age of Shania Twain, Cameron Diaz or Patsy Kensit within seconds, or find out what year George Michael went solo. 'Viv *has* got the internet now, hasn't she?'

'Yeah, she has. But without a surname...'

'Could you trawl through *all* the Olivias in London or Milan on Friends Reunited?'

Daniel's sheepish look revealed he already had. 'I even walked down Charing Cross Road the other week when I didn't need to, that's where her college is.'

Jim winced for him. 'Oh buddy...'

'I know, I'm a dick. Never mind. Plenty more fish in the sea!' Daniel brushed off.

'There's a girl over there checking you out,' Jim said excitedly, nodding unsubtly to a table in the corner of four young women who looked like they worked in PR, all blonde straightened hair, Anna Sui eye gloss and Mulberry handbags. Daniel didn't look round. He didn't need to say it.

She's not Olivia.

'Anyway your news is great,' he said. 'Don't feel bad for me. I'm really happy for you – this Wesley sounds like a catch. Tulips and all.'

'Oh Daniel!' Jim's big Bing Crosby eyes grew. 'You're so lovely and so handsome. I want you to find love too!'

Daniel laughed and changed the subject.

'Where does Wesley live?'

'Wandsworth, not far.'

Daniel anticipated The Look that came from Jim as he speared a grape with his straw and did a double take. 'Fuckin' grape?! In Pimm's?!' Jim then got back to the business of persuading Daniel to move to London.

As soon as Jim left Elmworth and the *Echo* to start his job on the showbiz desk at *The Sun*, he moved from his flatshare by the church to a flatshare four times the price in Tooting Bec – and loved it. He was always trying to get Daniel to move down there too. Daniel was slowly becoming accustomed to London. Since traversing from King's Cross to *The Sun*'s HQ in Wapping five times a week and sometimes meeting Jim beforehand, he was becoming more familiar with the city, even if he wasn't ready to move there.

'Don't worry don't worry, I'm not going to say it – but just remember the offer is always there, as soon as Dull Dean moves out, that room is yours, even if I have to drag you from Elmworth myself.'

'Thanks mate,' Daniel said, as he looked up at the TV. National anthems were being boomed out from a stadium in Nantes as a group of American tourists started cheering as unconvincingly about 'soccer' as Jim had.

'Must we watch this *ghastly* game? I'm still exhausted from the Holland one.'

'Yes. We do. The first half anyway.' Daniel looked at his watch and rubbed his eyes. 'It could be worse, it could be England playing and it'd be rammed. At least you have a seat. And Pimm's.'

'Wales should be there,' Jim joked, finishing up his drink.

'Wales are never there!'

'Cheeky bastard.'

'Your round.'

Jim looked at his watch. At 8 p.m. on a Thursday there was little else to do but get tipsy with a friend. He had time to kill before Chinawhite, Madame Jojo's or The Ivy got swinging and he'd already filed his non-time-sensitive stories to his showbiz editor. He just had to get the big splash, hopefully one for the cover if it was a really good night, and he usually got those when he was half drunk.

'OK, I'm meeting the ugly one from Boyzone at 11 p.m., you're in luck.'

Jim straightened his blazer and got up to go to the bar while Daniel looked at the screen. The comfort of watching sport, the feeling that he was never alone, the shared experience of a uniting moment, getting him through a few minutes of solitude. He looked from the screen to the table in the corner, and blushed to see one of the blondes looking at him before lowering her head in a huddle with her friends. He looked at Jim, waiting at the bar and clutching his new mobile phone tightly – Jim was the first of Daniel's friends to have one – while he seemed to be in an animated chat with the barmaid beyond him.

Daniel looked back to the television; the game had kicked off. He didn't see the harangued-looking barmaid, the last of the cigarette smoke she had enjoyed on her break exhaling from her neat nose. She was tall and willowy with bronze skin and deep red hair, falling messily down to her small chest.

'What do you want?' she asked Jim accusingly. She stood out even more because her accent was unusual – and not Australian, like many of the barworkers in Central London.

She looked grumpily at Jim while he hesitated, as if she had 4,000 better things to do tonight than to pull pints; as if it were *he* who had shouted at her to come back from her break. Jim narrowed his big blue eyes to study hers, of a colour he'd never seen before but must have heard about in a book, or somewhere, because there was something familiar in her uniqueness.

'A Pimm's, and... erm... a vodka tonic please,' he said, flustered.

'We're out of Pimm's,' the barmaid replied unapologetically.

'Sorry Liv, can I just squeeze by, get some ice?' asked a bearded barman with horn-rimmed glasses. Jim looked between the bearded barman and the woman pressing a glass against an optic, and was hit by an exhilarating thought.

'Hey, what's your name?' he asked.

'Not interested,' she shot.

'Nor am I,' Jim replied, as quick as a flash, and let out a booming laugh that jarred with his baby face. The sound caught Daniel's attention again.

'Look, what do you want instead of the Pimm's?' Her eyes were hostile and fiery.

'A cider please, he'll have a pint of Magners,' Jim said, as the barmaid rolled her eyes and grabbed a pint glass. She obviously preferred serving shorts. 'And *please* tell me your name,' he said, clasping his hands together. 'I promise I'm not a creep. I just might have a nice surprise for you.'

The barmaid's curiosity got the better of her, and a little smile curled into the corner of her mouth as she placed the pint in front of him like a challenge.

'Olivia,' she said, as she straightened out the bar mat and leaned on the pump. 'My name's Olivia. Why the hell are you asking?'

'Olivia from Milan?'

'What the fuck?'

'Fashion student?'

Olivia checked herself for giveaways but her thin cream slip dress held no clues. 'Who the fuck are you?'

Jim punched the air.

'Olivia from Milan, you have just made my day!'

Daniel looked up to see Jim do a little dance at the

crowded bar, but didn't know why. Jim handed over a tenner.

A playful, perplexed smile crossed Olivia's face and Jim noted she looked totally different to the woman who'd come back from her break.

'Get on with it!' barked a man behind the bar with spiky hair dyed blond at the tips. 'You spent too long on your break as it is.'

'I'm serving!' Olivia spat back.

'And tie your hair up! It's not good practice to have it loose near food and beverages.'

Olivia ignored the man and pressed buttons on the till.

'Here, two-seventy change. Now how do you know me?' Olivia smirked. 'I didn't get off with you at that party last night, did I?!'

'Erm, no. I have never met you before in my life.'

'So how do you know me?'

'Please, Olivia, would you do me a *massive* favour by bringing this pint over to my friend?'

'*Vaffanculo!*' she laughed dismissively.

'Olivia!' asserted her boss, jangling a chain of keys looped onto his slacks.

Jim gave Olivia his most dashing smile.

'It would mean more than you know, and then everything might make sense.'

Olivia raised an eyebrow as she picked up the pint. She couldn't remember most of the shit she chatted to punters in the pub she worked in; she must have spoken to this one before.

Jim didn't know if she was going to carry the drink over for him or throw it in his face.

'Over there. I think it'll make you smile.'

Olivia walked to the end of the bar where she followed Jim back to his table, hoping that whatever this guy was playing at would be worth winding up her boss for.

'Well, I fuckin' hope it'll make you smile,' Jim muttered to himself under his breath.

'Olivia!' snapped the landlord. 'It's not table service! Get back behind the bar!'

The tall woman in the cream satin slip dress slipped through the pub, pint in one hand, pushing her hair back with the other.

'Olivia! Thirsty punters here!'

'Just there, that table there,' Jim directed as he came to a halt to one side, letting Olivia through. 'There you go,' he said proudly. Daniel was staring at the football open-mouthed, but had kept glancing at the bar to see if Jim was OK and who he was in conversation with. And then he realised as he saw her approach.

'What?!'

'*Vaffanculo*,' she whispered. 'Dan-i-el?'

Yugoslavia scored and the American tourists in the corner shouted at the TV.

'NOOOOOOOO!' yelled one.

'USA! USA!' chanted another two in unison.

'Olivia!' Daniel gasped.

'Hey. How are you?'

Daniel coughed on a strawberry stalk as he stood and gave Olivia's bare shoulders an overenthusiastic hug. She looked more sophisticated than the backpacker in the denim cut-offs and paisley shirt, the ribbed vest and tie-dye trousers. Her nose ring had gone and her English sounded better. A

London twang outweighed the mid-Atlantic one. She seemed a bit thin and slightly wooden, but pleased enough to see him.

Over her shoulder, Daniel could see Jim smiling, as he gave two thumbs up and rose on his Campers.

Jim looked on but couldn't help feeling it was all a bit Danny and Sandy in *Grease*, only 80 per cent confused enthusiasm from Daniel and a casual vagueness from Olivia. And then he felt bad. There was an awkward pause.

'It's so cool to see you! Do you *work* here?'

Daniel was baffled – if a Pirelli tycoon's daughter could live in a flat in Soho, why was she working behind a bar?

'Yeah…' Olivia looked almost embarrassed, as if she could read Daniel's mind. 'Keeps me out of trouble,' she laughed.

'*Did* work here!' shouted the landlord as he called last orders on Olivia's employment. 'Sling yer hook! There are homeless out there who'd pull a better pint.'

Olivia turned back.

'Yeah, well fuck you!' she shouted, making a hand gesture Daniel had never seen before. 'Then *give* them a job, you fuckin *testa di cazzo*! I gotta gig to go to anyway…'

'I *love* her,' Jim mouthed at Daniel.

Olivia marched to get her leather biker jacket from out the back but the landlord threw it at her face before she could even reach the bar. She just caught it before a zip hit her eye, and cursed something else in Italian.

'Bring your drinks with you,' she commanded Daniel and Jim. 'We're outta here.'

'You'll pay for those glasses!'

Daniel and Jim looked at each other, worried about

stealing from the pub but too enchanted to ignore Olivia's diktat, so they downed their drinks, which was easier for Jim and his vodka than it was for Daniel and his pint, and followed her out onto Rathbone Place.

'How the *hell* did you manage to set that up?!' Daniel marvelled as he wiped cider from his mouth.

'You're welcome,' Jim almost sang, taking full credit for the coincidence as the pub door slammed shut behind them. Daniel didn't care about the football anymore. He didn't care about his shift. He stood there, unable to wipe the smile off his face. The girl he had been obsessing about for two years had just walked across the pub with a drink for him and right back into his life.

'I can't believe I've bumped into you!' Daniel enthused, while Olivia lit a cigarette and scowled down the barrel of it, not looking as surprised as Daniel felt. Jim checked his phone to see if Wesley had messaged or his meeting had changed. The downside of having a mobile phone? The ugly one from Boyzone kept changing their rendezvous.

The three of them stood awkwardly on the summer-stained pavement of Fitzrovia. 'Where are we going then?' Daniel asked, rubbing his hands together, as if they had just broken out of prison.

'You not going to work?' Jim looked surprised.

'My friend has a gig at the 100 Club,' Olivia nodded down the road towards Oxford Street as she took the first, soothing drag. 'They started ten minutes ago.' Olivia looked at her watch. The colourful Swatch Daniel remembered from Dunedin had been replaced with a chunky gold one that looked like it might have been her father's.

Daniel looked up and down the road, torn by what to do.

'Have you got Will's number in your phone?'

'Sorry Daddy-O – only the showbiz desk…'

Daniel and Jim looked at each other and winced. Despite Will's bank of freelancers and night journalists, Daniel would never get away with going AWOL for the night. Fort Murdoch was like a prison, you had to sign in and you had to sign out.

'Sickie?' Jim suggested helpfully. 'Showbiz or News can pass it on. Although it is getting a bit late…'

Olivia looked at them impatiently.

'Well, you could eat soup or you could jump out of the window,' she shrugged.

'Huh?' they said in unison.

'Take it or leave it. But I know which I'd rather be doing…'

Olivia threw her cigarette into the gutter and put on her jacket.

'What's the band?' Jim asked.

'The Horizontals, they're awesome,' she said with a frown. 'My friend is the bass player.'

Jim hadn't heard of them yet, but he was always interested in seeking out the next big thing to oust the tabloid fodder he usually had to put on a pedestal: the girlbands, the boybands. The European DJs, Blur and Oasis.

'I'll come for an hour,' Jim said.

'Dan-i-el?' she asked. Three syllables as she levelled him with her gaze. He was still shocked and confused and smiling at her in disbelief.

Daniel remembered Olivia wiping mustard from her lips as they ate burgers at the bottom of the world; the glitter in her eyes when she saw her ankle chain; the wetness of her tears against his neck on the steps of the train station; the taste of her kiss before she ran for her train. He looked at her angry cascade of hair as she pulled each lapel of her jacket together over her flimsy dress, and knew he'd never see her again if he let her walk off now.

'Jim, give me your phone,' Daniel said, as Jim delved into his chinos pocket and whispered 'Uh-oh.'

'I'm calling in sick.'

Eighteen

September 2017
London

'A*y, amore mia*, is there anything else you need?' asked a fretful Maria. 'Do you want some more figs? Another bottle of water perhaps? Is there anything I can get you, *tesora*?'

Olivia lay in her hospital bed in London, waiting to go to theatre, while her two mothers sat at her side. Nancy, perched on the mattress by Olivia's pillow, had pale skin and red hair in the short, pageboy style she had had all her adult life. Maria, sitting on a chair stroking Olivia's hand, looked like a Sicilian peasant, despite the fact she clutched a Mulberry bag she had picked up in the West End yesterday. The dark corridors and basement cafe of the National Hospital for Neurology and Neurosurgery on Queen Square had been stifling for the past week of appointments, scans and pre-op assessment, so Nancy and Maria, Mamma Una and Mamma Due, had appreciated some fresh air and light relief, while feeling guilty about doing so without their daughter. It wasn't right stroking the ties in Liberty or having a slice of cake in John Lewis if Olivia wasn't with them.

Both women were practical and pragmatic, powering Olivia on in different ways. Nancy was the mother Olivia would turn to for advice about money, university applications, car insurance or political discussion. They would talk at length on the phone about Scottish independence, Hillary for President or rising populism in Italy, and she was a good, if matter-of-fact counsel in parental questions or worries Olivia might have about Flora and Sofia.

Maria was the mamma Olivia turned to as a child when she needed ointment on a cut, a new party dress fashioned out of nothing, boyfriend wisdom, or to cry into a plate of pumpkin doughnuts or almond cannoli (tears of sadness would soon turn to joy as Olivia inhaled the sweet ricotta filling). Maria had a recipe for every heartbreak and disaster, and Olivia sought comfort in her cookery, and most of all, the hum of her sewing machine. And it was Maria who Olivia turned to for guidance and creative direction when she started her own clothing brand: helping her name it ('Olivia Messina *ovviamente*!'), sourcing fabrics, feeding back on sketches, advising on embellishment and where to have the clothes made – even though she vehemently believed that no workshop in India would be as good as the ateliers of Milan.

From under her polyester hospital bedlinen, Olivia looked at the faces of the women she tried not to take for granted and marvelled.

'I'm fine, really. I'm not meant to eat now anyway,' she scorned Mamma Due the feeder. Maria made a face as if to say, *oops*. Daniel returned to the busy ward and Olivia's bay with a coffee in a cardboard Costa cup.

'We'd better get back for pickup,' Nancy said, looking at her watch. Timekeeping was also more Nancy's domain. She gave Olivia an apologetic smile.

'Really, it's fine, go get our girls.'

'You'll be all right?' Maria retied her headscarf and tried to hide her tears.

'Really. I'm as ready as I ever will be. I have peaches I'm not allowed to eat. I have *Oggi*, *Grazia* and *Hello!*. I have three bottles of water and six cans of Aranciata I'm not even sure I'll be allowed to drink when I wake up. I have a book that I haven't started yet. I have Daniel. And I have enough *torta setteveli* to feed the entire surgical team for a month. Go!'

Daniel laughed away the tension and put his cup down on the side table among Olivia's book and magazines.

'She'll be fine,' he said, taking Maria into his arms while she stifled her cry.

'I will Mamma. I'll be out of here before you guys know it.'

Two hours later, Daniel was still sitting by Olivia's bedside, patiently waiting for her to be taken into theatre. It was the lack of urgency that he found hardest to cope with, the most frustrating.

There hadn't been an ambulance waiting on the tarmac on their return from Ibiza to Stansted. There was no melodramatic rush down a corridor with medics talking in a vernacular of 'units' and 'lines'. There wasn't any sense of hurry, despite the worry that Olivia might have another seizure at any time. The woman on the desk at Guildington

GP surgery had put up her usual barriers when Daniel and Olivia walked through its doors the day after landing, while Flora was watching Sofia watch cartoons at home.

'We don't have anything for three weeks, I'm afraid,' said the woman who looked like a goblin, without much remorse at all.

Olivia laughed – even terrified, she was so *laissez faire* and flighty about her illness.

'Erm, that won't be good for us,' she said with a smile.

Daniel interjected, a tense pallor on his sun-kissed faced. 'No – we need to see Dr Humbolt as soon as possible. It's urgent,' he said behind gritted teeth.

'Well, what's it regarding?' The goblin looked pained, expecting the harangued husband to complain that his wife had a bladder infection or a bad cold, because she'd already had to fend off a load of time wasters today.

Daniel was about to object.

What business is it of yours?!

He looked behind him and scowled at the waiting queue. A little sign saying 'Please stand behind this barrier to give the person in front some privacy' stood only a metre behind him. Olivia put a calm palm on his chest to stop him and smiled at the goblin.

'I have a brain tumour. I collapsed at an airport in Spain. I've been in hospital there for the past week while they discovered I have a tumour the size of a walnut. I'm on anti-fitting drugs and I need brain surgery. Urgently. You need to find me an appointment with Dr Humbolt *today*.'

The goblin was silenced, and told them to sit in waiting area B.

Dr Humbolt had been their GP since they moved to the

village thirteen years ago, the day Flora was born. He was scruffy, sympathetic and helpful, and got Olivia into the system at Addenbrooke's hospital in Cambridge on the list of Dr Okereke, a consultant clinical oncologist with grey braided hair, sparkling brown eyes and deep purple lipstick, who said Olivia's surgery would be done three weeks later at a specialist hospital in London, where Daniel waited anxiously now.

What if it's too big to remove now?

What if all that time sitting around made the astrocytoma grip too deep?

Why is there no urgency from anyone?

Can brain surgeons start operating at two in the afternoon?

What if they're not concentrating so well?

What if she never wakes up?

Daniel finished his third coffee; his eyeballs were tired yet wired, and he hoped his wife wouldn't notice his stomach's plaintiff rumblings for food.

Maybe I should have one of those peaches.

Olivia let out a sigh, closed her eyes and turned her head as she tried to get some rest, tried not to think that soon, someone would be going into her skull, into her brain. Her hair was crammed into a blue cap bursting at the seams, her white hospital gown peeling away from one shoulder. Daniel looked at her and remembered the night in the 100 Club. Her brown collarbone holding up her cream slip dress. The night that started with the most amazing surprise but turned ugly.

'You look beautiful,' he whispered out of nowhere.

Olivia's eyes flickered open.

'Me?'

'Yes.'

'My brain doesn't look big in this?' she joked, pointing to the bulbous mass.

'Your brain is perfect.'

'No it isn't.'

'It will be.'

'They shaved a chunk out of my hair, did you see?'

'Yes, but no one will notice under the rest of it. Besides, all the hip mums at school are rocking an undercut.'

Olivia closed her eyes again and turned her head.

She'd had lots of visitors to her bay since Nancy and Maria had left. Dr Okereke and the senior consultant neurosurgeon, Mr Greene, had been round, along with two junior doctors, followed by a chat with the anaesthetist and what felt like four hundred nurses delivering pills and potions, all wanting to discuss Olivia, mostly as if Olivia weren't in the room. Finally, two nurses and the anaesthetist returned, and said it was time.

'Would you like a minute?' asked the anaesthetist from behind a bushy moustache. Daniel nodded, pulled his seat closer to his wife and tried to think of something profound to say while the medics lingered around a corner.

'I love you, you know.'

'I know.'

'And the girls love you more than anyone could love a mother.'

'Flora doesn't.'

'Don't say that! She does. She's just 13. It's the law – she has to give you shit.'

Olivia gave a look as if to say, *I know*. That she knew her daughters loved her, despite the different ways they showed it. Daniel's smile made way for sincerity again. 'Jude loves his mamma too,' he said, his eyes filling with water. A greyness washed away Olivia's smile. 'He will be watching over you, our beautiful angel.'

Olivia squeezed Daniel's hand.

'At least if this isn't a success, I will be reunited with him.'

'Don't say that.'

'Well, I meant to say, if this *doesn't* go to plan... then, well, I've left letters for the girls in my knickers drawer.'

'What?'

'If I don't wake up or if I'm soulless or a vegetable.'

'Don't!'

'Well, there are letters to the girls. And, well... I'm sorry I let you down.'

Daniel let out a desperate sigh, a sound that showed he was trying to suppress a sob, and his eyes welled up. This was the first time either of them had said it out loud. He scratched his nose and looked down at Olivia's hand, hooked up to cannulas and wires, and he clasped it in both of his.

'You are *not* going to let me down. You are the strongest and bravest woman I know.' He clasped tighter. 'I would be a *mess* if it had been the other way around – if I was the one going into theatre. Look at you! You could *never* let me down. This will be fine, *you* will be fine. And we will be laughing about it next week.'

'You think?'

Daniel held Olivia's weary gaze. She hadn't felt a single headache, a single bit of pain since her diagnosis – apart from that caused by needles and prodding and claustrophobic scans in tunnels – but the fatigue she felt, the exhausting nature of being told you're ill and being put through a system of hospitals, even if you didn't feel ill – well, that had been draining.

'I know it.'

Now wasn't the time for Daniel to show his anxiety, so he held her gaze lest he show the terror he felt; kept his eyes firmly on his wife's, and did the last thing he would expect to do in such circumstances: he broke into Dolly.

'Islands in the stream...'

Or was it Kenny?

Self-consciousness seeped away from him for a second, he didn't care that the other patients behind their moth-eaten curtains might be laughing, as he carried on singing.

He had pitched it an octave too high and they were both trying not to laugh as he continued to sing badly.

Olivia laughed. Then she cried.

The nurses and anaesthetist returned to wheel her away and Daniel stood, leaned over the trolley bed and kissed Olivia firmly on the lips. She gave a little wave.

'I'll be here when you wake up!' Daniel shouted down the corridor.

That was what he had meant to say.

Nineteen

June 1998
London

'Olivia Messina,' Olivia announced to a man with broad shoulders and a battered clipboard at the entrance to the dingy underground club.

Daniel and Jim gave each other a pointed look and made the mental note.

Messina.

The doorman looked down his list and drew a line through Olivia's name on it.

'And you two?' he asked gruffly.

Jim stepped forward.

'Jim Beck, showbiz reporter, *The Sun*.'

Olivia, who had already started walking down the stairs to the club, turned back to look at Jim and raised an eyebrow.

'Want to see my press pass?'

'No, you're good,' the man said, waving Jim and Daniel in, who followed Olivia into the basement.

The band had already started playing to a misty haze of dry ice and blue lighting.

'That's my friend there!' she pointed proudly. 'Mimi!'

Daniel and Jim looked up at the small stage in awe. Mimi's bass guitar was almost as tall as she was, and she leaned back to take it in her slight arms as she played, holding it against her white vest and tight dark jeans. Her hair was black and poker straight, contrasting with her pale skin as she whispered haunting harmonies into the mic as the blue lights captured the brightness of her pale eyes. Daniel didn't realise yet that he had seen Mimi before, in a cafe in Sydney.

The band sounded good. Jim was taking note.

Singer and guitarist Nate took the lead under a jagged fringe, while morose Tommy stood behind a synthesiser and buff drummer Nik pummelled the drums as a small crowd danced with great enthusiasm.

Mimi spotted Olivia and smiled in surprise as she sang into the mic. She wasn't expecting to see her, even though she had put her name down.

'Whoooo-hooo!' Olivia cheered.

'Double Jack Daniel's?' Daniel asked cheerily.

'Vodka tonic!' Olivia shouted. 'But yes, double thanks.'

Daniel looked to Jim expectantly.

'Same please!' he said, with a cheeky sparkle. Neither of them could really believe how the night was turning out.

'Japan baby!' cheered Olivia at the end of her favourite song, as she took her jacket back off, looked at Jim and swayed. He could see why Daniel was so enchanted, Olivia was unlike anyone he'd met before.

'Japan?'

'They're off on tour tomorrow, three weeks in Japan!' she said, slinging her jacket onto a raised barstool at a vacant high table next to them. Jim raised an impressed eyebrow.

Maybe The Horizontals *were* going to be the next big thing.

'How cool. I like them!'

The Horizontals were embarking on a tour of Japan, where they had struck gold; all the groovy Harajuku girls and boys were loving their synth pop ditties, even if Mimi had to work the soft toy department of Hamleys in London by day, to make ends meet.

All eyes were on the band – mostly on Mimi – but Daniel made a beeline for Olivia as he returned from the bar and handed out the drinks.

'Thanks buddy,' Jim said.

'*Grazie*,' Olivia said with a flirty smile. She was about to ask Jim whether the business about *The Sun* was true, but the mobile went off in his pocket and he weaved upstairs to take the call.

Olivia downed most of her drink in one and went to light another cigarette. Daniel marvelled at her. He couldn't believe he'd bumped into her. Again. On this side of the world.

'So surreal – I can't believe you're here!' he said.

'Nor can I!' Olivia laughed, although Daniel wasn't sure if she meant meeting him or the fact that she was in the 100 Club and not at work.

'How have you been?'

'OK,' Olivia said unconvincingly as she exhaled smoke and reached for the remnants of her drink in the plastic cup on the table.

The band finished another song and Olivia clapped and shouted.

'Go on treacle!' she added in a mockney accent, cheering and whooping. 'Play anuvva blinder!'

Daniel laughed.

'You've taken to London then?'

'Oh yeah,' Olivia answered. 'I've got the lingo down guv'nor,' she said in a terrible East End accent. Daniel smiled as he sipped his pint.

'I know that "cream crackered" means I'm tired; a man is now a "geezer"; and "pissed" doesn't mean angry anymore, it means loaded.'

'Loaded?'

'Drunk, guv!' Olivia protested. 'Loaded means drunk among the kids I went to school with... but they mostly speak American.'

'Yeah, loaded means something else here. But you might be that too.'

Olivia didn't answer that, because it was obvious she was. She didn't really need the job she had just been sacked from. She had taken it to add some rhythm to her week, because her mammas were worried about her erratic schedule and her lack of meaningful friendships. Nancy in particular had recommended she get a job, not realising that barwork was conducive to neither good timekeeping nor making friends.

'I might not fit in, but I just know to never – *ever* – say "fanny pack" again.'

They giggled.

'Ooh and I know what "sling yer hook" means now I've been fired!'

Daniel smiled, then remembered his own pitiful employment situation, and wondered if Will would be firing him. The longer the set went on, the less Daniel cared. He wouldn't have missed this for the world. Jim came back in and made his excuses. 'Gotta go. Boyzone cancelled on me but I've just taken a *very* interesting call from Geri...' He was hoping for the exclusive on why she had recently left the Spice Girls.

Daniel feigned interest but all he cared about was Olivia. He wouldn't leave her side for anything tonight.

'Olivia, I can't tell you how wonderful it is to meet you,' Jim said formally, taking her hands in his and looking her in the eye. They were the same height.

'Good to meet you too, er...'

'Jim.'

'Good detective work Jim,' Olivia said. 'Or should I say Inspector Montalbano...' Daniel and Jim looked puzzled.

'Well quite!' said Jim. 'Now please – please – give this man your email address, before the night is out.'

Olivia's eyebrows knitted together. Daniel blushed.

Jim kissed her on each cheek, then Daniel too.

'MESSINA!' Jim shouted to the low ceiling, as he walked out, as if he were chanting hallelujah to the heavens. Daniel was saved from having to make an explanation by the band.

'We're just gonna take a short break,' Nate said into his microphone. 'We'll be back with some more beastly tunes in about... fifteen!'

Mimi removed her bass and propped it on its stand, before the band dispersed to the bar to chat to friends, followers and groupies.

'WHOOOOOP!' Olivia cheered and hollered as Mimi approached.

'You're here! I put your name down but thought it was optimistic.'

They hugged.

'You're on fire!' Olivia answered, as she slipped on her flat shoe and one leg gave a little.

'Oops, watch it there!' Mimi cautioned. She looked at the stranger propping her friend up and back at Olivia with concern, awaiting an explanation.

'Oh, this is Daniel. Daniel, this is Mimi.'

They smiled a hello at each other, then Mimi turned back to Olivia.

'How come you made it?'

'You're on fire – I *was* fired,' Olivia said with a smirk.

'Oh Livvi!' Mimi lamented.

'Fuck it. It was a heap of shit job in a heap of shit pub, I was only in it for the free booze.'

Mimi had a look of concern in her bright eyes, but turned to Daniel, as if she were seeking help.

'How did you two meet?'

'New Zealand,' Daniel said.

'Australia,' Olivia chimed.

Mimi looked between the two of them.

'Well, both...' Olivia shrugged.

'Wow, small world,' Mimi said, seemingly relieved that they had actually met before and Daniel wasn't one of Olivia's waifs or strays she liked to pick up.

'Nice to meet you. You're excellent – I love your sound,' Daniel said awkwardly. He wished Jim hadn't left. Jim was better at this. 'Would you like a drink?' Daniel offered.

'No I'm cool thanks, and I have water on stage. Thanks though...'

Olivia shrugged and noticed the drink Jim had barely touched and picked it up. Mimi made her excuses.

'I'm just going to say hi to our promoter, be right back.'

Mimi weaved through the crowd and Olivia felt the vodka coursing through her veins. She put her hand on Daniel's shoulder and appraised his face.

'Soooo, how's newspapers going?'

She remembered.

'Great!' Daniel lied.

I'm fucked.

'How's Central Saint Martins?'

Daniel thought of his recce down Charing Cross Road, how he had walked past The Spice Of Life, The Cambridge and The Porcupine, wondering if that's where the fashion students hung out and drank, not knowing that Olivia often did.

'It's shit.'

Olivia didn't lie.

Daniel was taken aback.

'I only just scraped the year. Again. My tutors are impossible. The people on my course are mostly horrid and I don't have supermodel friends to walk in my graduation show next year.' She said it all with a laugh that belied the severity of how much she hated it. The sadness she felt. If Mimi wasn't living in Brixton, if she didn't have her best friend from school to hang out with, or a familiar face in Vaani in the corridors, she would have sacked college off a year ago and gone back to Milan. Olivia was dreading Mimi going on tour to Japan, even for a few weeks, but she didn't say that out loud.

'Oh man! I'm sorry to hear that.'

'I went to a graduate show this afternoon, before my shift…' She put her hand to her brow and closed her eyes, as if she were trying to steady herself now. 'It was amazing.

So adventurous and original. I'm way off doing that kind of thing.'

'Yeah but you have a whole year to get to that surely?'

'I dunno,' Olivia shrugged as she tied her hair into a bun on top of her head. 'I live in this amazing city but I have so very little inspiration, I hate to admit it. I'm not enjoying it.'

Olivia's brow creased and Daniel wanted to smooth his thumb along it. To kiss it better and tell her that he was sure she was amazing.

'Oh. That sucks. I'm sorry.'

'Yeah, it's a real "pea-souper"...' mockney Olivia said, although Daniel was pretty sure she'd got this one wrong.

They went quiet as he watched her secure her hair artfully with a drinks straw, and Daniel pondered that if she, this goddess, felt like a fish out of water at fashion school, how much of a dork he would feel like there.

He looked around the hazy room, feeling self-conscious that he wasn't wearing a Breton top like Kurt Cobain, a crushed velvet suit like Jarvis Cocker or a Harrington jacket like Damon Albarn. He didn't rock the football-casual sensibility of a Fred Perry shirt, an achingly hip parka, Adidas Sambas or a glam-rock leather jacket. Daniel wore an inoffensive chambray shirt, black jeans and grey and pink Converse. The men all around him were carved in their tribes. The women too. Apart from Olivia. She seemed to be the leader of her own. No one else looked like her in her cream slip dress and metallic gladiator sandals, holding together her pub-stained feet.

The sandals.

Daniel remembered seeing them, close to his nose on the podium in the nightclub, in a place called King's Cross on the other side of the world. She wasn't wearing her ankle chain tonight.

Daniel's Pimm's, cider and beer were making him feel braver.

'Your birthday. You were going home for your twenty-first. How was it? I thought about you a lot. How you were getting on... without your dad.'

Olivia looked surprised.

'I told you about my dad?'

'Yeah.'

Mimi, Nate, Tommy and Nik took to the stage again to cheers and whoops from the crowd, which had filled up since the first half, and struck up another catchy tune.

'Well... I got home and we had a small party – my mothers and me.' Olivia read from Daniel's face that she had told him about them too. 'We went to church. Lit some candles. But it was shit. I missed my dad. I still do.'

'I bet you do,' Daniel said, as Olivia held his gaze and tried not to cry. 'I'm so sorry.'

Daniel had a kindness Olivia hadn't seen in the faces of friends she had made in London. If she told them her dad died, they would cock their heads to one side, squeeze her arm, pout their bottom lip, and change the subject. Only Mimi and Vaani genuinely seemed to care. And Daniel.

'I'm lost without him,' she confessed, as she bit her lip.

Daniel gently shook his head.

Olivia couldn't speak. Instead she flung her arms around Daniel's neck, pressing her body against his. He was taken aback, unsure what to do, but he wrapped his arms around her waist, squeezed her tight and rubbed her back, surprising them both.

Olivia pulled back.

'I'm sorry,' Daniel apologised.

Olivia waved as if to say *it's nothing*.

'You know you say sorry a lot, Daniel. Even for an English person.'

'I'm—'

'Shh!'

As Daniel gave his temple an awkward rub, Olivia felt her sharp shoulders drop a little. 'Another drink?' she asked, her pupils glassy.

'I'll get them,' Daniel said.

'Cool. Although after this set I gotta go to an end-of-term party on Frith Street, kind of celebrating the shows.'

Daniel's heart sank.

'You'll come with me?'

'Of course.'

'I'm only going if I'm fucked first.'

Daniel looked taken aback.

'You know, loaded?'

'Oh right. Yeah, I'll get us a drink then.'

'So do you work at *The Sun* with your friend now?' Olivia asked, as they dodged the night buses along Oxford Street, knocking into each other as they huddled in. The June evening had taken a chilly turn, Olivia hugged her ribs under her leather biker jacket; Daniel's flimsy burgundy bomber only just did the trick.

'I'm still at my local paper – the one I was about to start on when we met...'

Daniel didn't want to sell himself short this time. It wasn't *just* potholes and gates that sounded like Chewbacca. But he hated it, he couldn't lie about that.

'Up near Cambridge.'

'Oh yeah,' Olivia said, as a black cab driver beeped at her for stepping out onto Wardour Street. She gestured at the driver and swore in Italian under her breath. 'Of course,' she said, regaining her composure. But clearly she couldn't really remember.

'I do night shifts at *The Sun* though, not with Jim. He's showbiz, I'm sport.' Daniel had a feeling he wouldn't be doing another sport shift any time soon. 'Until the daytime, when I'm back at the local paper.'

'It's down here,' Olivia said, as they walked south, zig-zagging Soho's streets, past pizzerias, jazz clubs and sex shops.

'I can't stand it,' Daniel admitted, feeling an unexpected liberation from being honest. Olivia looped her arm into Daniel's.

'Oh. Why would you do anything you couldn't stand?' she asked, as if it were perfectly obvious; forgetting that she was living a misery she didn't admit to.

'It's a job, I suppose. A good grounding.'

'But why do you hate it so much?'

Daniel looked up at Soho's lights as a drizzle started to fall, illuminating them a little, and pondered.

'It's not the boring stories...' Daniel found their sedate tone reassuring. Elmworth wasn't the type of place where handbag snatches or stabbings took place. 'It's my editor, the boss.'

'What's wrong with your boss?'

'She's exhausting. Makes staff feel like nothing is good

enough until you start to believe nothing is good enough. Then when you have a glimmer of what actually *is* good enough, you realise it's all just a mind game. It's all very tiring.'

'Sounds like a *porca puttana*.'

'Well, that sounds like a pizza to me, so I think that's too good for her.'

Olivia hit Daniel playfully on the chest with her free hand.

'Fucking pig whore!'

'Oh yeah, that's more like it. Although it sounds sexier in Italian.'

'Everything is sexier in Italian,' Olivia said as she nudged her arm into Daniel's with more force than she realised. He steadied himself on the pavement.

'Speaking of *porca*...' Olivia raised her index finger and pointed at a dumpling bar they were approaching on Old Compton Street. 'If I don't eat soon I'm going to be sick.'

Daniel didn't object, and followed Olivia up a small step into the dumpling bar, where she placed an order with a middle-aged woman with glasses.

As they waited for their pork buns and chicken gyoza, Olivia resumed the conversation; trying to give Daniel a strategy.

'You need to get out. Change your job. See if your night job can become your day job if you like that one more.'

'I think I might have blown that option.'

'So look for something else. Get another job. Another newspaper.'

'Easier said than done...'

'Why?'

Daniel didn't have the sense of entitlement that Olivia's International School education had afforded her. But then he couldn't think of a 'why not'? And he really didn't want to be living at home anymore. He hoped she wouldn't ask about *that* and he'd have to pretend he was living in a very cool flatshare like Joey and Chandler in *Friends* and not with his parents.

'I suppose I've done two years on the *Echo*, I do need to get out.'

'The guest is a fish who smells after three days.'

'Huh?'

'It's time to move on.'

'Yeah I suppose so.'

Olivia looked at her chunky gold watch and laughed.

'Shit, we'd better get to the party. Is our order ready?' she asked the woman behind the counter.

'Just here Miss,' she said, handing over two small boxes of steaming hot dumplings.

In the tatty bar on Frith Street, Olivia and Daniel sat side-by-side on a well-worn green banquette at a table full of students. Everyone looked totally different to the person they were sitting next to, but they were all uniformly fashionable.

Olivia had introduced Daniel to those whose names she could remember – there was Dev, with brown skin, a tweed suit, and the luscious long locks of a Miss World contestant; Edie, the girl on Vaani's course, whose red lipstick made her teeth look yellow; and Cate, who wore a vest and tutu and whose hair was cropped in a white-blonde pixie cut. Others smoked and conversed so intently they hadn't looked up to say hi. None of them seemed interested in talking to Daniel and Olivia as they sat in pockets of twos and threes around two pushed-together tables, locked in conversation, punctuated by sudden urges to go to the loo in the basement bar. A steady stream of young women and men clomped up and down the rickety wooden staircase, nodding to each other as they passed. Everyone seemed to know each other, but Daniel observed the salutations were all superficial and fleeting.

He didn't care. He was next to Olivia.

'*Ecuador*' came on the bar's speakers and Olivia began to sway.

The rudimentary synth piano started to pulse through Daniel's soaring heart. Was this really happening? Had he really bumped into Olivia by chance?

'When's your birthday Daniel?' she asked, arms in the air in celebratory mode. Her eyes were demanding, she slurred her words. Olivia's flirtation was now more imperious, harder to read, more... London.

'The 1st of March.'

Olivia looked disappointed. She loved other people's birthdays; the 1st of March was too far from June to get excited about.

'How old are you? I can't remember.'

'Twenty-four.'

Olivia raised a flat dark eyebrow into a question mark, as if Daniel weren't telling the truth, and he wasn't sure why. He had always pretty much looked his age.

'How did you spend your last birthday?' he asked, preferring not to talk about himself. Olivia couldn't remember how she spent her last birthday, so she too shifted the focus.

'You'll have to come out for my next one, next month,' she said, her hand on his thigh. He didn't remind her that he knew when her birthday was.

'I'd really like that.'

They looked at each other.

'Can I give you my email address?' Daniel suggested.

'No, I'll never message you.'

'Oh.'

'I'm rubbish with the *tecnologia*. You take mine. That was your friend's command... wasn't it?'

Daniel rubbed his chin and smiled bashfully.

'I'll get you a pen.'

Daniel looked around. He hadn't brought his backpack out tonight; he used the office stationery at News International if he were meeting Jim in the pub first; he worried about bags and pickpockets in London pubs.

'Oh it's OK, I'll use this...' Olivia took a stumpy kohl eyeliner out of the small cash purse in her jacket pocket and started to write on the grease-tinged napkin from their bao buns. 'My Hotmail is shit,' she mumbled. 'I'll give you my college one...'

Daniel watched her write a long Central Saint Martins email address, letters formed beautifully, in a foreigner's hand.

Olivia Messina.

'Here you go.'

'Thanks.'

He studied the long email address, committing it to memory, before folding the napkin and zipping it in the pocket of his bomber jacket, which he had taken off and tied around his waist. Olivia shuffled in closer, put her palm on Daniel's sternum and opened a button on his denim shirt. She pressed the eyeliner against his chest, writing her email address again among the smattering of hair in an arch over his left nipple.

'And there.'

Olivia's writing looked like a tattoo around Daniel's heart.

'Oh and here, just to be sure...'

Olivia edged up onto Daniel and straddled his lap, pushing his hair upwards as she wrote her email address on two rows across his forehead. The kohl was getting blunt now, the end rough and sharp as it retreated into its pencil crater. Her script started to scratch a little but he didn't object. He was happy to be so close to her. He put a hand on each of her thighs as he looked up at her.

Olivia's dilated, glassy pupils fixed on Daniel's forehead as she used her free palm to lean on him as if she were carving into a tablet. Her tongue poked out of the corner of her mouth towards the mole at the end of her lip. Daniel looked at that mole. He wanted to kiss it, as he had in the middle of the train station in Dunedin at the end of the best night of his life. But he didn't have the courage to make the leap. She was still so far away, even when she was up in his face.

None of the other fashion students around the table, nor those emerging up the stairs from the basement bar, looked up at Olivia straddling Daniel; no one batted an eyelid.

'You're a bit sweaty, it will probably smudge,' she said.

'But there you go, three places. On paper, your heart and your head.'

As the end-of-term party went on and the intimate conversations became more raucous, Olivia led Daniel by the hand downstairs to the basement bar where people had started to dance. It was also conveniently nearer the toilet, and Olivia's trips to it were increasing in frequency. As they stood at the bar, her sharp shoulder almost level with his, Olivia started to become repetitive. She kept trying to counsel Daniel through his woes, but as her slurs elongated, he wondered if she were running away from hers. But she did seem to be enjoying the party she had dreaded, and kept going off to the loo with friends as they passed.

The last friend she went off with was a guy. He was about six foot five, with muscly arms, a tight T-shirt and a shaved head. He'd stopped by the bar and beckoned Olivia to the toilets by taking her hand, without having the manners to acknowledge Daniel or ask if he wanted to join in on whatever they were up to.

As Daniel waited, longer this time than the last, he didn't know where to look. There was no comforting screen playing a sport he could get lost in. Olivia's fashion friends hadn't made him feel particularly welcome. They'd just looked him up and down, seen him as something of a cute civilian, then walked on, looking for someone more interesting to talk to.

A short woman with brown skin, cropped black hair and enormous eyes stopped next to Daniel at the bar.

'Tonic water please,' Vaani said to the bartender, before giving Daniel a suspicious sideways glance.

'You're with Olivia,' she stated accusingly.

'Sort of...' Daniel shrugged, embarrassed at having been left alone for so long. 'Are you a friend of hers?' he asked.

'Sort of.'

Vaani let out a little laugh to herself. 'I went to school with her.' Her tone was curt and functional. She seemed to be the only sober person in the room and her abrasiveness was fast sobering Daniel up too.

'In Italy?' he asked excitedly.

Vaani nodded with an air of disdain, as if she were already bored of this tedious conversation. They stood in silence and watched the barman get her drink, before Vaani turned to Daniel again.

'You've got something on your face,' she said, making a circle with her forefinger in front of her own.

'Thanks,' Daniel replied, wiping the corner of his mouth.

'No, up there.' She gestured to his forehead.

'Oh yeah.' Daniel didn't do anything about it other than stand tall, so he could see his reflection in the long thin mirror behind the bar.

The writing made Daniel look like Mr Worry from the *Mr Men* books he loved as a boy. Two rows of simplistic black squiggles, undulating across his anxious brow.

Fuck.

He tried to flatten his hair.

Where is she?

Vaani paid the barman, picked up her tonic water and walked off with a flippant, 'See ya,' as Daniel waited, unable to work out what the hell he should do.

He had sacked off his shift and now it felt like he'd been dumped. He'd probably blown his sports opportunity and if he didn't go in the next ten minutes, he'd miss the last train home. He felt like an idiot. An imposter.

I've got to go.

But he couldn't leave Olivia, not when she had walked into his life tonight.

Where the fuck is she?

Daniel looked at the fashion students dancing. He wondered if the bar would ever close. Fatboy Slim pulsated his brain and he felt a tightening in his chest. He thought about Viv Hart, how he didn't want to sit opposite her tomorrow feeling hungover while she crunched apples loudly and asked him to rewrite his stories. Everything felt horribly familiar and repetitive and he struggled to breathe.

I've blown it.

Ten minutes later Daniel decided.

Fuck this shit.

Aside from the South Asian girl with the massive eyes, no one else had made an effort to talk to him and he was feeling increasingly stupid, increasingly unable to breathe – ashamed of himself for being dropped, for not making an effort to talk to anyone else. He wasn't One Of Them. Olivia was from another world, and it was obviously not one he would ever fit into. He lived at home with his mum, dad and brother. He was neither Joey nor Chandler. He was dull and English and not rich and not fashionable. Had Olivia cottoned onto this and made an escape?

Agitated, Daniel walked over to the ladies' toilet and knocked on the door.

'Olivia!' he banged. 'Are you there?' An angry-looking girl with pink hair came out of the ladies' at the same time as Olivia and the tall guy came out of the men's, giggling conspiratorially.

She was drunker, higher, darker, than when she went off.

'Heyyyy,' she slurred, adjusting her slip dress.

'I'm just heading home, you'll be all right yeah?'

'Dan-i-el... you're not leaving, are you?' Olivia looked taken aback.

The tall guy straightened his jeans and walked across the bar and off up the stairs, three at a time.

'Yeah, I've got a shitload of stuff on. Big day tomorrow...'

Daniel could barely look at her, he felt so sad, so insignificant. He felt for his wallet in his back pocket, untied his bomber from his waist, finished his bottle of beer, and made for the stairs.

I have her email.

'See you around yeah?' He had to get out of there, he was desperate for air.

His foot struck the bottom step of the creaky staircase that led up to the ground floor.

If I even want to message her.

'Hey, don't go!' Olivia lurched, as she reached out to grab Daniel's arm, her hand almost swatting him as she misjudged the distance and fell onto the stairs at the heel of his Converse. She hit her forehead on the sticky bottom step, ripping one of the spaghetti straps of her now-grubby dress. Daniel stopped.

'Shit, are you OK?'

'So soon!' Olivia laughed erratically, as she shielded her forehead to stem the blood, to contain the throb.

'Yeah I have to go. Shall I get you a cab?'

'No, no! I can walk home, it's near here somewhere.'

Olivia clutched her forehead and Daniel saw a thin and gloopy trail of blood oozing from her hairline to her eyebrow. He hesitated, torn by the urge to make the last train home versus the urge to scoop Olivia up.

'You're bleeding! Are you OK?'

She looked at her fingers and smeared her hands onto her satin slip dress as she slumped.

'Olivia? Olivia? Want me to walk you home?'

She didn't answer, but she didn't need to. Her lids kept flickering and Daniel felt a panic rise.

'Shit.'

'I'm sorry,' she laughed, eyes rolling maniacally.

'Jesus! Where's your jacket?'

Olivia didn't answer.

'Is it upstairs?' Daniel looked around; Olivia was almost bent double and no one else seemed to care or notice. He propped her on the bottom step and leaned her head against the stair post.

Where's her mate?

He scoured the room for any of the people they'd been sitting with upstairs – for the friend with the huge eyes, for Olivia's jacket – but it was hard to see through the haze of beer and people. He searched the seats at the edge of the room.

There!

She'd flung her jacket in a corner. He picked it up and gathered Olivia from her post. The schoolfriend wasn't down here anymore. If she wasn't upstairs, still in the pub, he would have to find out where she lived for himself.

Daniel walked the thin and dimly lit pavement with Olivia draped around his shoulders. He'd propped her up through Old Compton Street, up Wardour and onto Brewer Street, before turning right onto Lexington.

Lexington.

She had told him about it in New Zealand, and made it sound like New York.

He stemmed the blood with a paper towel from behind the bar upstairs, the staff quick to oblige, wanting her out of there as fast as possible, and she murmured and mumbled on his shoulder all along the route, her face burrowing its blood into his neck. Her ramblings reassured him that at least she was conscious. Daniel stopped in front of an arbitrary doorway.

'Is this it?' He held her chin and turned her face so she might see it. 'Olivia! Is this your door?'

When Daniel had thrown her biker jacket over her shoulders, he rummaged in the pockets and found a set of keys. They didn't have a name or building number on them, but two Yale keys glimmered on an AC Milan chain, and he hoped they were the keys to her flat.

'This door – look!'

She rolled her head and mumbled in a language that sounded neither Italian nor English.

'If you can't tell me the number, tell me the colour. What colour is your front door? Can you remember?'

Daniel felt increasingly despairing, as he looked up the street and noticed all the doors were black. He'd never been to this street before. He didn't know its grand doorways, looming in recesses and arches.

'Lex. Ing. Ton,' she murmured, sounding Italian now.

'We're *on* Lexington Street. This is it, but which is your flat?'

None of the buildings, the little closed bistros or hidden doorways looked like they might be student digs. 'Can you remember your door number Olivia?'

He clutched the keys and let out a sigh of anguish. Short of trying every keyhole on the street, he needed a solution that wouldn't get him arrested. He looked up and down the road again, edging up to the next property, but there was no one respectable around he could ask at 1.30 a.m.

'*Quello!*' she pointed accusingly at one shiny black door tucked away in the shadows. Struggling under the weight of Olivia's long and lifeless limbs, Daniel fumbled with the key in the lock. He almost cried with relief when it turned and the door opened.

'Here we go!' he sighed. 'Your flat.'

For a fleeting second he felt like he'd won a prize until he saw the task ahead. Facing them was a flight of stripy carpeted stairs, and Olivia fell onto the third one up with a dramatic thud.

'Hello?!' Daniel called up in front of him. He didn't believe a student and – until tonight – a barmaid could live alone in such salubrious surroundings. He flicked a brass light switch. The carpet looked expensive. An elaborate lampshade illuminated the hallway. Olivia put one cheek against the soft carpet and closed her eyes, congealed blood mopped up by her hair.

'Hello?!' Daniel called again; he didn't want to alarm a flatmate, and couldn't remember if Olivia lived alone.

'Who there?' she mumbled, her lids fixed shut.

Daniel set Olivia into a restful coil and swept up the flight alone, to scout out his route for getting her up the stairs. This apartment was cooler than anything in *Friends*. It had high ceilings, clean lines and expensive-looking furniture. The telltale signs that a fashion student lived there were its smattering of clothes and chaos, empty takeaway boxes and bottlcs, overflowing ashtrays and haughty semi-naked mannequins.

Daniel turned on the lights in every room, to check there was no one elsc and to get his bearings. The bathroom had elaborate tiling and a turquoise rolltop bath. The bedroom had a low futon and would have looked minimalist were it not for clothes strewn across it. The kitchen and living space at the top of the stairs had state-of-the-art tech that was clearly never used.

Daniel dimmed the bedroom light and propped the door so he could carry Olivia in, then rushed down the stairs to check on her.

'Hey, I think we need to clean up your forehead, so I can see how deep the cut is.'

Olivia didn't respond.

Is she asleep?

'Olivia?'

Daniel crouched down and lifted her face with one hand, angling the cut so he could see it under the light. 'Olivia?'

She opened her eyes but they were gently rolling upwards, like she might be in a dream. Daniel pressed her cheek lightly and repeatedly with his other hand. 'Olivia?' Her eyes returned to face forward; she looked at him as if she didn't know who he was.

Olivia slurred something in his face, something undecipherable, and leaned in, pressing her forehead against his.

'What the *fuck* were you taking?' Daniel begged.

She whispered again, something that sounded almost like a song.

Disco 2000.

Daniel held her cheeks and remembered it from the karaoke bar in New Zealand.

'Olivia? I need to get you upstairs, to the bathroom, yes?'

Olivia mumbled something about meeting in the year 2000.

Daniel lifted her off the bottom step, his arms under her armpits, until they were almost the same height.

'Olivia?'

Daniel heaved her up.

As she sang something about a fountain her heavy lids lifted and her eyes widened in alarm as she put her hand to her mouth to suppress a stream of sick.

'Fucking hell!' Daniel half shouted.

A spurt of vomit escaped between two fingers, beyond Daniel's shoulder as he deftly ducked and it hit the wall.

Olivia, startled by herself, seemed to regain some awareness.

'I'm so—'

'Let's get you to the bathroom.'

Olivia retched, her stomach contracting violently, as Daniel rushed her up the stairs as quickly as he could, almost dragging her into the bathroom behind his shoulder where she slumped on the cold tiles against the toilet. There she vomited and cried and cried and vomited.

'*Cazzo...*' she muttered to herself between the bursts of bile and horror waking her up.

'Shhhh, it's OK, it's OK,' Daniel said, as he rubbed her back, although they both knew it wasn't. The spine protruding from the top of her slip dress felt rough and jagged. 'Shhhh, shhhh, don't worry. Shhh...'

She continued to retch.

'I'll get you some water.'

'My hair!' Olivia wailed. Daniel looked for a hairband to tie it with, which he found next to the sink. He had never tied hair back before, but gently pulled it and did an OK enough job considering the pressure he was under. Olivia was too drunk to feel how tightly he'd tied it, how it pinched her forehead and pulled at the cut on her hairline – alcohol had numbed the pain.

Daniel went to the kitchen to get a glass of water and wondered if tap water was drinkable in London – he never drank the tap water at Wapping – before reasoning on that being the least of her worries. There was no bottled water in the futuristic barren fridge.

'Here you go.' Daniel sat on the edge of the turquoise bath, holding the glass out for Olivia while her stomach pumped itself. From his rolltop perch, as he rubbed her stegosaurus spine and looked around the room, waiting for her body to do what it needed to do, he noticed an assortment of empty bottles: big ones, little ones, vermouth, vodka and gin, all empty, secreted on the other side of the bath, between its clawed feet and the boxed-in plumbing at the wall.

'What the fuck?' he whispered to himself, wondering

if he should phone an ambulance, wondering if there was someone he could call. He didn't know how to contact Mimi; he imagined she would have long since packed up and left Oxford Street.

He wondered if the boyish girl with big eyes lived nearby.

When Olivia finally stopped retching, Daniel put a cold flannel to her forehead to clean the wound, relieved to see it wasn't as deep as the blood would have him think. As he held her in his hands and she closed her eyes again, she looked strangely fresh-faced; she looked young. She looked like someone in need of a mother or two, and it made Daniel feel sad. She seemed to have no one.

Olivia rested her head on his thigh while he rinsed the flannel and cleaned the residue of sick from one side of her mouth and then the other as he tilted her head, before ringing out the flannel, hanging it over the taps, and lifting her into the bedroom.

He wanted to get the broken grime-and-blood-stained slip dress off her and into something clean, but it didn't feel right, so he carefully lowered her onto the futon and rolled her to her side, facing the window onto the street. She looked like a bag of bones. Her hair looked darker and her swarthy skin was pale – from London or from puking, he hadn't noticed it earlier – and he contemplated lying next to her, so he could protect her, stroke her, to make sure she was OK. The confident girl from the cafe on the Blues Point Road, with saltwater sun-kissed hair, seemed so vulnerable and incapable. So young and silly. But it felt too opportunistic. Too uncomfortable. Instead, Daniel switched off the light and returned to the bathroom to wash away the sick; to clean up.

He looked in the mirror, his reflection tired and harrowed. Black kohl and the imprint of brown blood had smeared into a sweaty and indistinguishable mess across his forehead. What was left of Olivia's email address danced, in reverse, blurred and violent like a bruise. But that didn't matter. He had it on the piece of paper in his jacket pocket; he had it around his heart. Plus it was already committed to memory.

Not that I know what to say to her.

Daniel scrubbed the mess from his forehead, fastidiously cleaned up the rest of the bathroom and tipped the bleach he found under the kitchen sink into the toilet, then returned to the bedroom and closed the Roman blinds. Olivia was already asleep. Daniel propped a pillow behind and another in front of her, to keep her on her side, pulled the eiderdown up over her, and kissed the mass of hair on top of her head, before letting himself out so he could walk away, to walk through the night and get the first train out of King's Cross.

Twenty

September 2017
London

Any news?

Daniel sat in the empty bay where Olivia's bed had been, looking at his phone. Mimi. Nancy. Maria. Silvia. Vaani. All of them had texted in the past two hours, messages of love, support and inquiry. An army of women who wanted so much for this operation to be a success for Olivia, for the young women who deserved to have a healthy mother, for Daniel.

There was nothing to report.

He looked around his curtain cage and returned to the sports pages of his newspaper. England v the West Indies. The Singapore Grand Prix. City and United at the top of the table. None of these events he had covered, or even watched, since his boss at BBC Online had asked the deputy sports editor to step up and cover Daniel 'for a few weeks'.

He couldn't take any of it in, he kept re-reading sentences and still being none the wiser. So he put the paper on top of

Olivia's magazines on the table next to the gap where her
bed had been and noticed someone had tidied them up.

Who was it?

When did they come?

Are they getting ready to clear her stuff out?

Do they know something I don't?

He looked back at his phone and checked in to see if he
could read those sports stories online. To see how his deputy
was managing. How it all looked. But it looked like a blur,
the scrolling hurt his eyes. His wife's skull had been drilled
into and surgeons were touching her brain, *right now.*

He felt sick. His heart raced.

I've had too many coffees.

Daniel looked for the kidney-shaped cardboard bowl
that had been lying around, in case he threw up. A rising
nausea sloshing in his belly. A piercing pain to his forehead.

She's not even had so much as a headache.

He listened to the low chatter on the ward, to see if he
could hear the nurses' station, and whether they might be
talking about Olivia, and how to break it to the husband.

Surely the surgeon would tell me first.

He thought about life without Olivia.

Oh god.

He remembered how mundane the days of young
adulthood were, spent on his parents' sofa when he
daydreamed about Olivia and how he could find her again.
He remembered stagnation, Annabel and quiet cups of
tea. He saw his past in black and white and thought about
how Olivia's laugh and her honesty brought all the colours
of the world into his life. His nausea worsened as he thought
about her pulsating brain, exposed from its beautiful shield,

as medics in masks hacked away at it. The cancer and its tendrils.

He thought about her serene yet scared face as she was wheeled away, and remembered the last time he saw her looking so vulnerable on a hospital trolley. In a birthing suite, having been through the agony of delivering their dead son. He wanted to see her, to hold her, to pull her into him, but panicked that he might never be able to again. His body filled with dread as he pictured the scene of Olivia not coming round, of that being It. Of having to tell the girls. Of life going back to black and white.

He rubbed his eyes again and looked at his phone. The messages.

Sorry. No news. Still waiting x

Twenty-One

June 1998
Cambridgeshire, England

'Do you want a cup of tea, love?' Silvia asked her son's girlfriend, Annabel. 'I've got a million reports to read, I need another cuppa to get me through.'

Annabel shook her head but kept her eyes glued on her Catherine Cookson book. Daniel looked from the TV to Annabel, sitting on what had become 'her chair', to see if she was going to say anything to his mum, or just keep her head in the book.

How about, 'No thank you'?

He took a swig from his can of Boddingtons. Matt and his dad were already on their third.

'Want me to make it, Mum?'

'Oh don't worry love, I need a break. A change of scenery.'

Silvia took off her reading glasses, dropped them to the chain around her neck and made her way to the kitchen. Daniel nudged Matt with his foot, sitting at the other end of the long cream sofa, to tell him to turn over from *Blind Date* to Brazil v Chile on BBC1.

'Has it started yet?' asked John, their dad, as he walked in from the garage with an assortment of sticks. He liked to fashion pieces of wood into chopping boards, chess sets and percussion instruments with his plane, lathe, coping saw and clamps in the garage. It was a nice outlet to offset number crunching in the bank.

'Build-up's just starting,' said Matt jovially.

'Well, move up then son.'

'Only if you put that sharp stick down!'

Daniel pulled his legs in to let their dad sit between them and looked over at Annabel again, unmoved. Oblivious to family life – *his* family life – around her. Lasagne, beers, marking books and Saturday night telly.

'You too Matt!' John ordered. 'Move along.'

Daniel knew that at 24 and 26, both he and Matt ought to have moved out by now, but wondered what their parents thought of *another* adult living under their roof rent-free, as Annabel was always there. In the best chair. Not engaging.

Annabel stared, absorbed by her book, her small brow furrowed. Her face would have been quite pretty if it weren't so sullen; her blue eyes might have sparkled were they not hostile; her small mouth might have looked cherubic were it not downturned. Daniel often wondered what Annabel looked like when she laughed; what Matt was doing with her; what she was like in bed. Because he couldn't for the life of him see what his brother saw in her. They were a strange pairing. Matt was sociable and chipper – the one who always wore a Santa hat at Christmas, started a cheer of 'Oggy oggy oggy!', and knew most of his supermarket customers by name.

'Yes Mrs Pilch, I'll carry the turkey to your car for you.'

'Is there anything else I can help you with today, Mr Bailey?'

'Ooh, don't worry about that, Sue, I'll put it back for you.'

Annabel was the frostiest employee of every month and the rest of the staff were glad when she finished her studies, left the cheese counter and started working at the accountant's full-time.

'Funny little thing,' the Safeway's stalwarts would say, although never in earshot of Matt.

As Matt lifted one buttcheek and let a fart out into the upholstery, his dad tutted and Daniel got up. Perhaps he used all his charm up at work.

'Gross. I'll go help Mum.'

Annabel hadn't even batted an eyelid at the noxious fart, and it annoyed Daniel that he was spending Saturday night with her and not Olivia. He hadn't stopped thinking about Olivia since he left her flat two nights ago; since he sent her an email first thing the next morning. Was her forehead OK? Did she sleep it off? What if she puked and choked on her own vomit? What *had* happened with the guy in the toilet? What did she take? What was with all those bottles? Who was looking after her?

Daniel walked into the kitchen.

'Want a hand?'

'Oh thank you darling, yes please. See if anyone wants some Battenberg cake, will you?'

'Sure.'

Daniel poked his head back around the living-room door.

'Who's for Battenberg?'

His dad rubbed his hands together in glee; he didn't need

to answer that. Battenberg was the way to John Bleeker's heart.

'Ooh, I'll have a cup of tea with it as well, son.'

'Mum's already making a pot.'

'No thanks,' chirruped Matt, watching the national anthems.

Annabel scrunched up her face, didn't look up, and said, 'Yuk.'

She'd made the same face at the dinner table when Silvia presented her with a vegetable lasagne, and she asked for a cheese and tomato pizza instead. Annabel was that curious anomaly of a vegetarian who didn't like vegetables, and who didn't appreciate Silvia's efforts to be inclusive.

'I'll just pop a pizza in the oven,' she had said, apologising to Annabel that she would have to wait another sixteen to eighteen minutes for her dinner.

'What did you say?' Daniel asked from the doorway.

Annabel glanced up, a contemptuous look on her face.

'I'm not a fan of marzipan.' She pretended to gag.

How about, 'No thank you' then?

Back in the kitchen Daniel rubbed his mum's back. He'd felt sorry for her with lasagne gate, busting a gut to make two different types when she had thirty reports to write. Making a round of tea for an ungrateful rabble. No one made tea for her.

'What's that for?' she asked fondly, surprised.

'Nothing Mum, just trying to help.'

'Ahh, well you check the tea in the pot then, while I take that into your father.'

Silvia stopped to appraise her son.

'Are you all right?' she asked, looking up and rubbing his forehead.

'Yeah, fine.'

Silvia wasn't sure, but she took the cake plate into John anyway.

As Daniel stared at the teabags swirling in the pot, he felt agitated, not fine. He hadn't stopped thinking about Olivia in the forty-eight hours since he'd left her flat. The Friday at work had been dreadful. After he walked around King's Cross, waiting for the first train home, he slumped on his bed and slept for two hours before going in late at 9.30 a.m.

Viv had given him a bollocking for poor timekeeping and suggested maybe he go on a time management course. He smiled and said it wouldn't happen again. And spent the day fretting about Olivia – how she was – while he tried to write his stories.

He sent her an email as soon as he got to work, to let her know that he hoped she was OK, but he hadn't had a reply all Friday, and the internet was down at home. It was rarely up. He would have to wait until Monday to see if there was a response.

She probably wouldn't have gone into college on Friday.
Not in the state she would have been in.

Daniel stirred the tea and got lost in a trance, of water and whirls and china and chinking, as he thought about Olivia and wondered if anyone was checking in on her. If she was up and out again. Had she watched Italy beat Norway earlier? Was she happy?

His mum walked back into the kitchen.

'Annabel wants a Diet Coke.'

'Well, why doesn't she get it then?'

Silvia stopped and looked at Daniel, shocked by his uncharacteristic snappiness.

'It's fine, love, I was coming for the tea anyway.'

'I'll take it in, Mum.'

Daniel took the tea tray into the living room and poured out three cups. As he sat down to watch Ronaldo's Brazil take on Zamorano's Chile, he wondered what the fuck he was doing there. At home with his parents, with Matt and Annabel. Again. On a Saturday night. Even the usual soothing salve of football wasn't helping.

That's it. He needed a plan.

If I don't hear back by Monday, I'll email again. Then I'll go into London. See if she's OK. Tell her how I feel. Maybe have a look at some estate agents and see about flatshares.

Twenty-Two

September 2017
London

'What's this?'
'It's a grape.'
'In Italian?'
'*Uva.*'

Daniel smiled, although he wasn't certain of the word *uva* himself, he knew Olivia was right.

'Remember once, you couldn't remember the English for them and you called them "little green bubbles"? So cute.'

'Very funny.'

The fact that Olivia recalled both the word *uva* and the incident he was talking about – during her early days with him back in London – was all Daniel needed to assure him they hadn't cut out the wrong part of her brain.

The relief was thick in the air, unhindered by Olivia's grogginess, as she sat up drinking bad coffee and eating limp toast. A chink of light got through the small, high window leading to street level outside, highlighting her toast on its plate, as shadows regularly dulled it, from people walking the pavements of Bloomsbury.

'I miss the baked hake, the sunshine. Antonio Banderas...' she said, looking around the redbrick recovery ward.

Daniel smiled. Further relief. Although he wasn't quite as fond of Dr Lorca as his wife had been – he was the bastard who delivered the terrible blow back in Ibiza.

As Daniel sat watching Olivia cautiously eating, shunning the cheese rectangle in its sweaty packet, he waited for the consultant to come by. He needed confirmation that this most horrific of days had been worth it.

Daniel tried to focus on Olivia's face, and not the tube that made a suction noise as it pulled and drained liquid along its tunnels, jutting out of a mass of hair under a bandage. Daniel wondered if particles of the tumour were draining out along it, or whether it had all come out in one clean slice. The thought made him nauseous again.

Olivia had remembered who her husband was. That he was 43 and she was 42. What grapes were. That the operation was over and what it had been for. She had asked after Flora and Sofia, and Daniel had assured her that Mammas Una and Due had collected them from school and they were in the Huf Haus in Guildington, doing their homework. She seemed to understand everything about this scenario, to Daniel's huge relief.

The urge to go to the toilet was pressing on Daniel's bladder but he daren't go in case the surgeons came around to evaluate Olivia, so at 10 p.m., when the team visited her bay, Daniel almost wet himself in relief.

'Ahh, here you are!' said Mr Greene, the small, senior consultant neurosurgeon, even though he knew that's exactly where Olivia would be. He was accompanied by

Dr Okereke, Olivia's consultant from Addenbrooke's in Cambridge, although this was clearly Mr Greene's patch. He had a cold authority about him; reassuringly competent, but not as good as Dr Okereke or Dr Lorca at looking his patients in the eye.

Daniel stood up and Dr Okereke shook her head, urging him to sit down. Her dark purple lipstick had worn away but for the corners of her mouth and her look of compassion and kindness made Daniel feel fearful. That the operation wasn't a success.

Would they know that by now?

'How are you feeling, Mrs Messina?' asked Mr Greene cryptically.

Daniel didn't like the formalities. He preferred it when they called her Olivia. Treated her like a human rather than a name on their daily list. Dr Okereke always called her Olivia back in Cambridge. Daniel hoped she would today.

Cut to the chase.

'Bit groggy – drunk like a monkey really. But otherwise OK.'

Daniel smiled to himself again. It was one of those phrases Olivia would translate literally, and not notice when people didn't understand.

Ubriaco come una scimmia.

Olivia hadn't been drunk like a monkey for years.

Mr Greene and Dr Okereke took her humour to be a good thing, and Dr Okereke laughed.

'She said she doesn't even have a headache,' Daniel piped up proudly, but Mr Greene didn't smile, he continued to look from data charts and clipboards to Olivia's face, his face not giving much away. He didn't respond to Daniel, but Dr Okereke gave him a warm smile with her sparkling brown eyes as if to say, *Funny that isn't it?*

'Yes, you're going to feel woozy,' said Mr Greene, looking up over his glasses at Olivia. 'A soreness of the head, but mainly external, where the incision was made and where we went in through the scalp and skull.'

Daniel looked at the liquid in the vacuum tube coming out of Olivia's head and wanted to be sick again.

'But the operation went *terribly* well. I'm very pleased with what I've done.'

Daniel and Olivia exhaled huge sighs in unison and exchanged a look.

'We removed a mass of almost five centimetres, as expected, and we feel we got it all out and are pleased with how tidy the bone flap looks.'

Olivia was a bit too groggy to speak now, so Daniel spoke for her.

'Bone flap?'

'Where we went in through the skull – but it's all been replaced with titanium miniplates and stitched up – Olivia's hair will eventually hide the scar,' Dr Okereke reassured them. Olivia pushed the toast away and Mr Greene continued.

'The tumour will now be looked at in closer detail; next steps will be some radiotherapy to the brain – just as a belt and braces approach.'

Belt and braces?

Olivia didn't know what that meant. Daniel's heart sank. He'd so hoped this was going to be the end of it.

'You can do that back at Addenbrooke's, under me,' said Dr Okereke, wide-eyed and enthusiastic despite her fatigue after a long day of surgery. 'About three or four sessions, depending on how things look.'

How things look?

Daniel opened his mouth but didn't know where to start.

'It's perfectly painless,' dismissed Mr Greene, seeming keen to move onto his next brain, or home at this hour. It must have been a gruelling day for him too.

But he does this every day.

'We'll talk you through all that in a few weeks, give you time to recover from the surgery,' added Dr Okereke. 'You did really well,' she said, giving Olivia all the credit Mr Greene was taking for the success of the operation.

'I'd like to keep you here for two or three nights,' Greene interjected, reminding everyone of the pecking order. 'But let's play that by ear, and I'll see you on my rounds tomorrow.'

'The nurses will watch your pain relief,' Dr Okereke added.

'Thank you,' Olivia and Daniel both said, although they weren't really sure if this was a good thing, and what radiotherapy actually meant. Daniel knew he would spend another train journey online, googling meanings and explanations, through tunnels of fear and despair until he arrived home.

He stood up. He didn't know what the etiquette was for someone who had seen the inside of his wife's head and taken a five-centimetre tumour out of it. Did he hug the surgeons? Pat them on the back or arm? It all seemed very formal, but Dr Okereke took the dilemma away by extending an elegant, precise hand.

'Take care Daniel, you get some rest too.'

'Thank you,' Daniel said, clasping her hand with both of his. Mr Greene nodded and went on his way.

Daniel slumped back into the chair and tried to look at Olivia without looking at the suction tube coming out of her head. She gave a woozy smile. Through all this she had been optimistic and casually upbeat; Daniel didn't know how she'd done it. And today, after going through actual brain surgery, she was managing to sit up in bed, attempting to eat.

They looked at each other.

'Fuck!' they both said, marvelling at the wonder and terror of the day.

Twenty-Three

July 1998
London

R at-a-tat-tat.
    Daniel's hand rasped on the shiny black door, sunk into the oblong lines of an archway in Lexington Street. He hadn't remembered the vegetarian restaurant next door, nor the French bistro, tanning shop and salon opposite, all of which had been closed at 3 a.m. on a Thursday night last month. So why would he? He had only noticed the black door, jumping out in a sea of black doors, when Olivia had picked it out. Dazzling like the right answer on a gameshow as she finally recognised it as *hers* and the relief of warm shelter lifted the darkness of Soho.

A month later, but a different time of day, the street was bustling. People spilled out onto the pavement, waiting for tables at the restaurants, hot and bothered customers covertly stepping out from their sunbeds with an air of guilt, excitement and melatonin, the gay and the groomed exiting the salon with freshly waxed backs, sacs and cracks.

Rat-a-tat-tat.

There was no answer.

There had been no answer to Daniel's email he sent, the day after he left Olivia sleeping. No answer to the subsequent emails he sent in the four weeks after, until one bounced back with Failure Notice written in the subject line and a message that said: Sorry, we were unable to deliver your message to the following address.

Daniel had wanted to cry at his desk at the *Elmworth Echo* when that one came back, and wondered what the hell had happened. He had memorised that Central Saint Martins email and had checked and double-checked. None of the other messages had bounced back until then. What had he done differently?

Rat-a-tat-tat.

A little more confidently this time.

Tomorrow would be Olivia's twenty-third birthday and Daniel thought it fitting to go and see her today. The 28th of July. A date that would give him the confidence and a reason, given they met this night, two years ago. This would be poetic and maybe – just maybe – he wouldn't let her go a third time. A seventh time.

His heart raced. France had won their World Cup. The school holidays had started, which meant kids ruined his peaceful lunchtimes by the river and his mum was home from work. Plus it was even sillier season in local news. This Tuesday evening was close and muggy.

Rat-a-tat-tat.

Louder this time. He had spent £17 on a travelcard. He wasn't going to let it go to waste.

Shit. She's out.

Daniel was about to turn around and slink off back to

King's Cross, or to see if he could meet up with Jim and return later, when he heard footsteps padding down the stairs he remembered carrying Olivia up.

She's coming!

Daniel panicked and realised he was woefully unprepared for something he had spent a month building up to. He didn't have any flowers, he didn't even have a card or birthday present. He was just so focused on getting the courage to go and knock on her door.

Shit, I should have bought a birthday present...

He wouldn't have known what to get the girl who could afford to live in a flat in Soho. And it was all so last-minute anyway. He had only decided, this lunchtime by the river, that today would be the day. He couldn't pass up this date.

The door was about to open when Olivia must have realised she put the latch on it, and the fumble of a key chain went on for a bit longer than Daniel expected.

'Oh, hang on!' said a male voice on the other side. A chain rattled. A heart tightened. And a puzzled-looking man in his fifties wearing only a maroon dressing gown opened the door cautiously.

'Yes?' he asked, pushing his glasses up his nose and tightening his fluffy belt to preserve his modesty.

'Oh.'

Daniel was confused.

He couldn't be her dad.

Surely he couldn't be her lover.

'Is Olivia in?'

'Olivia?'

The man narrowed his eyes and scratched his head, before looking down to check nothing was on show.

Daniel felt his face go hot. A rage rise in his throat.

I never should have left her. I should have come sooner.

'Ahhh,' said the man. The penny dropping. 'Olivia Menzies?'

'Olivia Messina.'

'Oh yes, Messina. She moved out.'

'She moved out?'

'A few weeks ago now. I'm the new tenant.' The man gave a sympathetic shrug and, despite his kind demeanour, Daniel felt a frustration that made him want to kick the door open.

FUCK.

'I didn't actually meet her, but if you know a forwarding address...' The man stopped himself, realising that if the former tenant's gentleman caller hadn't even known she had moved out, he was unlikely to have a forwarding address for the mail he was getting.

Calm. Down.

The man gave Daniel an apologetic smile.

'Don't worry. I'll catch up with her another time.'

'Sorry old chap,' the man said, before looking down to check his old chap again and closing the door to get back to his bath or his friend or whatever it was he was doing in Olivia's flat. Daniel looked back up at the lofty and symmetrical windows and pictured Olivia in there. Her low futon. The turquoise tiled bathroom.

Did she remove the bottles?

He imagined what the apartment might look like without Olivia there. Without her mannequins and makeup and empty bottles secreted and strewn all over the place.

Where's she gone?

Daniel walked up towards Broadwick Street and left onto Carnaby.

He's lying. She was in there.

But he knew she wasn't.

Did she *make that email bounce back?*

Why was Olivia Messina so fucking elusive?

And he realised. Because people came to her. She didn't have to make an effort.

Except he had seen her at that fashion party. He had seen her get the sack. He had seen her dirty secret hiding behind the bath. He knew she was as vulnerable as everyone else, and he so wanted to see her, to see if she were OK.

If she wanted to contact me, she could have found a way.

He felt at a total loss.

Daniel pulled his new mobile phone out of his pocket and dialled the only number he knew. Jim Beck. He had made a good case to Viv for letting him get a mobile phone for work, being a journalist and all – Jim told him all the journalists in London had one, no, *needed* one. But despite having one herself, she had said no. That employees tended to play games on them rather than use them for work; that they'd never take off.

'Nothing is more powerful than face-to-face Daniel, you have to get out there on the doorsteps…' she said, before suggesting he might want to go on a course if he wasn't feeling confident enough doing interviews.

That lunchtime, after sitting by the river and contemplating his options, Daniel went to the new Orange shop that had opened on the high street and got himself a little Nokia that didn't look anything like the bricks the Americans wielded in the movies. He charged it up at work and he did play

Snake on it, but only on the train going into London that evening. He punched Jim's number from a piece of paper into his phone contacts list of one.

'Hey, it's Daniel,' he said as he walked up Carnaby Street, unaccustomed to the act of talking into a mobile, face still hot from the panic of Olivia having moved out. From the email bouncing back. From the sight of her broken and bony as she slept in the recovery position.

'You got one!'

'Yeah. Weird.'

'That stingy cow gave in, did she?'

'No, I had to get it myself.'

'Fucking bitch.'

Daniel didn't laugh as usual.

'Hey, where are you?'

'Soho.'

'Oh, me too!'

It wasn't all that unlikely. If Jim wasn't at his desk in Wapping he was scouring Soho for a celebrity story, and within ten minutes they had met up in The Sun & 13 Cantons for a pint. Except Jim was doing something called the Carol Vorderman 28 Day Detox, so his pint was of lime and soda.

'Can you get us into Brixton Academy tonight?' Daniel asked. He'd seen in *NME*, The Horizontals were back from their trip to Japan and had been given a slot for an up-and-coming bands night. 'Olivia might be there.'

Jim looked at his watch. It was already 8 p.m., he would be hard pushed to get hold of The Horizontals' PR.

'Are you sure this is a good idea? Surely if she'd have wanted to—'

Jim looked at Daniel's sad, khaki-green eyes, his kindly smile and handsome face, and couldn't bring himself to say it.

'I'll see what I can do.'

He pulled out the aerial on his fancy flippy Motorola and stepped outside the pub so he could hear.

On the side balcony at Brixton Academy Daniel and Jim watched The Horizontals rock out. Turned out Jim was doing the PR a favour by getting some press attention for them, as the gig was only half sold. The Horizontals could sell out stadiums in Japan but were still niche on the UK circuit.

Daniel sipped warm beer from a plastic pint glass and looked around. There was no flame-haired girl cheerleading her mismatched best friend. No shining light in a cream slip dress.

After the gig, while the band's manager – a fat man with a square head – was pressing Jim to write a story on the gig, Daniel took his chance.

'Hey, Mimi!'

'Oh, hi!' she said with a quizzical half smile. Relief and champagne made her bright eyes sparkle.

She obviously couldn't remember his name, so he helped her out.

'Daniel – I saw you at the 100 Club, last month.'

'Yeah I remember. Hi...' Mimi said, looking up at him and wondering how he got into the VIP bar.

'You were... erm... awesome tonight.'

'Oh thanks. Shame it's not a great crowd. Think they wanted the Lighthouse Family but got the wrong day.' Mimi laughed at her joke. Her slightly upturned nose shook delicately as she did. On stage she had looked like a porcelain doll wielding an enormous bass.

'Well, I thought you were amazing.'

Mimi blushed. 'How come you're here?'

'Oh, my mate Jim works at *The Sun*. Showbiz section. Caught fifteen minutes of you at the 100 Club and wanted to see more.'

Mimi's eyes widened excitedly.

'Oh, really?' She looked over to her manager chatting to him. 'He'd better give us a good review.'

Daniel winced internally at his half lie. He didn't think The Horizontals would be sitting alongside Geri and Robbie in the paper tomorrow. But he only had one thing on his mind.

'I was hoping to catch up with Olivia to be honest.'

Mimi smiled hesitantly as her eyebrows knitted together. She did remember now. He was the guy at the 100 Club who Olivia had met in New Zealand. Or Australia. Or wherever. He seemed cute. But Olivia met a lot of cute guys. And Mimi was often having to fend them off for her. She didn't quite know how to play this one. Olivia hadn't really talked about him.

'Oh sorry... Daniel, was it?'

He nodded.

'Olivia's not here.'

'Yeah, cause I went to her flat...'

Mimi looked surprised that Daniel knew where she lived.

'Her flat?'

'She wasn't there.'

'Yeah she wouldn't be. Livvi's gone back to Milan. She's not in a good way.'

'Not in a good way?'

'No, I think everything caught up with her.'

Daniel shook his head as he took in the news; the concerned look on Mimi's sweet face made him measure his own.

'Has she gone home for the summer?' he asked hopefully, suspecting what was coming.

'No. She's gone home for good. I'm sorry Daniel,' Mimi winced. 'Livvi dropped out. She's gone back to her mums. You know, to get herself sorted.'

Twenty-Four

October 2017
Cambridgeshire, England

'Will you come inside with me, Mummy? I can show you my clay model.'

'Of course,' said Olivia from under her hot bobble hat.

'The head was a bit wobbly, so you have to be careful picking it up, but Miss Cave said it would dry out over the weekend, so it should be fine.'

Sofia talked at a hundred miles an hour as she led her mother by the hand up the path towards her Year 3 classroom, almost breaking into a skip she was so excited. It was a different response to Flora, who clearly hadn't wanted Olivia and her embarrassing bulbous bobble hat anywhere near *her* school.

Olivia had wanted to walk both of her daughters on the two-kilometre trip from one school to the other. The sunny autumn morning, with its crispness, conkers, and last of the apple fallers on the pavements, was the first of this school year that she had been able to do it. That she didn't have an appointment, an operation or recovery to stop her. The

Mammas had gone back to Italy and Daniel was back at work, at a big online strategy meeting in Salford.

I can do this, Olivia reminded herself, as she pulled on her coat and looked in the hallway mirror. Simple tasks she had thought nothing of before her fall at the airport.

'I'll go from here,' Flora had said as they came through the park and onto the road her school was on. 'You'll make Sofia late.'

Sofia was jumping onto a pile of red and brown leaves with abandon, clearly not worried about being late. But Olivia knew it was that Flora didn't want her friends to see her with her mum. That it had been embarrassing enough to have a mum with brain cancer, let alone have people looking at her, checking out her bald shaved patch under her stupid bobble hat.

'OK,' nodded Olivia acceptingly.

'And I'll walk myself home,' Flora said flatly. 'You'll have loads to do anyway.'

Olivia craned her neck and looked up the road at the secondary school behind the hedges. Her daughter's new life in Year 9, a step up that she knew nothing about since being plunged into her cancer vortex.

'All right, love you. You've got your key, yes?'

'Yep,' Flora said with a low wave, already halfway down the road.

As Sofia skipped down some steps and through a gate to the classroom, Olivia struggled to keep up. She was still tired and could feel the synthetic fibres of the hat rubbing against her head and her healing wound.

What if it's hot in the classroom?

What if I have to take off my hat?

I really don't want to talk to any—

'Olivia hiiiiiiiii,' said Charlie's mum, Caroline, her frame even taller, her limbs more willowy than Olivia's, her face close and her head cocked to one side. 'How are you getting on? Sofia told Charlie you'd been poorly.'

Poorly?

It wasn't actually Charlie who'd told his mum that Olivia was poorly. Isabella's mum Genevieve had overheard Daniel telling Miss Cave on the first morning back, that Sofia had had a tough summer and his wife was awaiting brain surgery. Genevieve had told Caroline, and asked Harry's mum, Julie, if she knew anything about it, because Julie lived near the Bleekers' Huf Haus and might have seen some of the comings and goings if ambulances were involved.

As word got out, Phoenix's mum Nikki started a WhatsApp group, just so people would know that she knew the most about it, under the guise of starting a collection so they could buy Olivia some flowers. By Harvest Festival, it had got around the entire playground.

'Oh, I'm good thanks,' Olivia said, stepping back gently. 'Recovering well.'

'Gosh, you look well. We thought it was a *lot* worse,' Caroline said almost gleefully. Olivia couldn't really think of many things that could be worse than brain surgery, dying aside, but she smiled and gestured towards the open classroom door, so she could follow Sofia in.

As she did, out stepped Laura, a parent governor, and therefore a self-professed authority on the matter ('She had a stroke – but apparently her face isn't wonky').

'Olivia, hiiiiiiiii!' said Laura, her high blonde pony swishing behind her. 'How are *you*?' She cocked her head to one side and made a sympathetic face as she squeezed Olivia's arm.

'Yeah, feeling great,' Olivia smiled, as she scratched the bobble hat. It was a hot mess under there.

'That's super!'

Laura scrutinised Olivia's face, waiting for her to give her more. 'Yah, Pete said he saw Daniel in Waitrose and that you were doing amazingly…'

She awaited further detail with bated breath.

'Ah, so you already knew.'

Laura looked a bit flummoxed and Olivia felt bad. *She's just being kind.*

'If there's *anything* I can do…' Laura had an eager face. She was the parent governor who was also the class rep and the head of the PTA. She was earnest, if pushy, but all Olivia wanted Laura to do was to move aside and let her into the classroom, so she could see Sofia's clay model.

'Mamma!' Sofia called, shouting from inside.

'Oh, I'll let you get on,' said Laura, with another squeeze of the arm. 'So jolly to see you back, and you look a-maze-ing.'

Olivia nodded wearily and stepped inside the classroom.

'Olivia hiiiiiiiii!' said Evelyn's mum Rachel, who was head-to-toe in Lilybod leisurewear. 'Welcome back! You look fab! Gotta run, but we must catch up. Coffee soon?' she said as she headed out of the door.

Sofia came running over, with her model in one hand.

'Look Mamma!' she said proudly, as the big cat's head

wobbled off and fell onto the floor.

'NOOOOOOOO!' Sofia shouted. Miss Cave stepped forward and gave Olivia a knowing smile that said *welcome back to the mad house.*

'It's BROKENNNNNN!' Sofia slumped into her mother's waist.

Miss Cave picked up the decapitated tiger's head and put it on her desk.

'Don't worry Sofia, I have just the thing for it, and if it doesn't work, you can make another one in Golden Time. You were so good at it!' Sofia's tears abated and Olivia smiled gratefully – as grateful to Miss Cave for not going on about her bloody brain as she was for placating Sofia.

Olivia wrapped her arms around her daughter.

'Bye-bye *cara mia.* Shine brightly today.'

Olivia kissed Sofia's nose and Sofia threw her arms around her mother's neck, almost pulling her down.

'Whoa, easy!'

'I don't want you to go!'

'I'm not allowed to stay, darling. You have a good day. Love you.'

Olivia tried to disentangle herself from her daughter's tight grasp.

'Shall we go find my magic glue?' asked Miss Cave. 'See if we can fix that head.' Sofia's tears stopped at her cheeks and she nodded a subdued yes.

'Wanna coffee?' asked Olivia's friend Henrietta, as she handed her son Albie the PE kit he'd forgotten.

'Shit yes!' Olivia muttered, as they both stepped out into the refreshing morning air, as Ethan's mum Vicky, The One

Who Was Always Late, rushed into the playground with Ethan's little sister in a buggy.

'Olivia hiiiiiiiiiii!'

Twenty-Five

December 1999
London

Daniel stood on the deck of the party boat and looked at the golden glow of the Houses of Parliament, lit beautifully at night. He was surprised by how close he was to the building; how close a corporate party boat full of drunks and mischief-makers could get to a chamber of such importance as it glimmered and flirted with its reflection on the Thames. Or was it an optical illusion? Was the building really much further away? Terrorist acts and gunpowder plotters felt like a thing of the past, The Troubles consigned to history since the Good Friday Agreement, IRA Christmas campaigns and bomb scares in schools left behind in Daniel's childhood. Maybe the world was a safer place now.

It felt calming to be so close to something so solid, a place of such grandeur. Daniel had wrestled with a feeling of discord and fear for much of the evening, but the icy air was refreshing and restorative as he looked at the beauty of the Palace of Westminster and the new skyline springing up along the river around it.

In October, Daniel had been despatched to the South Bank to cover the raising of the Millennium Wheel for the *Echo*. An Elmworth engineer was part of the team charged with lifting it after a failed attempt had caused it to suddenly slip. Derrick Tilbury had been the hero of the hour, his team of engineers finally managing to raise the wheel successfully, and Daniel had covered the story in his hard hat and hi-vis yellow coat for the paper.

It was now December, and Daniel looked between the Houses of Parliament on one side and the new 'London Eye', further away on the other, fully upright now and ready for its official big reveal in two weeks' time on Millennium Eve. He breathed in the chill and appreciated a moment of calm while the DJ inside the Silver Sturgeon played '1999' by Prince for the fourth time that evening, as revellers danced under a purple starsheet.

The *Elmworth Echo* Christmas party hadn't started well. The coach to take the staff into London had no heating and no way of clearing its steamy windows, so Viv Hart had to wipe the windscreen with a chamois all the way down the A1 to The Strand, pretending that she didn't mind, knowing that she should have stumped up a bit more for a better coach. At the back of the bus, the advertising and editorial staff were drinking Archers miniatures and playing 'I Have Never'. One of the salesgirls Becca had already fallen out with her boyfriend Gavin, mainly because she didn't want Gavin to be there because that quashed her chances of getting off with Duncan who covered the obituaries. Duncan was single, so didn't have a significant other with him. In fact, all the staff were shocked when Viv said partners were invited too. Daniel didn't know why he regretted telling Kelly that, even before she started puking on Savoy Pier.

'I'm just not good with boats, am I?' she said, on her knees, her burgundy faux-fur box coat riding up her back, her new neat bob skew-whiff. A streetlamp on Embankment lit the patchy fake tan on Kelly's bare legs as she leaned over the jetty and vomited.

'We haven't even boarded,' said Daniel, as he rubbed her back.

In September, Kelly had turned up at the *Echo*'s top-floor offices with two packs of sandwiches, two cans of Dr Pepper and a selection box of miniature Scotch eggs, pork pies and cocktail sausages, to ask Daniel if he'd like to go for a picnic lunch by the river.

Daniel was shocked. He hadn't heard from Kelly in the three years since he had last seen her scrunched-up face in a nightclub in Sydney. He didn't even know where she lived now, though he knew her parents and sister were still in Elmworth – he would sometimes see her mum in the library, or her dad in the Post Office or the Red Hart.

'Erm, I guess,' Daniel shrugged, looking around the office, relieved to see Viv was out. Lee sat awkwardly at his desk while the girl with the bob and the matter-of-fact voice stood wielding snack foods and determination, and gave Daniel a supportive smile as he grabbed his coat to use it as a blanket by the river.

'I called your house,' Kelly said as they watched ducks turn in a circle. 'Matt answered.'

'Oh, did he? He didn't say!'

'He said you worked at the *Echo*. I felt so proud of you.'

Really?

'Don't you remember, I had an interview before we went travelling?'

'Yeah but I didn't think you'd actually get the job.'

'Oh.'

'But you did! You're a proper journalist now.'

'Thanks,' Daniel said.

Kelly went on to explain that it hadn't worked out with Ian. They'd had the *best* time travelling – they stayed two years in the end – but Ian wanted to move back to Brighton, do a year's teacher training, and she didn't. She wanted to put her speech and language therapy degree to good use. Get a job. Buy a car. Start earning some 'bucks' as she called them. She explained how she had moved back in with her mum, dad and sister, and was starting her own business as a private speech therapist. She spoke with a slight Australian twang, ending her sentences as if they were questions, and told Daniel that the quarter-life crisis was very real, and it had woken her up to the fact that letting go of him might have been her biggest mistake.

'Really?' he asked, in utter astonishment.

'For sure,' she said, like a character in *Neighbours*, putting down a Scotch egg and taking Daniel's hand in her crumb-strewn palm. She stroked the back of it with her free fingers.

Daniel looked at Kelly in the sunlight of the riverbank under the gaze of the church and was touched. That she had never stopped holding a flame for him. He thought of everything they had been through together, through A levels and uni – how their families knew each other, how easily they slotted into each other's lives. That maybe his crazy obsession with the spoilt Italian was just that – an obsession he needed to cure himself of. He didn't really know anything about Olivia anyway, not the way he knew Kelly: the childhood photos that adorned the walls of her parents' home; that she had watched *Dirty Dancing* more than two hundred times; that her favourite curry was a chicken korma; and that she cried happy tears every time he made her come. It had been well over a year since he had last seen Olivia, her spine facing him as she said a violent farewell to London. Maybe, at 25, he was ready. Maybe the whole Ian debacle was just a blip he could forgive her.

And Kelly looked good. Self-assured. Like she had a plan, and that was attractive. Her swishy pony was now cut into a bob and she looked like she was going to be a success.

Standing on the deck of the Silver Sturgeon, while Kelly was passed out on a banquette indoors, Daniel wiped soft snowflakes from his suit shoulders, inhaled the air, looked at the Houses of Parliament and thought about a new millennium ahead. What hopes and dreams Kelly had for them – she already had six clients – what his own hopes and dreams might be. Kelly had been talking about moving in together; she had suggested looking at flats in Elmworth, Cherry Hinton, or even Cambridge. Perhaps Daniel could get a job on the *Evening News*. 'You don't need Viv Hart and her tinpot job! You could move to the city and write about so much more.' It had only taken a couple of months for Kelly to change her tune; for Daniel to need to up his game. For the confidence he had unlocked on his travels, the confidence he had discovered while soaring over a shipwreck on a surfboard, to start to diminish.

'All right mate?' asked Gavin, Becca's South African boyfriend. 'You haven't seen my girl up on deck, have you?'

'No man, sorry,' Daniel shrugged, although he suspected Becca might be with Duncan on the starboard side.

'Your little lady is a bit worse for wear, yah? I think I saw her passed out in there!'

'She'll sleep it off,' Daniel assured Gavin.

'OK fella, catch you on the dancefloor, I'm freezing my tits off here. If you see Becca…'

'I will.'

As the boat passed Somerset House and Daniel watched couples ice skating arm in arm under a sparkling Tiffany tree, he saw a woman, with hair like Aphrodite, and wondered what Christmas in Milan might look like.

Twenty-Six

Millennium Eve 1999
Milan

'My darling, I think you could be a chef as well as an atelier!' said a man with neat white hair and bronze skin.

Olivia blushed.

He raised his glass and said '*Cin cin!*' to the gathering and a collection of glasses clinked while friends said, '*Saluti!*', 'Cheers!' and '*Kanpai!*'

It was the second New Year's Eve in a decade in which Olivia hadn't been drunk, stoned, or both, but the first in which she felt OK about it.

At the relaxed and refined table in the Messina dining room, the detritus of a meal at which friends had reflected on a year, a decade, a century and a millennium, looked satisfyingly dishevelled.

Maria's closest friend, her former boss and studio director Bernardo, was there with his partner Haruki, who had spent most of Millennium Eve teaching Olivia to roll sushi and onigiri, before an Italian/Japanese fusion feast was presented to their guests. Nancy had joined them as usual, with her sometime boyfriend Angelo and his pet Pomeranian called Maro. And Mimi, boyfriend Tate and his brother Nik, the drummer in The Horizontals who had hooked them up, called in for dinner. Mimi hadn't gone to Australia this year for a BBQ on the beach at St Kilda – she'd spent Christmas in Amalfi with Tate and distant relatives, and had stopped by Milan for a few days to show Tate her old haunts. It was a new relationship Olivia suspected wouldn't last, because Tate kept rowing with both Mimi and Nik, who spent most of the evening drumming his fingers on the table, happily, rhythmically, annoyingly, while Olivia, Haruki and Maria served up dinner.

'Well, you'll have to choose one or the other,' advised Nancy in a friendly, schoolmarm tone. 'You don't want nori sheets anywhere near those delicate fabrics you and Maria favour...'

At 11 p.m. Mimi, Tate and Nik left to go to an old schoolfriend's party, which Olivia was happy to eschew.

'Sure you want to stay here with the olds?' Mimi had asked, while Nik looked on with puppy-dog eyes. He had always had a thing for Olivia. 'It won't be old-school crazy – and I'll have your back.'

'No, I'm sure, thanks,' Olivia answered contentedly.

The morning after her lowest ebb, Olivia had woken up to pained confusion and a throbbing in her temples. The bathroom of her Lexington Street flat smelled sterile, of bleach, but she could tell from the remnants of vomit in her hair and the bloodstains on her slip dress that it had been another filthy and bleak night.

Who cleaned it up?

She remembered being fired.

She remembered bumping into Daniel from New Zealand.

She remembered Vaani's disapproving eyes in the basement bar.

She remembered being taken by the hand, by a guy she had got high with before, and following him to the bathroom. But she couldn't remember anything else. Which cocktail of drugs she had taken this time. Whether she had slept with the man whose name she didn't even know. How she had got home. She couldn't remember why a plastic bag full of precious fabrics she had bought earlier in the day from Broadwick Silks was next to her bed, filled with watery bile. She couldn't even remember what her father's kindly face looked like.

As she sat on the toilet and tried to decipher whether the blood on her dress was a result of sex, the cut on her head, or something else, she could only picture her father's face of disapproval. Of shame.

Olivia suspected Daniel from New Zealand had gotten her home, but she couldn't remember him being in the flat. As she cried in the bath and scrubbed her body, she smashed all the empty bottles secreted behind it until her hands bled and she was sitting in a bath tinged pink with blood and slashed skin. So she cried and scrubbed her body all over again.

When she hosed herself and the tub down, she got on the phone to Maria, and said she wanted to come home.

Nancy didn't believe Olivia had a drink problem – getting

drunk and kissing boys was just something students did. But her daughter hadn't told her the whole story. She hadn't told her that what had started innocently – staying at school with the boarders so she could drink in the dorms and kiss Mimi's brother Mike – evolved into *having* to drink, to take the edge off her nerves, so she could talk to the boys, or seem cool and calm. Which had in turn evolved into increasingly blacking out.

In London, if she ever popped out to Tesco Metro to get some food, she invariably came home with just vodka. Vodka that made her feel great and forget how much she missed her father.

Back in Milan she lay in bed for weeks, in some kind of malaise, too scared to meet up with schoolfriends because she didn't know how to be with them if there wasn't a drink in her hand.

'I think I have a problem, Mamma,' she told Nancy one evening, watching a film in Nancy's apartment on the leafy Via Eschilo.

'Darling, are you sure? It's not like you're *addicted*. When was the last time you had a drink?'

Olivia thought back to that hideous night in London and faces she never wanted to see again. Vaani had called her a few times since, just to check she was OK, but Vaani wasn't the sort of friend for confessionals or chitchat, so Olivia vaguely said she would see her in September.

Nancy talked to Maria at length about it, as they walked Angelo's Pomeranian around Parco Guido Vergani.

'She talks as if she's an alcoholic, but it's been weeks, months even, since her last drink. It's not like she's snaffling mouthwash... is she?!'

Maria pondered it. She had been keeping an eye on the drinks cabinet since Olivia had confessed the shame she felt, but she couldn't see any signs of it being touched.

'If she sees it as a problem, it's a problem.' Maria was softer than Nancy, more understanding.

'Yes but she's not an *addict*.'

'Is it not better go through life sober, believing you have a problem, than drink drink drink and convince yourself it's OK?' Maria asked, as she alerted Nancy to Maro's poo that needed picking up.

'But what if it *is* OK? What if she's overreacting? She does have a tendency to be melodramatic.' Nancy walked over with a little bag in hand.

'I think she hasn't told us the whole story,' said Maria sagely. 'And maybe we are not the right people to tell.'

As they continued their walk they both felt the wrench in their hearts, their lives, their evening strolls, caused by their worry about Olivia. Caused by the absence of Alessandro.

Tension rose when it became apparent to Olivia's mothers that she wasn't going back to London to finish her third and final year in the autumn.

'Why wouldn't you?' Nancy asked incredulously.

'It would be such a waste of your talent to give it all up now, *tesora*,' pleaded Maria.

But the final year started, and Olivia didn't go back. So Maria insisted that if Olivia weren't finishing her studies, she must help cutting patterns, toiles and fabrics, in the spare-room studio.

In October, Olivia tentatively tiptoed down the hall and

sat down at the spare Necchi. Soon she was cutting, sewing and stitching, sometimes driving samples and swatches across town to deliver to whichever fashion house they belonged to. Maria Messina's daughter, entrusted with Bernardo and the other studios' secrets.

As 1999 rang in, and Olivia stayed home for the first New Year's Eve in a decade, through fear of going out, she resolved to find a new way to live. She had shunned parties and socialising for six months, but missed the excitement and attention of friends. Olivia the extrovert. Olivia who loved being in school plays. Olivia who liked going dancing and talking to people.

She researched local AA meetings and went to church halls and old theatres to listen to other people's stories, surprised that not many of the addicts she met looked like alcohol would be a problem for them, either. There were other young women there. Mothers of young children. School teachers and high-functioning businesswomen, all among the haggard-looking men. Not all of them had dramatic stories either; some were like her and just wanted to stop – although some were horrific and Olivia cried when they shared their narratives.

The people she met were all so different, but one thing unified them: the desire to not drink again. Soon Olivia trusted in this common ground and got the confidence to speak, to tell her story. At first she was embarrassed, the privileged *principessa*. But some meetings were attended by people who were far more privileged than Olivia, all struggling with the same desire. Pop stars would pass through on their way to the Forum di Assago, Scala or San Siro; supermodels would drop in during Fashion Week;

rich and bored housewives would share their stories of addiction and self-loathing. And they were all treated with the same compassion as the homeless man, the woman whose children had been taken away from her, or the ex-convict. Olivia made a few friends among the regulars and the characters, and would drink coffee and eat ice cream with them, helping each other with new strategies for living with the bereavement of alcohol, of turning life on its head and reshaping recovery as something exciting.

With Mimi, Tate and Nik drinking Olivia's fair share of vodka, whisky and rum across town at a party, and Toscanini playing on Alessandro's beloved record player, Olivia drank sparkling water with her mothers and their friends and felt a contentedness she hadn't experienced since leaving London. Since her dad died. Since she could remember. Having made and eaten sushi, having enjoyed her own company and the company of others, Olivia felt there were things she was good at, and none of them involved alcohol.

Angelo's son Santino and his girlfriend Elisabetta dropped in just before midnight and Olivia felt completely comfortable opening a bottle of prosecco and pouring them each a glass.

'So what's it to be?' Haruki asked, with a kind and handsome smile. 'Sushi with me, or stitching for Bernardo?'

'I *am* trying to poach her you know,' Bernardo confessed to Maria. 'We need some vibrancy in the studio. New energy.'

'Ahhh Bernardo, but that would mean working just for you – my angel's wings are too big to tie her to one house.'

'I know!' he objected.

Just before midnight Nancy turned on the television, mainly to see firework displays from Rome and across the world, but also to see if it would work – all this talk about a Millennium Bug and Italy being the most ill-prepared country to face it had made them wonder. Olivia stepped out onto the balcony terrace for a moment of solitude; to see the fireworks erupting across the city let off by revellers who couldn't wait. As she gazed out to the cold and smoky night sky, the smell of gunpowder, sulphur and charcoal filling her lungs, she was surprised to think of Daniel. The guy who had rescued her ankle chain on her travels and had rescued her the night she went too far. She thought of his sweet and handsome face and wondered what he might be doing tonight, remembered that his New Year would come an hour later. She thought of London and didn't feel sick to her core as she usually did.

'*Funziona!*' Nancy cheered. And as quickly as Daniel had entered Olivia's mind, he evaporated again, as she turned back into the living room where everyone had congregated. As Alessandro's grandfather clock struck twelve and the needle still crackled over the turntable, Olivia knew that she was going to be all right in the year 2000.

Twenty-Seven

October 2017
Cambridgeshire, England

Vaani walked around the light bright downstairs of the Huf Haus with her hands in the pockets of her sleek Paul Smith trousers. In all the years she had known Olivia (thirty) and in all the time Olivia had lived in Guildington (thirteen), she had never ventured out of London to see her. Even though she had been rather interested in the 'Teletubby house' as she called it.

It wasn't that Vaani was lazy, or that she found meeting Olivia a chore. Business was thriving and they hadn't had a cross or misunderstood word since they went into partnership together soon after Flora was born. Vaani just didn't leave London unless she had to – and that was usually to go to Mumbai, Paris or Babington House. And although Olivia insisted she was fine, that she *could* make the journey into London and meet Vaani at their Belsize Park headquarters, Vaani felt an unusual sensation that was so strong, it made her take a train. Into suburbia. And that was guilt. Vaani couldn't make Olivia go back into London just four weeks after she had brain surgery there. Today she knew she had to dig deep and get a train beyond the M25.

'Journey OK?' asked Olivia, putting some fresh coffee in the machine that belched lovely aromas.

'Yes! Turns out I didn't have to pre-book,' Vaani answered in surprise. 'You can just *buy* a ticket and jump onboard. Choose any seat.'

Olivia frowned at Vaani in a half smile, to check if she was joking.

'But you already know this, of course...'

'Well yes, it's hardly London to Paris on the Eurostar.'

'And did you know that each terminal in London is famous for having trains that take you in a certain direction? So, say, Paddington is the one you always use if you're going to...'

'Bristol?'

'Yes! Places over... there.' Vaani took her hand out of her pocket and waved it towards the garden. 'And you go to King's Cross if you're going to Scotland,' she said, pointing to the high roof.

'And Cambridge.'

'Yes, who knew?!'

Vaani strode around the house, perusing the walls appreciatively, pleasantly surprised by how artists like Tracey Emin, Jeff Koons and Stuart Jones had made it out to the sticks.

'*I* knew. We're hardly in Scotland.' Olivia handed over the coffee in a shiny copper cup. 'Shall I show you the garden?'

Olivia often marvelled how Vaani – a businesswoman and style influencer with 100k Instagram followers, a well-dressed, savvy, competent citizen of London and Mumbai

– could live in such a bubble. She could bust investors'
balls in business meetings and hold her own sitting between
Anna Wintour and Victoria Beckham in the front row, yet
she couldn't take a train to Cambridge without a fuss. It
was certainly part of her charm.

Olivia opened the glass doors and felt the October chill
on the shaved part of her head that no one could see.

'This is nice, isn't it?!' Vaani said with surprise. Olivia
wasn't sure what Vaani had expected, but was glad she was
impressed, as they walked among autumn's gold and red
jewels, and looked back at the house.

'Yeah, we got lucky with this.'

'Really lucky.'

'So how *is* life in the big wide world?' Olivia asked keenly.
'How's the studio? Has Meg settled in yet? You should have
let me come in, you know.'

Just before the summer Vaani and Olivia had hired a
new assistant who cried on her first day when she mistook
Vaani's dismissive tone for a firing.

'Well, she's finally stopped whimpering around me.
Thank god.' Vaani rolled her enormous eyes. 'Sachin and
Meenu have gone back – I think it was definitely worth
them coming over, seeing the UK side of things. And it's
just business as usual. You got the sales breakdowns for S/S
2017, didn't you?'

'Yeah,' Olivia said unsurely. She couldn't shake the feeling
she was out of the loop. She'd missed the big visit from the
managers of their Indian workshop; she'd missed meetings
with investors, influencers and press interviews. She'd felt
bad for not having been able to do Meg's induction; she
knew she was a more welcoming face to the brand than

Vaani. She'd ducked out of daily life at Olivia Messina London – her own brand – for three months now, and felt as if she were neglecting a child.

'Well, come in before the chemo starts, yes?'

'It's radiotherapy.'

'I never know the difference. Which is the one where you lose your hair?'

'Well, that tends to be chemo...'

'Oh thank *god*.'

'But there might be a localised patch of baldness with the type of radiotherapy I'm having.'

'Shit, sorry.'

Vaani winced, then they both laughed. She was the only person who could get away with saying any such thing to Olivia.

'Well I'm definitely coming into London before the radiotherapy starts, I have such FOMO.'

'Oh, you haven't missed much.'

'I missed all of Fashion Week. We pulled the show!'

Vaani hugged her coffee cup to warm up.

'You know what, I don't think it will have made too much difference in the scheme of things. Makes us more of a big deal come Feb. People know why we didn't show – it's not like you couldn't be bothered. And buyers are still buying. The PR team did an *amazing* job.' Vaani took a sip and gestured to the studio at the side of the long leafy garden.

'Want to see what I'm working on?' Olivia asked. 'It's not much, just some sketches, but Ibiza got me inspired... well, until everything fell apart.'

'Good girl. I'd love to,' nodded Vaani, as Olivia unlocked the studio door with the big key in her cardigan pocket.

Twenty-Eight

May 2001
Milan

Hi Olivia,

I hope you're well. I met you at the bottom of the world the day before your twenty-first birthday, then again in London.

So I followed your advice and changed my job, I got out of my rut and moved to London. I'll be in Milan next week to cover a football match for *The Guardian*, I'm a sports writer here. It would be great to catch up for a coffee... if you're free?

Daniel

X

'Olivia Messina, you weren't a figment of my imagination!' Daniel said, as he took his hands out of his jeans pockets and opened his arms into a wide and welcoming embrace.

Olivia, surprised by how handsome he was, how he looked like a man, walked towards him, along a stone and sand path in Parco Sempione, her colour-stained hands outstretched. The neat green park set behind a fortress castle, touched by both Da Vinci and Napoleon, was Olivia's favourite outdoor space in Milan; her mind felt uncluttered and her breathing was always calm as she navigated the paths and ornamental ponds between the green lawns of Milan's lungs. In spring it smelled of orange blossom, in winter roast chestnuts. Jutting out of its western edge was *La Triennale*, a design museum for this perennially stylish city, where Olivia had spent hours finding inspiration in peaceful isolation. Sempione always provided a serene sort of assault on the senses, which is why she suggested it as a rendezvous to Daniel. Somewhere *tranquillo*.

'No!' she laughed. 'I'm very real.'

She wrapped her arms around his waist and hugged him, pulling into his chest, smelling his scent of cedar, mandarin and the sea through the shirt under his open jacket. As he rubbed her back in their embrace, her spine felt smooth under her shirt dress, her body softer. She wore a slouchy leather bag across her shoulders and silver trainers that shone in the evening sun.

She's here.

Olivia's accent sounded more like an Italian person speaking English again, her skin was olive and tanned. She pulled back so she could examine Daniel's face, planted a palm on each cheek, and kissed him vigorously on one side and then the other. Daniel blushed. She was friendlier than Daniel expected, there was a warmth in her he hadn't seen in London.

'Why? Did you think you had imagined me?' Olivia questioned. 'That perhaps I was the dark side of your alter ego?'

'Like *Fight Club*,' they both chimed, and then laughed.

Daniel tried to clarify himself.

'Well, we met summer 1996, then summer 1998. So according to our rhythm, we really should have met up in the year 2000. When we didn't, I wondered if I had, in fact, invented this amazing Italian character.'

Olivia raised her palms out to her sides and gave a philosophical shrug.

'Well, summer '98 was not a good one for me, I was a pig's misery.'

'Huh?'

'You know, when things can't get worse?'

She said it with such peace in her eyes, the golden hour of the Lombardi sunshine making them glimmer, that Daniel knew things must be *better*.

'Rock bottom?' he asked with a wry smile.

'That's right! Pig's misery *is* rock bottom!'

I get it.

'Then in '99, well I was kind of... trying to get my shit together. *Recuperando*, if you know what I mean.'

Daniel knew.

'And last summer?'

'Last summer, I went to see my grandparents in *Sicilia*.'

Olivia laughed at the simplicity of it and Daniel wanted

to kiss the corner of her mouth. The little mole that looked almost edible.

Daniel thought back to his summer of 2000. He had just started as a junior on the sports desk at *The Guardian*, and even though he was beginning at the bottom again; even though he wasn't invited to go to Belgium or the Netherlands to cover Euro 2000, he loved his new job, his new life renting a room in a flatshare with Jim Beck and Wesley De Boer, and the confidence it had given him to finally end things with Kelly. After a nine-month slog, transitioning from one millennium to another, Daniel soon realised that not much had changed about Kelly, and her demands and double standards were getting him down. When he remembered how much better he was without her, that he would rather be the Daniel he was when he was travelling, even if it meant he was on his own, he got the courage to end it. To move on as he moved out of Elmworth.

And here he was, in a park tinged all colours of orange and pink, with a sweet honeysuckle scent rolling on the early evening breeze, glad to be the man he was now. Relieved that Olivia remembered and cared who he was. Perhaps he hadn't been as insignificant to her as he feared.

He smiled and Olivia kept looking at his face, as if it had the answer to a question knitted in her eyebrows. Daniel definitely looked older. Twenty-seven suited him. He looked more mature and manly, with a light smattering of a beard now. Not one from the inertia of travelling. One that suited his face. His broad shoulders supported a heavy-looking backpack, and his strong legs anchored him to the soil and shingle of Sempione.

'Your hands!' Daniel said, breaking Olivia's gaze, scared he didn't have the answers. He knew he was always more needy, more reticent in their brief dalliances, but he took a deep breath, looked at her long hands, coloured with paint and jewellery, and remembered he was here on his terms. A grown-up. Nothing to feel needy about or to be ashamed of. He stroked the top of one of her hands as he looked at it and they both felt a charge run down their spines.

'*Si*, they get kind of... messy!' Olivia laughed, *that laugh*, as she looked down at her fingers, rings interwoven with yellow and blue dyes, from a day assisting the print and embellishment team at the Etro studio on Via Spartaco. Bernardo had managed to convince Olivia, in the spring of 2000, to liven up the studio he had managed for a decade, and she had loved it from day one.

Surrounded by moire, taffeta and heritage print – sequins, ribbons and handwriting textiles – with the hum of the Necchis in the sewing room, Olivia felt the most content she could remember since her father had died. And she was even being paid to do a job she loved. Daniel could see that joy in her placid face.

'I'm working for a fashion house. Embellishment, embroidery, threadwork – lots of colour assisting,' she said, holding up her palms as if to say, *you got me*.

But she did have him. She just didn't know it yet.

'Shall we walk?' Olivia said, as she dropped her sunglasses down from the perch on her head to the bridge of her nose and her hair tumbled. She gestured to a large pond beyond the bushes and pathways ahead of her.

'That would be lovely,' Daniel said, putting his hands back in his pockets. The park was filling up with people at the end of a busy day's work. German and Spanish tourists exploring the city before the big game. Children's laughter echoed as they played on a roundabout. Two binmen picked litter while each licking a gelato.

'I was surprised to get your message. I hoped you wouldn't remember me!'

'Oh, really?' Daniel felt disappointed by her bluntness, but realised her smiling face belied her words.

'Or rather I hoped you wouldn't remember how you last saw me. I don't think it was good.'

'You look better now.'

Daniel worried about being offensive, but as he stole a look from under his brown-bear hair, he realised Olivia hadn't taken it the wrong way.

'I was coming here for work, and then I remembered you.'

Daniel didn't say it was the other way around. That he hadn't *not* thought about Olivia for a day since the day before her twenty-first birthday, and he had done everything he could to engineer a trip to Milan for work. To cover Bayern Munich v Valencia in the final of the Champions League, taking place at the San Siro the next night. He hadn't had any luck, his hints gone unnoticed, until football's fortunes favoured Daniel, at the expense of his boss.

His sports editor, a Yorkshireman called Lloyd, who always kept the best sporting gigs for himself (he'd send Daniel to Queens but would always take Wimbledon), was a Leeds United fan, and so devastated when his team lost in the semi-finals of the Champions League, he couldn't face the heartache of going to a party his beloved Peacocks should have been at.

'You go, lad,' he'd said, putting the press pass on Daniel's desk, after returning from the drubbing in Valencia. 'I can't watch, I'll only be blubberin'.'

Daniel thanked his boss and clung onto the golden ticket. He finally had a reason to go to Milan. To seek out Olivia.

From his computer on the sports desk he looked on AOL, Google and Friends Reunited, searching for an Olivia Messina in Milan, and was shocked to find a Hotmail address that he duly etched into his brain and hoped it was the right Olivia Messina. He lingered on it for three weeks before writing his simple, hopeful message, asking her if she'd like to meet for a coffee.

He sent it from his work email address, to show he had done something right. He had got out of the clutches of a boss who had done everything she could to manipulate, belittle and strip her employees of their confidence. He had finally moved to the sports desk of a national newspaper, where he showed his determination, diligence and passion – and wasn't ever distracted en route to a shift. And he had broken down a broken Leeds United fan enough for him to send Daniel to Milan instead.

Thank you, Valencia.

Olivia had replied with a simple:

Perfect! I see you in front of the castle, Sempione Park.

They sorted the time and date, and didn't say anything else. And here they were, walking towards terrapins basking in the mud on a sunny spring evening.

'I can see you love your job now. I can tell it from your face.'

'You can?'

'Yes.'

'Funny, I was just thinking the same about you.'

'Well, isn't that wonderful?' said Olivia, with a wonderful smile.

'It certainly is. And I have you to thank for that.'

'Me?'

'Yes, you told me to get my shit together. To leave the *puttana* I worked for.'

Olivia choked on an intake of breath.

'I said that?!'

'Yes. I thought *porca puttana* was a pizza, but turns out it was a really nasty swearword.'

'Shit.'

Olivia curled her lip and looked surprised by herself.

'Yeah, you inspired me to look for another job, new opportunities. It took a while, but I got there.'

'Wow. I'm glad you did listen to me. But you shouldn't have.'

'Oh. Why?'

'I didn't know what the fuck I was talking about.'

'You didn't?'

'No! I was drunk as a monkey or stoned off my tits most of my time in London. I needed to get *my* shit together.'

'Oh.'

'To be honest I don't really remember you much from that night in London, mainly from New Zealand.'

'Oh.'

Daniel thought back to their hug on the steps of the Italianate train station in downtown Dunedin – their kiss in the deserted ticket hall. At least she remembered that.

'I'm sorry.'

'No, that's OK...'

'No, I'm sorry that I don't remember much from London. Apart from the fact I was miserable.'

'That's a shame.'

'And Flamin' Beef Monster Munch. I remember that, I lived on that shit. And vodka.'

'Well, I'm even more sorry then. Pickled Onion is clearly the best flavour Monster Munch,' Daniel said, nudging a flirty arm into hers.

'Don't be sorry. I'm happy now. You're happy now. Gelato?'

The sun was kissing the tops of the elm trees, lighting up the path in hues of gold and pink, as they strolled through the park towards an ice cream seller and her wagon, striding side by side but not touching. At the wagon Olivia chose a rose-flavoured ice cream, delicately coloured and less pink than the sky, while Daniel chose something called *stracciatella* he had never heard of before, but the way Olivia said it made it sound all the more appealing.

Olivia went to open her purse but Daniel quickly handed the elderly woman a five-Euro note.

'*Grazie.*'

'*Prego.*'

They licked their ice creams and started walking again.

'Hmmm, soooo good. What is this exactly?' He gestured his cone to Olivia.

'Like little stripes of chocolate in vanilla.'

'Ahh, strands,' Daniel said, feeling the texture of it on his tongue. 'How's yours?'

'Good, you want some?' Olivia proffered and suddenly Daniel felt self-conscious.

'I'm OK, thanks.'

He wasn't into floral flavours anyway.

'You want some of mine?' he asked.

'Of course!'

Olivia leaned to take a hearty slurp, as a light wind whipped up and some strands of her hair blew across the strands in his ice cream.

'Oh, I'm sorry!' she laughed, ice cream now dragging across her face as she removed it, stopping to savour the taste of *stracciatella*.

He was so close to her again, he felt a beat pummelling in his chest. He wanted to wipe the threadlike ice cream strands off her face and kiss her clean. But he pulled back.

'It's good,' she declared. 'But not as good as mine.' Olivia winked, and stuck her pink tongue out. Daniel wished he'd tried some, that he hadn't been so self-conscious. So English.

They carried on walking through the park, past high horse chestnut trees and low fragrant verbena bushes that smelled of orange blossom, Olivia leading the way around the paths and little woodland bridges.

'So those fashion types... they got you down, hey?'

'Yes, quite a lot. But it wasn't their fault. It wasn't even *my* fault. It just wasn't the right place for me. Or maybe it wasn't the right time. I didn't fit in.'

'I guess it's a hard place *to* fit in.'

Olivia didn't know if he meant fashion college or London, but actually he meant both. 'Yeah, well Paul McCartney wasn't my dad. I didn't want him to be my dad. I just wanted my father back. Full stop. So I was pretty sad.'

'Oh, right.' Daniel didn't know why Olivia was talking about Paul McCartney.

As they walked, Daniel noticed the ankle glimmering gold, pink, green and yellow above her silver trainer. 'So how are you getting on... without your dad?'

Daniel's expression was thoughtful and caring. Olivia gave him a sideways glance.

'Well, it's been five years. Five years since his heart just stopped. I can't believe it. It feels like yesterday but it's five years.' She said this as if it was almost funny. 'Sometimes it seems like a lifetime ago I jumped on a plane and went travelling, to escape the pain in my heart, but it didn't really work. I had to be here. In *Milano*. Facing it.'

Daniel looked across at Olivia as he finished his ice cream.

'My mammas have been amazing – Mamma Due especially. It was hard for them both, but she felt the absence the most. Papa no longer in the apartment. The smell of his cigars, his neroli. His laugh and his presence. Mamma Una too, but she was most worried about me. She didn't have the emptiness of the space a great man filled.'

'Where does she live?'

'In *Milano* too – but another apartment across town. She has lots of friends and "gentlemen callers", she calls them. But they were both heartbroken, worried for me, both affected by his loss. The silence of his absence. I made the silence worse, by leaving.'

'You did what you needed to do.'

'Well – I was a bit of a *puttana* myself. I left them when

they needed me. But we've reconnected. It's been good to slow down. Be back here. To work. Although to many *Milano* is crazy.'

Daniel looked at the sedate park surrounding them, glancing back at the former castle and ice cream vendor they'd left behind, the balloon seller and artists in front. The fig trees and bushes. Milan looked pretty civilised and serene to him.

'It's not crazy compared to London.'

'Well, exactly. My father's parents – and Mamma Due's – are from *Sicilia*. They think this place is crazy. Imagine if they ever went to London!' Olivia threw back her head and laughed, picturing her Nonna Renata crossing Oxford Circus at 6 p.m. on a Thursday. Arms brushing and squashed in the throng bustling for the underground. A scene she knew would never happen. They had only ever left Sicily once, and that was for their son's funeral.

Daniel looked around the park.

'I love it.'

His eyes rested on Olivia. He wanted to tell her he loved her, but he knew that was ridiculous.

'It really is beautiful here. And not what I expected.'

'You've never been to *Milano*?'

'Never. It's my first time.'

Olivia gasped.

'How can that be?'

'Well...'

'What do you think of it?'

'I thought it would be all supermodels in gaudy clothes and smoking factories and industry, but this park feels like...'

He was thinking *home*, that he could imagine going about his business here. *Their* business. But he didn't want to use that word and he couldn't think of another. Fortunately Olivia interrupted, as was her way.

'In which case, I'll give you a tour.'

'Really? Don't you have things to do?'

'That's my thing to do! To pop my *Milano* virgin's cherry.' Daniel blushed.

'How long have we got?' she asked, wiping the last of the ice cream cone from the corner of her mouth.

Daniel looked at his watch. He'd covered all the pre-match press conferences he needed to at the San Siro, but he did need to write his copy up for 11 p.m. and send it to his editor. 'I have a bit of work to do tonight, but I reckon I have a couple of hours spare...'

'Then let's walk, before sunset, and you can come back to ours for dinner. Work from our apartment if you need to.'

'You live with Mamma Due still?' Daniel didn't want that to sound judgemental, not when he'd only moved out of his parent's house and in with Jim and Wesley in Tooting Bec last year.

'Of course!'

Daniel felt silly, for desperately wanting to impress her, to show her that he had moved to London, when all the while the woman he was trying to impress was proud to be living at home. And he so wanted to see her home. Where she lived. To not have a miserable parting of ways again.

Daniel didn't know what to do. He felt the urgency of his deadline, how he couldn't let Lloyd down with this first amazing trip. But he didn't want to leave Olivia's side either.

Not ever again.

Don't blow it.

'Well, that sounds great, thank you,' Daniel said, from under his hair. 'As long as you're sure your mum or mums won't mind.'

Olivia had already moved on and started her tour.

'*Guarda!*' she said, pointing to a man sharpening a pencil with a thin razor blade. 'First thing to do in Parco Sempione is to get a portrait.'

'A what?'

'This guy, he's been doing it for years...'

Olivia looped her arm through Daniel's and led him to an artist, sitting on a tripod stool in a shady corner. He was a weathered man with tight white curls popping out from under a flat cap and bags under his eyes that carried a lifetime of stories. 'He's super funny.'

'Funny?'

Daniel wasn't sure the artist would want to be called funny.

Olivia spoke to him in Italian and he stood up slowly to push two chairs together. A board behind him displayed samples of his work, celebrities in caricature form. Zinedine Zidane. Princess Diana. Elton John. Silvio Berlusconi. One of Kate Winslet and Leonardo di Caprio at the bow of the Titanic. All with the same grotesque features.

Daniel wasn't sure about this. His parents had a caricature of him and Matt on the wall of their stairs at home, but they were 8 and 6 at the time, which seemed OK. He looked across at Olivia and realised she made everything feel OK, so he sat down in the chair next to her and the artist started to draw. Daniel would never normally get a portrait of himself, but then Olivia did make him do things he'd never normally do.

As they sat and talked, Daniel wondered if the artist minded them chatting – shouldn't their mouths not move – while he held his A3 pad close to his chest and sketched conscientiously. He didn't seem to.

'So where are you living now?' Olivia asked, as she tried to sit still.

Daniel told her how he'd moved in with Jim. 'Remember my friend from the pub you worked in? The one who realised you were the Olivia I had met travelling...' Daniel's cheeks turned pink. 'The one who came with us to see The Horizontals at the 100 Club?'

Olivia didn't remember Jim, although she did remember the misery of working in that pub.

Daniel explained where Tooting Bec was, and that Jim and Wesley were going great guns, even though she didn't know them. Jim was now deputy editor of a women's glossy. Wesley had given up magazines to retrain as a teacher. He told Olivia how glad he was to get away from Elmworth, from the claustrophobia of Saturday night TV; how his brother was marrying his monosyllabic misery of a girlfriend this summer, who still spent most of their evenings on the sofa in the family home, despite owning a flat around the corner. He didn't mention the Kelly blip. And he didn't know Olivia had never had a significant boyfriend, although he assumed there must have been several.

Olivia told Daniel that Mimi had bought a flat in Brixton, but she didn't know if that was near Tooting Bec or not, but it didn't matter anyway as she spent most of her life on the road.

When the artist finished, he silently nodded and turned the pad around, his sombre face hard to read, and Olivia looked at Daniel, awaiting his reaction with excitement.

'Ummm...'

Daniel was taken aback.

'Well...'

The artist hadn't drawn Olivia and Daniel. Not even a grotesque caricatured version of them. He had drawn a woman and a man, neither of which were Olivia nor Daniel. Olivia smiled, studying Daniel's face and he felt aware of her eyes on him as well as the artist's, unsure as to whether it was a joke.

'Wow. Just wow.' He applauded heartily. 'Very good.'

'*Bravo*,' Olivia said, taking ten Euros out of her purse and handing it to the artist. He gave a modest nod and rolled up the picture.

'Let me get that,' Daniel said, reaching for his backpack and his wallet.

'No, *really*,' Olivia replied, giving him a knowing look. 'My treat.'

Daniel tried to suppress his laugh so as not to offend the artist.

'Just wow...' he repeated.

'*Grazie mille gentile signore*,' Olivia said, as she took the rolled-up tube and put it under her arm. Daniel stifled a cough as they walked off and out of earshot. They didn't get very far, he was laughing and coughing so much he couldn't walk.

'But...'

'Yes!'

'Is that...?'

His face crumpled and eyes started to water.

Olivia laughed too.

'Is that who I think it is?'

'*Siiiiii.*'

'Was that not...?'

'*Si!* Did you notice how he never once looked up?'

Daniel held his stomach while he laughed, looking back in the hope the artist couldn't hear them beyond the bushes.

'I wondered why he didn't mind us talking!'

'He sees a woman with red hair, he draws Nicole Kidman.'

'But you look nothing like Nicole Kidman!'

'He sees a man with dark hair and light skin, he draws Tom Cruise.'

'But—'

'I *know*!' laughed Olivia. 'He did Mimi as Courteney Cox.'

'What?! Does he just have stock famous people he draws?'

'I'm pretty sure that's *exactly* what he does. Mind you, my dad *did* look a bit like Silvio Berlusconi.'

'No!' said Daniel, stopping to see that she was actually being serious behind the tears of their laughter.

They stopped in the middle of a pathway, around a corner and a bush from *Signore* Caricature; Daniel bent over double with his palms on his thighs, Olivia hugging her body as she shook, as locals and tourists walked past them and smiled at the scene. Daniel and Olivia's laughter was as infectious to strangers as it was to each other.

'Tom Cruise!' he howled through the tears. 'My nose!'

Neither of them had laughed like that in years, as they held their tummies full of ice cream, the ice truly broken.

Olivia sighed and caught her breath while Daniel ruffled his hair.

'Too funny,' she said, wiping a tear as the sun disappeared. 'Come on, let's go home and eat.'

As dusk evolved into night, and the scents of spring's fragrant bushes were overpowered by the heady smell of mopeds and cigars, the lights of the city's traffic illuminated the wide leafy boulevards along which Olivia led Daniel, on pavements, across tramlines and past *gelaterias*, *pasticcerias* and 7-Elevens. With her arm looped through his, they wound, her guiding him past now-empty playparks and closed newspaper stands, through the Buonarotti district of Milan and its villas and imposing apartments. Buildings that were grey and grand, with high ceilings and pretty balconies. The well-heeled women they passed walking their toy dogs gave way to young people heading out for the evening, and Daniel could tell that a new life cycle was emerging during rush hour in Milan.

'Home,' Olivia announced, as she stopped at an ornate, dark green gate between two pillars. On top of each pillar was a statue of an urn full of abundant fruit, all turned to stone, although it was hard for Daniel to see the grapes, pears and pomegranates in the shard of light emitted from the elegant, grey lamppost further up the street. Behind the gate he could see a tall, cream villa nestled among a small, manicured garden. Shutters framed the lofty long windows on every floor, in the same dark green shade as the gate and its railings.

'Is this your *home*?'

'Partly. My dad bought the building, before I was born. He hoped to do it up and fill it with children.' Olivia put her key in the little round hole on the gate and it squeaked open. 'He decided it would be more economical to split it into apartments. Mamma Due and I live in the one at the top.'

'Wow, it's incredible.'

A garage with a wooden door sat recessed at the back and Olivia led Daniel past it along a terracotta paved path between small neat green lawns from which fig, laurel and lemon trees burst. Cicadas brought the evening song to the flowering dogwood. Daniel felt like he was walking into paradise and wondered what the garden might look like in the sunshine. He hoped to see it so.

Through another door, this one made of glass and ornate metal, Olivia led Daniel into a marble hallway, eschewing the narrow old-fashioned lift with a sliding bronze grill, for the large staircase ahead of them. As Daniel followed her up, past apartments on the ground, first, second and third floors, he followed Olivia's silver trainers; watched the sway of her hips, the pull of her calves, and marvelled at the beauty and strength of her. How *she* wanted to spend the evening with *him*. To invite him into her home, to meet her mamma.

'*Mamma! Abbiamo un ospite!*' Olivia shouted, as she unlocked the tall, thin door at the top of the stairs. She turned back excitedly to Daniel, beckoning him in with an encouraging nod. She looked proud to have brought a friend back for dinner.

Maria came out of the kitchen, a pinny hugging the waist of her black tight dress.

'Ah, *tesora! Buon tempismo!* Oh—'

Maria stopped and inspected the man in the hallway with an oven-mitt-clad hand on each hip, her waist small and her eyes big. 'Who are you?' She was so matter-of-fact, Daniel wondered if she were Olivia's birth mother, but she looked too Italian. Neither answered, so Maria started rambling in a flustered bustle, pushing a wild black curl off her forehead. 'The ossobuco nearly ready,' she said in English. 'Your mother here too.'

'We have enough for one more?' Olivia asked in English.

It was a silly question, Maria always had enough food for one more, so she shot Olivia a look to say *of course* and Daniel followed them both into the kitchen.

The modern sleek lines of the state-of-the-art kitchen juxtaposed with the primrose-yellow and pale blue tiles of the original floor. At a small table against the wall sat a woman with smooth red hair in a pageboy haircut, zesting a lemon.

'Hi darling,' she said in a soft barely Scottish roll.

Nancy paused from her task in hand and looked up with expectant eyes. Maria returned to the hob to stir her saffron risotto.

Olivia kissed her mother on both cheeks and slung her bag and keys down. 'I didn't know you were coming for dinner.'

'I didn't know you were,' Nancy said, with a raised eyebrow. Half schoolmarm, half playful.

'Oh Mammas this is Daniel – he's from England.'

Dan-i-el.

'Daniel, this is Nancy, Mamma Una, and Maria, Mamma Due – who you met.'

'Hi.' Daniel gave a bashful wave from the doorway.

Nancy stood up, charmed and softened by the man at Olivia's shoulder, even though she didn't like the English much. She put a hand on each of his arms, as if to hold him in place while she stood on tiptoes and kissed each cheek.

'Where are you from?' she asked. Nancy did like to talk to Brits in Milan, just to show off how she had ended up living there, how she could speak the language and knew the city inside out.

'Near Cambridge.' Daniel smiled politely, before putting a fist to his chest to clear his throat. 'But I live and work in London.'

'Delightful,' Nancy said with a stringent smile.

'Come!' said Mamma Due, beckoning Daniel to the hob. 'Stir this, we need a strong hand to keep this risotto going.'

'Mamma!' Olivia protested. 'Papa didn't *ever* stir the risotto! We're tough enough.' Although she knew Maria was just trying to take the edge off Daniel's nerves.

'Let me get that.'

Olivia took Daniel's backpack off his back, slid his jacket down his arms, and put them on a kitchen stool. He rolled up his sleeves and looked for soap at the sink.

'Here,' Maria pushed it along the worktop and appraised him as she watched him wash.

'Oh my god, it smells *stunning*, Mrs Messina!' sighed Daniel, returning to the hob and inhaling warm aromas of saffron, shallots and marsala that made his stomach rumble. Maria studied him as if he were trying out for a job in the kitchen.

'You're hungry,' was her conclusion.

'Erm, well…' Daniel was hardly skin and bones. 'This is

enough to make anyone hungry.' Truth was he was starving. All day he'd been too nervous about meeting Olivia to eat.

'You'll stay for dinner.' It was a given, but Maria was just making sure he knew he had passed his test.

'Thank you, I'd love to.'

There was an air of excitement as Daniel stirred sweet saffron stamens into carnaroli rice, grateful to have something to focus on when he knew he was under scrutiny. Maria and Nancy were so pleasantly surprised to have company, they made a conscious effort to *not* look at each other. Olivia hadn't socialised much since she'd been back in Milan. She would meet the odd friend from a meeting, or have coffee after work with some of the other atelier staff. She hadn't even mentioned she was seeing a friend this evening; they'd assumed she'd gone to the mall. It was pure luck Maria had felt like cooking something welcoming and bountiful.

Nancy picked up the zester again and continued to scrape it against a plump lemon, as Olivia pressed two glasses against the fridge door to get some icy water.

'So, how do you two...' Nancy asked, trying to sound blasé. She shook the peelings into a small bowl for Maria. Nancy wasn't a cook, but she was a doer, and liked to help with the little jobs while the two of them were gossiping in the kitchen.

'From London,' Daniel said, relaxing his shoulders as he stirred and inhaled. Each inward breath sent anticipation to his stomach, making him feel more and more at ease among the women in the kitchen.

'From travelling.' Olivia countered, wanting to give Daniel a better chance. 'New Zealand, right?' she said, looking at Daniel, knowing perfectly well that it was.

'And Australia...' they both chimed, then laughed nervously.

Nancy and Maria looked from Olivia to Daniel and back again, entranced by the unusual turn the normal spring day had taken and the bashful, handsome man standing at the hob. Olivia was unusually lost for words and wanted to break the tension.

'Come on, I'll show you around,' she said, pulling Daniel by the arm like an excited puppy.

'Taste it!' Maria insisted, handing Daniel a pink enamel teaspoon.

Daniel looked at Maria and smiled as he scraped a teaspoon of jewelled risotto up the inside of the thick pan.

He felt very self-conscious and scrutinised, but weirdly comfortable. This was the hearth, the home he had always hankered for. He tasted the risotto and looked at Maria.

'Delicious.'

Maria almost swooned.

'You can go now,' she said, clutching a tea towel to her heart before shaking her hands to shoo them away.

Olivia picked up Daniel's backpack and jacket and her soft leather bag and slung them on a chaise longue in the hallway.

'First, I'd better wash my hands again.'

After she had tried (and failed) to get the last of the fabric dye off her fingers, Olivia returned to the living room, where Daniel was looking out of the long tall door that led to the balcony terrace.

'Such a cool view. Such a cool city.'

'Isn't it?' Olivia said proudly. 'I'll save that for last. Come on…'

First Olivia showed Daniel the stitching room – a room that would once have been another bedroom, but ever since Alessandro and Maria Messina bought the rundown relic in the early 1970s and did it up, and the children they hoped for never came, it was Maria's room, for pattern-cutting, toile-making, fabric-chalking and stitching. It was the room Olivia had sought comfort in after the summer of 1998 and the room where she felt most comfortable. A large workbench occupied the middle with two sewing machines on top of it and another at a low wood-and-wrought-iron sewing table by the window. Faceless mannequins stood in different states of undress, and a large plastic mat was laid out in one corner, held down by what looked like pots of paint.

'Wow, is this where your mum works?'

'Yes,' Olivia said as she raised her chest and drew the curtains closed. 'Less so now she's retiring, her eyes aren't as precise as they used to be. More and more of those are mine.'

Daniel looked at the half-formed dresses on half-formed dummies. Some wore frothy layers, some had unfinished sequin embellishment. All were fashioned out of black tulle and netting. He didn't know what to call it but they looked like high-drama shapes harking back to another era, forming an army around them. Perhaps they were unravelling, but it very much looked like progression.

'They're amazing,' he gasped self-consciously.

Daniel didn't feel qualified to comment on fashion, he

didn't know much about it – but he knew that what Olivia was creating was spectacular, as he dragged his fingertips through a sea of black sequins that were scattered across the workbench.

'This is very much my own stuff – not what I do in town. I'm doing more dye-work there.' She held up her stained hands. 'It's quite traditional where I work. But these are just tiny ideas – my ideas – starting to form.'

'They're big ideas,' Daniel said, looking at the magnificence of the mannequins. 'You're very clever.'

Olivia smoothed her hair behind her ear as her long lashes swept onto her cheeks.

'My mamma is very clever. She created some works of art in here.'

Daniel stood back and took in the room where Maria was entrusted to keep the early secrets of Versace and Etro; the evolutions of Missoni and Prada. It was the room in which she stitched early prototypes of Dolce & Gabbana's Sicilian widow dress in the mid-1980s, as well as projects for herself: cinched-in skirts that augmented her large bosom, party dresses for Olivia, trousers and shirts for Nancy. 'She's the best,' Olivia whispered in delight, before closing the door. Daniel was struck by how an only child could seem like part of such a big extended fashion family. 'But my clothes seem to have somewhat taken over. Oops.'

Daniel looked at her in the darkness of the lofty hallway, their noses almost touching, his heart pounding.

'Come on, I'll show you the rest.'

They walked along the tiled floor where bedrooms with dark wood furniture – mahogany bureaus and marquetry chests of drawers – juxtaposed with the clean lines of sleek beds, modern artwork and high, light walls. Olivia showed Daniel her bedroom, with dresses hanging from every possible space on the high picture rails, like ghostly patrons at the opera. They peeped into Maria's room and saw the double bed she still only slept on one side of. The guest room had a single bed under the window, where Nancy sometimes stayed if she'd drunk too much to drive or cycle home, and next to it a plush bathroom and the dining room that was saved for special occasions.

Back in the living room with bookshelf-covered walls, an old record player set deep in its wood console and a large flat-screen TV, Olivia took Daniel's hand.

'Here...'

With her free hand, Olivia cranked open the handle on the balcony door and stepped out onto the noise of Via Tiziano below. 'Mind the plant pot,' she cautioned, as she led Daniel out onto the wrap of the terrace.

'Shit!' Daniel gasped, appreciatively.

At one end of the balcony they could see into the apartment's slickly lit kitchen. Nancy was getting plates out of a cupboard while Maria was checking on the veal shanks in the oven, pushing her hair back with a mitt. Olivia and Daniel peeped in, looked at each other and laughed like children playing spies, each silently wondering what the mammas were saying.

At the other end of the long thin balcony and the edge of the Messina villa was a side street dividing their building from the next set of buildings. They looked down at a moped waiting to turn right, and Olivia squeezed Daniel's hand before letting go and sweeping her arm towards the lights of the city.

He hoped his palms weren't too clammy.

'I give you, *Milano*!'

'Incredible! You grew up with this view?'

'The San Siro is... that way,' she said, pointing westward. Daniel pictured himself walking around the press room, tunnel and stands earlier in the day, gathering quotes, team news and a feel for tomorrow night. It had filled him with a fizz of excitement, the anticipation of the game. The anticipation of meeting Olivia Messina in Sempione Park later that afternoon, with little knowledge that tonight his vantage point would be even more wonderous.

'*Piazza del Duomo* is... that way. But you can't see it.' They looked inwards, into the apartment, where Nancy was now setting the table at the far end of the living room, much to Olivia's relief. The dining room would be too staid, too terrifying, for their guest tonight. As they watched her, thin scarf elegantly tied around her neck, sweater over a shirt and tailored trousers, Olivia and Daniel gave the conspiratorial giggle of children knowing the adult couldn't see them, and wanted to kiss each other, although neither said it.

'*Allora*, dinner is ready!' hollered Maria, towards the hallway, as she carried a pot into the living room. Daniel and Olivia stepped back into the apartment and its aromas of meltingly soft stew, mostly wafting above the black cloud of Maria's buoyant hair. 'Ah! You're there!'

'Anything I can do?' asked Daniel, clearing his throat.

'Yes, you get the risotto, it's settling on the hob.'

'I'll get it,' Olivia chipped, almost skipping into the kitchen.

'Wine, Daniel?' asked Nancy, taking glasses out of an elaborate armoire made of marquetry wood and glass.

'Yes please, just the one thanks.' He had stories to final read and file.

Nancy took a chilled bottle of white out of its freezer sleeve and opened it with great pride and flair, while Maria and Olivia went back and forth to the kitchen for the risotto, vegetables, and the focaccia for soaking up the juices.

'You came on the perfect night,' Nancy said discerningly – playing her outsider cards to her favour so Daniel would have an ally, while also enjoying her authority as an ex-pat. 'This is *Milanese* cooking typified!'

'Oh really?' Daniel enthused, pulling his seat out and rubbing his hands on the thighs of his jeans.

'Yes, although we usually eat this with polenta,' Maria clarified.

Olivia poured iced water from a jug.

'Maria, you must have had a sixth sense we would have company,' Nancy joked. 'She's a good witch that one,' she added with a wink.

Throughout dinner, the mammas fussed over Daniel, ensuring he had enough stew, risotto, asparagus and wine, while Olivia sat opposite him, drinking Orangina from her wine glass, grateful to see him, and to her mothers for asking all the questions she loved hearing the answers to. Nancy asked Daniel about his job at *The Guardian*; about the upcoming General Election that Daniel assured her would be another socialist landslide; what the British press thought of Italy's own recently re-elected prime minister.

Maria asked Daniel whether he had ever been to Italy before and he told her once, to Lake Garda, as a child, falling even deeper in love with it during Italia '90 as a teenager. Maria asked whether Daniel had seen much of Olivia in London and he answered diplomatically. That period was still much of a mystery to Maria, and she wondered what Daniel had been privvy to.

'It's a brutal city,' Nancy said dismissively, as if London had spurned her too.

When Maria didn't understand the turn of conversation or a phrase, Olivia and Nancy would translate for her, and vice versa if Maria was trying to explain something to Daniel, who she couldn't stop looking at, as if a rare creature had stepped over their threshold.

Daniel had never sat at a dinner table that felt so unlike home – dinners at the Bleeker house were brief and transactional. Or the television was often on and the family bonded over football, rugby union, *Popstars* and *The Royle Family* while they ate sofa suppers. Yet he'd never felt so comfortable somewhere so different.

As Daniel helped Olivia clear up the plates, and Alessandro's grandfather clock ticked 10.30 p.m., he realised he had to get his stories sent back to the office in London. He asked Olivia for an adaptor and sat at the table finishing off his work, so he could send them over to Lloyd on the sports desk. The pre-match banter. Selection dilemmas. How Milan was being taken over by Bayern and Valencia fans. Soundbites and vox pops from some of them ahead of the final.

Maria and Nancy took their glasses to the sofa to watch the news while Olivia joined Daniel at one end of the dinner table, flipping through colour and fabric swatches while she tried to work out something in her head and he pressed send on each story.

The two of them worked comfortably in peace until midnight, when Nancy heard the chime of the grandfather clock.

'Is that the time? I'd better be off.' She offered to drop Daniel back at his hotel near Milano Centrale train station, and Daniel took his cue.

'Yeah, I'd better get back, big day…' he said, closing the lid on his laptop and shovelling it into his backpack with his notebook, Blackberry and pens. He handed Olivia her adaptor and gave a shy, 'Thank you,' as if they were back to square one. Olivia wasn't so hesitant.

'It's OK, Mamma, I'll take him on my scooter.'

'Are you sure?' interjected Maria, stitching on the sofa, although the dimly lit room was playing havoc with her eyesight. Her niece in Syracuse had recently given birth to a baby girl, and Maria was embroidering the name 'Valentina' onto a bonnet. 'It is late.'

'Mamma, I'm almost 26! It's fine,' Olivia brushed.

Nancy seemed less worried, and would rather Olivia were out with Daniel than sitting at home on her own.

'She'll be OK.'

Nancy put on her blazer and picked up her handbag.

'I'll leave you lovebirds to it then,' she said with a soft and rolling Edinburgh lilt and a glint in her eye as she kissed her daughter twice. Olivia didn't even seem embarrassed. She was just at peace. Nancy kissed Daniel goodbye too.

'Wonderful to meet you,' she said, squeezing his arm. 'See you soon, no doubt.'

Nancy called to Maria on the sofa while Olivia dug out her helmet and a spare from a concealed cupboard in the walls of the hallway. 'I'll drop a card for Valentina tomorrow, and a little thing to go in the parcel. I'll be off!'

Nancy waved and left the apartment while Maria waved from the sofa, put down the bonnet and removed her glasses.

'Ah, here it is, should fit you, it was Papa's!' Olivia said, pulling something out from the cupboard. Daniel wondered if there was any point in wearing the beige and brown vintage helmet, but he took it all the same. It felt like an honour.

'You'll be careful, won't you?' pleaded Maria, as Olivia grabbed her keys.

'*Non preoccuparti, Mamma, tornerò presto!*'

'Come here,' Maria said to Daniel, pulling him into her bosom. He blushed. 'Thank you, Daniel, you have certainly been a beautiful house guest.'

'Thank you for dinner, it was delicious.'

'Do come again,' she said hopefully. 'And you—' she released Daniel and pointed at Olivia. 'Come home safe.'

'*Cosa certa, Mamma.*'

Olivia blew Maria a kiss before slinging on her jacket and helmet.

'Ready?' she said as she skipped downstairs. Daniel put his bag onto his back and remembered the sensation of Olivia sliding it off him in the kitchen earlier, her imprint still travelling his spine, as he watched her spiral down the stairs, her silver pumps sparkling on each marble step.

'Ready.'

In a parking bay outside Daniel's unremarkable business hotel, close to the rather remarkable Centrale train station,

Olivia put her Vespa on its stand and took her helmet off, shaking out her hair as Daniel got off the back.

'That was fun!' Daniel laughed. The ride through the midnight traffic had been exhilarating as he clung to Olivia's waist, simultaneously shielding her and holding on for dear life.

'Only way to travel in this city,' she smiled, launching a leg over so she could get off too.

Daniel took his helmet off and handed it back to Olivia, and she looped them both on the handlebars of her moped like baskets.

'Thank you so much.'

'*Prego.*'

'I had a really lovely evening. I didn't expect—'

'So did I,' she interrupted, halting him, making him even more lost for words. He looked at the face he loved. This was it. This was the moment. Gone half past midnight during the bustling Milan midweek.

'Would you like to come up?' he asked awkwardly.

Olivia got lost for a second. In the hesitation of Daniel's face. The sheepish look in his sparkling khaki eyes.

I so want to.

'You know... I won't.'

Daniel nodded.

Of course she wouldn't. This was how their evenings ended.

She's out of my league.

'I have work tomorrow and it's a big day for you with the match...'

Olivia felt like she owed Daniel an explanation.

'Oh, don't worry about it,' he said, trying to sound

indifferent. He was now more worried about Olivia getting back home. 'Will you be OK—'

Daniel didn't have a chance to finish his question as Olivia pressed a long index finger to his lips. Blue hues of faded paint dye weaving around tanned hands.

'Shhhhhh,' she commanded.

He obeyed, through closed lips.

Olivia liked how Daniel's lips felt under her finger, but lowered her hand to his chest so he could breathe.

'I just don't want to ruin a perfect evening. I feel so happy I could cry.'

She pressed her hand onto the top of his chest, her eyes filled with fire and water.

'You could come up and cry with me?' Daniel suggested.

'No, I'm going to have a little cry on my moped,' she said, pulling her hand away.

'Can I see you tomorrow?'

'We both have to work.'

'I'll ask if I can get you into the game somehow.'

'I don't want to see the game.'

'Oh.'

'But I want to see you. So of course I will come.'

Daniel was flooded with relief. For the first time in the five years he had not stopped thinking about Olivia Messina, he felt assurance. A calmness. That he would see her again. Nothing would come in their way.

'Plus, I need to give you our portrait. You left it at the apartment.'

'Do you?' Daniel winced, as if she really ought to keep it.

'Nice try, but it's my gift to you, you *have* to accept it.'

'OK, well thank you.'

'You're welcome,' she said, before quickly pecking him on the cheek and kicking out the moped stand.

'See you tomorrow?' Daniel asked as he rubbed his temple.

'I'll meet you at the San Siro after work,' Olivia declared, as she jumped on the moped and turned on the ignition. '*Domani.*'

'*Domani,*' he repeated coyly.

As Olivia pulled away on her Vespa she started crying.

'I love you,' Daniel whispered to the space where she had been.

'Dan-i-el,' Olivia whispered to herself in breathy joy as she waited at a set of lights. And cried all the way back to the villa on Via Tiziano.

Within the spiralling concrete coils of the San Siro's four pillars, Olivia tried to focus on the football, when all she wanted to do was watch Daniel work. The press area around them was fascinating. High tension and deadline hitting. Everyone striving to do their jobs well. Banks of commentators, writers, pundits – and beneath them, the sports photographers waiting to catch the money shot from European football's biggest night.

Daniel had spent all day concocting a story on how to get Olivia into the game. What rouse he could make up so she could watch the sold-out match alongside him. He thought about claiming she were his translator, and that he had forgotten to bring her credentials with him and it was all his fault. But when he went to the gate to meet her, a navy jersey dress making her bronze skin dazzle, she said something in Italian to the steward in a fluorescent yellow tabard, and he opened the gate to let her in.

Having Olivia by his side put Daniel in his element – he was more assured and confident than she remembered him. She felt an urge to put her arm around his neck and stroke the soft hair at the nape of it, as if it was the perfectly natural thing for her to do, but she didn't want to interrupt him, to prevent him from doing his job, so she held back and took in the atmosphere of the stadium. Looking around she reminisced about pivotal moments in her life within those pillars.

She had seen Duran Duran there as a child, a happy privileged princess under the arm of her papa, one reassuring hand on her back, the other holding a fat cigar by his side. When she closed her eyes she could almost smell the sweet richness of his Toscano; when she opened them she could see his smoke rolling past her nose – but perhaps that was from the firecrackers the exuberant fans had let off.

Olivia remembered repeat trips to see Vasco Rossi and Eros Ramazzotti with her mammas; the day Michael Jackson came to Milan and she and Mimi went wild. She wanted to tell Daniel all about these memories, but filed them under *later*. For now she was content to see him. Daniel Bleeker was the star of the San Siro, and he didn't even know it, as Olivia watched his gaze flit between the pitch and his laptop, checking to see if she were OK, as he made notes, as he typed, as he revelled in doing a job he loved. This was much more exciting to Olivia than the football on the pitch.

Valencia scored an early penalty, then Bayern Munich missed one, but equalised shortly after half time. Daniel didn't want the game to go to extra time, he wanted to get to the end of the match, do the post-match interviews and hope it wasn't too late to steal a few more hours with Olivia before his flight home in the morning.

'Penalties!' he said, half excited, half defeated. Penalties were the order of the night; the late finish would penalise him for preferring to be with Olivia.

In a brief pause while the team managers decided on orders and outcomes, Daniel felt the urge to put his arm around Olivia. To weave it under her hair and across her shoulder, and pull her into him – but he didn't want to ruin what was so far the best night of his life.

Olivia's interest in the game was piqued a little by the excitement of a penalty shoot-out. The high drama. But she felt the tension rise in Daniel as his print deadline loomed closer.

'Are you OK?' she asked.

'Yes. Yes, I'm OK. Are you? Sorry it's such a late night.'

She gave a half smile that Daniel couldn't read.

Is she about to go?

Bayern Munich missed their first, then four went in until a Valencia shot was saved by the German keeper, who Olivia observed had hair like Mamma Una's ginger bowlcut.

Five more went past the keepers like bullets. Olivia wanted to hold Daniel's hand in the suspense but he was furiously typing away, not knowing how his match report would end. Then an Italian playing for Valencia sent his penalty straight to the keeper's gloved hands. A crowd roared and groaned. The German giants had done it.

Daniel hammered on his keyboard, watched on by Olivia

as crew and stewards built a makeshift stage in the middle of the pitch, and the photographers poised their lenses on it, waiting, waiting, waiting…

'Done!' Daniel said triumphantly, pressing return as if he had just deactivated a bomb. The relief. He so wanted to stop time. But he had more work to do.

'Can we go?' asked Olivia innocently, looking from her watch to Daniel.

Daniel let out a sigh.

'That was the match report. I've got a few minutes before the interviews… but they won't take long.'

Please don't go.

Defeated players stepped onto the platform to collect their runners-up medals. Dignitaries and officials gave consolatory smiles. The Bayern Munich men filed up, the photographers raised their cameras, propping the heavy lenses on their knees.

The captain raised an enormous trophy and under the firecrackers of the grand finale, under a sparkle and whizz of blue and red tickertape, Daniel turned to Olivia by his side, pointed at the pitch and said, 'Exciting, hey?'

But Olivia wasn't looking at the hero goalkeeper lifting up the cup. She didn't care for the crescendo of Handel's choral harmonies and the roar of the crowd. She was looking at Daniel, her whole body turned into his, and kissed him, firmly, passionately, fully for what felt like the first time.

'I'm coming with you, you know.'

Olivia looked across the back seat of the taxi at Daniel and stroked the stubble on his jaw. She was wearing yesterday's navy dress – her hair rampant and her olive skin glowing from the exhilaration of being up all night exploring each other's bodies. Daniel rubbed his eyes – both bloodshot and sparkling – and smiled.

'What?'

'Not right now, on this flight. I need to go to work.' Olivia nodded to the sliding doors of Malpensa airport departures terminal through the open window of the car. The morning sunshine shone on the silver façade. 'But I'm coming back to London.'

Daniel paused, his hand on the door handle, his eyes locked with Olivia's. Elation thumping in his heart.

'Are you sure? I thought you hated it!'

'I did. Three years ago. But then I hated *me* three years ago. I will love London with you there, I know it. I'm pretty sure I love—'

'*Sono cinquanta euro...*' interrupted the taxi driver.

Daniel and Olivia both laughed, and got out of their respective doors while Olivia explained to the driver she wanted him to wait, before taking her to work back on Via Spartaco in the city.

The driver nodded and put the radio on while he attacked his teeth with a toothpick. Olivia joined Daniel on the pavement.

'Are you sure?'

The pavement outside the departures hall was bustling with families, businessmen and football migrants all flooding into the terminal around them, while Daniel and Olivia gazed at each other in a bubble.

'Yes! I've never been more sure about anything in my life. I'm not letting you go again Dan-i-el.'

Daniel opened his mouth to speak but was silenced by surprise. By happiness. By Olivia's kiss. And by the thunderous roar of a plane taking off overhead.

Twenty-Nine

November 2017
Cambridge, England

'**B**est faggots in the Fenlands, I tell ya!' a bald man with thick bottle-lens glasses shouted along a line of chairs. In the five seats between him and the man in a wheelchair he was talking to were five women. Women reading: two silver-haired friends hunched in towards each other, one reading Jilly Cooper, the other *Woman & Home*. Women scrolling: one in her sixties checked her Twitter, her adult daughter with the same face shopped for winter boots. A woman knitting: but she was the wife of the man in the wheelchair, and grateful that someone else was talking to her husband for now.

The two men at each end of the line had realised by coincidence – when one had to give his postcode to a radiographer – that they had lived in the same street in the past, although not at the same time.

'Juicy faggots, those were. My Barb would serve them with mash and peas, oooh and some really pokey mustard...' The bald man with the thick glasses went misty-eyed.

The man in the wheelchair said little. Ever since he had given his postcode, he had been talked at by the man who liked faggots, as he talked over the women sitting between them.

'And game pie, did you ever try Allington's game pie?' He didn't wait for the man in the wheelchair to answer. 'I loved that on a Saturdee...'

Olivia and Daniel sat on the row of chairs opposite, a small table with magazines separating them. Olivia's hackles were rising.

'You don't get game pie – nor faggots – where I live now. I miss those I do... best faggots in all of East Anglia, I dare say.'

For almost an hour the man had talked incessantly about pubs, potholes, window cleaners, the Friday market. And faggots.

'Shut up about your fucking faggots,' Olivia urged through gritted teeth under her breath to Daniel while he scrolled through BBC Sport and squeezed her leg.

The man alongside her, reading Felix Francis, smiled to himself when he heard Olivia's whisper, and let out a subtle puff of air as if to say *he's annoying me too*.

No one wanted to be in the waiting room of the radiology department at Addenbrooke's hospital, let alone being talked at, or across or over, as they waited for their turn, their room, their machine, to blast a delivery of radiation therapy to mouths, breasts and brains. This was Olivia's first session and she felt nervous enough as it was. All she wanted to do was flick through her copy of *Vogue*.

A fortnight ago, nurses had fashioned a mesh plastic mask called a shell, in the mould of her face, that would hold her head in a precise position so she wouldn't move during treatment. So they didn't zap the wrong part of her brain. So memories wouldn't be erased. So that all she would feel would be stifled and buried alive, while dressed as an Egyptian mummy.

Olivia didn't like the anticipation, the dread, of having to put the mask on for real, it was awful enough when it was being cast. But she knew that this was what she had to do.

She had escaped surgery without losing any of her faculties – without forgetting who her children were, that Sofia was coming up for 8, how to speak Italian, or the lyrics to 'Islands in the Stream'. She had got lucky. What if this was the stage now when they slipped up? One wrong blast.

I must lie very still.

It won't take long.

Shut up about your fucking faggots.

'What are faggots anyway?' she whispered to Daniel. 'I thought that was what Americans called—'

Daniel cut her off and whispered a quick low, 'I'll tell you later. He doesn't mean *that*.'

'Why doesn't he just shut up? Why is he talking over all of those poor women?'

Daniel was worried that the man would hear Olivia's griping.

'He's probably just nervous too.'

That was a thing Olivia found both adorable and irritating about Daniel. He always saw a situation through a compassionate lens, even when someone was getting on his tits.

Olivia accepted it and looked back at the magazine on

her lap. But she couldn't focus on fashion or her fellow style-makers. She could only think about Sofia's birthday party and how desperate she was to be well enough for it. For Sofia to have the swimming party she wanted. To manage thirty children. To sort party bags and parents who hadn't yet sent an RSVP. To decorate an elaborate cake – or better still carry the one Mamma Due had made, although she wasn't coming until Christmas, dammit.

Olivia channelled her fear by focusing on the birthday party when a radiographer with shaggy blond hair and a light beard ambled into the waiting room from the corridor with the treatment rooms beyond it.

'Olivia Messina?' he called out from behind his rectangular glasses, although he already guessed Olivia was the woman with the long red hair on account of not having seen her before. She was a fresh face. A newbie. Fairly young compared to most, although not as young as some – he treated children with cancers in the morning clinics. But hers was the only new face today, and he would definitely have remembered it, had he seen her before.

Olivia put her hand up and went to stand.

'Oh no, don't get up,' said the man with shaggy hair.

He crouched on his knee by the table at Olivia's lap and Daniel squeezed her leg tighter. She looked at his kindly face and tried to find his small eyes behind the beard, glasses and hair.

'Sorry, just to let you know, we're running a little late – one of the machines broke down this morning, so it'll be another half an hour.'

'Oh.'

Olivia felt a strange mix of relief and disappointment.

'How are you feeling? Are you OK?'

I'm far from fucking OK.

Looking around the waiting room had confirmed what Olivia had felt since her first diagnosis from the handsome Dr Lorca at the hospital in Ibiza: this was not OK. She was too young for cancer. The woman scrolling on her phone with an *adult* daughter was too young for cancer. Even *fucking Faggots Man* who must have been at least seventy was too young for cancer. This was an outrage she didn't quite believe. But still she had to sit, in a welcoming and sterile chamber, deep in the depths of Addenbrooke's hospital, waiting for the first of her four radiotherapy sessions, to 'mop up' any cancer cells from her brain. It had to be *OK*. She had no choice.

'A belt and braces approach,' the rather cold consultant Mr Greene had said in London.

Olivia wasn't OK. She didn't want any of this. But the man with 'Graham' on his name badge had a face too gentle and altruistic to snap at, he was an NHS hero she was grateful for, so she nodded acceptingly, while trying to remember who would collect the girls from school if her treatment ran on. *It's OK. Henrietta said she could.*

'Well... I am a bit nervous actually.' Olivia conceded, surprising herself. Daniel squeezed harder. He liked the look of Graham too.

'That's perfectly understandable, but really, you won't feel anything at this stage.'

Olivia nodded compliantly.

'Do you have kids?' Graham asked.

Olivia's eyes welled up.

'Yes, two girls.'

'How old are they?'

'Thirteen and seven. Almost eight.'

'Well, try to see treatment as lying down for twenty minutes – which I'm sure you rarely get to do with kids.'

Olivia smiled and Graham got back up. 'Les, you can come with me now, I'll take you down to machine nine.'

'Right you are, young Graham!' waved Faggots Man, as he stood up and picked up his beige coat and shopper. The two men went off through the set of double doors Olivia hadn't yet been through.

'It won't be long, I'm sure,' said Daniel, having no better idea of how long it would be than Olivia did.

She took a pen and piece of paper out of her saddle bag and started writing notes about Sofia's birthday party. The yeses. The nos. The party bags. The food allergies. The timings. The number-eight candle. Then she started sketching a dress – a party dress she might like to make Sofia, that wouldn't be fit for any swimming pool party, but that didn't matter, Sofia would love it and wear it over and over. It had ruched shoulders and a tiered skirt. Draping and a sash. She hadn't sketched a child's dress in a long time – she'd been so lost in ideas for her own new collection, inspired by the majolica of Ibiza, and had spent much of the past month drawing in her studio, recovering and rewiring her brain while Daniel brought her cups of tea, listened to her ideas and cooked dinner – but this party dress was a brilliant tonic for waiting-room nerves.

She'd love it!

Fifteen minutes later Les came back through the double doors, back from the Other Side, and put on his coat ceremoniously. He cleared his throat, as if he were about to make a speech, and Olivia saw the mother and daughter sitting opposite her shrink a little in their chairs.

'A few of you know me... well, you know I like to joke. Some might say I'm a bit of a character.' He rose on the balls of his feet a little.

Wanker.

Shh!

Oh god, he really is going to do this.

The man reading Felix Francis looked up.

'And, well, I've been here every day for the past six weeks, so some of you are probably tired of my jokes by now... my "unique" sense of humour as you call it, eh...?' He turned around to see if any of the radiographers were in the waiting room, but they had gone back to adjust machinery, shells and beds.

'But today's me last session. And... well... it's been a bit of a journey, I'd say.' Les brushed his eye with a knuckle. Olivia wasn't sure if he were joking or being serious, but her left hand clasped Daniel's right as the notebook teetered on the magazine on her knee. 'And I can't fault the staff. Really. Marvellous people. Everyone's been marvellous.'

Oh.

Olivia felt a bit bad.

'So best of luck everyone. Wherever you are in your treatment or whatever you're being treated for.' Graham came back into the waiting room as a nurse walked through from the opposite corridor, carrying a jug of squash. They both stopped, realising this was a monumental moment for one man. 'I just want to say... god bless, you couldn't be in better hands with this team, I'm... I'm...' Les' watery eyes were magnified further by his thick lenses, as he became lost for words.

Graham came to his rescue. 'Ahhh, do come back and see us Les – just visiting, mind!' he added, his tiny eyes twinkling. 'There's the Macmillan stand on the way out and we're always having cake sales and events – do come back for cake, won't you?' Les nodded, unable to speak, finally silent. He buttoned up his coat and looked to his comrade in the wheelchair, who had fallen asleep. His wife kept her gaze on her knitting. The silver-haired friends carried on reading their book and magazine.

Daniel put his arm around Olivia and gave Les an encouraging nod, only Les didn't notice it as he fastened his coat and tried not to cry.

'Best of luck, eh,' Daniel said, with a warm smile, wondering whether Les had anyone helping him through his radiotherapy treatment. What had happened to Barb?

The mother and daughter looked up from their phones at Daniel, then back down again. The man reading Felix Francis got up to go to the toilet. And Graham told Olivia that they were ready for her now.

Thirty

June 2002
Tokyo, Japan

At a plastic galley table in a bustling Shibuya sushi bar, Mimi, Nate and Nik perched on tiny high stools, while Daniel and Olivia sat opposite. All of them were watching the carousel of aburi salmon nigiri, coriander seared tuna and mixed maki whizz past on colourful plates at one end of the table, like cats being teased by a ball of wool. Tommy had sacked off dinner and gone home after rehearsals to be with his Japanese girlfriend Kaoru. Tommy was a man of few words anyway, so his absence was barely notable.

A petite girl with a timid face approached the group, her shiny pockmarked skin reflecting Shibuya's neon lights outside, as she handed Mimi a shirt it looked like she had just bought for herself.

'Can I give you this?' she asked in a sweet and uncertain voice.

Mimi looked at the girl, her hair in bunches and braces on her teeth.

'Sorry?' Mimi asked affably.

'Can I give you this?' she giggled, and then turned to her friends who were standing in an encouraging huddle outside the restaurant, peeping through the gaps between bright stickers on the window.

'If you're sure? Yeah!'

'I am,' the girl nodded politely.

'Well, thank you,' smiled Mimi, who jumped down from her stool and gave the girl a hug. The girl stood awkwardly, then giggled, nodded, and ran back to her friends. Nate and Nik didn't take their eyes off the conveyor belt of food, like cheetahs about to make their kill. All too used to Mimi being approached by shy teens and Harajuku girls, wanting to bestow gifts on their bass player.

Daniel rubbed the small of Olivia's back as they both watched the scene in awe. Everything about Japan was awesome. Daniel had been in the country for five weeks already, preparing for and covering the Japan and South Korea World Cup for *The Guardian*.

He'd started in Tokyo, like most of the press pack, where they dispersed to different stadia and Daniel reported on England versus Sweden at Saitama, and drank sake until he was sick. From there he flew to Sapporo in the north, where he saw England beat Argentina and visited a hot spring that helped lift the demons of the sake. In Osaka he struggled to report anything exciting about a 0-0 draw against Nigeria, but immersed himself in the local art of *kuidaore*, or 'eating until you drop'. And from Osaka he took a bullet train to Niigata, and found solace in a stadium that looked like a swan, before heading back to Tokyo, where Olivia joined him for a few days' downtime, catching up with Mimi and the band who were touring again.

*

Their reunion at Haneda airport was feverish – Olivia dotted Daniel's face with frenzied kisses. They hadn't been apart for more than three days since Olivia had returned to London to be with him. Five weeks of intense work, intense travel and intense partying had been a drag for Daniel, despite the excitement of the World Cup. He missed Olivia hugely.

'Does this happen often?' Olivia asked, seeing how blasé Mimi's bandmates were about the encounter.

'All the time,' sighed singer Nate, as he looked something between bewildered and boastful. 'You can't walk down the street without girls bestowing clothes, cuddly toys or Pocky on Mimi…'

'What's Pocky?' asked Daniel. He hadn't come across it yet.

'I have Pocky!' declared Mimi, eyes wide as she remembered the couple who had given her a packet at Ginza station this morning. She took a box of chocolate covered sticks out of her bag and handed them to Olivia.

'Hmmm, maybe for dessert…' she said, eyeing the box, before looking back at the prawn tempura on the carousel.

'It's lucky I'm a Japanese size,' said Mimi. 'I don't have to pack much when we tour here as my wardrobe is easily supplemented.'

'That's handy – nothing fits me in these shops!' Olivia laughed.

Mimi turned to Daniel as she nimbly scooped up the seaweed starter with her chopsticks, strands of translucent green that looked like they could be glass.

'How are you finding it here, you know, working?'

'I bloody love it! It's incredible.'

Mimi nodded.

'But I've been in a bit of a football bubble. It's just a load of press, from all around the world, asking the same questions to these absolute *stars* we're all in awe of. But because it's work, I've felt like I'm on a school trip. Until now.'

He pulled Olivia into him.

'All these cool things I wanted to show you.' Daniel turned to Olivia and remembered the flower fields outside Sapporo, bubbles of vivid purple and pink moss phlox as far as the eye could see. The sight of it made him want to tuck his legs in and bounce across it like in a dream. 'You'd have loved hiking in Hokkaido.'

'I knowwwww...' she groaned.

Olivia hadn't been able to justify the cost of all those internal train trips and flights on top of the international one, or to take time off work for the whole six weeks Daniel would be there, from the team training camps in mid-May to the final in Yokohama in ten days' time. He'd even missed the first anniversary of them getting together, but booked a table at The Ivy and arranged for Jim and Wesley to take Olivia there for dinner.

When Olivia left Milan to be with Daniel, two weeks after their kiss at the San Siro, she moved into the Tooting Bec flat he shared with Jim and Wesley, and spent her days at the local lido, walking to Wandsworth or Wimbledon

Common, or at the V&A, seeking inspiration in galleries and historical gowns.

At the Radical Fashion exhibition that autumn, Olivia got talking to another museum-goer, a languid blonde called Phoebe, a London College of Fashion alumni who was looking for a print and embellishment designer to join her expanding team at her up-and-coming label. Olivia and Phoebe immediately clicked: Phoebe's vision and energy were uplifting and infectious, and reminded Olivia of the person she wanted to be; Phoebe was fascinated by Olivia's fashion heritage and everything she had experienced at the houses in Milan.

Phoebe offered Olivia a job at her label, East of Eden, mostly in the Shoreditch studio but sometimes helping out in their Carnaby Street store, and Olivia didn't hesitate in saying yes. It felt like a lucky second chance. She had taken a gamble going back to London, giving up her job at Etro, but Bernardo – a deep romantic who loved the story of the boy at the bottom of the world – understood and said the door would always be open for Olivia. Having met Daniel, Nancy and Maria understood too – he was much lovelier, much more grounded, than any boy she'd brought home before. They could tell that night over dinner how in love with their daughter Daniel was; they suspected it wouldn't be long before Olivia felt it too, and they knew she would be OK in London with Daniel by her side. The move, and the new job, felt right.

At the studio Olivia got stuck in. She loved the smell of the workshop, the British banter and sense of humour, the rhythmic hammering of the sewing machines, and the comfort they brought her when she thought about being in her baby basket on Mamma Due's table. London finally felt like home too. A different sort of world to Milan: more exciting. Edgier than Etro.

She missed Daniel terribly whenever he was away for a couple of nights with work, but Jim and Wesley kept her company. They took her to the cinema and out for dinners, never harassing her to drink or share a bottle, respecting that this was the way she wanted to live her life. Her job at East of Eden was enough to keep her mind occupied, inspired and excited. Life with Daniel, Jim and Wesley – and Mimi between tours – was wonderful, and she finally saw through sober eyes, all that London had to offer.

Olivia booked tickets for Mamma Due to visit. She'd never been to London before but the V&A was hosting a Versace retrospective over the winter, and Olivia knew how happy it would make Maria to see some of the pieces she had stitched from the archives on display.

After a few months, Mimi decided to rent out her Brixton apartment, given she would be touring for much of the following year, so Daniel and Olivia happily moved in to the Victorian maisonette on Brixton High Road with its parquet flooring and views out onto the Academy. The flat in Tooting Bec had become a bit crowded for all of Olivia, Jim *and* Wesley's beauty products, but they still met up. Jim was launch editor of *Popcorn!*, a new celebrity weekly that was flying off the shelves, while Wesley had qualified as a teacher, and Jim took great pleasure in flirtatiously calling him 'Mr De Boer'.

Olivia had never missed Daniel as much as she did while he was in Japan, and their reunion, their stolen week

together in the Far East, only cemented what she knew –
that he was the best thing that ever happened to her.

'How's my flat?' Mimi asked over dessert of coconut mochi
rice, green tea and Pocky.

'Great,' said Daniel. 'So easy to get to gigs!' That wasn't
Mimi's point, but Daniel and Olivia had seen Neil Young,
Basement Jaxx and The Strokes since they had moved in.
'We only have to cross the road, soooo cool!'

'Yeah, I meant how's it looking? Has the mad lady next
door died yet?'

'Hmmm, don't think so,' Daniel mused, thinking of when
he last saw Mrs Macdonald walking the stairwell in her
nightie and banging a broom against the railings.

'Did I tell you about The Pogues at Christmas?' Olivia
asked Mimi, stroking Daniel's cheek as she remembered the
reverie of a 'Fairytale of New York'. It was a turning point
for her. She had settled in at East of Eden and found her
own rhythm – commuting with Daniel until they had to
change tube lines at King's Cross; meeting up at galleries
or the theatre or cinema after work; grabbing dinner from
the coolest new eateries. They had learned to live together,
to make ossobuco together, to argue well and make up
passionately, feeling stronger and more unified every day.
She realised it as Shane MacGowan swayed on stage –
that she was blissfully happy in London and that it was the
first time she enjoyed the truly giddy spoils of feeling drunk
and carefree, despite being sober.

'Oh, they play every Christmas!' Mimi rolled her eyes.
'But yes, you did,' she said, squeezing Olivia's hand across

the table and feeling truly happy for her that she had found a good egg and was seemingly settling down. Life on the road hadn't been conducive to romance for Mimi. Nate, Tommy and even Nik had girlfriends now – but since Mimi dumped Nik's brother Tate, she had been single. Only shy Japanese girls seemed confident enough to approach the pop star. Men were too in awe of her on stage and assumed she was with one of the band.

'Right, karaoke?' suggested Mimi, while Nate settled up. Olivia beamed. Daniel groaned.

'"Islands in the Stream", my darling?' Olivia asked.

'No,' waved Daniel, bottle of Asahi in one hand as his cheeks went pink. 'Mimi's got all the harmonies. Sing with her!'

Daniel, Olivia, Mimi, Nate and Nik huddled in their Hello Kitty themed room at the karaoke bar on Udagawacho, with three Japanese businessmen they'd never met before.

Mimi was already scrolling through the songlist. A pint-sized connoisseur of karaoke, the businessmen weren't going to get a look-in with Mimi on the mic, but they were genial and welcoming, and kept ordering bottles of Yamazaki whisky for everyone.

Mimi belted out 'Hanging on the Telephone' by Blondie, one hand on her small hip, while Olivia, looming tall next to her, accompanied, laughing more than she was singing.

Nate swayed and Nik drummed, two fingers on the low table, while the businessmen slung their arms around them and topped up everyone's glasses.

As Daniel's face got hotter and hotter, he looked at Olivia

and realised. This woman. Singing in front of him. He loved every fibre of her. Her truth. Her curiosity. Her sass and her smile. She was laughing again, carefree. Only not like the girl in the cafe in Sydney because that girl was miserable. She was truly happy now, lemonade in one hand, mic in the other.

'*Hangin' on the telephone...*' Olivia and Mimi harmonised, badly. Olivia was not the performer Daniel had first thought she was on that podium, jiving to Chuck Berry.

At 11.59 p.m. Daniel tipped the scales between reserve and recklessness, Yamazaki outweighing any shyness.

'My turn!' he called, standing, smoothing down his T-shirt, crumpled from life on the road.

'Get out!' gasped Mimi, her jaw dropping.

'What?!' Olivia hollered, perplexed. She wasn't drunk like the others but she felt happier, more invincible, than she felt anyone possibly could. She and Mimi bowed to Daniel's surprise statement, while he pulled up his jeans, strode over to the television, and pressed some buttons. The synth strings of a bad backing track to Dean Martin's *That's Amore* struck up and everyone sat down and cheered.

Daniel held the mic like an old Rat Packer as a tinny chorus of women opened up the singing on the video, echoing in the room and making everyone laugh. As he took his cue, he looked quite the crooner, to everyone's shock. The businessmen looked at Nate, Nik, Mimi and Olivia and howled with laughter.

'Outrageous!' one shouted.

'Yes sir!' said another.

Daniel sang off-key but with newfound confidence,

looking from the screen to Olivia, a whirligig of their relationship spinning in his mind as his audience echoed 'That's amore...' back at him.

He saw her, looking up from a campervan in a gold and dusty haze on the highway. He saw the opulent tiles of a train station departures hall, spinning in a circle as their lips first touched. He felt the heat of the fireworks and the roar of a crowd in the San Siro, so he kept on singing. He saw Olivia and Mimi, swaying in unison at one end of the cushioned seating. The businessmen at the other started too, although they were going the opposite way, so they bashed into Nate and Nik in the middle like the metal balls of a Newton's cradle.

'I can't believe you're doing this!' yelled Olivia as she clapped and Daniel kept on singing, finding his stride with every 'That's amore...' his audience replied, an octave too high and out of tune.

'You're a natural!' shouted Nate, to hysterics from the businessmen.

Daniel nodded in feigned arrogance, knowing he was terrible as he sang with a twinkle. During the choral interlude, Daniel picked up a fresh bottle of beer and took a big swig while Olivia mouthed, 'I'm so proud of you' and he gave her a wink before rejoining Dean for the last verse.

That last sip of Asahi made it harder to read the lyrics on the screen, but Daniel decided to get creative with them anyway.

'Excuse-y me, Oliv-livvi-lee, will you ma-ha-marry me? That's amore...'

'WHAT?!'

Daniel didn't sing anymore. He stopped, gave into his

fears, and soaked up the smile on Olivia's face.

Mimi turned to Olivia and hit her, thinking she must have misheard, but from Olivia's smile it was clear she hadn't. Their eyes locked as she nodded, stood up, threw her arms around Daniel for knowing how brave he had been, and kissed him. 'Will you marry me?' he repeated, in a whisper.

'*Si*,' she said in his ear, before kissing it repeatedly, and then his lips, to great cheers from the room, the drunkest of the businessmen joining Daniel and Olivia in their blissful huddle.

Thirty-One

December 2017
Cambridgeshire, England

'Happy birthday to you...' A swarm of 7 and 8-year-old children stood around the table, all eyes wide on the circus-themed cake in front of them. Olivia wasn't the best baker – she didn't like to cook much since nothing was ever a patch on Mamma Due's hearty dinners and pastries – so celebration food was a team effort for the Messina Bleekers. Daniel would cook the beef or veal centrepiece for the Sunday roast and all of the trimmings; Olivia would fashion a ring out of bay leaves and clementines to go around it. Daniel would bake sponges for the girls' birthday cakes; Olivia would decorate them elaborately. Daniel always created the solid base; Olivia would give it flair and make it look standout. Daniel had made three tiered sponges; Olivia had iced them.

She had intended to make the cake colourful: a red and white big top; sugarcraft animals and bunting in primary colours arching over a number eight, but her artistic edge shunned the Pinterest board and its garishness for something altogether more gothic. Pure white icing wrapped smooth sponges then a palette of smoky grey shades worked their way in an ombre to the top, like a mist clearing on the blackest of nights in a snowscape. At the top, Olivia modelled two ladders from royal icing and between them, the black silhouettes of two trapeze artists, a woman and a man, hands meeting in the middle mid-swing. It was quite beautiful, fit for a wedding more than a kid's birthday party.

'Happy birthday *to* you...' Flora stood next to her mother, a good way taller than her sister and classmates, holding a knife and a stack of paper napkins, her serious face cracking in fondness. Daniel tried to take photos on his phone while chatting to some of the parents who had come to collect their children. Thirty kids with wet hair and tired eyes lisped and spat as they sang a hearty and tuneless rendition of *Happy Birthday*, while all marvelling at the almost-spooky centrepiece. A blond boy called Buzz stole a white Malteser from the base of the cake, and was met with a stern glare from Olivia.

'Happy *birthday* dear Sofia... happy birthday to you!'

Everyone in the cafe clapped while the empty swimming pool beyond the glass panorama looked weirdly still.

'YAY!' they cheered. Sofia beamed. Flora broke into a smile.

The blond boy went to take another Malteser – he was the boy who had been shouting 'TURRRRRRRRD!' while dive bombing onto people in the pool earlier, and Daniel and Olivia had speculated if he knew what the word meant; whether he knew he was the biggest one at the party.

'Erm, hands off please!' said Olivia wielding a knife. The

boy gave her a princely and petulant stare.

Jesus!

In the excitement and chaos of the situation, as Olivia sank the large knife through vanilla and raspberry sponge, all she could think was how *tired* she felt.

While radiotherapy and the shell mask had been claustrophobic and frightening, it was painless, and Olivia hadn't really believed Dr Okereke or her deputy, a softly spoken Irish doctor called Marian McQuillan, when they warned her about the side-effects of fatigue. How could lying down for twenty minutes just four times render you so weak?

But weak she was. Her head felt foggy, her limbs heavy. And even though she still hadn't had a single headache since collapsing in Ibiza and being diagnosed with brain cancer, her eyeballs hurt, as though she were wearing Sofia's swimming goggles and they were too tight.

'You OK?' Daniel whispered, seeing the grey haze wash over Olivia's face.

'So-so. Get the party bags and give Buzz one first, I'm done with him. Little turd.'

Olivia sliced finger portions and Flora wrapped and put them into the thirty party bags that were waiting on a table by the door. Kids were becoming impatient. Kids were becoming tired. Parents started to trickle in to see how their little darlings had behaved and whether they had had a good time.

This was the milestone Olivia was wanting to get to – treatment over and Sofia's birthday. Sofia was born after a time of trauma, after Olivia and Daniel had lost the second child they were expecting. Sofia's birthday was always a signpost of relief. She was their rainbow baby, their gift. A gift for their 5-year-old to dote on and to cuddle after the heartbreak of dashed hopes. A baby brother they had to explain away. Sofia's arrival, and every birthday since, always heralded celebration and relief. Perhaps that was why Olivia had focused so intently on getting through surgery, radiotherapy and recuperation with this day in mind. Now she was here, feeling exhausted, wanting to bat away the irritating children when she knew she ought to feel fortunate. All she wanted to do was run away. Or crawl out given how she felt. Take her daughters home to the Huf Haus, cut herself off and isolate with her tribe.

Deep breaths.

Parents walked in and cocked their heads to one side. They had known it hadn't been easy for the Messina Bleeker family. They were surprised Olivia was going to the effort of throwing a whole-class party.

'Was Buzz OK?' asked his well-meaning mother. Olivia went to open her mouth.

'Great!' interjected Daniel.

Thirty-Two

May 2003
Tuscany, Italy

'*My baby just cares for me...*'

Mimi crooned to the castle dancefloor, where Daniel led his new bride onto the thick stone floor, wearing her first proper Olivia Messina creation. She couldn't find a wedding dress that felt *right*, so she set to work with silk chiffon and lace, creating a bohemian, tiered dress that was perfect for the relaxed bride she was. Her deep red hair tumbled onto her shoulders as the champagne silk plunged at her chest and thin straps revealed a low back and freckled shoulder blades.

Daniel cried when he saw Olivia approaching in it, a simple wreath of peach blooms and lavender berries adorning her crown. As the sun lowered and the silver olive groves and vineyards turned golden, Olivia walked up a cypress-lined path flanked by her mothers, her father's gems anchoring her ankle, to Daniel and Jim, standing next to the registrar on a terrace in front of guests.

Olivia hadn't wanted to get married on Lakes Como

or Maggiore; she'd been to four hundred Pirelli weddings there when she was a little girl, and springtime in the lakes was too busy. So when Gili, an Israeli schoolfriend from Milan, offered up her vineyard, Olivia and Daniel flew out for a romantic weekend to check it out.

Gili had moved to Bordeaux to study viticulture, but knew that her heart was in chianti, so she moved back to Italy and restored an old castle in the grounds of a vineyard, falling in love and marrying her cellar master, Andrea, in the process. Olivia and Daniel's weekend spent exploring Tuscany was heavenly: meandering in their Fiat 500 hire car past villas of terracotta, yellow and peach; drinking coffee in courtyards under pine trees that looked like green canopy clouds; walking through forests abundant with wild capers, asparagus, chicory and fennel; tasting chianti Andrea had lovingly produced and proudly poured. As they flew back to London there was no question where they would wed.

Gili and Andrea staged the most beautiful celebration for Olivia and Daniel, who took their vows while guests looked out onto the fruit and fertile earth of the rolling Tuscan countryside behind them. As the shadows from the burnt-orange and brick exterior walls of the castle grew long, the wedding party tucked into cured meats, cheeses and fried zucchini flowers at trestle tables, washed down with prosecco and frizzante. Ravioli and rabbit followed, and before Jim gave a rousing best man's speech, Daniel paid tribute to his wife, and Olivia said some words in memory of her father. Guests tucked into *torta nuziale* and kept cheering '*Evvia gli sposi!*'

Daniel didn't have many school or university friends at the wedding, since he spent most of those years with

Kelly, travelling between Farnham and Brighton to see her at weekends. A few of his newspaper colleagues from *The Guardian* flew out – his sports team, the picture and travel editor, the fashion editor Lillie who had taken a shine to Olivia, and her actor boyfriend. Plus, Andy, Duncan and Kathy from the *Elmworth Echo*. Daniel had bumped into Viv Hart on a weekend back visiting his parents, and she said she was disappointed she couldn't make it: 'Half-term, I'm away with the kids...' she apologised, even though Daniel hadn't invited her.

Matt and his wife Annabel were there – she mostly sat looking bewildered by all the foreign food and outpourings of love and emotion. Annabel was seven months pregnant and rather inconvenienced by having to travel to Italy so close to her due date, but Matt was the reliable and charming usher who performed his responsibilities with pride, until he discovered a penchant for limoncello, drank his way through the cellar and forgot the rest of his jobs.

'Is there not pizza?' Annabel had hissed into Matt's ear when waiters proudly presented their table with a platter of *fritto misto antipasti*.

Annabel didn't 'do' vegetables, so she was put out by the fried courgette flowers and pumpkin as she pushed them around her plate in disdain. Surely in Italy of all places, she could get a cheese and tomato pizza?

Matt was too merry to be weighed down by it, but his parents fussed around Annabel, excited by and nervous for the imminent arrival of their first grandchild, so they asked a waitress if she could get anything for their pregnant daughter-in-law and put it down to cravings. The waitress brought out a focaccia steeped in olive oil.

'Foreign muck,' Olivia saw Annabel mouth to herself, angrily.

Olivia had more friends at their wedding, given her youth had been so misspent, her life so sociable and her education so rich. Milan's International School diaspora had spread far and wide. Friends from Chile, Sweden, Hong Kong and the US mingled with Olivia's sleepy and shrunken grandparents from Sicily. Alessandro's parents, Vincenzo and Renata, were older than Maria's parents, Flavio and Veru, but all four sat quietly at trestle tables on the terrace, being looked after and talked at by bright young things from around the world. Nancy's parents, Jean and Archie, had flown in from Scotland, and found the whole notion of their granddaughter marrying a Sassenach quite bizarre.

There weren't any children at the wedding – not because the bride and groom didn't welcome them, but few of their friends had become parents yet, and those work colleagues who had kids revelled in leaving them at home in favour of a weekend in Tuscany.

As the wedding band took a break and filled their platters, Gili joined Mimi at a second microphone and joined in with 'My Baby Just Cares For Me'.

They'd had their 'official' first dance to 'That's Amore', but as Mimi and Gili crooned Nina Simone, and Jim and Wesley joined Olivia and Daniel on the rustic castle's stone floor, the bride and groom spun within a circle of tea lights.

Olivia looked at Daniel, handsome in a tux Maria had made him, and knew that this was all they both wanted in life. To unite their families, from Lombardy to Cambridgeshire; Lothian to Sicily, and to forge the bonds of a unique family of their own.

Thirty-Three

December 2017
Cambridgeshire, England

'She's *awfully* antisocial, isn't she?' Nancy whispered as Olivia shook the roast potatoes in a tin on the hob. 'Hasn't stopped looking at her phone. On Christmas Day. *At the table!*' Nancy had to talk quietly as there were no dividing walls separating the Huf Haus kitchen from the long dining table on the far side of the living area, and she looked down over her spectacles as she spoke. 'Here, mind the oven.'

Olivia shook the aged tin with all her might and felt the tired pull on her limbs again. Her mother always sounded more Scottish when she was being critical; it was something that made Olivia and Daniel chuckle – unless she was being critical of them, of course.

'It's OK, I've got it.'

Olivia slid the heavy tray back into the oven for the final crispy push and Nancy shut the door for her.

'I'd never noticed the extent of it before. Mind you, she was a misery when I first met her at your wedding.'

'Twenty-one years!' Olivia said, putting an oven glove to her brow.

'You haven't been married twenty-one years.'

'No, *they've* been together twenty-one years. Imagine!'

'Urch!' Nancy said, scrunching up her face as the steam from the Brussels sprouts pan covered her glasses.

'Daniel says she was like this from the off.'

'Urch!' Nancy added again for emphasis, as she cleared her lenses on the corner of her Oxford shirt. 'But Matt seems so... *warm*.'

'He is.'

'Surely he must be screwing someone at work?' Nancy speculated, her rrrrs of *screwing* and *work* rolling more and more as she became more outraged.

'Not everyone does that, Mum,' Olivia said, raising one eyebrow. Nancy hit her on the arm with a tea towel.

'Ow!' Olivia feigned pain and laughed, but she could actually feel the impact on her aching body.

'What does Matt do now? Is he still big in Safeway?'

'Well, they were bought out by Waitrose. But he's at John Lewis now. Store manager in town. Most of our Christmas crockery and decorations came via him.' Olivia nodded her head towards the table in gratitude.

'Well, surely he's screwing one of the Saturday girls.'

'Annabel *was* the Saturday girl. Twenty-one years ago.'

'Old habits die hard...' Nancy said with a wink and the two gossips laughed.

'Mamma, is it ready yet?' Sofia bounced to the kitchen.

'Yes! Five more minutes. Here, take these spoons. Ask your sister to top up drinks. And tell Papa he can start carving.'

*

Christmas was always an elaborate feast in the Messina Bleeker household. The family tended to alternate between Maria's apartment on Via Tiziano – the spare room now decked out with two single beds for Flora and Sofia – and the Huf Haus in Cambridgeshire. The Milanese Christmases of crostini with liver pate and tortellini followed by lamb, broke the fast of Christmas Eve, when Olivia, Daniel and the girls would accompany Maria and Nancy to the Duomo for mass: Flora and Sofia loved getting a stocking from San Nicolas, or if they were staying until Epiphany, La Befana would come bearing gifts. It was a more religious and a more culinary affair, which Maria especially made magical. And always somehow *easier* without the English pressures of consumerism, five-bird roasts and tense dining tables.

Christmases in Guildington were lively but stressful. The advantage was Flora and Sofia could play with their toys and see their friends over the holidays. The downside was the circus. Nancy and Maria would come and stay, weighed down with ridiculous amounts of presents and panettone, pandoro and panforte – sometimes with a boyfriend in tow if Nancy had a significant other. Maria had never looked at another man since Alessandro's death, but Nancy had dated the odd Italian banker, American art critic or like-minded widower from her cycling club. Daniel's parents, Silvia and John Bleeker, would come because the Huf Haus was much more accommodating than the house on Albert Road in Elmworth, and Matt would turn up wearing a jolly Christmas jumper with Annabel and their son Bertie, a rotund teen with a large head and pink cheeks.

It was a large and convivial table, apart from the spectre at the feast, Annabel, who had the bitter resting face of someone who didn't want to be there. Olivia and Daniel often pondered why she came, and imagined the terse conversations between Annabel and Matt in the run-up to Christmas, him trying to persuade her that it was her best offer, given they had no intention of hosting. Regardless of where they were in the world, Nancy always made a Cranachan trifle, doused in amaretto instead of whisky.

This Christmas mattered more than any before. The Messina Bleekers needed to be at home after the fright of the past six months. Despite the fatigue of shopping, cleaning, filling the fridge and hosting, Olivia didn't want to go away, this of all years. This Christmas needed to be low-key and slow, a reminder to be grateful for their health.

Sofia's birthday, then Christmas.

It had been the milestone Olivia wanted to hit through her most awful of autumns.

She had memories to make, a worried family to calm, A/W 2018 to finish – a colourful new direction away from muted tones and bridal gowns, inspired by her heritage and her holiday – and a business partner to reassure. A brain to heal.

Daniel feared hosting Christmas would be too much; Olivia had been so tired since the radiotherapy and had never been one to find respite and relaxation in cooking. He worried that the pressure of having everyone over would take its toll. He even suggested they go away, and Daniel wasn't the sort to go away at Christmas – he liked the turkey and trimmings too much.

'Somewhere exotic!' he said, as they were unpacking a Tesco delivery. 'The Caribbean perhaps?'

But that all felt a bit… terminal to Olivia. Too last-ditch. Like a final hurrah of a holiday *just in case* the operation and radiotherapy hadn't actually been a success. Plus Olivia was booked in for an MRI and CAT scan at Addenbrooke's on Christmas Eve, and she just wanted it out of the way.

As Daniel finished carving a citrus-ringed turkey and Annabel looked at her phone, the rest of the family tucked into the main event, thanked the hosts profusely, and reflected and reminisced about Christmases past. The presents they had given. The plays and shows they had performed in. Bertie proudly told the table he had been Joseph, all three wise men *and* Buttons in various school Christmas productions, because he's 'a better actor than Ben, even though Ben goes to drama club'. Silvia said Bertie must have got it from his father, because there wasn't a school play Matt hadn't shone in, and perhaps that was why he was such a success as a store manager. 'You have to be a bit of a showman to juggle everything in an operation like that,' she said proudly. Sofia laughed at the prospect of Uncle Matty dressed up as PT Barnum.

Flora mostly kept quiet, remembering Christmases of her childhood fondly: the time Daniel dressed up as Santa for the school grotto; going to see *Frozen* when she was ten; Warren the shire horse at the Guildington Christmas market, trussed up in jingle bells and taken for a walk on Christmas Eve with the Town Cryer.

'Do you remember, *tesora*,' said Maria, scooping plump and pink cranberry sauce onto her plate – a curiosity she only enjoyed in England. 'When you were little and your papa would take you to the Pirelli Christmas parties…'

Olivia nodded and smiled, a face full of chestnut stuffing.

'That time the reindeer ate your corsage?'

Heads all turned to Olivia.

'A real reindeer, Mummy?' Sofia asked, excitedly.

'It was real. *La verità!*' Maria howled, bringing her hands to her cheeks as her dyed black curls bounced. 'The reindeer was so still Olivia thought it was a stuffed model.' Mamma Due told the story, even though she hadn't been there – the Pirelli parties were Nancy's domain, so she interjected.

'You should have seen your mother's face when the reindeer moved. The shock!' Nancy clapped her hands together and Sofia's mouth hung open. 'It tried to eat the flower brooch on your mummy's lapel, and her little face crumpled! She'd never cried so much.' Nancy chuckled behind her hand. 'It could have been worse, it could have been *Signore* Carelli's wig…'

Maria and Nancy laughed across the table to each other. Flora couldn't help but smile. Silvia looked on in awe at Olivia's mothers, and Daniel's dad John worked up a meat sweat and searched for one of the three gravy jugs on the long table as if it were a puzzle.

'Remember last year, Mamma, the Elf on the Shelf ate all the chocolates from the tree, in *one* night?' said Sofia, half bemused, half annoyed. Daniel suppressed a guilty smile while Olivia gave Flora a knowing look as if to say, *shhhh.*

'Elf on the Shelf?' scoffed Bertie, as he stacked five pigs in blankets onto his fork. 'You don't believe in Elf on the Shelf, do you?'

Annabel scrolled through her phone looking at the influx

of emails about Boxing Day sales.

'Huh?' asked Flora, whipping her head towards her cousin in disbelief, giving him her most scathing of teenage stares – to shut him up more than anything.

'Next you'll be saying she still believes in Father Christmas,' quipped Annabel in a flat voice, eyes still fixed on her phone screen.

The clatter of cutlery silenced. The conversation stopped. Flora turned sharply again, this time giving her aunt a scornful frown.

Sofia looked up. Puzzledom and heartache fluttering across her face.

'Ummm…' Her voice wobbled.

Bertie, who was heading towards 15, wore a waistcoat, slicked-back hair under a wonky Christmas cracker hat, and a knowing expression. He blinked furiously as he took great pride in educating his younger cousins.

'Don't tell me you *still* believe in Father Christmas?' he puffed. He turned his large face towards Flora, whose reproachful look was all the answer he needed to *shut up*. He turned back to Sofia, his cheeks flushed but his face defiant.

He's not really going there, is he?

'Bertie, shhhh,' hushed Matt. 'Not the time.'

Bertie ignored his father, as was his custom.

'I knew Santa wasn't real when I was, like, five.'

'Bertram!' snapped Silvia. 'Shush.'

While Annabel preferred the company of a book or her phone to people, she was never more present in the room than when someone else was disciplining Bertie.

'What?' Annabel glowered at Silvia, who kept her disappointed gaze firmly on her grandson.

'What?!' gasped Sofia. 'You're saying Father Christmas doesn't...?'

Nancy and Maria shot each other a look.

The atmosphere turned suddenly as prickly as the holly centrepiece Nancy had picked from the garden.

'Oh please!' Annabel snorted, as she shot her mother-in-law a sideways look. She'd relied on Silvia to look after Bertie all these years, but she still couldn't stand it if she ever told him off, which wasn't as often as she ought to. 'Let's get some perspective here...'

'But he came last night!' Sofia protested. 'He brought stockings! He left a narwhal Fingerling!'

Bertie guffawed with wet and mocking lips.

'If that's what you want to believe, sweet...' Annabel said knowingly, without an ounce of sweetness in her downturned mouth.

Enough.

Olivia threw her weighty knife and fork down onto her plate with a crash that made everyone jump.

'Sorry,' she said, acknowledging the smash to her daughters. Olivia put her hand to her brow and pushed her hair back, trying to calm down, but she was livid.

'Santa is *very* real, Sofia.' Olivia said it with such fervour, the anger of a lioness, that Sofia would have believed anything her mother told her right now, but her mother's temper disconcerted her, so she gave her dad a quizzical look, searching for comfort in his eyes. Daniel nodded gently, concurring with his wife.

'So will you just *fuck off*?' Olivia said, holding both hands out as if begging to the sky.

'Mummy!' gasped Sofia.

Matt laughed, almost in shock.

Flora inhaled a deep breath.

Silvia, Nancy and Maria froze.

Bertie looked up in disbelief.

John waved an empty gravy jug nervously, as he realised now wasn't the time to ask if there was more.

Annabel looked up, her face pale and pained, her small features and downturned mouth open and rounded like a Polo mint.

Sofia clasped her hand to her mouth as silence fell on the table for what felt like an eternal minute.

Daniel tried to conceal the admiration in his eyes.

Nancy stood and graciously started to pick up the empty plates, not stopping to check if anyone wanted seconds or thirds.

But Olivia's gaze remained on Annabel, at the far end of the table, who was looking back at her with the shock and discomfort of confrontation.

Three months ago Olivia had had brain surgery. A month ago she finished a draining course of radiotherapy. She and Daniel had just cooked Christmas dinner for eleven people, and Annabel had turned up sullen and empty-handed.

Annabel gasped, a small whistle of disbelief echoing through her Polo mint mouth.

'Wha—?'

'I said, will you just *fuck off*?'

Matt put his head in his hands. Daniel looked at Sofia sitting opposite him and winced apologetically.

Olivia stood up, pushed back her hair, and pointed accusatively down the table.

'My girls have had an extremely tough six months. Sofia

has been SO looking forward to Christmas. We all have. And you try to ruin it?!'

'I just—'

'Don't come into *our* house and sit on your *lazy* arse, scowling at *my* children, sneering at food *you* would never dream of going to the effort to cook, and tell my daughter that Father Christmas doesn't exist.'

Flora looked both in awe and embarrassed. She wondered if someone might mention Father Christmas *doesn't* exist, but knew that wasn't the point.

'How dare you! How dare you try to suck the life and joy out of everything and contribute nothing?' Olivia didn't take her eyes off Annabel, who broke her stare to look for her handbag under her chair and start gathering her things. She didn't realise she was scooping the party hat and novelty paperclip into her bag, along with her phone.

'Oh Olivia, no, no...' said Silvia, back in primary school headteacher mode, despite having long since retired. 'That's not necessary, I don't think Annabel meant to... I don't think you meant to say that...'

Maria stroked Sofia's hair from the seat next to her, while Bertie sat, wet lips still drawn open, as he looked from Olivia to his mother and back again.

'I absolutely did!' said Olivia, exhaling an air of relief.

'Now, now,' said Matt, putting his palms mid-air in front of him, to suggest everyone simmer down.

'Well, what *does* she contribute Silvia? You've looked after Bertie, after school and in the holidays. *Your* summer holidays. Always working like a donkey, cooking Sunday lunch for them, spending your retirement ferrying Bertie around the place. I hope she's contributing something, that she's grateful to you at least...'

John nodded at his empty plate, as if Olivia might have a point.

Silvia was paralysed, not wanting to say the wrong thing, wishing this awful situation wasn't happening. Olivia looked back to Annabel, now standing at the other end of the table.

'You are repeatedly welcomed into other people's warm and loving homes and you sit and sneer. And never give anything back. Or smile. Or ask how anyone is. You haven't even acknowledged my little brain issue or asked how I am...'

'Oh, so that's what this is about!' Annabel laughed bitterly. 'I didn't give you the attention you were seeking about your op?'

'Ha!' Olivia snapped. 'Are you joking? *Che stronza...*'

Daniel shook his head and shot Annabel his most disappointed of looks. His wife hadn't had a brain tumour for attention.

'I'm *not* going to be spoken to like that! Come on Bertram, get your blazer. Matthew, we're leaving!'

'Can I not even have any of Nancy's trifle?' Matt said, trying to make light of it.

'NO!' barked Annabel, her face apoplectic and rash-red, as she squeezed against the glass wall at the far end of the table.

Matt edged out of his seat, looking longingly at his plate, as he stood up and gave his brother an awkward smile. Daniel averted his eyes and busied himself with the dinner detritus and turkey carcass in front of him.

Maria, Sofia, Flora, Silvia and John sat gobsmacked while Olivia sat back down in her chair, gaze now fixed to the garden beyond Annabel's empty seat, and continued to eat.

In the kitchen Nancy put a tea towel to her mouth and pretended to be looking for something in the larder, to hide her face and stifle her cheer. Daniel walked over with a pile of plates.

'I've got a system,' Nancy said, looking busy, pointing to worktops and indicating where the empties and food waste should go, ignoring the elephant in the room. The stoic Scot kept calm and got dinner cleared as the front door slammed shut. Daniel looked at his mother-in-law and saw the twinkle in her eye.

She's back, they both thought.

Thirty-Four

April 2004
London

'Olivia Messina, well I never...'

Olivia turned to the boy in her peripheral vision and realised he was in fact a woman. A woman from her past.

'Vaani! Oh my god!'

They had been standing side-by-side for a good five minutes, admiring a tattered cropped T-shirt, designed by Jamie Reid, Malcolm McLaren and Vivienne Westwood, with a Union Jack on the front, ripped, stitched and held together by safety pins – then modified by Johnny Rotten – in the Vivienne Westwood exhibition at the V&A Museum. As they'd stood studying the punk and power of their birth years, they hadn't realised that the gold thread of school and university in their past, and the business of their future, bound their destiny.

'What are you doing here?'

'Er, checking out Westwood,' Vaani said, her usual curt tone not giving much time to silly questions. Olivia marvelled at her face. Vaani had barely changed in the almost twenty years since Olivia had first met her, in the large pristine garden of the large pristine International School. Back then, Vaani's style was suitably Eighties and boyish: jumpers and sweatshirts in geometric stripes and patterns, peg-leg trousers that finished above her skinny ankles, soft brogues from the best cobblers in Milan. Eighteen years later, that Eighties aesthetic shone through in the cool of the gallery. Her chest was still flat and her haircut boyish, but womanhood brought an elegance to Vaani, her beauty startling and bare, but for a swipe of nude gloss on her full lips. Her eyes were as curious and as wide as they were in those early days, fresh from Mumbai, but now they contained a cynical glint, probably caused by London life.

'I see you've been busy,' Vaani said, nodding to the protruding belly poking out of Olivia's mac.

'Yes, eight months, I'm fit to pop.'

Gone was the slight Italian twang Vaani remembered Olivia by at school and in their days at Central Saint Martins, before Olivia Messina disappeared from the social circuit and Vaani didn't realise for weeks.

Vaani felt bad when a mutual friend told her she had spotted Olivia back in Milan, that she had dropped out of college. But it was the summer holidays anyway, it's not like she should have missed her around Charing Cross Road. And Vaani wasn't in with that crowd. The white girls who did coke.

'Wow, amazing,' Vaani breezed, not showing much interest in Olivia's pregnancy or impending birth. Although she did try hard to remember the questions she ought to ask.

Olivia felt fortunate to have fallen pregnant so soon after marrying Daniel. Only two disappointing periods later, she sat on the toilet in the back room of the East of Eden store on Carnaby Street, marvelling at the blue lines on the pregnancy test.

Positive.

She called Daniel, beckoning him from *The Guardian* offices in Farringdon to the Liberty cafe off Regent Street half an hour later, under the guise of a stolen lunch.

'Newlyweds' prerogative,' she had said.

As they ate club sandwiches, a giddy Olivia slipped Daniel the blue and white capped pregnancy test under the table.

'Positive!' she declared. Daniel looked down at his lap and beamed.

'Really?!'

'Really.'

She rummaged in her bag and handed him something else under the table. Another positive pregnancy test. And then another.

'I did six,' Olivia laughed. 'All positive.'

Daniel dropped his club sandwich on his plate and the three plastic sticks fell to the floor under the table.

'Oh my *god*!' he shouted, walking to Olivia's side of the small table, dropping to one knee, and taking her face in his hands to kiss her.

'Yes!' she squealed between kisses.

A table of two elderly American couples enjoying afternoon tea looked on and applauded.

'Oh, did you see that Bob?' said a woman in a pale green twinset. 'He asked her to marry him!'

'Wonderful!' exclaimed the other woman.

One of the men dabbed his mouth with his white napkin, while the other, the most frail of the group, pushed his chair back, painfully slowly, and stood up to walk over so he could shake Daniel by the hand. He was so old and so feeble, his approach took an excruciatingly long time, giving Daniel the opportunity to scoop up the used pregnancy tests and drop them in Olivia's bag so they could go along with it.

'Thank you!' Daniel said with a hearty handshake, almost propping the old man up. 'I'm the luckiest man in the world.'

Olivia blushed demurely. For now, their baby would remain their exciting secret.

'Do you know what... *it* is?' Vaani said with a crease in her nose, and they both broke into laughter. Olivia wasn't offended by Vaani's crispness. She had always found her economy with words and pithy sympathy refreshingly honest.

'Yes, a girl. We think.'

'You think?'

'Well, they never say for sure what you're having.'

'Oh. Well, is it a girl, a boy or a potato?'

Olivia laughed.

'The sonographer said "keep the receipt", as they can get mixed up that way around.'

'Oh right,' Vaani said blithely. 'Stunning exhibition, isn't it?'

The exhibition had been a triumph, the first ever complete

retrospective from the textile and dress collections at the V&A, as well as Vivienne Westwood's own archives: the towering platform shoes Naomi Campbell had tumbled down the catwalk in; a 1972 T-shirt embellished with chicken bones; the clock from the old King's Road store that had 13 hours and hands that travelled backwards. Westwood's sartorial subterfuge shone through.

'Yes, incredible. I loved the corsets!' Olivia said assuredly.

'You would,' Vaani said with a joke roll of her eyes. Olivia's style had always been more feminine, more dramatic than Vaani's. 'My friend curated it...'

'Oh wow. Your friend did a good job.'

'Yes. I could stand and look at these for hours. In fact, I have stood and looked at them for hours, I need a drink. Fancy one? I imagine you ought to get off your feet too.'

Olivia was touched by Vaani's uncharacteristic concern. Maybe the past six years had softened that hard shell.

'That would be lovely.'

In the Gamble Room cafe Vaani tucked into a ham and Emmenthal baguette with vigour while Olivia tried to ignore her heartburn in favour of her quiche. She looked up at the majolica ceramic tiles that adorned the grand columns propping up three ornate archways, not knowing they would later influence her. She loved the coloured tinglazes of the tiles, flashes of the Italian Renaissance in this very English corner of the world. She took a deep breath to steady what felt like a heart attack in her ribcage.

'So are you back in London for good?' Vaani asked, not noticing Olivia's physical discomfort.

Olivia pointed to her belly.

'Yes, I'm kind of stuck here now.' She laughed and tied her hair up in a bun on her head to ease the heat of being overdressed for a sunny spring afternoon. The hormones and heavy belly made her feel burdened. 'I got married last year, we live in south London. Brixton.'

'Oh,' said Vaani disappointedly. She was still a northwest London kind of girl.

'We're moving out to the sticks though.'

'Oh.' Vaani's aversion grew, as if she'd just found a slug in her baguette.

'Nearish my husband's parents, but on the trainline to London. We're buying one of those modern, flat-pack houses.' She said it in the hope of winning Vaani over.

'Oh, cool. One of those German ones that look like a Tellytubby house?'

'Yes! Well. Sort of. It's a Huf Haus. We're buying it from a couple who are divorcing – due to the stress of having it built apparently.'

'Oh dear, I hope it isn't cursed.'

'I just hope it stays up. I can't be doing with a new baby and walls made of plastic if it all falls down...'

'German engineering. They're very solid – and very chic – apparently. What does your husband do?'

'Daniel – he's a sports journalist. At *The Guardian*.'

'Oh, my friend is fashion editor there.'

'Lillie? Lillie Carter?'

'Yes, Lillie!'

'She was at our wedding!'

'Shut up!' scoffed Vaani.

'No really, she's a friend of Daniel's. Small world.'

Olivia marvelled at how Vaani must have friends everywhere, but wondered how they fell out of touch. Perhaps this was where Friends Reunited might do well. Perhaps the internet might help with these connections; Daniel had done a search on Olivia to find her in Milan after all.

'So where are you working?' Olivia asked, as she put her hand to her chest to fight the spike within it.

'God, you're not going to give birth here, are you?'

'No, no, it's just my lunch.'

'Oh good,' Vaani said unsympathetically.

'And people don't "just give birth" – it takes ages to kick in. So I'm told.'

'Fine.' Vaani took a sip of her sparkling water. 'I work for *Drapers*, the industry magazine.'

'Oh wow, you really did stay on your course pathway. The business of fashion.'

'I know, right? So predictable.'

'Vaani, you are anything but that. What do you do there?'

'I'm deputy editor. Snooping around the industry. Moaning about business rates. Checking out what the parental leave policies are at the retail giants. Calling out the sweatshop proponents. Looking at the marketing successes... All very interesting for a geek like me. What about you? What do you do, apart from getting knocked up? Don't tell me you're working for Philip Green. Rumour is he's going to get a knighthood...'

'No, thank god. I work for East of Eden, in their Shoreditch studio.'

'I know Phoebe! She's great, isn't she?'

'No way, how funny!' laughed Olivia, as she rubbed her belly.

'I love what she's done, giving a boutique brand an egalitarian edge. Not my kind of clothes mind, all those cargo pants and utility... stuff...' Vaani made a face. 'But she's a *very* good businesswoman.'

'She is. I met her here in fact! Shortly after 9/11. We got chatting and she offered me a job.'

'Small world.'

Olivia smiled to herself and thought again how it was. How she had bumped into Daniel at opposite ends of it. How Vaani seemingly knew everyone. How bizarre it was that they hadn't crossed paths in the three years she had been back in London. Phoebe had been on maternity leave for most of that time, having a baby followed by accidental twins. Olivia had stepped up quickly and had been so busy helping to run the studio that she hadn't had any time to schmooze the trade press.

'She's just come back from mat leave actually, I'm handing back over to her now.'

'Well, I never. Olivia Messina has been the East of Eden caretaker all this time and I didn't even know it.'

'Working for Phoebe has taught me so much. The clothes aren't really my style either, but that doesn't matter. Her passion is inspirational. I don't know how she does it with three babies. I don't know how I'm going to do it with one.'

'Oh, you'll be fine!' said Vaani with a nonchalant wave. 'Just give it to a nanny or something.'

Olivia frowned.

'So what *is* your style?' Vaani asked, finishing off her last bite of baguette.

'Mine?'

Olivia had been working so hard for Phoebe – getting her drawings through to production. Meeting accountants and investors. Liaising with PR and marketing teams. Seeing stock numbers through to the Carnaby Street showroom and holding events there. Keeping the business afloat. So much so that no one had asked Olivia about *her* own style, not since she tiptoed from her bedroom to Mamma Due's sewing room, as she came out of her malaise at the end of the century.

'Assuming you're still drawing that is. Is it all Westwood-style corsets, like your binbag dress?'

'That dress!' Olivia laughed. 'No, it's...'

Olivia looked at Vaani and felt able to open up to those large probing eyes.

'Less structured. More floaty, I think.'

'Yeah?' Vaani wanted to hear more.

Olivia thought about her own sketchbooks and swatches. She'd drawn a few pieces, but only made one creation of her own since leaving Milan.

'Quite muted in terms of colour, but quite frothy in terms of fabric. I designed my wedding dress last year – we got married in the Tuscan hills – and the whole place inspired a style direction I guess.'

'Sounds... A Midsummer Night's Dreamy?' suggested Vaani.

'Yeah, dreamy, that's it. I love it, when I do get to do it. But I've been so busy with East of Eden and buying this Huf Haus in Cambridgeshire and the baby coming... my own drawings have gone on the backburner.'

'They sound lovely,' Vaani said warmly.

Lovely? Vaani? She really must have softened in her twenties.

'It doesn't sound like the sort of style you'd find lovely,' Olivia said honestly. Vaani was wearing a shirt buttoned up to the collar and skinny chinos. Her wardrobe palette a different sort of muted: mostly black, navy and beige.

'It's not for me – but look at you! You're a floaty maxi-dress-in-a-Tuscan-olive-grove kind of woman. I think *your* passion is inspiring and I'm sure your own style is too. To some people.'

'You think?' Olivia blushed. Her freckles flashing with her heartburn.

'Yes – you should explore it. Work on it while you're off. Women are meant to be creative when they're creating babies, aren't they?'

'That's what Phoebe says.'

'Well then, get stuck in. It would stop you becoming one of those awful bores who talk about *night feeds* and *nappy rash*.'

'Yeah, I will.' Olivia mused, while her baby kicked the insides of her and her heart burned in its cage.

Thirty-Five

January 2018
Cambridge, England

'Come this way please,' said a Macmillan nurse with a small face under a thick bob and a name badge that said Jackie. Olivia hadn't come across Jackie before. She didn't like having to start again with new faces in these cavernous corridors. She liked who she knew. Graham the radiographer. Dr Okereke and her beautiful, sage face. Her assistant Marian McQuillan. Their dashing Canadian student Jordan Lo. Kay, the Macmillan nurse she had first encountered in the corridors of Addenbrooke's, who also had two daughters, although hers were grown up. Olivia couldn't see Kay by the Macmillan station today and worried Jackie might be a bad omen.

Olivia and Daniel followed Jackie down the corridor, Daniel carrying both their winter coats over his arm, as she opened the door to a cramped room where Dr Okereke and Dr McQuillan were already waiting.

'Mrs Messina!' Dr Okereke said warmly. 'Sit down.' Her grey braids had new jewel adornments near the tips, which tinkled like a wind chime as she proffered a seat.

She called me Olivia before.

This too felt like a bad omen. She looked at Dr McQuillan perched on the desk, her smile warm and sympathetic. Olivia took the chair nearest to the desk, Daniel the one next to Olivia.

Them and us, he thought, as he sat down, too nervous about the blows ahead to make chitchat. Daniel was never good at chitchat.

He flopped their coats over the arm of the blue plastic chair as Jackie closed the door and leaned back against it.

Hemmed in.

Olivia looked at the vertical window blinds behind Dr Okereke, and the grey day and car park beyond it, and felt this room was not fit for the news that was delivered in it. Daniel put his hand on Olivia's.

'Thanks for coming in today,' said Dr Okereke, always authoritative and warm. 'Looks pretty horrid out there still...'

'It is,' said Daniel bleakly.

'It's been horrid hasn't it?' Jackie wittered and Olivia wanted to scream at everyone to stop talking about the fucking weather.

'So, for the benefit of Jackie, who hasn't been following your case as she's new to Addenbrooke's, this wonderful woman had a seizure in the summer, caused by an astrocytoma on the parietal lobe. She had surgery under Mr Greene and myself at Queen Square in September, which was a great success, topped up by some short bursts of radiotherapy, as a belt and braces approach...'

Belt and braces. She's saying it now.

Olivia still didn't know what it meant and reminded herself to ask Daniel.

'Mrs Messina…'

She called me Olivia before, I'm sure.

'…had an MRI on Christmas Eve…'

Why so formal? thought Olivia.

Why isn't she showing us on the screen? Daniel worried.

Dr Okereke shook the folder in her hand, even though the digital images were on the sleeping computer behind her – old methodology was hard to move on from. 'And I'm really happy with what we've seen, happy with how you're doing, and as far as we know it, today your brain is tumour-free.'

Olivia stared into space.

Belt and braces.

Daniel breathed out a sigh of relief that turned into a shake in his chest.

'Oh god!' he said, pulling Olivia into his arm before clutching his face with his free hand. 'Can we see the scan? Does that mean it's gone?'

Olivia said nothing. From a high corner of a cramped room she looked down on herself, sitting still on the plastic chair; looked down on Daniel and the relief flooding him as he rubbed his face, his smile travelling to the corners of his eyes.

'It's wonderful news,' Dr McQuillan said warmly, urging Olivia to feel able to celebrate.

'It's out,' confirmed Dr Okereke. 'There was no residue of the tumour we removed, nothing visible at all on the scan, and there are no signs or shadows to be concerned about. I can show you on the screen...'

As she clicked a mouse to awaken the computer, the images she'd been discussing with Dr McQuillan before Jackie brought them in flashed up. Nine brains in a tile.

'OK so this was August, your imaging from the hospital in Spain. This is the mass, the glioblastoma which was removed in September.'

Daniel looked at the small cauliflower floret Dr Lorca had first shown them, when he said it might not be anything serious. Olivia looked out of the window.

'Then if I just go to the image now...' Dr Okereke clicked on another tab, and the white mass looked bigger, the cauliflower had grown.

Daniel gasped and squeezed Olivia's hand.

'Oh, hang on...'

Dr Okereke fumbled, flushed and embarrassed, looking bemusedly between her mouse and screen. 'No, sorry, that was the September image just before your surgery, where you can see it at its largest. This should be December...'

Daniel saw Dr McQuillan's smile fade to a wince while Dr Okereke sang like a bird as she searched and clicked.

'Brains I can do. Computers... There!' she exhaled with a sigh of relief.

'This is December, as you can see, there is some scar tissue but nothing to be concerned about – we are *very* pleased to inform you.'

Olivia came back into her body and spoke.

'It's gone?' she asked flatly.

'It's gone,' smiled Dr McQuillan, in a soft Irish accent.

'Will it come back?'

Dr Okereke cleared her throat.

'Well, what we say as medical professionals is that you are "cancer-free". Any one of us in this room could have cancer in six months' time.'

Daniel frowned – Dr Okereke didn't need to put such a downer on it. Dr McQuillan interjected.

'Olivia, this operation and your treatment has been an amazing success, you have done brilliantly...' She squeezed Olivia's arm from her perch on the desk. 'And if I were you, I would go and book a holiday because you bloody deserve one.'

Olivia smiled.

'I really don't need any more treatment?'

'You'll be kept an eye on, three-monthly checks to start with,' said Dr Okereke, pressing her purple lips together.

Olivia thought of everything she wanted to do for her label – new designs she wanted to put into production and have made. All the reconnecting she wanted to do with her daughters.

'I don't have to come in sooner?'

'You can come in sooner if you like,' she chuckled. 'Word is Jackie's cakes are up there with Nigella!' No one laughed, although Jackie gave a modest smile from her post against the door. 'But no, get that holiday booked. You certainly deserve it.'

Daniel and Olivia stood up, gathered their coats and her bag in a huddle, still shocked, then Daniel launched himself at Dr Okereke, opening his arms and giving her a broad hug.

'Thank you.'

'Not at all.'

As Dr Okereke squeezed Daniel back, her large bosom pressing against him, Olivia saw a hesitation in her eyes, which she hoped was just down to his surprising embrace.

Thirty-Six

May 2004
Cambridgeshire, England

Sitting on the L-shaped sofa, boxes by her feet, Olivia held her baby girl to her breast and hoped the latch was correct. It looked correct, as Flora furiously suckled and released a deep fart into her tiny nappy. The key turned in the front door.

They're here.

It was the first time Daniel had left Olivia since Flora Jean Luciana Messina Bleeker was born three days ago, three weeks early, so he could go to Stansted to collect his mothers-in-law. The silence of the house, save for the little grunts and snaffles of her newborn, and the birdsong in the garden from the blue tits and black caps, filled Olivia with a sense of peace.

I did it. I made you.

'Sorry, it's a total mess...' Olivia heard Daniel say to Nancy and Maria as they came through the door.

'This is *spectacular*!' Nancy looked up, all the way to the ceiling of the modern gabled roof. German flat-pack houses that generated more energy than they consumed were rare in the UK, but even rarer in Italy, although Nancy had seen one on a cycling trip to Switzerland.

'Mind you don't trip over any boxes...'

Neither woman cared, they just wanted to get their hands on their granddaughter, so they dropped their bags and almost raced past the floating staircase to the expanse of the family room and kitchen at the back.

'*Allora*,' Maria said, rolling up her sleeves.

'Let me see her...' said Nancy, with authority.

They walked into the sun-dappled room to see their daughter sitting on the sofa with her daughter.

'Ah!' Nancy gulped.

'*Bambina miaaaaaa...*' Maria cooed.

Flora, soft hair in auburn swirls, flinched from her drunken slumber, eyes still shut, as her nonnas suddenly became speechless and cried silent tears.

Olivia looked up, barefaced and tired. Her hair parted and twisted. Nancy was struck by how young her daughter suddenly looked at 28. How tiny her granddaughter was. Olivia started to cry. She was so, so proud.

Olivia suspected as she climbed into the cabin of the removals van on the Friday morning, that something was rumbling, but she didn't want to worry Daniel, so she rode it out. Paid attention to the twitches. Felt the pull of her tight tummy while the driver made jokes about her not going into labour and Daniel sat between them.

They weren't sure if the other two removal men should be transported in the back like stowaways, but Olivia wasn't going to go in there.

'No mate, she's not due for another few weeks. You're all good.'

But as the van weaved its way from Brixton to Peckham, along the Old Kent Road and East India Dock; while Kelly Clarkson, Eminem and Kelis alternated between the adverts on the radio, the twinges started to hurt, and Daniel noticed from Olivia's uncharacteristic quiet that something wasn't right.

On the M11, the driver stopped to check the pressure on a back tyre, and while he was on the hard shoulder, shouting to his colleagues through the roll-down back of the lorry, telling them that the tyre was OK, Daniel insisted Olivia tell him what was going on.

'Have your waters broken?'

'No, I don't think so, but I think it's started, it hurts…'

Daniel went white. They didn't have a car and weren't picking up their new one until tomorrow from the dealership in Cambridge.

As they passed Elsenham, Olivia turned up Usher's 'Yeah!' on the radio and half sang, half howled, to cover the groans of her pain while the driver thought she was somewhat weird.

'Mate, can you drop us at the Rosie?' Daniel asked coyly.

'The what?'

'Addenbrooke's, the hospital… it's the maternity ward.'

The driver went as white as Daniel, and put his foot on the accelerator, to the protest of the men in the back with the furniture.

Flora swam into the world only four hours later, in a lowlit room with a birthing pool. The Andrea Bocelli CD

Mamma Due had sent over was god knows where in the back of the van, but the midwives put on a calming playlist of their own while Olivia yelled, sweat and swore. Lots. Words they didn't know, but they got the general gist of.

'What colour are her eyes?' asked Nancy. 'Has she opened them yet?'

'Barely, we can't tell. They just look a murky colour at the moment.'

'She's dark like your father,' said Maria. 'They'll be brown.'

'Her hair looks red!' said Nancy proudly, each woman laying their claim on the baby.

Olivia stroked the swirls and smiled.

'I feel so sad that she will never know Papa.'

'She will,' said Maria calmly, as she caressed Flora's scrawny cheek.

'Anyone want a cup of tea?' Daniel asked from the kitchen behind the sofa, as he rummaged to find two more cups, he grinned to himself, thinking about a beautiful world surrounded by beautiful women.

Thirty-Seven

January 2018
Cambridgeshire, England

'You heard Dr McQuillan, we need to book a holiday.'
'Holiday?' Flora said as she sauntered into the living room.

'I thought you'd gone to bed?' snapped Olivia, trying to remember that this stuff didn't matter. Today she had been given the all clear. Permission to book a holiday she so needed after the disaster of the last one.

'I just came down for my charger!' Flora lashed back.

'Flora…' Daniel pleaded – so often caught in the middle of two titans. She gave a look to say 'What?!' as she skulked through to the kitchen in her new Christmas pyjamas, unplugged the charger and walked over to the dining-room table, where Daniel was checking the website and Olivia was closing her sketchbooks for the day – final Polaroids planning the first collection since her illness; new drawings she had been tweaking while Daniel was sorting dinner.

'Caribbean please,' Flora said, leaning over her dad's shoulder.

'What?!' Olivia laughed.

'Arabella went to the Caribbean for New Year. Barbados. She said it's so cool.'

Olivia could tell Flora wanted to burst into smiles and descriptions, as she would if she were talking to Arabella or any of her friends. But she couldn't bring herself to let them out, to let her guard down for her parents.

'Lucky Arabella!' Daniel joked, raising his glass of red wine. 'Her daddy obviously isn't a journalist.'

Flora shot him a sarcastic smile.

On the way home from their appointment with Dr Okereke and Dr McQuillan, Daniel pulled up in the Waitrose car park and went inside to get the ingredients for his signature dinner (spaghetti carbonara, even though Olivia told him an Italian would *never* put cream in it). Olivia waited in the car. She called Maria first, then Nancy, to tell them she had been given the all clear, hung up, and dissolved into tears, sobbing so vigorously her body shook and a passer-by tapped on the window to check she were OK.

Flora ignored her dad's witticisms and slunk out towards the stairs, phone charger trailing behind her like a tail.

'Your phone shouldn't be in your room either, Missy,' said Olivia, still wondering why she was sweating the small stuff, picking fights.

'It's DEAD!' Flora hissed. 'The battery *died*, I can't do anything with it anyway!'

'OK, well charge it down here then. Good girl.'

These mother/daughter tensions had been increasing

over the past year, and although neither said it, both Olivia and Daniel were surprised that her brain cancer hadn't abated the arguments. Perhaps they were a healthy sign of normality, Daniel had wondered, but he kept out of this one, and cleared the leftover dessert plates from one end of the house to the other while Olivia slammed her phone onto the kitchen island.

'Night night, gorgeous,' he said.

'Night Papa,' Flora replied, pointedly giving her dad a hug while she gave her mother stink-eye.

'Another drink?' Daniel asked, shaking a bottle of rose and elderflower pressé.

'Yes please.'

They were celebrating after all, so Daniel poured Olivia a more flamboyant drink than usual, with ice cubes and mint, topped up his glass of red and brought them back to the table.

'So where are you thinking?' he asked, looking at the travel section of the newspaper Olivia had picked up. 'Welllll, I ought to go see Nonna Renata in *Sicilia*...'

'Yeah, but that's not all that relaxing, is it?'

'No. So what I really want to do is go see Mimi and Udo in Switzerland. Go skiing.'

'Skiing? Is that a good idea?'

'Of course! The girls have never been.'

'No, I mean for you.'

'I'm fine! I'm the only skier in the family. You heard what Okereke said, *you're* as likely as me to have cancer in the next six months.'

They both knew that wasn't true.

'Gee, thanks,' shrugged Daniel.

And still, skiing seemed so... dangerous for a fragile skull.

Daniel had only been skiing once, on a school trip to Austria, and hadn't particularly fallen in love with it. His cautious heart made him ski with trepidation; he preferred drinking acidic glühwein and getting his first kiss, in the store cupboard of the youth hostel kitchen with Amy Hill. He was too thoughtful and too nervous to let go and relax his knees.

Olivia on the other hand flew down the Dolomites as a precocious child, surrounded by women in fluoro and fur, and wondered why they had never taken the girls.

Life, I suppose.

And the business. And Daniel's job. He was so often away.

'Look, you'll be spending the summer in Russia, we won't get much of a holiday then...'

'The World Cup will be over by the time school breaks up!'

'OK, so we have two holidays. You heard what they said. We *need* it. The girls need it. Life's too short.'

Daniel shot Olivia a fearful look.

'Plus it would be great to see Mimi and Udo. We can go in half-term, after Fashion Week has wrapped up, get away from it all...'

Olivia did have a point.

She got up from her chair and sat on Daniel's lap, looping her arms around his neck.

'Come on, the girls need a holiday after what happened in Ibiza, something totally different, to take away from that. And I miss Mimi. She did so much for us last summer – the least we can do is go see her in the mountains.'

'Hmmm...' Daniel was coming around to the idea.

'Skiing is amazing and liberating and beautiful, the girls will love it! Maybe even you will one day.' Olivia kissed his lips tenderly and he nodded.

'Are you sure you're up to it? Half-term is only a few weeks away.'

'I think the question is, are *you* up to it?' Olivia replied with a wink.

Thirty-Eight

July 2005
Cambridgeshire, England

'SNACK!' bellowed Bertram in Olivia's face, spitting crumbs of the toast and Marmite she had just handed him back onto her. She wiped the yeast and grease splutter from the bridge of her nose and examined her finger.

'Pardon me?' Olivia said, hoping Bertie's mother would discipline him before she had to.

'SNACK!' he bellowed again, more crumbs projecting from his puffing wet lips. His big blue eyes stood out against his round rosy cheeks.

Olivia had been graced with a rare visit from her sister-in-law Annabel and nephew Bertie, under the guise of seeing his cousin Flora, but Olivia couldn't help wondering if there was an ulterior motive. Annabel had shown little interest in her niece since she was born fourteen months ago and she'd only ever shown disdain for the modern lines of the Huf Haus; the lack of curtains on the back windows looking out into the field. It wasn't a place she visited unless pressed to. Let alone on a weekday when she was usually at work.

Olivia's weekdays in Guildington were usually slow. Daniel would go off to the station to catch the 6.42 a.m. so he could be at his desk for 8 a.m. Olivia would get Flora up and sorted; take her out for a walk or meet up with Henrietta, a mum she had met while recovering from the water birth in the Rosie – her baby boy Albie was a day older than Flora. She'd usually spend Flora's naptimes working in the garden studio. Her days were quiet and gentle. She'd decided not to go back to East of Eden, although Phoebe said the door was always open.

Today Olivia could have done without an unexpected visit. On Friday she was due in London for a meeting with Vaani and a potential investor, and she needed her portfolio and business plan to be tip-top – she was hoping to work on them during Flora's morning and early afternoon naps.

'What do you say, sweet?' asked Annabel, slumped on the low sofa still wearing her coat.

'I's big boy,' Bertie answered proudly, seemingly unrelated to his mother's prompt. 'I wear pants now.' Perhaps he thought wearing pants exonerated him from the need to say please or thank you. He was almost a year older than Flora but took pride in his place as the eldest grandchild, and was doted on by Daniel's parents, who had looked after him for much of his life.

Bertie tugged on Olivia's shorts.

What are you even doing here?

She tried to soften as she looked down at her nephew's entitled face.

It's Thursday morning. I'm not even dressed.

Olivia wore cotton shorts and a thin white vest that Annabel seemed to disapprove of when she walked through the door and looked her up and down.

She had been in no hurry to get dressed. She had planned to go through the portfolio in her pyjamas and hope that a City investor with little interest in women's fashion would love her clothes – and Vaani's business vision – enough to give them £150,000 to get up and running.

'What do you say?' reiterated Olivia, holding another piece of toast and Marmite in her hand.

'SNACK!'

For fuck's sake.

Annabel sat on the sofa reading a magazine, so Olivia ate the toast herself, to plaintiff grizzles from Bertie and went to do the mounting washing up. She had left it to pile up last night after Daniel called to say he wouldn't be coming home.

Daniel had phoned around 4 p.m. sounding merry. The sports team at *The Guardian* had been out for a long, boozy lunch to celebrate London winning the Olympic bid. The paper had been covering it in detail, with Daniel often called off football to work on it. He hadn't been invited out to Singapore with his sports editor Lloyd for the announcement of the IOC, but back in London the staffers – the whole city – froze for a few nervous minutes to gather around televisions in newsrooms, offices, banks and schools – to see who had won.

'Paris,' said Jeremy, the political editor, as he'd breezed through the office and slapped Daniel on the back in commiseration. Jeremy was always a know-it-all. Except he was wrong this time, and when London was announced as the host city of the 2012 Olympics, the entire editorial and advertising teams erupted like fans in a football stadium.

This was a big deal. Olivia could understand why Daniel was drunk.

Just after 7 p.m. Daniel sent a text to say goodnight to Flora, which definitely meant he was too drunk to speak, and Olivia relayed his message with kisses and raspberries as Flora drank her bedtime milk and kicked her legs out on the sofa.

The last Olivia heard was at 12.41 a.m. Daniel had missed the last train home, and was checking into the Premier Inn on Euston Road.

Sorry tesora. See you after wrok tomrrw.

Daniel only ever used Italian when he was drunk, and Olivia wasn't all that happy. She needed him home. She hadn't expected motherhood to be quite so tiring. The move out of London on the day of giving birth. The sleepless nights. A house that felt pretty isolated. She was pissed off as she turned out the lights, and saw leaving the washing up as a little *fuck you* to the patriarchy. Except now she had to do it. At least it was a distraction from Annabel and Bertie.

She switched on the radio and stood at the sink.

'Why did you say you'd called by?' Olivia asked, as blunt as her younger self, but under the noise of the radio, the ferocious tap, and Bertie's bumblings, Annabel didn't seem to hear.

'I's wear big boy pants.'

Olivia smiled and nodded as the suds rose. She wasn't interested in seeing how well Bertie had taken to wearing big boy pants. She wasn't impressed that the nursery staff and Daniel's recently retired parents had done all of the potty training for Matt and Annabel, when she knew it was something she would be taking on with Flora alone. Annabel didn't notice any of Olivia's antipathy as she read her magazine and ignored her son's shouts for more food.

'What are you up to today?' Olivia asked, *mezzo forte* now, as she washed the glasses first and gazed out of the window, into the fields beyond their garden. A small muntjac was bounding for cover into the bushes.

'Huh?'

Annabel twisted her head.

'What are you up to today?'

'Not sure, are we, sweet?' Annabel nodded to Bertie, who was toddling about smearing buttery hands across the television screen.

'Fireman Sam!'

'What do you normally do on Thursdays?'

'I *work*,' Annabel answered pointedly, as if Olivia had never done a day's work in her life.

'Yes, but it's Thursday today.'

'Oh yes. The staff are having a training day at nursery. Whole place is closed.'

She looked back at the magazine she was hunched over. She preferred it to watching Olivia wash up in her pyjamas. She found Olivia's long legs and braless state a little... showy.

The penny dropped.

Their in-laws were on holiday in France – and Annabel obviously didn't know what to do with her son for the day.

'Oh right, that sounds nice. A nice Mamma and Bertie day then?'

Annabel scowled.

'A lot of parents are up in arms about it, *actually*. We're not sure why they have to shut, but they do it every July. They say it's for "training".' She made quotation marks with her stubby fingers. 'But we're pretty sure they're just on a summer *jolly*, courtesy of their extortionate fees.' Annabel said the word jolly in a rather unpleasant way.

'Oh well, they probably deserve it after all that potty training and wiping arses.'

Annabel's expression hardened further, and she returned to the magazine.

'MUMMY, SNACK!'

Olivia continued to wash up, hoping Bertie's shouts wouldn't wake Flora.

As she listened to the radio, she felt an irritation in the pit of her stomach. Irritation about this impromptu visit. Irritation about Daniel not coming home. Irritation about the fact he hadn't called this morning when he knew Olivia and Flora would have been awake since 5 a.m. Irritation that he hadn't answered his phone when she called him from their bed this morning.

Why didn't he answer?

This wasn't like him.

This wasn't like her.

'SNACK!' bellowed Bertie again, picking up an apple from the fruit bowl, taking a bite, then launching it on the floor with a thud and a bounce.

For fuck's sake.

Olivia looked at Annabel. Her nose stuck in Victoria Beckham's latest diet secret.

'What shall I get him then?' Olivia asked flatly.

Annabel looked blank.

'Huh?'

'Bertie. He keeps harassing me for food. Shall I make him something else?'

'Erm…'

'Does he like eggs? Shall I scramble him some, call it brunch?'

'Oh, I don't know if he likes eggs.'

Olivia knew that Flora loved eggs in every form.

'How can you *not* know?'

Annabel looked up and glared. Olivia realised she needed to diffuse things. 'Flora eats so many eggs I'm surprised she doesn't turn into Dumpty Humpty!'

Annabel didn't raise a smile. She didn't correct her. She didn't say anything, she just looked blank, waiting for someone to entertain Bertie.

'Well, I can make him some, if he wants…' shrugged Olivia, turning back to her washing up.

'Oh, go on then.'

Go on then?

Olivia smiled through clenched teeth and went to the fridge to get the eggs. She turned up Radio Five Live to make a point. That if Annabel was just here to hang out, Olivia had better things to do or to listen to than Bertie's demands. A plastic bowl with Weetabix remnants sat in the sink.

She whisked and added a grind of pepper.

Scrambled eggs. She thought. *I'm making your kid scrambled fucking eggs and you don't even know if he likes them.*

WE'VE GOT SOME BREAKING NEWS COMING IN FROM THE PA NEWSWIRE, THAT THERE HAVE BEEN REPORTS OF AN EXPLOSION NEAR

LIVERPOOL STREET STATION IN LONDON. WE HAVE NO MORE INFORMATION AT THE MOMENT, AND THERE ARE NO DETAILS OF WHETHER THE POLICE WERE INFORMED OF A WARNING, BUT AMBULANCES, FIRE SERVICES AND BRITISH TRANSPORT POLICE ARE HEADING THERE NOW.

Olivia looked at the radio as if that might offer more information, her violent whisk froze.

'SNACK!' bellowed Bertie, toddling up to Olivia.

'Shhh, quiet Bertie, hang on a sec,' Olivia hushed her nephew. Annabel's ears pricked up at Olivia disciplining her son.

LONDON AMBULANCE SERVICES HAVE CONFIRMED THAT THEY HAVE SENT RESOURCES TO THE SCENE. NO FURTHER DETAILS ON WHAT CAUSED IT, OR INDEED IF THERE ARE ANY INJURIES, HAVE BEEN RELEASED.

Olivia tipped the egg and milk into the frying pan and moved it around with a spatula.

EYE WITNESSES SAY THERE WAS A BANG DURING RUSH HOUR AND THAT IT'S 'POWER RELATED', ACCORDING TO REUTERS.

'SNACK!' Bertie bellowed.

'It's just coming!' snapped Olivia.

Annabel looked up again and shook her head, seemingly shocked by Olivia's curtness.

WE'RE ALSO HEARING ABOUT A FURTHER INCIDENT AT RUSSELL SQUARE. ALSO DESCRIBED AS A 'POWER SURGE' – AND THAT THE WHOLE OF THE LONDON UNDERGROUND IS NOW SHUT.

'Power surge? That's a strange use of words,' Olivia said,

as she put another slice of bread in the toaster.

Annabel looked completely nonplussed. London was a world away from her bucolic bubble.

BRITISH TRANSPORT POLICE HAVE SAID TWO TRAINS ARE STUCK IN TUNNELS AT EDGWARE ROAD. IT IS NOT KNOWN IF THEY COLLIDED.

'*Cazzo...*' Olivia muttered to herself.

'More snack!' spat Bertie.

For fuck's sake.

Flora's cries came over the baby monitor next to the radio as Olivia hurried to finish Bertie's eggs on toast.

'There!' she shoved the melamine plate onto the kitchen island. 'Annabel you're going to have to watch him, I need to get Flora, she's woken up,' Olivia said pointedly.

WE'RE NOW HEARING REPORTS THAT A BUS HAS BEEN RIPPED APART IN AN EXPLOSION NEAR EUSTON STATION. ALL OF LONDON'S TRANSPORT IS DISABLED.

'Euston?!' Olivia went flying out of the room and up the stairs, where she grabbed Flora from her cot. 'Shhh, shhh, hey baby, good sleep...?' She had a horrid feeling in the pit of her stomach. Daniel had stayed on Euston Road last night.

He didn't answer.

She hurried back downstairs, Flora swaddled in her Grobag.

'Bertram, are you going to try some of this?' Annabel asked with a distrustful snarl.

The dumpy toddler with the red face waded over in his big boy pants and clambered up onto a stool. Annabel separated the food with a fork, cooling it with her downturned mouth.

'Shhh, shhh, *bellina*...' Olivia kissed Flora's teething-pink cheeks. Flora looked at her cousin and pointed in recognition. 'Burbee!' she said.

'Flora!' he replied amiably, before crumpling up his face and spitting out his egg into a dribble down his T-shirt. 'Yuk!' he shouted, swiping the plate on the floor. Egg flew and melamine spun. Olivia bit her tongue and put on the TV.

'Fireman Sam!' shouted Bertie.

Annabel didn't acknowledge Flora had woken, nor did she look at her niece. Olivia did see her brush a bit of scrambled egg under the kitchen island with her foot though.

Olivia turned on BBC One.

THERE IS A SUGGESTION THAT THE EXPLOSION ON THE BUS HAS BEEN CAUSED BY A SUICIDE BOMBER. IF THAT'S CONFIRMED, THEN THAT WOULD BE THE FIRST TIME A SUICIDE BOMBER HAS STRUCK IN THE UNITED KINGDOM.

'Fireman Sam!' protested Bertie, toddling over to the television and slamming his fist against the screen.

'No!' barked Olivia.

'I beg your pardon?' said Annabel. Olivia didn't know – or care – which of them she was talking to. All she could think about was Daniel. How she hadn't heard from him.

On the TV screen a map showed circles, where chaos was congregating; one was right on the area Daniel had spent the night.

'Shit!' Olivia said.

Olivia thought about the terse word she'd ended their text exchange on last night. A sarcastic, 'Thanks'. How she'd been annoyed that it was fine for him to go partying and leave her in the sticks. She was trying to grow a business and take care of their baby. Flora tangled her fingers in her mother's hair and looked at the television too, entranced by sirens and bright lights and people running along London streets.

'Why don't you try a bit more, Bertie?'

'Yuk! Don't like it.'

Olivia pressed her nose to Flora's head and inhaled the sweet smell of her scalp as she swayed from side to side, her daughter on her hip. Her heart raced as she thought about Daniel, where he might be. And for the first time since she had known him – since she had seen him standing alone, looking out to the storm over the sea beyond the Otago Peninsula, she had a hideous realisation that the reliable man, the man she took for granted, the man who always came back to her, would one day not exist.

Thirty-Nine

February 2018
Swiss Alps

'THIS IS AMAZING!' yelled Flora, in gay abandon as she sat between her dad's legs.

Udo had gone down first, clutching Sofia in the curved basin of his wiry arms, as he held the leather reins of the wooden sledge and led the way. Udo was a Tony-award winning showtunes songwriter and a demon on the slopes – and since he and Mimi had settled in the mountains to write, hike and ski together, he was a trusted pair of arms around Mimi's goddaughter.

I heard it. I'm sure I heard it.

Olivia wanted to shout ahead to Daniel, to see if he would look around and confirm Flora's rare outburst of happiness and joy, but he was concentrating too hard on the bends of the snowy mountain path; trying to catch up with Udo and Sofia, who was shouting 'WEEEEEE!' all the way down. Mimi brought up the rear on her own wooden sledge, her singsong laugh the soundtrack to this frozen idyll.

There was no one else on the mountain – the runs were closed at the end of a busy day. The chair and ski lifts had shut, and the only people heading down to the picture postcard town at the bottom were the six people on four sledges, weaving their way, with the odd stop to take in the view and nibble on the honey and almond chocolate Udo had packed.

It had been an amazing few days. Olivia was right – they did need it, it *did* do them good, and although she wasn't sure if Flora would have relaxed into her arms down the mountain the way she had her father's, she knew the girls had loved their holiday. They had thrived, skiing under the Matterhorn's majestic gaze, the girls going gung-ho down the mountains. Daniel had been more wary, more fearful of the splendour of his surroundings, but Udo and Mimi taught him to relax just enough to enjoy it.

Olivia was struck by how hard she found skiing, how her coordination was sometimes a little bit off, how she kept misjudging turns and overshooting or falling over – she used to fly down the slopes of Cortina d'Ampezzo, winter after winter, with her father and mothers. Perhaps that was too long ago and she was too rusty, or motherhood had made her cautious and clumsy.

She curved around a bend, hearing Mimi's high laugh still echoing behind her, and saw that Udo and Sofia, Daniel and Flora had pulled up.

Udo was lowering his palm gently as if to say *shhhhhh* and *stop*.

Olivia slowed to a halt and tried to look at what the others had spied in a snow filled glade.

'You see it?' Daniel whispered excitedly.

Olivia shook her head as she struggled to take off her mittens.

'Over there!' said Udo. His piercing blue eyes, bleached by the snow, were locked on the still figure of a deer that had looked up, startled and alert. 'It's a roe deer. The roebucks shed their antlers in November or December – if you look you can see new ones starting to form.'

Mimi came sledging around the bend, her singing suddenly stopping when she saw Udo's stance.

She got off her sledge and quietly walked over; the crunch crunch crunch of the snow under her boots was a satisfying sound to everyone.

'Amazing, isn't it?' she whispered, looking up at her friend.

Olivia smiled back and put her arm around Flora – who didn't even flinch.

'Mummy, I love it!' Sofia whispered, from her position next to Udo, trying not to jump up and down. 'I wish we had deer as a pet.'

'You pretty much do,' Daniel whispered, referring to the muntjac that occasionally danced through their garden.

As they watched the roe deer browse for berries and lichen in the snow, Olivia looked at her daughters and felt a strange concoction of bliss, gratitude and terror.

In a cosy wood-panelled restaurant back in the village, the Messina Bleekers, Mimi and Udo sat at a rectangular table, all eyes on the raclette in the middle. Heady wafts of cheese permeated the room, absorbed in the red curtains that looked like they might have been there in Whymper's time.

Half the diners ate in ski gear: fur-lined jackets slung on the back of chairs, ear mufflers pushed up into the hair above their ruddy cheeks; the other half wore evening wear. It was a bizarre mix, and a world away from Mimi's Brixton, Milan or Melbourne. Olivia loved how contradictory the Swiss Alps were to where she imagined urbanite Mimi would end up – an Australian who loved the tropical heat, settling in the snowy mountains. Olivia loved how thoughtful Udo was compared to the long line of self-centred rock stars Mimi had dated – but how she was happier than she had ever seen her. How contentment oozed out of every bare and mountain-kissed pore.

'Right, so you're coming back then girls? You like skiing?' Mimi asked, carving a sweaty slice from the raclette.

'Try stopping them,' Daniel said, winking at Flora.

'You should come in the summer,' Udo said enthusiastically, his black thermal vest clamped to his sinewy frame. 'The walks we do up towards the Matterhorn and Jungfrau are simply the best.'

Olivia pictured Udo and Mimi, rolling in fields of wildflowers, songsheets and notes fluttering around them as they sipped from pints of creamy Alpine milk, and smiled to herself.

'Oh, can we Mamma?' begged Sofia. Flora suppressed a hopeful and shy smile.

'Well, maybe we can come when your dad's in Russia huh?'

Daniel looked a little disappointed, but agreed it was a good idea.

'Yesssss!' Sofia screwed her little hand into a fist and punched the air.

'Oh you must!' assured Mimi, pulling Sofia into her. 'You girls could even come on your own while your dad's at the World Cup. Give Mummy a little break.'

'We'll sort something!' Olivia said breezily, as she tied her hair up off her face. It was all getting a bit toasty inside the restaurant – raclettes and fondue pots were causing the windows to steam up. 'But this first...'

Olivia raised her glass of sparkling water. She was always the first to raise her glass, whichever coffee shop, restaurant or dining table she sat at. Brain cancer hadn't quashed her love of a toast. 'Thanks so much for having us. Udo, you're a hero – Mimi, I love you and I miss you.'

Mimi smiled, her sparkling eyes welling up.

'Yes thanks guys, it was just what the doctor ordered,' Daniel added, not meaning to be literal. 'It's been amazing.'

Sofia and Flora thrust their glasses of orange juice and lemonade into the centre, Udo, Mimi and Daniel their white wines. As glasses chinked and hands felt fiery over the raclette, Daniel's blissful world suddenly turned grey. He couldn't help noticing the stem of Olivia's glass, shaking in her hand, and with it brought a rattling realisation and a sick feeling of dread.

He'd noticed it when she struggled to do up the clip on her ski helmet on day one; he'd noticed when she was getting a biscuit out of a packet for Sofia yesterday; he'd noticed when she struggled with the simple coordination required for taking off her mittens as they sledged. And he noticed it now, in the cosy cocoon of the restaurant, as joyful cheers and splatters of drink cooled hot hands and swelled hearts.

Cancer-free, he thought, as he pictured the serene face of Dr Okereke as she said it. *For now.*

'Cheers!' the girls laughed, one more loudly than the other.

'*Saluti!*' Olivia said.

'*Prost!*' Udo nodded.

And Mimi didn't say anything. Words failed her. As she looked across the table at Daniel and their eyes met, they both knew they were struck by the same terrible fear.

Forty

December 2006
Cambridgeshire, England

Olivia put a fresh coffee on the workbench, rolled up her sleeves, and looked around the studio. The white tongue and groove walls were pinned with designs, fabric swatches, measurements, collection sheets and numbers. A large slate board had a list of deadlines in order. 'Brief'. 'Sample due'. 'Fits'. 'Red seal'. 'Approved'. 'Shipped'. Another wall was entirely covered in magazine tears and pages photocopied from books, the early inspiration for a second collection, if this first one takes off. A rail of luminescent samples in shades of rose, cream and nude lit up the darker wall. A bench in the middle was covered in rolls of fabric, a sewing machine, a laptop and lamps. Headless mannequins and dressmaker's dummies, in varying states of undress and amputation, lingered happily around the studio. One wore a white toile template, another just a skirt. Olivia's favourite mannequin, which she named Giulia and occasionally spoke to because Giulia had a head, wore Olivia's wedding dress. Her first Olivia Messina London creation.

So much to do!

Olivia had just done the frenetic drive and drop-off of Flora at nursery and felt so excited by what was in front of her, what was to come. She inhaled the aroma of coffee while she waited for it to cool, and put a scratched copy of INXS' *Kick* into the paint-splattered CD player, speckled from past experiments with fabric dyes.

When they bought the Huf Haus, Olivia knew she wanted to turn the garden studio into a workshop, but assumed it would be for sideline projects or clothes for her baby. But a serendipitous encounter with Vaani Bhalla at the V&A got Olivia thinking, and took her down a different path.

While she was on maternity leave, in Flora's first year, she revisited her sketch books from Milan and felt all the emotions again of that time spent at home. Struggling with shunning going out. Ashamed of how few un-adjusted, raw and true memories she had of her life in London; of her life before that. She hated her designs from that period – they felt dark and dated – but they gave her the impetus to start again. Draw through fresher, sober eyes. As a romantic. As a mother. Dresses that would have meaning to the women wearing them.

As her maternity leave came to an end, Olivia didn't want to put Flora in full-time nursery; she didn't want to ask her in-laws to look after Flora as well as Bertie. She wanted to be with her daughter. To create around her daughter. To believe Vaani's vision, that the Olivia Messina label could be something. It could offer women elegant, ethereal and affordable occasionwear that would make them feel as happy as Olivia did in her wedding dress.

Olivia put Flora in nursery two days a week as the Skype

calls with Vaani and the meetings with investors, suppliers, retailers and tastemakers became more regular in London. Vaani registered the company to her address in Belsize Park, and the day after the London bombings, Olivia Messina London secured a £150,000 investment from one of Vaani's fashion finance contacts through *Drapers*.

Through her work at East of Eden, Olivia had learned enough about what happens *after* the drawings. She learned how to cost garments, how the supply chain worked – and how to change the elements that weren't working. She learned how to merchandise a collection and ensure it was stocked in the Carnaby Street store, as well as the department stores who were increasingly taking it on – and she knew how to harness those good relationships with her honesty, her laugh and her charm.

As the investment came in, and Olivia's second baby grew, she finished the designs for a twenty-five-piece launch collection and engineered the patterns. Vaani had been to-ing and fro-ing between London and India, where the intricate threadwork, embellishment and embroidery was to be executed in a small studio in Maheshwar. Olivia had the creative ideas; Vaani the business sense and understanding of margins to make those ideas commercial. To make A Midsummer Night's Dreamy sell.

They planned to start small. Vaani secured a three-month pop-up in Selfridges, and hoped the department store chains and new etailers would take notice and fall for Olivia's whimsical, affordable, cool event dresses that looked like high-end ateliers had made them.

While the first collection was being made, Olivia started working on the next.

'If these sell like I think they will, we can't take our eyes off the ball,' heeded Vaani. 'So many people are asking me about this…'

When Flora was at nursery or in her bed, Olivia was in the garden, cranking up the music and talking to Giulia while she sketched, made toiles, prototypes and designs.

As she surveyed her studio, Olivia took in the soft colours that had started to emerge. Her second collection was feeling more botanical – pale greens and dusky pinks were creeping in like ivy, with subtle botanical embroidery, metallic threadwork and hand-dyed pressed petals on bodices and hems. Perhaps this was a by-product of being in bloom. Phoebe had always said pregnancies were her most creative periods.

'*Tutti bene,* Giulia?' Olivia asked, as she took a sip of coffee. Giulia didn't answer, and Olivia smiled, as she sat down at her workbench, her bump heaving between her legs. She looked through Polaroids of the final twenty-five chosen pieces on models, shot for their first ever lookbook, and felt pure excitement. Soon these pieces would be with the retailers, she would have a new business and a new baby. She felt on the edge of an exciting precipice as she drank her coffee and thought about everything she had to do before her son arrived: check that the collection had been put on the boat. Research tulle suppliers to improve their margins. Look at the CVs Vaani had sent her for the merchandiser they were recruiting. Develop the dimensions and drawings for the second collection; start to think about a third. Get all of Flora's baby clothes out of storage.

She put the photos to one side as she looked at her laptop and listened to the agony and optimism in Michael Hutchence's voice.

Kick.

And Olivia had the sudden and horrific realisation, that she hadn't felt her baby kick for hours.

Forty-One

May 2018
Cambridgeshire, England

'Right, are you sitting down?' The precise and perfunctory voice of Vaani on the other end of the phone had more than a hint of excitement in it, and Olivia was intrigued.

'Well no, I'm walking down the high street, just picking up school shoes for Flora.'

'Urgh, how ghastly.'

Vaani hadn't ever had children, but she had enough nieces and nephews to know that school shoes might just be the most dreadful insult to fashion on the planet.

'I know, I know,' groaned Olivia. 'They're vile. And I have to pay fifty quid for the pleasure, but I couldn't bind her into the old ones for another two months, she's a size seven now like me.'

'Oh, you should have sent her to school in your D&G flats. Those rubberized rivets would fend off the Mean Girls.'

'Don't!' Olivia laughed. 'Anyway, *I'm* too scared to wear

my D&G flats – she's not snaffling them. Look, I'm just at the shop, I'll call you back in a sec…'

'OK well hurry, this is too cool and too important to be usurped by unsightly footwear. Call me right away. I'm pacing the office.'

'OK, will—'

Olivia looked at the screen and realised Vaani had already hung up. She pictured her walking up and down their light and airy office in Camden.

They outgrew Vaani's flat in Belsize Park shortly after the first collection launched in 2007, and moved into an office around the corner from there, where they stayed for ten years. Last year they moved to a converted Georgian building on Arlington Road, spacious enough for a label that had just hired a business development assistant and a head of ecommerce. Olivia Messina London now had twenty employees in the capital, ten in India, and Olivia in her studio in Guildington. Last year's health hiccup and LFW no-show aside, they were booming.

Olivia was so impatient to know Vaani's big news, she hurried into the shop and walked straight to the till.

'School shoes for Bleeker,' she said, while a fizz of excitement danced in her belly. The AW18 collection had gone down a storm in February and industry insiders spoke in happy hushed tones how Olivia Messina's return to health had heralded her best collection yet. The new website was up and running and looking amazing. The right kind of celebrities were wearing Olivia Messina on the red carpet. The checks and balances were all bubbling along buoyantly.

What could it be?

A mousy young woman came back from the storeroom.

'Size seven, yes?'

'That's right.'

She opened the box but Olivia didn't really care for what was inside – they looked ugly online, they looked ugly in the shop – so she waved her hand as if to say 'fine'. At least these would see Flora through to the summer holidays.

'That's just fifty-five pounds please...'

Fifty-five?!

Olivia took out her wallet, paid and looked at the screen of her phone, willing the shop assistant to hurry up.

'Would you like a bag?'

'No thanks, I'll carry the box.'

The phone rang again and Olivia answered instantly.

'I can't wait either – what is it?'

'Hello, Mrs Bleeker?'

'Oh. Sorry,' Olivia said, frowning into her phone and realising from the number on the display that it was the school office calling. 'Yes, that's me. Is everything OK?'

'We've had a bit of an incident.'

A chill ran down Olivia's body, shooting into her legs.

'I'm afraid Sofia has a head injury.'

'A what?'

'A head injury. She's OK, but we have decided to call an ambulance as there is a lot of blood.'

'Oh my god.'

The shop assistant busied herself, stapling a receipt to a piece of paper as she felt the ill ease of the customer.

'She fell over and cut herself on the play equipment at lunchtime.'

'Play equipment?!'

Olivia pushed the shoe box back at the shop assistant and walked out onto the high street.

'She is all right, and she is conscious – we just want you to know so you have the choice whether to come straight to school, or meet Sofia and Miss Cave at A&E. I suppose it depends on where you are...'

Olivia thought of the crowded A&E department in the hospital she had been to for so many appointments in the past year, where people always snaked and smoked outside the door. It was a good twenty minutes away, by car, which was back home on the drive.

'I'm coming,' she said without hesitation, as she broke into a run, out of the shop and into the May sunshine. Running running running. Past banks, bakeries and opticians, her yellow trainers thumping with every horrified step. She ran with the image of Sofia, bleeding from a neat cut above her eyes until the conjured scene became darker. Her head was split open, her bare and pink brain entrails tumbling into the hands of her horrified teacher, her face pale and lifeless, her mouth clamped open.

Olivia ran faster, legs pummelling the pavement as she thought of the dead baby she had held in her arms.

'No Sofia, no Sofia,' she whispered to try to keep rhythm. She had never run before unless she had to. Her breathing was frenetic and laboured.

No Sofia, no Sofia.

'My baby!' she cried, as shoppers turned their heads to look at the maniacal woman pelting down the high street. Olivia wasn't even aware of them. Only that her cries hindered her running now, so she closed her mouth to gain speed, faster than she had ever run in her life.

My baby, my baby.

Panic engulfed her until she could barely breathe. She *had* to get to school before the ambulance did, even though she wanted the ambulance to be there in a flash. She didn't want Sofia to go to the hospital alone, or for Sofia to die alone, without her.

I can't run!

Olivia's legs whirred in a blur, past the pub with scaffolding on the outside, past the park with the water fountains, towards Sofia's school.

My baby.

The image wouldn't go away. Sofia's blue face. A goodbye to Jude in the delivery suite, blood and afterbirth on the floor, and all for what? Sandwiches in a pub – the pub she was running past – after the cremation. He should have been 11 now. He ought to have been at big school with Flora.

Not my baby!

At the far end of the long winding high street was a bridal shop. A black slate love heart hung from the door saying 'By appointment only'. An Olivia Messina London bridal dress hung on a mannequin in the window. Based on the wedding dress Olivia had worn to her own wedding. Her first creation. Her most favourite creation, after her children.

As Olivia ran past the bridal shop, knowing she wasn't even halfway there, one leg buckled, sending her kneecap crashing to the paving slabs, followed by the smash of her arm and cheek. The mannequin wearing her dress looked down on her as she passed out. The phone in her bag buzzed with excitement.

Forty-Two

August 2009
Cambridgeshire, England

'Happy birthday Dad!'

Daniel raised a bottle of Peroni in the pizzeria next door to the bank his dad used to manage. Olivia, Matt and Silvia raised an assortment of glasses and bottles, while Annabel looked out of the window, onto the high street, bored. On the blue banquette side of the table, Flora peered over Bertie's shoulder, to try to fathom what the game on his iPad was all about. But subtle, repeated nudges indicated he wanted to be left in peace.

'Thanks son,' John said, as he stroked his new chisel set as if it were a thing of beauty.

'Happy birthday to you for last month too Olivia!' Silvia raised her wine glass again. 'I don't think we've seen you since, have we?'

'No. But thank you. And for the candle. Did you get my card?'

'Yes, we did love. Did you have a nice birthday? What did you do?'

'Blissfully, nothing!' Olivia laughed.

Silvia smiled back approvingly.

Silvia quietly adored Olivia, ever since Daniel first took her to Elmworth to meet his parents in the summer of 2001. John had fired up his new barbecue set for a family party to celebrate his mother's eightieth birthday, who kept saying unwittingly xenophobic things and asking Olivia questions about 'that Mussolini' as if Olivia's family had known him. But Silvia and John Bleeker were fascinated by Olivia: her upbringing, her family, her job, as if she were some kind of heavenly creature their son had captured in a net.

'What's that type of pasta called that's not twists but curly spirals?'

'Do you celebrate pancake day in Italy?'

'Have you ever been to the Pantheon?'

'Is the Mafia still a "thing"?'

They were always full of questions and wonder for Olivia, and loved how happy she made their youngest son.

Olivia enchanted everyone in the garden that day – apart from Daniel's bigoted grandma – and Annabel, who had barely broken a smile for Olivia, and had gone home claiming she had a migraine.

Eight years, two grandchildren and one deceased grandma later, Silvia's warmth and Annabel's hostility had only blossomed.

Olivia tried to bring Annabel into the conversation – she seemed cut off beyond the noise of Bertie shooting dragons.

'Are you back at work tomorrow?' she asked cheerfully,

hoping to strike up some joy. The most animated Annabel ever got was when she spoke about clients.

'Yeah, can't wait,' she said in a tone so flat that Olivia couldn't work out if she were being sarcastic or not.

'Long summer eh?' Olivia asked conspiratorially, although hers had been delightful. After three busy years of growth and development – Olivia Messina London was on its sixth collection – Olivia had decided to take a month off so she could enjoy Flora's first summer since starting school, so she could rest properly.

'What's the point of being the boss if you don't make the most of it?' Vaani reasoned, sending her off with a promise that they would be fine without her.

Daniel didn't have a football tournament he had to travel to and cover; it wasn't an Olympic year – summers ending in odd numbers were always Olivia's favourite – so he worked normal hours and Olivia would spend days out with Flora at Linton Zoo, Shepreth Wildlife Park or the Fitzwilliam. She took Flora into London a couple of times to see Daddy's office and have lunch with him – but mostly Olivia would tinker in the garden studio, while Flora played Lego on the workbench or dress up her dolls in silk, tulle and ribbon.

Daniel made it home in time to read Flora's bedtime story and kiss her delicate nose goodnight, before sitting on the sofa, holding Olivia tight and trying to reassure her that, this time, it would be OK.

The horror of her second baby's arrival, early and sleeping, was too much to bear. A boy she and Daniel called Jude. His heart had stopped, sometime in the night, before the morning Olivia realised she hadn't felt a kick, at thirty-six weeks.

Olivia had gone back into the house to get her doppler out of the bedside drawer, the one Daniel bought them when she was pregnant with Flora, but she couldn't hear a heartbeat. There was no sound of galloping horses rushing along the beach.

Sometimes I didn't hear it with Flora.

Just silence, as she frantically moved the probe across her distended belly.

The position might not be right.

But Olivia had a terrible feeling, it had been too many hours since she last remembered a kick, so she called Daniel, got in the car and raced to the Rosie. The sonographer waited for Daniel to arrive from London before confirming the news, and the consultant recommended a natural birth, as it would come with fewer complications; increase Olivia's chances of having future children.

'I don't want any more children, I want him!' she cried, but three days later she was induced. The atmosphere was subdued, the birth harrowing. In the delirium of pain, Olivia feared they might take her baby away, they might put him in the bin.

'I MUST HOLD HIM!' she screamed, as she kept pushing through.

The midwives and consultants assured her she could, for as long as she wanted to, and Jude was born, sleeping and silent. A beautiful treasure, his arrival heralded a strange sense of peace over the room, and Olivia held him tight.

'I love you so much, I love you so much,' she kept whispering soothingly, apologetically.

Daniel was encouraged to take photos he didn't want to take and to cut a lock from his baby's dark and bloody hair. A young midwife noted Jude's weight and measurements in a memory booklet. An older midwife asked Daniel to help her make handprints and footprints, holding limp limbs that didn't move.

When Jude was taken to the chapel of rest, Daniel followed him out to the corridor and let out an anguished cry, while Olivia wept into the arms of the silver-haired midwife, who held her firmly until Daniel came back in.

During Jude's funeral Olivia thought if it weren't for Flora she would jump in that furnace with him.

This summer, with the trepidation of growing a life, yet not allowing themselves to enjoy it, to become *complacent*, they slowed down, didn't travel, and met family for simple celebrations, including John's sixty-fifth birthday and Olivia's thirty-fourth.

'Well, I took Friday afternoon off, but that was enough to be honest. What with the Bank Holiday today.' Annabel's mouth barely moved as she talked. Olivia's gaped open in disbelief. She really wasn't sure if Annabel were joking, her sarcastic, caustic manner made it hard to tell. 'The summers are so long,' she complained. 'Especially with His Nibs' school.' She nodded to her six-year-old son, engrossed in shooting dragons. 'Can't wait to get back to work tomorrow to be honest.'

After one long weekend?

Olivia looked at Bertie's wide and mesmerised eyes, lost in a game, and suddenly felt terribly sorry for him. It was his parents' decision to send him to a school where you paid to have long holidays they complained about. His parents' decision to send him to Granny and Grandad's and summer camps instead of taking time off. His parents' decision to joke about what a pain he was to entertain, even for just one Friday afternoon in the entire summer holiday.

Bertie gave Flora another jab with his shoulder and suddenly Olivia didn't feel so sorry for him.

'Erm, Bertie…'

He gave his aunt a petulant stare.

Olivia turned back to the conversation at the adults' end of the table. Silvia was telling Daniel and Matt about a holiday they had booked.

'Thailand, in October… we'll be back in time for half-term…' Silvia nodded reassuringly to Matt and Annabel. They had plans to go to Bangkok. Do a river cruise. Take in some shopping. Visit some temples. The beach. It all sounded wonderful, and goodness knew they deserved it.

Flora slipped under the table, tired of her cousin's prods and shoves, and climbed up at her grandad's feet, to sit on his lap and look at his chisels.

'Hmm, I don't think these are for you my petal!' John chuckled, as he perched Flora in place on his lap. Daniel moved the carpenter's tools out of reach.

'Hey!' protested Bertie. 'He's *my* grandad!'

'Er, he's Flora's grandad too,' chuckled Matt, with a bemused and adoring smile. Bertie slunk under the table, emerging by his grandad's legs, and edged Flora off his lap.

'Now, now…' said John, without too much protest.

Daniel took Flora onto his lap as a waitress brought doughballs and calamari.

'Remember we booked a similar trip for Easter 2005? The tsunami decimated the whole resort.'

'Oh yeah,' remembered Matt.

'Is it the same resort, did they rebuild it?' Olivia asked.

Silvia lifted a doughball with a manicured finger and dipped it gently into a dish of butter.

'No, they never did – we're going somewhere else, the other coastline I think…' Silvia said philosophically, as she took a bite.

'Well, maybe it was for the best,' piped up Annabel to everyone's surprise. The table turned to her, to see if she was about to say something momentous. They could feel it coming.

'That holiday after the tsunami – maybe the first hotel was shonky, maybe it's not as good as the holiday you've booked now. Like with Jude…' Annabel nodded to Olivia's bump.

'*Shonky?*'

'Some things just aren't meant to be.'

Olivia felt a punch to her stomach and a kick from within it as the whole family fell silent.

'Two kids' margheritas?' a chirpy waitress asked.

'Mine!' Bertie shouted.

Forty-Three

June 2018
Cambridgeshire, England

'Sorry Daddy, sorry...' Flora smirked as she slinked into the car, dressed like Dua Lipa with an auburn topknot.

Daniel was so livid he could barely speak. He glared at the car's large digital clock display as he inhaled the smell of fruity booze and cigarette smoke.

Ten past midnight.

'Jesus Flora...' He shook his head as his daughter fumbled with the seat belt, clumsily scrabbling to clunk it into the buckle in the dark, while simultaneously arching her body towards the door so her dad might not tell she was tipsy. That she had smoked five cigarettes while standing in the garden with George Burford-Mason.

Daniel pulled away from the kerb with unusual carelessness, rubbing his chin between changing gears. Flora chewed wildly on minty gum.

'It's just it took me ages to find my jacket. It's a big house. Amelie said she'd put all the coats—'

'Save it!' Daniel shouted, with such rage it startled Flora, pressing her spine into the back of her seat. Her dad never shouted at her, not like that.

They drove from Amelie's house two villages away back home to Guildington in fifteen minutes of tense and stifling silence, Flora waiting, for Daniel to tell her off for drinking – or perhaps he had realised she had been smoking and she couldn't passively blame it on her friends. She concocted excuses as she looked out of the window at the inky summer night through fuzzy eyes, but all of them felt flimsy. She knew her dad was no fool.

They pulled onto the gravel drive in front of the glass house, lights switched off, save for the dull red glow of Flora's lava lamp in her bedroom upstairs. Daniel turned off the ignition as his shoulders slumped.

'I'm sorry, Papa...' Flora conceded.

'Your sister is sleeping up there,' Daniel bowed his head to look up at the house through the windscreen. 'I've practically left her home alone, in the middle of the night, to get you from a party I didn't feel comfortable about you going to. And you kept me waiting forty minutes...'

Flora was surprised; that wasn't the thing she thought he was most angry about – she had thought she was only a few minutes late.

'I said I'd be waiting in the car outside. Eleven-thirty. You knew that.'

'But she's not home alone. Mum's there!'

'Your mother can't look after your sister at the moment. Your mother is very frail. I left two people who aren't capable of looking after themselves home alone in the middle of the night, for well over an hour...' Daniel shook his head.

'I'm sorry Papa. I just lost track of the time and then I couldn't find my—'

'Why does she annoy you so much? Why are you so horrid to her?'

Flora was taken aback, and the feeling of giddiness at having kissed George Burford-Mason on the decking at midnight seeped away as the blood drained from her face. Her mouth gaped open. She felt a little bit sick.

'She's poorly, you know. I thought you might be angry about it, that this was your way of taking your frustration and anger out – on her – but this started before Mamma got sick...'

Flora's fast-sobering eyes welled up.

'She loves you, you know.'

Flora couldn't speak; her bottom lip started to wobble. Daniel grabbed his phone and house keys from the cubby in the middle of the car. 'And she needs your love and kindness – now more than ever. Tomorrow we're going to London for the night; on Monday we get her test results back. She—'

'I DON'T KNOW WHY I DO IT!' shouted Flora, stopping herself from crying by frantically fanning her eyes.

Daniel was shocked by Flora's outburst of honesty and paused, his hand hovering over the silver door handle.

'I know when I'm doing it but I don't know why!'

Startled by the fear and softened by the beauty in his daughter's face, Daniel retreated. They sat crippled in silence for almost a minute, before Daniel spoke.

'Well, can you try to stop yourself next time? We need

to pull together. Can you do that? Can you stop yourself? Please!'

Flora nodded, cheeks flushed with Bourjois, fury, Apple Sourz and shame.

'Great, well let's get to bed then.'

Forty-Four

December 2009
Cambridgeshire, England

'I haven't forgotten you my darling...' Olivia stood next to the young magnolia tree in the icy garden. The moon was lighting up the frost so it sparkled on the grass around it; she and Daniel hadn't taken off their winter coats since coming home, paying the babysitter and putting her in a taxi.

They had been out for an early dinner – pie night at their favourite pub, The Victoria, in the village – before Olivia's 10 p.m. eating curfew ahead of her C-section the next morning. At dinner Olivia told Daniel she would like to visit Jude's tree before bed and Daniel wrapped his hands around Olivia's and pulled them in for a kiss.

They had planted the magnolia in memory of Jude's birth and death, three years ago next week. A forever reminder that he was stillborn but still loved. Now the tree was burgeoning, if not yet blooming – winter was never kind to it – and Olivia stood in front of it, side-by-side with Daniel, holding a small candle. 'You're always in our hearts. You always will be.'

She let out a sigh, like a warm *libeccio* wind raging across the Mediterranean, enveloping Jude's tree with a veil of love.

Daniel rubbed the small of her heavily burdened back, her belly low and distended, and nodded. Flora was upstairs asleep in her bedroom.

'Is there anything you want to say Daniel?'

Olivia turned to him, pained.

'No, no – you always say it best.'

Olivia nodded in agreement and turned back to talk to the tree, to Jude.

'This baby will not replace you... you're always here in our hearts and we will never forget you. We won't, will we Daniel?'

That was what worried Olivia most – apart from tomorrow going hideously wrong – that Jude might be forgotten.

'I didn't beg you to open your eyes because I knew they wouldn't!' Olivia lamented, as if she were apologising.

'It's OK Liv, you did everything right!' Daniel interjected, worried his pregnant wife would get distressed.

'I know. I just wish I knew what those eyes looked like. Whether they were like yours or mine or neither of us. So we could see him and reassure him we loved him. So we could see how lovely his soul was. How lovely it *is*.'

'I think we know how lovely your soul is, Jude,' Daniel said to the tree, and Olivia, cold hands clutching the warm and comforting candle, huddled into his neck. 'We will *never* forget you,' Daniel affirmed, as Olivia nodded against his skin. 'We will always keep your memory and your story alive.'

Forty-Five

June 2018
London

Daniel stepped out onto the busy pavement of Euston Road and scoured it for a taxi among the buses, people carriers and cyclists. None of the black cabs had their lights on, although it was hard to tell in the reflection of the summer morning sunshine.

He let out a sigh, and through the blur of traffic, Daniel could see the Premier Inn on the other side of the road. He looked up to the window of the room he stayed in the night before the bombs went off.

Daniel had missed the last train back to Guildington and got the cheapest, cleanest hotel option he could find. A £79 Premier Inn room within stumbling distance of the station. He'd got to his room, eaten two custard creams from the packet by the kettle (to soak up some of the alcohol) and flopped on the bed, passing out in his clothes.

He woke to beeps of traffic, the anger of a hot July morning, the jostling of people onto buses and towards the tube. He thought he'd only been asleep for five minutes but suddenly it was morning – his head was thumping – so he showered and put yesterday's clothes back on before heading back to work. As he walked past King's Cross station he didn't realise four men with explosive devices in backpacks were congregating there.

Daniel had already got to the newsroom in Farringdon when PA and Reuters newswires came through, talking about a power surge over near Liverpool Street.

The picture editor called from Aldgate East to say it was more serious than that and she was going to stick around to see what she could find out. One colleague, half deafened from being on the tube between King's Cross and Russell Square, stumbled into the office shell shocked and barely able to speak, but he was too scared to go home. Daniel started to worry about his junior sports reporter – who was always at her desk with a soy latte and some bircher muesli by 9 a.m. – and was relieved when she burst in shortly after 10 a.m., saying she had seen the bus explode on Tavistock Square, and had run for her life.

As the vernacular changed from 'power surge' to 'terror attack', and injuries became fatalities, Daniel desperately tried to get through to Olivia at home, to let her know he wasn't one of them, but the landlines weren't working; the mobile networks were down.

He looked across the traffic blurring between him and the Premier Inn and remembered that day. The panic of the days that followed. Fifty-two lives taken, almost 800 injured. A terrified wife at home.

'Taxi!' he shouted, as one driver set a passenger down outside the British Library, but it was too far away, someone else jumped in first. He looked back up at the grey blackout liner behind the inoffensive hotel room curtain, drawing a line under the memory, wondering how he was going to get through today.

Daniel and Olivia had stayed in a different sort of hotel last night, something more comfortable. A plush room with a view of St Pancras' peaks. Daniel wanted a comfortable bed and a bounteous buffet breakfast for his wife, to see if that would pique an appetite in Olivia. Her frame had become so thin since her fall, he worried about her lack of strength, her 'bouncebackability' as they called it in sport, but he was sure she could. He'd seen those strong thighs, twisting and jiving with a drag queen on a speaker podium in Sydney; he'd seen them straddle him on steamy nights at home and on holidays; he'd seen them birth three babies. He knew Olivia had the strength in her to get better.

'Taxi!'

Olivia still wasn't interested. She'd only nibbled on a corner of brioche to humour Daniel. Her lack of interest in food was as alien to Olivia as it was to him; she had always tucked into whatever was in front of her. But that moment Olivia had hit the ground running, her desire for cannoli and brioche, for fig tart and ravioli, evaporated into the concrete.

'Taxi!' bellowed Daniel, knowing how ridiculous it was, that drivers would never hear him. They stopped on a hand gesture or a whim.

Daniel looked at his watch. They had half an hour to get from the hotel to the appointment, only a mile away, but it wasn't walkable. He should have been flying to Russia today, to cover the build-up to the World Cup, but he didn't want to be away from Olivia and the girls, not until they knew more, so he'd sent out the deputy sports editor alongside the chief football correspondent.

If the results go our way, I'll go out for a game or two. Moscow or Ekaterina.

A taxi finally pulled up and Daniel waved through the glass wall, to the square sofa on the other side of it, where Olivia was sitting, leaning on a metal frame in front of her. She propped herself up onto it as Daniel spoke to the driver, her thin shoulders hiking up like a V around her shrunken neck. Olivia didn't look tall anymore.

With the frame in front of her she slowly walked out. Her trousers loose, her feet bony, and the taxi driver waited patiently, meter on, for her to get in with Daniel's help.

'Queen Square please mate,' he said, as he lay the metal frame on the floor of the black cab and arranged their legs around it before closing the door with a hefty pull. He looked at Olivia and gave her a reassuring smile, while squeezing her thigh and noting that it must be thinner than Sofia's now.

'So we've had a look at the MRI and CT scans. And I'm afraid, as suspected, there is a new tumour. Several actually.'

Olivia and Daniel sat on plastic chairs in a long thin office within the redbrick walls of the National Hospital for Neurology & Neurosurgery, while consultant neurosurgeon Mr Greene leaned against a table strewn with piles of papers. Greene was flanked by two doctors perched on desks. Three wise men, their faces drawn, as they did their best to look Olivia and Daniel in the eye.

She missed the handsome doctor from Ibiza, with a grey beard and a sparkle in his warm brown eyes, and almost wanted to laugh when she remembered how beautiful he was, how much easier this all was back then. How she didn't understand what Mr Greene was saying.

My girls.

Daniel wanted to hit him, for failing at trying to be nice about it when this was news he delivered every single day.

Actor cunt.

He did have his most sincere face on.

A foppish younger surgeon who Olivia imagined had a high-achieving wife propped himself between stacks of papers on Mr Greene's left. His face was one of sympathy and apology. Another medic with a bald head found some space to Mr Greene's right. His face was so indistinguishable Daniel and Olivia knew that they would never remember it. It was all such a blur.

Where is she? Where is Okereke?

Olivia inhaled a long breath and closed her eyes.

This isn't happening.

Daniel tried to squeeze Olivia's hand but his was shaking and clammy and he knew it wouldn't be calming at all, so they sat side by side not touching like schoolchildren trying to pay attention. He ruffled his hair and looked at the consultant accusatively.

'But Dr Okereke said... we were told in January...' the words wouldn't come out. 'What treatment plan do you have then?'

His question was aggressive. He still wanted to punch the surgeon in the face.

She said they'd got it all out.

'I'm afraid, with these types of tumour, and with the location of them… it's not always possible to operate. Ergo, we won't at this stage.'

'At this *stage*?'

Daniel's aggression turned to hope.

The surgeon read the situation. As the most experienced brain surgeon in the country, he had led hundreds of conversations like these.

'It's not that we're not bothering to treat your wife Mr, er, Messina. It's that we can't. I'm terribly sorry. There are multifocal glioblastomas and they're very delicately placed, some in the very centre of your wife's brain.'

'*You* said – Dr Okereke said – she was cancer-free. Was she fucking joking?'

'Daniel…' Olivia put a hand on his arm.

'No. She – Mrs Messina – you *were* cancer-free then. These are very aggressive and very fast-growing cells.'

A thick silence hung in the room, a question hanging over the diagnosis that Daniel desperately needed to know the answer to. But Olivia didn't want to ask.

'What about chemo?' he asked. 'You said at an earlier meeting that chemo might be an option down the road. Is this the time for chemo?'

'We have discussed this, my colleagues and I – and we don't think your wife is strong enough or fit enough for chemo at the moment.'

She can get fit. I'll force-feed her if I have to.

'Are you saying you would turn her down for it?' Daniel felt so agitated, like a frustrated toddler banging at a wall to be understood, he wanted to cry.

Mr Greene looked grave. Like he was searching his brain for diplomacy rather than a solution.

'I'm not sure it would help at all.'

'You're not sure or do you know? Can she have it or not?'

'I would say...' He stroked his neck and turned to Olivia. 'That as long as you are able to walk into this building yourself and ask for chemo, you can have chemo.'

'I can't walk anywhere at the moment by myself,' said Olivia, almost laughing, as if this surreal conversation wasn't about her.

He knows that, the cunt.

'We'll get you fit enough, my love,' Daniel said defiantly, almost to spite the medics. 'Do some physio. I'll cook, we'll get your weight back up. Get your mums over.'

The young doctor with the floppy hair wanted to give Daniel a hug but couldn't.

'Get you well enough for chemo, we can do it.'

Olivia let out a sigh of submission.

'Oh. If you think so.'

The doctors said nothing. The one with the blurred face looked down at the floor. Maybe that's why Daniel and Olivia would never really remember him – he wasn't even there. He hadn't said anything. Just observed. Maybe the Grim Reaper doesn't wear a hood and a cloak. Maybe he's so bland and nondescript, people don't see death looming at all.

Forty-Six

December 2009
Cambridge, England

Olivia lay on the operating table looking up at the ceiling. The plinky plonk opening chords of Florence + The Machine's 'Dog Days Are Over' made her almost rise off the slab in elation. Daniel was in scrubs next to her. The heartbeat was strong. She would never have to go through labour again after she begged her midwife and consultant not to make her.

The fear of it had been plaguing her dreams increasingly as her pregnancy progressed. Jude's face as he lay still, in her arms. She used the doppler most nights just to check. She had spent a restful if nervous summer, not quite believing this day would come.

'*Please* can I have a C-section?' Olivia pleaded with the consultant obstetrician, a thin man with a translucent face and cloud of white hair. 'My baby is due on the day my son died. I can't go through that again.'

Mr Kristiansen pored over the paperwork. There hadn't been any explanation as to why Jude's heart stopped beating, but he assured Olivia it wasn't due to her work, or Flora's rambunctiousness. It wasn't bad nutrition or that she didn't sit down enough. It wasn't Olivia's penance for a period of creativity. After short consideration, Mr Kristiansen agreed.

'Yes, fine,' he said, reading the fire and fear in Olivia's eyes, and booking her in for a week before the due date.

The weeks waiting, beyond thirty-six when Jude had died, were the hardest. Every night Olivia went to sleep she feared her baby would stop kicking, even though Sofia barely stopped doing cartwheels, even in her tummy.

The day finally arrived, and Olivia and Daniel were at hospital at 8 a.m. as instructed. They hadn't found out the gender this time. Olivia didn't know how she'd feel if she were told she were having a boy.

The anaesthetist spoke softly by Olivia's ear. Telling her what he would be doing to Olivia's spine and how it might feel. He asked her if she could feel a cold spray on her thigh, her tummy, her shoulder and she said she couldn't. She didn't feel the incision or the ripping of her placenta. She didn't feel the violent tear as Mr Kristiansen pulled her apart. Daniel winced as he watched the consultant's face as he tugged.

Olivia didn't feel that 'washing up in your stomach' sensation she had been warned about.

All she felt was a strange sense of calm. That this was going to be OK.

The dog days are over.

As Mr Kristiansen lifted Sofia out, screaming and crying and bloody and blue, the silver-haired midwife who had held onto Olivia three years before cheered, 'A girl!', and she placed Sofia onto Olivia's chest. She was moving. Crying.

Limbs flailing. Her swollen and scrunched face put out by the interruption, the cold room and the stark lights.

Olivia didn't think this clinical birth would be the one she enjoyed the most. A healthy baby, coming into the world to the soundtrack of her pregnancy.

'A girl!' Daniel marvelled, looking at their pale waxy daughter – her hair not red like Flora's; dark but more abundant than Jude's – as if she were a thing of magic. Olivia held Sofia's naked body against her clammy cold chest and cooed. She had an impish look about her, a funny face. Olivia stroked her nose and inhaled the bliss of relief as Daniel cradled them both and cried.

'Girls! My girls!'

'Flora's going to adore her,' Olivia said.

Daniel laughed.

'Our girls...' he said, as he grinned to himself, thinking about a life outnumbered by women, knowing he was the luckiest man on the planet.

Forty-Seven

July 2018
Cambridgeshire, England

'Do you want another blanket? It's getting chilly...'
Jim stood wielding an assortment of throws he'd
gathered from the various chairs and patches of lawn they
were dotted on all over the garden, tearing apart his sons'
teddy bears' picnic as he went along.

'Shh, don't tell them it was me...' He winked at Olivia,
who lay on a lounger, her legs bound in striped merino wool,
a chunky oversized snood enveloping her jagged shoulders.
'No thanks, I'm comfortable.'

As the late afternoon sunshine lit the corn in the field
beyond the garden, Olivia sat still, watching a tennis ball
rise – followed by the top of a child's head as they leapt to
catch it.

She looked through her large sunglasses and didn't move;
she was mesmerised by the playful peekaboo limbs of her
daughters and their friends.

Wesley's tanned arm sprung up as he released a ball with
power, into the air, each time higher than the last; more of a

challenge for the children to catch. He was leading a game between Flora, Sofia, Elliot and Finley – his and Jim's twin sons who had recently turned ten.

It had been a beautiful afternoon – apart from the wasps – but they had spiralled away, drunk on apple juice from the fallers and ice cream detritus from the teddy bears' picnic, back to their nests to take cover, and now the soft evening sun was the colour of nostalgia as the cornfield was lit by a deep and gentle glow.

The Beck De Boers had come up from London for Olivia's birthday, to bring some distraction and cheer. Wesley packed a feast big enough for a *Bake Off* finale, Jim brought the flowers, booze and giant water guns. They were both terribly worried about Daniel and held him in a triangular huddle when they arrived, all three of them trying not to cry.

Flora, Sofia, Elliot and Finley all got along well – the boys were feral and funny, climbing trees, doing silly impressions of the adults, bundling in a ball and rolling away in it when their rough and tumble went a bit far. The girls loved their get-togethers, even if boys could be annoying sometimes. But Elliot and Finley gave Flora permission to unleash her inner roar when she wanted to be boisterous; Sofia was their biggest fangirl and loved to play 'red panda rescue' with Finley during rare moments of calm. Their reunions were fun and exhausting, and as long as Wesley was around, the chaos was controlled. Olivia listened to his instruction from the field but couldn't see his face, and imagined him to be a wonderful teacher.

'Have you had a good birthday?'

Olivia nodded. It would have been perfect, were she not

terribly worried for Daniel too.

'You?'

'It's not my birthday.'

Olivia turned her head and rolled her eyes.

'Have you had a good day?'

'Beautiful,' Jim sighed sadly, as he slunk down on the lounger alongside her. 'Budgie up!' he said with a sparkle in his wide blue eyes.

'Oh come on, I haven't said that for ages!'

She shuffled along a tiny bit and curled on her side facing the field, Jim mirroring the zigzag of her form so he could hug into her. He wrapped his arms around her shoulders, throwing himself onto her like an additional blanket.

'I don't think they have much longer,' Olivia said, looking to the looming shadows.

'That ball is fluoro, the boys will be playing at midnight if they can,' affirmed Jim. 'Although I'm not sure Wes has much more staying power.'

'Sofia is so tired.'

Daniel was inside, clearing another round of the plates in the kitchen in case anyone got a second wind for birthday cake or fancied cheese and crackers.

'Anyone for tea?' called his distant voice.

'Ooh bloody yes,' whispered Jim, almost punching the air, before hollering, 'Please! I'll come help you!'

Olivia nodded but couldn't muster up the energy to shout.

'Olivia too!'

'Me three!' shouted Wesley from the field. He hadn't heard the question but guessed what it was from Jim's enthusiasm.

Olivia pushed her sunglasses up on her head, before rolling to her other side, to face Jim. Her moves were cumbersome and strained.

'How do you think he's doing?' she asked, acute eyes piercing him.

Jim knew what she meant.

'As well as anyone could. I think...' Even with a lowered voice, Jim's Welsh diction was crisp. 'He's seemed genuinely happy at times today, fussing around the birthday girl.'

Olivia gave a mournful smile.

'It's a strange thing. Daniel always puts such significance on my birthday. I think because of the five we spent apart more than the eighteen we've spent together. My birthday is such a big deal to him.'

'Do you think?'

'Yes. And it's so sad.'

Jim looked away, to the field, hoping not to make Olivia sad. Hoping she wouldn't say what he thought she was going to say.

'He's not understanding that it will be my last.'

'Don't say that,' Jim said, his voice faltering, as he looked back at Olivia and frowned.

'It's funny because Daniel has always been more cautious, more negative than me, but he's flipped. He thinks this is fixable.'

Jim shook his head.

'People change their behaviour during times of extreme stress. When life is turned on its head. Except for you...' Jim stroked a strand of Olivia's hair and tucked it behind her ear. 'You've always been a badass.'

Olivia smiled.

Flora came out of the field, cheeks flushed and legs bare in denim hotpants, and Olivia and Jim both felt relieved their conversation had reached a natural finish. They smiled up at Flora.

'They never stop!' she said, nodding to Sofia and the boys in the field with Wesley, colluding with the adults.

'*They're* the reason I turned grey, Flora. You won't remember – but I used to be gloriously flaxen-haired...' Jim winked, as he got up from the sun-lounger and tucked his Wayfarers into his pocket. 'I'll go help Daniel with the tea.' He kissed the top of Olivia's head before he walked up the garden into the house.

Flora, a bronzed picture of health and vitality looked down at her mother, who she was the same height as now, but Flora's limbs were growing stronger while Olivia's appeared to shrink, and her youthful smile fell into a frown as she studied her mother's weak frame. Flora opened her mouth, as if she were about to admonish her. But it hung open, half in horror.

'What's the matter, *tesora*?' Olivia asked, making a shield over her brow, even though the sun had gone down. Flora looked at her, lost for words, as if she had been petrified and couldn't speak. Her bottom lip began to tremble as she was utterly speechless. 'Darling? Are you OK?' Flora shook her head defiantly, as if speaking would reveal a secret, and clambered onto the sun-lounger, mirroring her mother's form before grasping her around the ribcage and clutching onto her for dear life. She threw one gawkish leg over Olivia's, and cried.

'I'm so so sorry...' Flora sobbed into the blankets and the bones of her mother. 'I don't want you to... to go away...

I love you… I'm sorry…' Her cries were muffled in the hair and flesh between them, but Olivia heard, as her heart swelled, and shrank with every beat as she wrapped her jagged arms around her daughter's back and pulled her in.

'I know you do. I love you too. So much. So so much. Never forget that.' They clutched each other for a few minutes both sobbing as quietly as they could so as not to worry Sofia in the field, Olivia crying at the thought of all she might miss, Flora desperately not wanting to let go. Olivia caressed the baby hair at Flora's temples. 'Don't be frightened,' she whispered. 'You will be all right. I love you, I love you, I love you.'

'Tea's up!' shouted Jim, as he and Daniel walked through the open doors of the back of the glass house, each carrying a tray.

'Right,' said Daniel, looking down at his offering. 'I can't make it look as pretty as Wes, but I've cobbled together a cheeseboard. I *think* the flowers are edible…'

Forty-Eight

August 2012
London

In a sandy play area in a corner of the Olympic Park, the morning sun poked between pillowy white clouds, lighting up their huddle within the boundary of laurel bushes. Daniel's arm was slung across Olivia's shoulder on the bench next to him as she ate black cherries from a brown paper bag, sandwiched between their thighs.

'Does it feel like a pilot's holiday?'

They sat watching their daughters play on the wood and rope climbing frame, set in an enormous sand pit in front of them. Flora was helping Sofia scale the stairs of the slide, before sending her down and meeting her at the bottom to rapturous applause and cherry-stained giggles.

'A pilot's?'

'You know, when you're doing what you normally do. Not so special.'

Daniel rubbed his eyes. He had spent most of the past two months at the Olympic Park, with regular site visits before that. Writing about the preparations. The budgets.

The selections. Whether the stadium would be finished on time. It reminded him of reporting on the Millennium Wheel for the *Elmworth Echo* – and the local engineer who had helped raise it. Now Daniel was sports editor for BBC Online – having wanted to transition from print to digital, as many of his peers were – and had spent much of the past few months being led around different facilities within the Olympic Park on press tours. The launch of the aquatic centre, the velodrome, the Orbit. The big unveiling of the athletes' village, the state-of-the-art press area, the futuristic amenities and family friendly playparks and garden spaces. He'd pored over press releases and interviewed the chairman of the organising committee what felt like a thousand times. Asking tricky questions yet hoping to get behind the once-in-a-lifetime celebration of sport that was coming to *his* country. On *his* watch. He'd studied the schedules. Had the artistic notes on the opening ceremony and watched the petals gracefully lit in Thomas Heatherwick's flame cauldron. He'd been at the Olympic Stadium and done live online reporting of Super Saturday.

And now he was here, as a punter, a father. With his arm around his wife, not having to think about work or press conferences as he watched his daughters play. Although Olivia had a point: if he were honest, it was a little hard to shake the feeling he should be dashing across the site for his next story.

'No, it's lovely,' he said, gazing at Flora, who was directing her sister to walk along a beam and leap onto wooden posts at the end of it, as if she were a show dog at Crufts.

'That's it Sofsof! Good girl,' Flora applauded, as she rubbed her sister's tummy.

'Anyway, we'll use the loos in the press centre, there has to be some perks to having spent more time here than at home this year. I don't mind it being a pilot's, or indeed a busman's, holiday. Not if you don't.'

'I don't mind. This is lovely. I just wish I knew it was so lovely before today. I would have pictured you here more happily.'

'Maybe if you expected it to be cool, it wouldn't be when you actually got here.'

'Or maybe it's not that lovely, but rather this moment in time is.' Olivia gestured to the girls and then pretended to take a photo of the scene in front of her, as she had on the Otago Peninsula, making a box with her fingers and a clicking sound.

'Yeah maybe...' mused Daniel, thinking about all the not-so-lovely hours he'd spent in the Olympic Park. Olivia dissolved her imaginary camera and grabbed another handful of cherries.

'You know I think if I died tomorrow, I would be happy.'

Daniel looked aghast.

'Don't say that! You're just 37!'

'No, obviously. And I never want to leave the girls or you. I just mean that if I die tomorrow I would die a happy woman. A fulfilled woman.'

'Really?' Daniel didn't understand it.

But what about...?

Olivia knew what he was thinking. Being fatherless. Sonless. The hard times.

'Yes, really. I have all that I could want in life Daniel. We got very lucky, to find each other. I adore you and you adore me. Even though you can be a bit boring about football sometimes. But I have two healthy daughters – and two healthy mothers. I have the dream career I wanted. I genuinely think I am the luckiest woman on the planet. Too lucky perhaps.'

Daniel looked scared as Olivia turned to him and put cherry-stained fingers to his brow.

'Don't be so frightened, Daniel, that you forget to stop and enjoy it.'

Olivia nodded to their daughters. Flora, long-limbed like her mother. Sofia, clumsy and clambering, a jovial sparkle in her eyes as she held out her arms, entrusting her big sister to lift her into the swing.

'I am enjoying it.'

'Good.' She untangled a cherry stone from her tongue and put it in the paper bag. 'Then kiss me and tell me where the posh toilets are. I need the loo.'

Forty-Nine

August 2018
Cambridgeshire, England

'Right, I've dropped Flora in Cambridge, Sofia is at drums – shit, I've got to remember Mr Spicer's cheque when I pick her up, that's three weeks now... and I'm going to quickly prep that broccoli and kale bake. Then I can put it in the oven while I get Sofia... the three of us can eat lunch when I get back.' Daniel nodded to the little coffee table he had bought and put by the window, with three bean bags dishevelled around it, so he, Sofia and Flora could eat some of their meals at the same time as Olivia ate hers, from the overbed table he'd bought from the mobility shop in Guildington.

Olivia winced and looked out of the large, triangular bedroom window, that went all the way from the floor to the high, pitched roof. One pane was angled open in its deep grey frame to let the air in. It had been a long and sweltering summer – June and July had been consistently sunny, and although August had brought some normality to British summertime and the rains had started and the temperature dropped, the field beyond their garden looked parched and barren. A kestrel hovered over what Olivia assumed was a field mouse.

Daniel plumped up the pillow behind Olivia and noticed her nose, still crumpled.

'Did you not like the bake last time I made it?'

'It was OK. A bit... earthy.'

Daniel looked perplexed. He'd been quite proud of it.

'I thought it was nice. And it's packed with manganese and sulforaphane. Remember the article I showed you about sulforaphane inhibiting histone deacetylase?'

'No.'

'Well, cruciferous veg are *packed* with it.'

Olivia's eyes stayed firmly on the kestrel, while Daniel kissed her nose to smooth out the creases of aversion.

'I'd better get on if I'm going to get this in the oven before twelve. Can I get you anything?' Daniel rolled up the sleeves of his raglan top. 'What do you need?'

'I need a poo.' Olivia looked back at Daniel with a heavy sigh. 'And I don't want you to take me to the toilet.'

'It's fine.'

'No, it isn't.'

She glanced back at the kestrel as it made its dive.

'I tried to go earlier, when the carers were here, but I couldn't.'

'I'll take you now.'

'No, you won't. I'll wait for them to come back later. I'll hold it.'

'They don't come back on Saturday afternoons, remember?'

Olivia shook her head. She couldn't remember what day

of the week it was, they all blurred into one at the moment.

'They won't be here until tomorrow morning, with the hoist for your bath.'

Olivia shook her head gently.

'Seriously my love, let me take you. You can't hold it in, it'll make you sick.'

'I *am* sick.'

'Well, I'll leave you in there – just hold the grips on the new surround and shout when you need me to—'

'No!' Olivia snapped. 'I'm not having you wipe my arse!'

Daniel slumped and sat in the space on his side of the bed and put his fingertips on his closed eyelids.

'Save me some dignity, Daniel.'

He opened his eyes and put one hand on Olivia's shin. He stroked it, longing for the muscles that used to hug the bone.

'I'm sorry, my love. I just don't want you to be uncomfortable.'

'I know.'

Olivia put her palm on top of Daniel's hand.

'You know, Linda – the nice carer with the helmet hair…?'

'Yeah…'

'It was her this morning, while you were at swimming. She told me a space has come up at the hospice.'

'The hospice?' Daniel rubbed his chin with his free hand.

'She suggested I might be more comfortable there.'

'Do you want to be there?'

Olivia shot Daniel a look as if to say *of course not.*

'Sorry,' he added.

'She said it doesn't have to be terminal, some people go there for respite, just for a few weeks, so their families have a rest, so you could relax knowing that I was being looked after twenty-four-seven.'

'You are being looked after twenty-four-seven. I'm under no pressure to go back to work.'

'I know that... But look at everything you're doing. Running around after the girls – their swimming and music lessons, all their parties and playdates – all you're doing for me. It's too much.'

'It isn't.'

'And you could visit day and night if you wanted to. St Margaret's is lovely. Remember when the girls sang there?'

Daniel nodded but couldn't speak. He'd seen what the men and women looked like in the common room as they watched the Guildington Primary School choir sing 'Time After Time' when Flora was in Year 6 and Sofia was in Reception. The anaemic faces and thin chests. The vacant eyes while they tried to take in uplifting rousing songs the children had diligently learned. Those sick people didn't look like they'd be ever leaving St Margaret's.

Daniel and Olivia sat on the bed, her half under the sheet, him on top of it, holding hands, not saying a word, looking into each other's eyes in desperation, until a jolly beep sounded from the washing machine downstairs.

'I'll make the pasta bake when I get back, I'd better get that washing on the line first.'

A dejected Daniel kissed Olivia on the forehead, got up, and sloped towards the bedroom door, where he stopped, turned back, and leaned against the thin width of it, almost hugging it.

'Cheque for Mr Spicer,' he said to himself quietly.

'So sexy.'

'Me? Or Mr Spicer?'

'You. Look at you. So sexy, looking all mean and moody in the doorway.'

Daniel tried to smoulder, but still looked a little harangued.

'I love you, Daniel Bleeker.'

'I love you too.'

Fifty

'Go!' whispered a voice in her ear. It was forthright and commanding, like Vaani's, except it was laced with a comfort and reassurance that tended to evade her partner's stringent tones. This voice was genderless, its urge gentle. Like Zephyr holding Aura so she could send Venus to shore on a gentle breeze. A Botticelli. A blow. Encouraging Olivia to step out from the shadows.

Olivia stood behind a grand column, peeping through a gap between a doorframe and its large door to a grand marble-floored museum entrance, where an audience applauded, gasping and buzzing and tweeting about the most talked about show of Fashion Week. Olivia Messina London's A/W 2015 collection, her first showing at London Fashion Week, or anywhere, after a steady rise from independent upstart to coveted couture.

It can't be Vaani.

Vaani had already taken her seat in the front row alongside Anna Wintour and Alexa Chung. She dashed there just as the last sheer sequin was being stitched onto a Puerto Rican model's ruched shoulder.

Olivia looked back to the chamber behind her. The aftermath of chaos. Rails of clothes. Boards pinned with style sheets and call sheets and beauty notes. Makeup artists with their brushes in their belts like weapons, chatting among themselves now their job was done. Puzzled, Olivia looked back through the gap in the door, waiting for the raised hand of her artistic director, a figure in black at the back of the room, to call her out for her final bow.

'Go!'

There it was again. Perhaps it was the unidentifiable voice of one of the many production coordinators, dressed in black jumpers and trousers, with headsets around their ears. These invisible women and men had helped turn Olivia's vision into a *show*.

And what a show it was.

Twenty-five models wearing 108 pieces, floated down the steps and into the grand museum entrance like a dream. Darkly romantic and deliciously decadent, dresses, skirts and tops sailed in synchronicity, the cream, dusky pink and dove-grey hues blurring into a whirl. Some of the models had pre-Raphaelite hair like Olivia – Vaani always thought she was the best poster girl for the brand – others had short crops and severe cheekbones. A model from South Sudan wore the only white dress of the collection – a flirtation with bridalwear from a label inspired by a wedding dress – with a haughty beauty, the white fabric billowing against her beautiful black skin. The last of the dresses streamed down the catwalk, almost in slow motion.

'It is time,' the voice echoed calmly.

I know that voice!

Olivia felt an encouraging hand press on her shoulder blade and turned around to see the face of her father, wearing one of his smart suits, his smile warm and charming. Her nerves dissipated. All she felt was reassurance. That she was ready.

Go!

Olivia emerged through the arched doorway and walked down the stone steps to great applause. A crowd on its feet. As the claps echoed, she looked up to the ceiling, cathedral like all the way to the sky, and felt startled by the space. Swamped by the expanse. Her size seven feet suddenly seemed tiny, as each stiletto echoed on the stone step she descended.

In front of her, the models were standing in formation, the shape of a V from the back of the room fanning out. Elegant hands clapping the creator as she strode the mosaic and marble floor.

Olivia looked to her right and saw faces, every one of which she recognised. Her staff, her contemporaries, her peers. Some faces from fashion school; others from Milan. Some were style influencers and tastemakers, other people she had encountered in a distant time in her past.

She looked to her left and saw Vaani, Mimi and Udo, clapping in slow motion, turning to each other and smiling. She saw Jim Beck and Wesley De Boer, leaning into him, style notes in hand as they gave a hearty and rounded applause. She saw her mothers, beaming. Nancy's neat hair shaking with every proud cheer. Maria the back-room seamstress, never before having attended a show, standing on her Dolce & Gabbana heels and shouting something Olivia couldn't hear. Maria's mouth moved slowly, but Olivia knew the pride of those Italian shapes. She wondered if Maria knew her husband was backstage, and looked in puzzlement for a second, wondering if she should tell her.

Further down the row, as Olivia approached the end of her long walk, and the models started to step in to congratulate her, she saw Daniel, a reverence in his adoring smile, peace in his face, as Sofia curled into his chest, tired from her big day out in London. They'd been to Buckingham Palace and the Science Museum en route to Mummy's show, and Olivia could see fatigue in those flushed cheeks and heavy lids, as Sofia sat up and looked at her mother longingly. On the other side of Daniel, beautiful Flora, looking as she did when she was ten, her soulful eyes studying her mother.

Always a wise and cynical soul.

Olivia looked at Flora and saw the fear in them as she clapped.

It's OK. It's OK.

Flora smiled, closing her lids to strangle her tears as she rested her head on her father's arm.

It's OK.

At the end of the catwalk, as the swirling fabrics came together around her in a whirl of applause, lights flashed and images were captured. And Olivia Messina's first catwalk show was filed away in the archives of one woman's brain for ever.

Part three

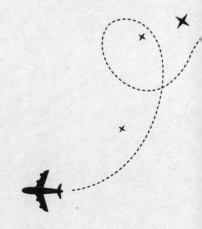

Fifty-One

September 2018
Cambridgeshire, England

'Go,' Olivia whispered softly, a peace washing over her pale face. Her freckles had almost been swallowed by her sallow skin; a blur of grey dots receding into the angles around her brow and cheekbones.

Fraser hadn't heard Olivia speak for days, and he looked at Daniel to see if he had registered it.

Of course he did.

Everyone sat up a little, from their position around the bed, and focused on her. 'Olivia Messina', said the red writing on a white board in a fat script above her. They looked at each other, stunned to have heard her speak in the little huddle of the small room. Olivia had a private room now, one of the rooms the St Margaret's Hospice staff saved for when they knew it was getting close.

Daniel squeezed Olivia's hand. It had been resting in his, cool and still, for hours.

'What's that, my love?'

'Go. It's time to go.' Her whisper was barely audible.

Daniel and the women around him poised their heads, sharpened their ears, to ensure they had heard it correctly.

'No!' bellowed Flora, slumping onto her mother's arm. 'Don't go!' she cried.

Fraser quietly let himself out of the room. His final checks and measurements noted. The apothecary's cart had nothing for Olivia Messina anymore, so he closed the door softly behind him, returned to the nurse's station and gave his colleagues a nod.

'Can you hear me, my love?' Daniel said hopefully, as he leaned in and brushed a wave of hair from her face, tucking it behind her ear. 'Flora is here, and Sofia. And your mothers.'

'Yes, hello darling,' said Nancy, softly. Maria couldn't speak.

Sofia yawned, not registering the severity of the situation, of her father desperately clutching and scrambling for something.

Nancy pushed her glasses up her nose and Maria cast her knitting aside, stifling a quiet sob, as they repositioned themselves around the head of the bed, Nancy stroking Olivia's cold, pale forehead while Maria recited prayers under her breath.

'We're here,' confirmed Nancy.

Daniel took Olivia's hand in his again and squeezed it tight.

'I've written it. I've written it up!'

Daniel hoped his enthusiasm, his swell of pride, would buy him a few more minutes. That it would bring comfort to Olivia, who opened her eyes, rolled her head slightly, and looked deep at him. The colour was there, but the fire had gone.

'I've finished it. The story you wanted me to write. For the girls.'

Daniel didn't say that there was one terrible part he hadn't yet written. He had hoped so hard that he wouldn't have to. But he knew now, and wanted Olivia to know that he had been writing, night and day, every minute he wasn't with her, to honour the task she had set him just a few weeks ago.

'I've written it up.'

Olivia studied Daniel as he clung onto her hand. He smiled back sweetly, encouragingly, desperate for her not to see the heartache in his eyes, the fear that was ripping him apart.

'Are you the torchbearer?' she asked, her teeth protruding through a parched and hollow mouth.

'It's me, Daniel.' His smile was starting to wane.

'Dan-i-el?' Olivia almost puffed on a sliver of air.

'Your husband. Flora and Sofia are here, and we love you more than you could possibly know.'

'No!' Flora sobbed again, clutching her mother's arm as Maria wrapped herself around her granddaughter. Nancy shook her head and repeated, 'No no no no no,' as she gasped.

Sofia looked at her dad, to check whether he were crying or not, but as Olivia closed her eyes for a final time and her fragile face sank a little into the pillow, he couldn't help it. He so wanted to reassure their baby that this would be all right, but as he broke down and crumpled, and told his wife he loved her for one last time, as he pulled his daughters into his sides, Daniel knew they had only just hit rock bottom.

Epilogue

December 2018

Your mother died on a Thursday. By the time her funeral came around in October, autumn's russets and reds lit up the whole village and made it glow. Your friends came to the church and cried for you. Mimi sang 'Ave Maria'; Jim sang 'Crazy in Love' at the restaurant.

Lots of fashion types turned up in silly hats. Photos were in the newspapers. I kept all the cuttings in case you ever want them. Annoyingly Mamma would have *loved* to have been there, raising a toast, surrounded by all the people whose lives she enriched. People who, in turn, enriched your lives. It would have been the best party ever, if only she had been there.

Everyone was so kind to us; people held you tight. I've never experienced an outpouring of so much warmth and so much heartache at the same time. It was both uplifting and exhausting.

Sofia, you shone in your party dress – you proudly told everyone it was an Olivia Messina original – you even managed a cartwheel in it in the cemetery. Flora, you made people gasp. We came home and collapsed in a heap on the sofa with a box of popcorn, all falling asleep at different times as we watched *The Greatest Showman*. Flora, you helped me carry your sister up to bed and decided to make you each a memory jar from two of the Kilner jars Mamma had in her studio, decorating them beautifully with your names on. And although none of us will ever forget such a traumatic day, there are pieces you might want to remember or fit together in future. As you will of her life – but we can help each other with that.

This is why your mother wanted me to write one account of it – and I hope this helps as you grow older. As will the letters she left you in her underwear drawer. Treasure them, even when you're angry and want to rip them up.

Tomorrow we go to London to collect Mamma's award. Vaani found out about the nomination the day you cut your head at school Sofia. The British Fashion Council Trailblazer of the Year. She didn't ever know she won it. But she already felt like a winner – you girls were her true prize creation.

Your *nonnas* will be at the awards. Aunty Mimi and Udo too. Jim and Wesley. You girls and I will go up on stage and we will collect Mamma's trophy with Vaani. I will hold your hands tight and you won't have to say a thing. All you will need to do is remember how Mamma was the trailblazer of our lives, not just for a year. And you are trailblazers too – young women she was so in love with and so enormously proud of – and your characters and colours carry the spirit of your mother and her infinite love with you.

Acknowledgements

Firstly, I'd like to thank my readers – not only for reading this book – but also to everyone who's been on any of my book journeys with me. I appreciate every review, every kind message and every little line on Instagram to say my novels have resonated with you. It's an honour that I get to follow my dream of writing, and that my stories touch lives beyond my kitchen table. I wouldn't have achieved that without the dream team who get my books out into the world:

Thank you to super-agent and everyone's best best woman, Rebecca Ritchie. I still marvel at how often we are on the same page, which is handy in this industry! I am so grateful to you for your faith and your brilliance. Huge thanks too to my editor Hannah Smith, who is so spot-on and sharp – her passion for great stories only matched by her enthusiasm for musical theatre – thank you for always being right. Vicky Joss (a great Catherine Parr to Hannah's Anne Boleyn – I *so* want to join in their Six The Musical singalongs...) is a whizz with a marketing strategy, a blog tour and a gif. And thank you Nikky Ward, Becky Clark, Christian Duck, Rachel Hart, Daniel Groenewald, Laura Palmer and Nicolas Cheetham – Aria/Head of Zeus heavyweights to whom I am so grateful.

Thank you Olivia and Tory at Midas for your magical touch last year; to Leah Jacobs-Gordon for your beautiful cover design; to copy editors and proof readers Annabel Walker and Dushi Horti. And also to my personal first-reader friends: Guro Eide, as ever you are a goddess, and Kathleen Whyman – I'm so excited for your publishing journey too. Ian Critchley: thank you for the ongoing chats over coffee and hot chocolate. And the U2 song puns. You are the Sweetest Thing (etc).

Big shout out to James Beck, aka Lovely James, aka Jim Beck in the book you have just read: poor James won a prize in an auction raising money for Bliss, the charity for premature and sick babies, to have his name in my next book... just after I had written two novels where the main character (Train Man) was called James. Sorry! Thanks for bearing with me and waiting for The Night We Met. And special thanks to Bliss fundraiser and fixer Anna Black who got in touch with me about the auction. Anna is so awesome, we soon quickstepped from author/reader emails to marathon running buddies, personal trainer and now friends. You are a pocket powerhouse in Sweaty Betty.

Harriet Jones - you're a hero. Thank you for the fashion retail vernacular and the use of Rockahula Towers when I needed urgent weekend writing space. You saved my bacon!

Thank you, Kate Williams. Who knew in April 2018, on a long walk through Milan with our menfolk, that the city would inspire a novel?! Thank you for that and the subsequent research chats about International School life. To Michelle Margherita, *tesora mia*, thank you for inspiration in the Alps; thank you Paige Toon for your wisdom (on publishing and puppy training) and to Tony Carelli for help with Italian swearwords: you are a filthy man.

This is a sadder story than I've written before: inspired by the loss of family and friends who died before their time. Doc and his kind, tolerant and beautiful mind. Melanie Barlow – a wonderful mother to her gorgeous children William and Francesca, and wife to Chris. And Neil Mercer, a strong and smouldering soul, whose spark went out too soon. The fragility of life is something I never take for granted, which is why I'm grateful for every healthy day with my family:

My parents, Judi Billing; Don and Gerlinde Smith; Gill and Derrick Folbigg. My army of siblings who made lockdown quizzes so… competitive! You're the best. And my world: my husband, IT support guy and best friend, Mark, and our boys Felix and Max. I am grateful for every day the sun rises with you; every time you come dive bombing into our bed at 7am; every laugh and cuddle. To be in a bubble with you is a bliss I cherish every day.

About the Author

ZOË FOLBIGG is a magazine journalist and digital editor, starting at *Cosmopolitan* in 2001 and since freelancing for titles including *Glamour*, *Fabulous*, *Daily Mail*, *Healthy*, *LOOK*, *Top Santé*, *Mother & Baby*, *ELLE*, *Sunday Times Style* and *Style.com*. In 2008 she had a weekly column in *Fabulous* magazine documenting her year-long round-the-world trip with 'Train Man' – a man she had met on her daily commute. She has since married Train Man and lives in Hertfordshire with him and their two young sons. Zoë is the author of *The Note*, *The Postcard* and *The Distance*. *The Note* was Amazon Prime's most downloaded book of 2018 and has sold over 200,000 copies.

Follow the author @zoefolbigg

Loved *The Night We Met?*
Then read on for a sneak peek of

the distance

Every love story has a beginning,
it's how you get the end that counts...

Under the midnight sun of Arctic Norway, Cecilie
goes online looking for friends, and stumbles across
Hector Herrera. They start chatting and soon realise that
'love at first word' might just be possible. But there
are two big problems: Hector lives thousands of miles
away in Mexico. And he's about to get married.

Cecilie's whole life has been anchored by sticking
to what she knows, and her job at the cafe in the town
in which she grew up. Can she really change her whole life
for someone she's never met? And will Hector escape his
turbulent past, not to mention his imminent marriage,
and make a leap of faith to change the path he's on?

This is a story of two people, living two very different
lives, and whether they can cross a gulf, ocean, sea
and fjord to give their love a chance.

One

March 2018,
Tromsø, Norway

So, ro, lilleman, nå er dagen over… Sleep tight, little one, now the day is over… Cecilie can't stop the blasted lullaby from spinning around her head, twinkling like a hanging mobile doing revolutions above a sleeping baby. *Alle mus i alle land, ligger nå og sover…* The song is rotating calmly and methodically in Cecilie's brain, distracting her from the couple sitting in front of her as they wait for her to take their order. It is also distancing her from The Thing That's Happening Today that she's been dreading for weeks, hoping someone will put a stop to it or change their mind.

The lullaby must have been swirling in Cecilie's head since she sang it in a quiet corner of the library this morning; to mothers with grey crescent moons clinging to their lower lashlines; to fathers, over the moon to be enjoying their parental leave in a much more relaxed way than they think their partners did. Mothers and fathers and gurglers, all joined in with Cecilie to sing nursery rhymes in the basement

1

of the library, but now those songs and the sweet and happy voices are taunting her.

So, ro, lilleman...

Cecilie thinks of the large print above the fireplace in the living room at home. The room is an elegant haven of greys, browns and whites, dominated by a long, wooden dining table that stands out against the modern touches of the alternate grey and sable plastic Vitra chairs around it. It's a table where everyone is welcome for heart-to-hearts and hygge at Christmas, although most of the time Cecilie eats breakfast there alone. She likes the grey chairs best and always chooses to sit on one of those while she eats her soda bread smeared with honey and stares out of the window, to the vast and sparse garden beyond. On the white wall above the fireplace hangs a print of a static Alexander Calder mobile that her mother Karin picked up on a trip to London.

'Isn't it wonderful, Cecilie?' she exclaimed, her blue eyes lighting up against the silver of her bobbed hair, as Cecilie's brother and his boyfriend lifted the black matt frame onto the mantelpiece with a heave.

'Wonderful,' concurred Morten, the partner of Cecilie's twin brother Espen, as he pushed his glasses up his little snub nose. 'The beauty and intelligence is astounding,' he added. 'I just wish I could see it in motion.'

Karin nodded with vigour; Espen had already left the room.

Cecilie looked at the print dreamily, her pale green eyes gazing up at the black Vertical Fern, while it didn't oscillate as it had in the gallery, or might have done in a breeze. Still, Cecilie imagined herself, fluttering up to the largest of its black fronds to see what it would look like to gaze down at her mother and Morten's faces from above. Cecilie had a knack for drifting out of position on a whim or a daydream, and seeing the world from above.

Karin, a pragmatist and a politician, found it hard to understand her otherworldly daughter.

'Cecilie?' Karin had urged.

Cecilie crinkled her nose and snapped back into the room with a blink.

'It's wonderful, Mamma,' she agreed, although she couldn't fathom why her mother had bought an inanimate print of something that ought to be in gentle movement. It seemed so unlike her. Karin Wiig was the least static person Cecilie knew.

'Well yes,' confirmed Karin with authority. 'They were just so stunning, you really ought to go to London and see them in motion before the exhibition ends,' she said with a wave of her hand, although everyone knew she was really only talking to Morten. Even if Espen had still been in the room to hear, he was too wrapped up in his life at the i-Scand hotel on the harbour to bother with the inconvenience of a weekend break, and Cecilie had never travelled to a latitude below Oslo, which was something a diplomat and an adventurer like Karin couldn't understand.

'Why is your sister so happy to stay in one place?' she once asked Espen in despair.

'Perhaps Cecilie's daydreams take her to better places than a flight ever could, Mamma,' Espen had replied.

So, ro, lilleman…

The flash of the frond in her mind awakens Cecilie and she wriggles her inert feet inside her black Dr Martens boots. The lullaby evaporates and disappears, and Cecilie is back with the couple sitting in front of her, at their usual table.

'Pickle, are you all right?' asks Gjertrud, her kindly weathered face looking up at Cecilie. 'It's just Ole asked you three times for the spiced Arctic cloudberry cake, but you seem a little... in the clouds yourself today, my dear.'

'Oh, I'm so sorry, so much to think about...' Cecilie replies, as she writes *cloudberry* onto a pad in a wisp of ink.

Gjertrud wonders how much can Cecilie possibly have to think about, as she studies the waitress's face; her eyebrows arch to her temples, framing pale green eyes that usually flash with the iridescent brightness of a dragonfly's wing – only, today, they are dulled by a film of pondwater. Her blonde hair is pulled into twists of rope, piled at the back of her head, exposing the loveheart shape of her face.

Gjertrud's round, purple cheeks flush with the heat of coming indoors when it's cold outside, and she gazes at Cecilie, and wonders what goes on inside that dreamy brain of hers. She can't be that busy in her quiet life here in this quiet town. She doesn't even have children like Gjertrud and Ole's daughters did by the time they were Cecilie's age.

Gjertrud and Ole see Cecilie every afternoon for coffee and cake at the Hjornekafé teashop after their post-lunch walk. They always take the table with four chairs against the far wall, so they can look out of the large expanse of glass onto the small backstreet of the Arctic harbour town. Each window panel has a little etching in the middle, an illustration of the exterior of the quaint corner cafe, the same illustration as the one on the cover of the menus Cecilie hands out. Gjertrud always chooses a seat so she can sit with her back to the wall, to hold court and see everything going on in the Hjornekafé. Ole sits facing his wife, although he can see cafe life back to front in the rectangles of the mirrors on the wall in front of